DECEMBER BREEZE

Marvel Moreno

DECEMBER BREEZE

*Translated from the Spanish
by Isabel Adey and Charlotte Coombe*

Europa
editions

Europa Editions
27 Union Square West, Suite 302
New York, NY 10003
www.europaeditions.com
info@europaeditions.com

Copyright © 2014, Herederos de Marvel Moreno
First publication 2022 by Europa Editions

Translation by Isabel Adey and Charlotte Coombe
Original title: *En diciembre llegaban las brisas*
Translation copyright © 2022 by Europa Editions

Library of Congress Cataloging in Publication Data is available
ISBN 978-1-60945-802-7

Moreno, Marvel
December Breeze

Art direction by Emanuele Ragnisco
instagram.com/emanueleragnisco

Cover illustration by Sandra Restrepo

Prepress by Grafica Punto Print – Rome

Printed in Canada

DECEMBER BREEZE

PART ONE

I

For I, the Lord your God, am a jealous God, punishing children for the sin of the parents, to the third and fourth generation." Because the Bible, as her grandmother saw it, contained all the preconceptions that could make man ashamed of his origin, and not just his origin, but also his innate impulses, urges, instincts, call them what you may, turning a fleeting lifetime into a hell of guilt and remorse, frustration and aggression. Yet that same book also held the wisdom of the world it had helped to create ever since it was written, and so it was important to read the words carefully and reflect on its assertions, as arbitrary as they seemed, to fully understand the hows and whys of all human suffering. So whenever something happened to cause ripples in the murky though seemingly calm mass of lives that had formed the city's elite for over a hundred and fifty years, her grandmother, sitting there in a rattan rocking chair, amid the din of the cicadas and the dense, drowsy air of two in the afternoon, would remind her of the biblical curse as she explained that whatever had happened—or more precisely, its origins—could be traced back a century, or several centuries, and that she, her grandmother, had been expecting this for as long as she could remember, ever since she had been capable of establishing a link between cause and effect.

This fatalism filled Lina with fear; not surprise—by the age of fourteen she was no longer shocked by the things her grandmother and aunts said—but a dark dread that tingled in her hands as she wondered for the thousandth time what misfortune she had already been condemned to by fate. Seeing her grandmother sitting across from her, tiny and fragile like a seven-year-old girl, her white hair pulled back and coiled into a modest bun at the nape of her neck, she felt as if she were listening to an age-old Cassandra; not animated or hysterical, in fact not even a real Cassandra since she wasn't lamenting her own fate or that of others, but a sage whose prophecies would inevitably be fulfilled. Someone who carried the past in her memory, assimilating and understanding it in order to divine the present and even the future with a vague sadness, like a goddess who is benevolent but outside of creation, and therefore powerless to prevent the mistakes and suffering of mankind. For this reason, her grandmother—convinced that everything was preordained, that a secret force controls every step we take in life, forcing us to go one way instead of another—refused to intervene when Lina asked her to save Dora from marrying Benito Suárez, although in theory she could have done, because there was no one in the world Dora's mother respected more than Lina's grandmother.

Lina thought that a single phone call, or just a note, would be enough to coax Doña Eulalia del Valle out of her seclusion and make her walk the four blocks to where Lina and her grandmother lived. She also thought that once Doña Eulalia told her grandmother the lengthy litany of woes otherwise known as the ordeal of her life, that is to say, if she felt she had gained the sympathy of not only her daughter or maids but also someone she admired for her "lineage" and "exemplary conduct"—terms she always used to describe Lina's grandmother—she would be willing to accept her advice. Even if that meant rejecting Dora's union, her idea of 'purification', with a lunatic like Benito Suárez. But her grandmother had refused to pick up the phone, telling Lina: If it isn't Benito Suárez, it'll be someone else just like him, because it seems to me that your friend Dora is bound to be chosen by the kind of man who will take off his belt and beat her with it the first time he sleeps with her.

Many years later, in the autumn of her life, having heard similar stories here and there, having learned to listen and express herself without prejudice or anger, Lina would suddenly be reminded of Dora as she watched a woman walk past the terrace of Café Bonaparte, and she would wonder, smiling, if perhaps her grandmother had been right: right in saying that Dora was destined to get together with a man who would beat her when they slept together, first for the act itself, and then again for having done it with another man. But not back then. Back then, she'd just turned fourteen, and nobody, not even her grandmother, could convince her that Dora was being drawn by some dark force towards the man who would surely be the cause of her ruin, as inexplicably as a cat is driven by instinct to risk its life on the flimsy branches of a guava tree simply because a bird is fluttering about between the leaves, knowing all the while it will never catch the bird, and despite already having a belly full of lunch scraps.

At that time, the forces her grandmother spoke of—the correct name for which Lina would learn reading Freud, and not without some scepticism—sounded like one of those enemies that stalk mankind, like disease and madness, forces that need to be warded off in the name of dignity, in other words, in order to make it through life with a degree of decency, trying where possible to not inconvenience others, the way a newspaper should be left as we find it, more crumpled perhaps, but never with its pages torn or missing. And not out of consideration for others, since nobody gave it to us and nobody expects it back, but because it is always best to guard against carelessness, even though we know that in the long run we will inevitably lose and the newspaper will end up being thrown away. In other words, back then, in her own way, Lina already saw any form of surrender as unforgivable, no matter how often her grandmother alluded to the intervention of those mysterious forces, and especially if that surrender meant marrying a man like Benito Suárez.

Because Lina knew him. She had met him on a Saturday during Carnival in unusual circumstances, although that adjective, which Lina deliberately used so as not to be accused of exaggeration when she later told her grandmother the tale, by no means described the dramatic way Benito Suárez had first appeared, bursting onto the scene to become a permanent fixture in her life. From that day on, as Dora's closest friend, Lina was in no doubt that Benito Suárez would cross her path again, always causing the same drama and occasionally provoking the same icy rage she'd felt when she'd seen him pulling up that day on the corner in his Studebaker, jumping out and chasing Dora, who was running blindly towards Lina's front door, having fled the car with her face all bloody. It took Lina a long time to understand the full extent of what happened, the fact that simply witnessing the scene had changed her, or more precisely, it had set in motion the process that was to change her irrevocably. This was something that only struck her years later, as she realised that she could still recall the tiniest details of that Saturday during Carnival when she first saw Benito Suárez: the blue Studebaker screeching to a halt on the corner as she watched from the dining-room window, stunned, sitting at the mahogany table big enough for twelve and littered with her notebooks and the roll of tracing paper she had just cut in order to draw a map of Colombia's rivers and mountains; then next to it, the rubber, the bottle of ink and the little heap of sand she was planning to stick on where the mountain peaks opened up into volcanoes. She would always remember the pen flying out of her hands and staining the polished tabletop, Dora running crazed, stumbling, Benito Suárez catching up with her in the garden and once more hitting her across the face, which was now bloodied beyond recognition, and then the two of them, Dora and her, running towards the front door, Dora from the garden while she, Lina, dashed up the hallway and flung the door open, suddenly striking Benito Suárez with one of the porch chairs, not to stop him from coming in—he'd already made it into the hall with a face so determined there seemed no way of beating him back—but to stall him. Yes. The shock of seeing her, a thirteen-year-old girl who had just broken a Louis XVI chair over his back, hissing, "Watch out, the dog's coming for you!" The shock and the impact, maybe the pain: that was enough to slow him down. Lina would recall the short seconds in which she managed to grab Dora by the hand, drag her down the hallway to the dining room and slip behind the sideboard where she used to hide when her grandmother came after her, clutching that dreaded bottle of Milk of Magnesia. Gasping for breath, suddenly soaked in sweat, with Dora's face resting in her lap and sticky blood staining her blue jeans, she whispered into Dora's ear: "Stop crying . . . he'll kill us both."

Because Benito Suárez did want to kill them, at least that's what he was shouting as he crashed around the deserted house, kicking the furniture and calling her, Lina, a little fucking bitch. She'd heard him shout it from the dining room as he sent her notebooks flying onto the floor with a swipe of his hand; she heard his panting breath, with an inflection in his voice that was devoid of any human quality and resembled the groaning of an animal, furiously trying to make sounds that almost morphed into sentences. Perhaps it was that rage-choked voice, not her realization that the setters were barking madly in the backyard, which had made Lina think of the dog: the mongrel had no name and never barked, but its silence held the same capacity for hate, the same murderous impulse as the man who was kicking the sideboard she was hiding behind, her hand over Dora's mouth to keep her from crying out. The dog came into her head, not impulsively, like when she'd bashed Benito Suárez over the back with the chair, but with a sudden, calculated coldness that would later shock her; that is, later on, when she told her grandmother how she'd crept down the hallway as soon as she could no longer hear the aggressive spluttering of insults, made her way to the tree where the dog was tied up, grabbed him by the loop of his collar and went looking for Benito Suárez until she found him in the hallway next to the overturned chair. She was surprised, even more surprised when her grandmother told her: "I, for one, can certainly imagine you setting that wretched dog on Benito Suárez."

But long before what she would come to call the first skirmish (there would be so many others that Lina would get used to seeing that man as a natural yet almost innocuous enemy because she could predict his reactions and, for some reason, had a strange soft spot for him), Lina had already started to get the measure of Benito Suárez. She'd closely followed his tumultuous relationship with Dora, being her confidante from the moment she started at La Enseñanza, when Dora, perhaps driven by a precocious maternal instinct, had taken her under her wing: for a whole year, she'd protected Lina like a mother hen—religiously saving her a window seat on the school bus, or sitting her on her lap. Then things started to change, because while Lina moved up to the first, second and third grades of elementary school, Dora kept repeating fourth grade, and that was where they found themselves—Lina aged eight and Dora aged eleven—when their relationship was inverted once and for all, and Lina realized that if she wanted to get her friend out of that predicament, she'd have to whisper the answers to her during tests, write her essays, explain division to her again and again, and phone her to make sure she'd done her homework. But she managed, in the end, with cheating and sheer tenacity, to drag her up to the seventh grade, when all her hard work went up in smoke because Dora got expelled from La Enseñanza for picking up a lollipop a boy had thrown to her from the school wall.

Lina had always thought Dora was too quiet: she didn't play at breaktime or take part in the pranks that Lina, Catalina and her friends meticulously planned, trying to cause a disturbance that would wind the nuns up and break the monotony of the lessons. In fact, Dora had never joined in anything that required movement or physical activity: she was a very calm child, almost plantlike, with the indolent appearance of an organism engrossed in something that was happening inside itself, pulsating in its own cells. She was fed so many vitamins as a child that by the age of nine she started maturing, and at fourteen—when they expelled her from the school for the lollipop incident—she was fully developed and had that languid air about her, that sway in her step which impelled the boys from Biffi to clamber up the school wall crowned with a veritable thicket of broken bottle glass, leaving the concrete strewn with the skin from their knees and the sweat of their longing, just so they could watch her for a minute during breaktime. She was not beautiful like Catalina, and she lacked Beatriz's refinement. She was not exactly graceful or seductive to look at. No. There was something more distant, more profound about her: the kind of thing that stimulated the first molecule to reproduce or the first organism to fertilize itself, that throbbed at the bottom of the ocean before any form of life appeared on land and then, throbbing, sucked in, absorbed and created other beings, expelled them from itself; as life in its rawest form, then later, as the primitive female; not necessarily the human female but any female capable of luring the rowdy and fractious male into her cave and momentarily calming his aggression, not only to make him perform the act that might be his raison d'être as part of nature, but also to remind him that there exists a more intense and perhaps more ancient pleasure than the pleasure of killing.

Dora seemed unaware of this, although she may well have suspected it: she always felt the eyes of men on her, and even as a child she realized it was impossible for her to go out into the garden alone without some passing beggar or tramp being unable to resist the urge to frantically unbutton his fly and start touching himself in front of her. Lina, however, got the feeling that from the moment Dora was born—or, as her grandmother had insisted on putting it—from the moment she began to exist, she had been marked by the same sign that determined her dog Ofelia's behaviour, or rather, the behaviour of the male dogs that lustfully circled around her. Ofelia was encircled, not followed: she did not need to walk around or make the slightest movement to keep them close to her, in a state of desperate anticipation. There was nothing special about the bitch's appearance: in looks at least, she was no different from the other setters that had been born and raised in their house, all of whom were named after the heroines in Shakespeare's stories, which her grandmother had read to her so often at bedtime. Ofelia was merely a sleepy creature with curly cinnamon-coloured fur, who loathed the sun and spent the whole day lazing on the cool tiles in the hallway. But when she came into season, a greedy glint appeared in her eyes and, suddenly alert, she would stand proud in front of the impassioned Brutuses and Macbeths who barked plaintively, baying for her attention, ignoring all the other bitches on heat—invariably brought into season by Ofelia—and losing all the refinement of setters imported from England, dogs whose pedigree equalled that of someone of Bourbon descent, her grandmother explained, not without some pride. Considering how unwaveringly faithful Ofelia was, always choosing the same mate, all the energy she spent chasing, then spinning around and yapping, might have been considered a waste were it not for the fact that once her choice was made, the setters eagerly turned their attention to the other females, every single one of whom (even the ones that could barely stand) became the objects of their urges and attentions. In other words, Ofelia seemed destined by nature to carry within her the incentive, motivation or lure that compels living beings to reproduce, regardless of their will, and of course, regardless of any form of knowledge.

Observing Dora, one might have said that a similar ignorance prevented her from realizing how little she had in common with most women. It came naturally to Dora to feel desired, and she would have been dumbfounded if someone had bothered to explain to her that the main reason the boys from Biffi College climbed up the school wall and risked skinning their hands on the broken glass was to see her. For Dora this was the natural order of things, like the tramps who unzipped their fly as soon as they saw her alone in her garden; moreover, it must have tied in exactly with what her mother had told her about male nature being essentially corrupt and intent on plunging women into wretchedness. But until the age of fourteen she was only allowed to travel between home and school, so she never had the chance to meet any of the individuals who were determined to offend her modesty. And, Lina would later say to herself, she had never managed to pinpoint the origin of her bewilderment, which kept her in a daze at her desk while a nun wrote on the board and she listened to the maddening hum of the bees. Sitting always by the classroom window, she would get distracted looking at the school yard with its motionless trees outlined by a strip of metallic sky; her eyes seemed to cloud over, her gaze lost in images that perhaps were not even images but something that vaguely signified waiting and, in a way, confusion. Her behaviour, however, left nothing to be desired: she sat up straight, carefully copied down the scribbles written on the blackboard by the nun on duty, stood up silently when the bell rang and lined up with the other students in an orderly manner. In an orderly manner, she entered the refectory and ate, went to the chapel and prayed: orderly and absent. She was not there, and one might wonder if she had ever really been anywhere. She seemed to live differently from everyone else, existing inside herself and listening, not to a voice—only occasionally did it seem that some clear sound reached her—but to a murmur that perhaps predated human language, where every new noise was an extension of the one that came before it, and the passing of an airplane in the sky was followed by a sudden breeze rustling through the trees, a flurry of rainfall or simply something more inaudible, more indistinct, like the crackle of a seed pod bursting in the heat or the falling of a leaf scorched by the sun.

Lina's grandmother explained to her that Dora could have carried on like that, hidden, undiscovered, in a limbo of sensations that she probably lacked the words to describe, until her mother managed to marry her off—or rather, until the ceremony took place and she could finally hand over her daughter and her terror to a man, like a grenade with the pin pulled, thrown into the hands of another with relief. Dora might have remained in this state, had the nuns been less dull-witted and were it not for Doña Eulalia: distressed by the presence of her quiet, nebulous daughter, who was quiet and nebulous enough for her mother to imagine that her chastity could be safeguarded long-term even away from her watchful eye, she decided to send her off to work in a kindergarten run by a relative, perhaps repeating to herself, despite her reservations, that in the end, idleness is the mother of all vices.

And it wasn't strange that she should think this, because Doña Eulalia came from a family where no one had worked for five hundred years, if work was to be understood as making a living by using one's hands to sow, gather or handle any tool designed to transform one thing into another. She and all her ancestors believed they belonged to a special category of people who, in their own right and by divine command, were responsible for ensuring the rule of order, leading by example in times of peace, or using swords and cannons in the event of unrest. They remembered very clearly that they had come from Spain not as explorers, not even as warriors: by the time of the Conquest, their extensive use of weapons had earned them certain privileges in the Court and they could turn up to govern the chaotic overseas provinces, or disdainfully send their seconds-in-command and bastard sons to do the job for them. Yes, it was as inquisitors and judges that they disembarked in the coast's major cities, where their sons acquired or were awarded the lands worked by slaves, and their grandchildren, during the ill-fated days of Independence, were forced to flee to Curaçao and stay there until better winds came, allowing them to return to their devastated plantations after cautiously changing their surnames. But even then, they did not work. Not because they lacked the strength: though gaunt and prone to meditation, almost to mysticism, they were still capable of commanding obedience in men, and over two or three generations they managed to keep their bloodline intact. The problem was that the world was changing and they could not adapt to anything that meant evolution or change, to any situation that upset the values that had long served them as a point of reference, a mirror in which they found and reinforced their identity. One of those values instinctively distanced them from work, which they found demeaning at the best of times, but which, in those merciless lands plagued by sun, torrential rain and vermin, seemed to eat away at men until they had been drained of any form of intelligence or dignity. And so as not to betray their principles, they gave in: little by little, from fathers to sons, they started preparing to surrender without ever waging a war. When the changes that were taking hold of the country's economy forced them to compete with businessmen, politicians and smugglers, they silently resigned; silently and proudly, that is to say, with no outward sign of missing their big, abandoned houses or the plantations they had been selling off, plot by plot. They retained the memories, not nostalgia, and it seemed these memories were enough for them to walk tall while the world only they could see vanished to dust, crumbled at their feet: they were men of distinction. At least that was what Doña Eulalia del Valle believed, and what Lina had heard her say more than a thousand times. And so, it was impossible to imagine her sending her daughter to work in a kindergarten to earn a few extra pesos, even though she was practically verging on poverty, because Doña Eulalia, out of principle and tradition, thought being poverty-stricken was preferable to any kind of work.

So, that decision had to be linked to Dora's personality. That daughter of dubious descent, her bloodline tainted by centuries of debauchery, by the distant sensuality of dances, drums and strong scents, had nothing of her mother's pale, ascetic, indistinct figure, and yet Doña Eulalia had projected herself onto the child as soon as she turned nine years old and began to blossom, to unfurl like a plant with its roots so firmly anchored in the soil that it could weather any storm. At first, horrified, she tried to stifle, contain or destroy the scandalous thing that seeped out of every pore of Dora's skin, but when she did not succeed—because despite the girdles and bandages her daughter's breasts were protruding, her hips were filling out and her hair was growing so abundantly that it snapped the ribbons of her braids and ponytails—she tried, fascinated, to make Dora belong to her: like a vine she crept over her body, tried to breathe with her lungs, to see through her eyes, to beat to the rhythm of her heart; she scrutinized her brain with the same obstinate determination with which she rifled through her drawers and read the pages of her books and notepads; she forced her to think out loud, to reveal her secrets and desires. And in the end, she possessed her before any man could, paving the way for all men to possess her.

Benito Suárez's blue Studebaker was yet to make an appearance, but already Lina had detected Doña Eulalia's desire to have total control over her daughter, a desire so fierce that her face would crumple at the slightest suspicion of deceit or concealment: Dora was forbidden to play outside the boundaries of their garden, which was surrounded by a six-foot-high stone wall with sharp, spiky shrubs growing along it, and the mere presence of Lina's cousins and friends would prompt Doña Eulalia to pop up out of nowhere like the genie from Aladdin's lamp, her expression alert, pupils dilated, and, unceremoniously violating the most basic rules of hospitality, she would order Dora back inside the house to sit for hours in a chair as punishment. All this, Lina already knew, but what made her reflect on Doña Eulalia's intentions for the first time was her discovery, one Christmas, that Dora had received a bicycle she was allowed to ride as long as she didn't leave the 150-foot stretch of pavement outside their house. Being restricted to that small area diminished the enjoyment of having the bicycle: she could not race around the streets, go flying down hills at full speed, experience the tiredness in her muscles from riding every day and the reward of the sweat, the messy hair and the breeze in her face. That gift and the restrictions that went with it, Lina's grandmother would tell her one afternoon, represented the contradiction that troubled Doña Eulalia, who was determined to turn Dora into a girl like any other while at the same time doing her best to prevent this from happening. Because it was taken for granted in that crazy society that no well-bred girl would be reckless enough to endanger the membrane she needed to keep intact if she wanted to marry well, and parental vigilance usually sufficed to protect that membrane, so no one imagined that riding a bike through the streets of the El Prado neighbourhood could pose a risk to their daughters' maidenhoods; if they did, no one would have been foolish enough to give them a bicycle in the first place.

So, from that Christmas on, Lina began to watch Doña Eulalia del Valle with curiosity, establishing a somewhat hazy connection between her presence on the veranda—where, eagle-eyed, she could survey all 150 feet of pavement—and the way she got inside Dora's head, constantly violating her privacy. Lina listened, mouth agape, to the conversations that played out in front of her whenever they returned from the country club or a party and Doña Eulalia interrogated Dora, mining her for details of not only what she had seen, but also what she had thought or felt when she saw it. There was something of the inquisitor in her attitude, and something impudent and hungry in her insistent questioning, constantly corralling Dora back and forth like a bird of prey circling in the sky. Faced with her mother's probing, Dora adopted a tactic similar to the one which allowed her to evade the nuns' control at school: she did not argue at all, did not protest against anything. Her resistance, Lina would later understand, lay in the scandalous silence of her submissiveness.

As if Doña Eulalia were aware of this—as if she'd suddenly realized that even by shutting her daughter away inside her house, not allowing her to have a single thought or desire that was truly her own, she would still never be able to dominate Dora completely because biologically a part of Dora would always elude her—she tried to confront the demon hidden inside that submissiveness using the only instrument at her disposal: words. It was a method that Lina later described as obsessive and demented brainwashing and one which left her dumbfounded, even though she knew it existed and was one of the worst burdens of humanity, which is what her grandmother told her as soon as she started school. Her grandmother explained everything the nuns would also tell her, advising her to pay as much attention to their delusions as one would to the hooting of owls: there would be the dead and the risen, hell and purgatory, much lamenting and the sound of chains being dragged by tormented souls. And she, Lina, was not to believe any of it. Because it was called indoctrination, and in all doctrine, there were more lies than truth.

What puzzled Lina when she listened to Doña Eulalia del Valle's rhetoric was not so much the style of the sermon but the aim of her preaching. Because Doña Eulalia must have had some aim in mind when, every day, she made Dora sit across from her, and spoke to her about men, using the foulest language as she compared their sperm to excrement and their genitals to the filthy phallus of the donkeys that could still be seen in the streets of El Prado in those days; not to mention the lustful slobbering, the fetid breath, the seeds of sexual promiscuity they were said to sow. The things that Doña Eulalia said had such a scatological quality, and there was such perversion in what was left unsaid or insinuated; never again would Lina encounter such depravity—not even when she walked by the shop windows in Rue Pigalle, nor in the blue movies that she would often watch years later. Thinking about it, she would even come to the conclusion that those ineffable Swedish and Dutch directors would be well advised to turn to the fantasies of the most virtuous of Latin American women if they wanted to reach new heights of obscenity in their work. But that would be later.

Lina couldn't have been more than ten years old when she heard Doña Eulalia's extraordinary monologue for the first time; she'd often seen her giving her daughter a lecture, but as soon as Lina came into the house, she would fall silent. That afternoon, Lina's curiosity was combined with the good fortune of finding the service door open, allowing her to sneak into the yard without anyone noticing and tiptoe towards the end of the terrace where Doña Eulalia usually liked to corner Dora. There she was, spouting forth with a kind of rabid glee about the tricks used by virtuous women to avoid temptation: everything from picturing the man they desired defecating on the toilet, to popping a mothball inside their knickers. Since

Lina did not know the meaning of most of the words she over-heard, she had to write them down in her sketchbook. But even later, when she consulted a dictionary at home, she still couldn't understand why Dora had to be lectured in that way. Her grandmother explained that Doña Eulalia was deliberately pursuing the same objective that she, Lina, had been unwit-tingly seeking when she found the roosters mounting the hens and furiously shooed them out of the yard, believing that they were pecking at their throats out of sheer aggression until the day when Berenice, the cook, shouted at her and told her to stop messing with them because nothing made the hens hap-pier. Ashamed of this comparison and remembering that the roosters had not changed their ways despite her stubborn attempts, Lina simply said, "It never did any good anyway," to which her grandmother replied with a smile, "I reckon what you heard today won't do any good either."

And so Lina suspected very early on, but without clearly understanding all the implications of the matter, that a threat hovered over whatever it was that chance had bestowed on Dora, placing her at a disadvantage when in fact, based on the hidden logic of her grandmother's assertions, that same essence could have been her asset and her centre of equilib-rium, contributing to her happiness and, in turn, the happiness of the man or men who came into her life—albeit only if she had been born in another space and time, but above all, if her mother had been someone other than Doña Eulalia del Valle. However, not even Doña Eulalia del Valle could claim full responsibility for the fact that Dora viewed her sexuality as such an abominable flaw that it justified or even merited the beating she received from Benito Suárez the first time they made love, in the back of his blue Studebaker, opposite the site where construction was soon to begin on the towering statue of the Sacred Heart, which would watch over the city from the highest point of its only hill.

Accepting her grandmother's relentless fatalism would have meant admitting that the origin of Dora's submissiveness to the belt that flogged her back—when, still naked, she felt Benito Suárez's acidic semen trickling out from between her thighs—could not logically be solely attributed to Doña Eulalia del Valle's influence, as that would be as inadequate as saying it rains because the sky is cloudy. She would have to remind herself of the biblical curse and go much further back in time, to that ill-fated day when the man who was to become Doña Eulalia's father—a man from Santa Marta with an evasive air about him, and the afflicted look of someone who, if he wasn't locked up in a monastery, was born or raised to lock himself away in one—appeared in the city and, kicking up the sand of the streets beneath his horse's hooves, made his way to the house of the Álvarez de la Vega family, where the first thing he saw when he dismounted was a girl with blonde hair playing in the yard with her doll. Because that encounter between the man who from so much fasting and self-flagellation had totally lost the power of his loins at the age of thirty, and the girl, who was newly formed but still in the fairytale haze of childhood, was not the root cause of that submissiveness, because the root cause dated back to the time when men discovered that exploiting women was the first step to exploiting each other. Rather, it was the most recent cause that her grandmother could pinpoint: the story of the twelve-year-old girl given to the man who asked for her hand in marriage the very afternoon they met, the same girl who, astonished, was to find herself dressed up in white six months later, as if still playing make-believe, leaving the church of San Nicolás on the arm of a stranger she had probably never spoken to before. A man whose great-uncle had been the Inquisitor General of Cartagena, the descendant of Spanish royalty on his mother's side and heir to a less pompous title, but a title all the same, who would that very night violate the tacit agreement to wait three years before demanding his marital rights from the girl. Finding himself disarmed by the inexplicable, diabolical desire that stiffened his flaccid crotch for the first and last time, he damaged the girl's vagina, causing her to haemorrhage, and he had to accept the services of the first healer his maid could find at that time of night—some poor veterinarian who crudely stitched up the wound while the girl's shock, which turned to horror, was expressed in screams that could be heard in every neighbouring house, causing echoes that insulted the fifteen families forming the coastal aristocracy of the day, thus destroying his honour for good and ensuring his ruin in the process.

Not immediately, but eventually. The dowry from the Álvarez de la Vega family and his personal fortune kept him afloat for several years, fifteen to be precise: enough time for him to squander the inheritance while sitting in front of the orange trees in his garden all day long, imposing a tomb-like silence on his surroundings and staring intently at those trees until, after so much time there gazing motionless, his sight began to suffer: the trunks blurred in his pupils, the branches disappeared from his retinas, the leaves dissolved into fog, and then one morning he finally realized he had gone blind.

Because he didn't want to see, Lina's grandmother told her. It wasn't his shame he was avoiding, because he believed he'd already paid for that over the years, cutting himself off and spending his fortune without lifting a finger, though truth be told he would never have lifted a finger to preserve it. His daughter had been conceived the night when, without any explanation or justification to himself, he had betrayed, trampled over and shattered the commandments in whose name he had flagellated himself since his youth. Because from the moment he set eyes on the girl playing with her doll, to the morning when he left the church of San Nicolás with her on his arm—yes, all that time—he believed his only interest was in marrying the heiress of the Álvarez de la Vega family and protecting her virginity while he waited for three years to pass until, as per tradition, he could impregnate her, knowing for sure that the child would be his. So, the explanation for his blindness was most likely connected to the new golden-haired figure who was suddenly wandering among the orange trees, giving off the unsettling scent of a fifteen-year-old girl. By allowing his eyes to cloud over, her grandmother concluded, he succeeded in killing two birds with one stone. He would no longer have to see his daughter (a likely source of temptation and an inevitable reminder of his shameful act) or endure the pain of witnessing her naturally heading for the depths he himself had tried to escape through flagellation; in this way, he could slow down that inexorable progression, because his daughter, Doña Eulalia del Valle, would have to become his guide.

Lina's grandmother chalked this error of judgement up to the fact that he had spent fifteen years staring at the orange trees in his garden, because only a man who was sick from the fear of his own body could imagine that Doña Eulalia would be destined for any kind of lust—even the kind that was theoretically likely to happen between the sheets of a marital bed. Doña Eulalia had been brought up by her mother, a girl who was raped by her husband on her wedding night, stitched up by a veterinarian, and impregnated with a child that would drag her womb and ovaries out of her belly with it nine months later, taking her from childhood to her twilight years with no transition. During the three years that she stayed in bed, lurching from one illness to another, oscillating between hot flashes and tremors of delirium, Doña Eulalia del Valle's mother learned to hate men. Coldly. Lucidly. And with the same lucidity and coldness, she passed on this hatred to her daughter.

II

If Darwin was not mistaken and a process of natural selection did in fact exist, it seemed only right to conclude that the men currently living had descended from those whose violence or cruelty—now defects, then virtues—had allowed them to conveniently massacre their rivals, passing on a gene pool that was capable of sowing the healthiest distrust in women: that these men should stone birds, pull the wings off flies or dismember the bodies of lizards was in keeping with tendencies once encouraged by natural selection, tendencies that modern society had not succeeded in inhibiting, continuing as it did to tolerate the dominance of the fittest, and accepting randomness and injustice to be part and parcel of everyday life. However, men could be tamed; in other words, they could be taught to be less aggressive with the help of religion or ideology, or even—and this option, albeit utopian, seemed preferable to Lina's grandmother—by simply demonstrating that solidarity is justified insofar as we all started from the same point and are bound to come stumbling over the same finishing line; they could be turned—at least some of them—into the kinds of harmless dreamers who fall in love, write books, compose music or discover penicillin. But not hated; hating them made no sense. There is no point despising the puma that kills a cow, or the cat that attacks a mouse. One must try to understand the animal, try to get inside the skin of the puma or the cat and co-exist with it, as far as possible, in a certain time and space: it is only to be destroyed if it tries to destroy us first.

Since her grandmother believed that hatred ruled out understanding, and understanding was the *sine qua non* of harmony, it was easy to explain why Doña Eulalia del Valle had always seemed so unhinged, so compelled to turn rabidly against men ever since she was a child, or at least ever since she realized that men existed, because the only man Doña Eulalia had known in her childhood was her father, who spent all day gazing intently at the orange trees in the garden. Only later, perhaps when she belatedly took first communion and started going to early morning mass with her mother, she discovered that men not only dressed differently, but they also strolled down the street, carried bags or pushed carts around, instead of cutting themselves off from the world in a garden of orange trees. And at the same time, Doña Eulalia's mother started to warn her, that is, to verbally transform, with affirmations and anecdotes, the climate of hatred that she inevitably endured in a house where her parents never exchanged a word, slept in separate beds and never had guests, where nothing even remotely resembling the masculine principle existed. Because when Doña Eulalia del Valle's mother finally got up—after three years in bed oscillating between hot flashes that soaked her body in sweat and sudden chills that made her shiver and tremble, her face pale as chalk, with that same bewildered expression she had at age twelve and would keep until the moment she died—she slowly hobbled through the rooms of her house, leaning on a maid's arm for support and, without uttering a single word, simply raised her hand and pointed at the pictures she wanted taken down immediately, those oil paintings in which nine generations of her husband's ancestors stood proudly amid the sombre finery of the Spanish court, all men, all haughty and marked, centuries earlier, by the decision to shroud themselves in a cloak of abstinence.

Distributed on muleback among Doña Eulalia's relatives, those paintings—some bearing the signatures of great masters—spent several years gathering dust in abandoned colonial houses before ending up in churches, where some pious paintbrush made the insolent faces sadder and transformed the mournful clothing into habits, replacing hats and daggers with halos and scapulars to personify those European saints the people of the coastal town were hard-pressed to believe in. That day, not content with getting rid of the vestiges of a past that had influenced or determined her husband's vile behaviour, Doña Eulalia del Valle's mother continued, like a vengeful poltergeist, to condemn books, statues and chinaware until finally, at the peak of her silent rage, she made her way down the four steps leading to the yard, called out to the gardener and, an hour before firing him, ordered him to chop the heads off all the male animals that lived there, not even sparing the exquisite parrots or the shy canaries from the massacre. Never again would any man set foot in her house: her father was already dead, and she had no brothers. She took to keeping watch over her maids and frantically sewing blouses and skirts for the orphans of the Buen Pastor women's prison, instilling her daughter with a very particular respect for the Virgin, barely mentioning Saint Joseph and merely giving Jesus Christ a supporting role; the rosary she and her maids prayed at six in the evening as they kneeled before a statue of the Virgin skipped over the "Our Fathers"— as the old priest discovered, much to his horror, when Doña Eulalia's mother decided to broaden her daughter's education and summoned him to teach her the catechism, inviting him to take over from the unassuming old spinsters whose lifestyle had been held up as an example to Doña Eulalia until then, a lifestyle which, in all likelihood, she intended to follow.

But something had to give. Eventually a shadow of restlessness caused cracks to form in the solid wall that was built on Our Father-less rosaries and female parrots, cats and hens doomed to absolute chastity in a yard where the only man in the house would doze off gazing at the orange trees, because later, while flipping through the huge volumes of Argentinian magazines that Doña Eulalia had collected and bound (perhaps in secret) since the age of twenty, Lina would discover, perplexed, that those volumes fell open, as if an invisible hand were guiding the reader to certain pages, more dog-eared than others, some marked by what appeared to be chocolate stains from grubby fingers, at the paragraphs where the romance novels reached the height of eroticism permitted at the time: kisses on the hand and forbidden glances that made the heroine ache with longing, and most likely Doña Eulalia del Valle, too, as she whiled away the afternoons, those long hours of unbearable heat that drew to a close in a brief burst of orange, those afternoons of dreams cut short and unsettling desires as she waited for the sheikh, the exiled Russian prince or the British fleet admiral to come looking for her in Barranquilla, to ravish her or ask for her hand in marriage, cover her feet in kisses on a cold winter's night, tumble down into an abandoned mineshaft with her and tame her with the strength of his character or his all-consuming (yet controlled) passion amid the darkness and the hunger, teaching her to renounce her independence as a modern woman and bend to the male will in a sublime surrender, one that would lead her to the altar and fill her life with children.

This was something that Doña Eulalia del Valle herself could not imagine ever happening, because even she had to know that fantasies are for dreams, not for real life. The worst thing about it was that the man she accepted—or rather, the man she found herself forced to tolerate when the hardship to which she and her mother were consigned finally became real hunger—did not remotely resemble the characters in Elinor Glyn's books and had never worn a sheikh's turban or travelled through the icy nights of the Russian steppes. He was not even distinguished enough for her to proudly introduce him to her family: a doctor from some backwater, with skin not quite light enough and hair more curly than straight, had nevertheless won the favour of the people of El Prado for being the first reliable paediatrician to settle in the city. He answered to the unremarkable name of Juan Palos Pérez, and though no one knew it, he had a formidable mother who, despite never leaving Usiacurí or ever having worn shoes, decided to give her son a head start by sending him to Bogotá to study, selling off a mysteriously acquired inheritance of cows year after year until he finished his degree in medicine and set up his clinic. Having specialized in an elite gringo teaching hospital that swore by boiling everything, Juan Palos Pérez did so too: nappies, teapots, water, milk, meat, vegetables; everything, absolutely everything, had to be boiled before it was allowed near a child's mouth, stripping anything edible of its nutritional value, because that was what those multicoloured vitamins were for, the ones he prescribed at his clinic, where he also advised the most rigorous asepsis—no walking barefoot or getting soaked in downpours——to make the children of Barranquilla's bourgeoisie look as lovely as North American babies.

All this made him quite popular with the locals. When the gringos sold their hospital and moved on, he was the only reputable paediatrician left, and his clinic in the 20 de Julio neighbourhood welcomed a daily stream of women who were used to counting their money in pesos rather than centavos and were more or less in love with him, with his white coat, his warm smile and his brand new Ford—although his mother over in Usiacurí still refused to wear shoes because she insisted on being true to herself and couldn't care less about appearances. He spent his days attending to the women and their babies and his nights talking politics with their husbands in the brothels, talking and nothing more because the asepsis prescribed by the gringos had given him a secret repulsion towards whores. These virtues were all extolled to Doña Eulalia when she started receiving those boxes of chocolates accompanied by a card whose letterhead, with its reference to the "paediatric doctor," provided a tantalizing glimpse of the house in El Prado, the Ford and three square meals a day, not to mention the confusing sensation of suspicion and attraction she had when she saw Juan Palos Pérez every Sunday at midmorning mass at the Iglesia del Carmen, which she had started to attend since someone—a female relative no doubt—convinced her that despite the dusty resentments her mother harboured, marriage was still a better prospect than the poorhouse. So, at this relative's instigation, or for some other reason, Doña Eulalia got her first ever perm at the age of thirty, bought her first lip pencil and asserted her social status by attending mass on Sundays; there, among the faces of men all hot and bothered in suits and ties, and women suffocating in hats and silk stockings, she hoped perhaps to see a troika suddenly appearing and rolling towards the main altar, or to glimpse the disquieting turban, the treacherous glance, the insidious smile which, overpowering her aversion, would make her a slave, but under no circumstances a slave to the doctor with his false air of self-confidence and his rather ordinary if not downright common looks, who nevertheless counted the wealthiest children in Barranquilla among his clients and had a Ford waiting for him outside the church.

Listening to Doña Eulalia del Valle in her period of great depression, in the days when Dora had been kicked out of her home by Benito Suárez and was anxiously trying to gain custody of her son, Lina would learn how Doña Eulalia had slipped into that courtship of boxes of chocolates and visits presided over by her mother, completely clueless about the man she was to marry or the woman who had given birth to him in Usiacurí and had a rather telling aversion to wearing shoes; powerless, above all, to see beyond Benito Suárez's seemingly polite exterior and recognize the uncouth individual who wasn't used to drinking and so would get blind drunk on their wedding day, before ineptly driving the Ford to the beach house his friend had let him use in Puerto Colombia, then falling into bed while she, trembling in her white silk gown adorned with little pink bows, finished preening herself in the bathroom and finally stepped out, after much hesitation, ready to be passionately ravaged by the sheikh of her dreams, only to find a drunkard snoring like a freight train.

From that moment on she started to hate him, that is to say, from then on she had the justification for the hatred that her mother had conditioned in her, which reached its definitive, irremediable climax a few hours later when Dr. Juan Palos Pérez got out of bed, vomited and, without even rinsing his mouth, came back to bed, heaved himself on top of her and did the deed with all the swiftness of a rooster. In fact, and perhaps this was what hurt her the most, Doña Eulalia's husband was a wicked lover who got a kick out of turning women on and knew how to touch and caress them just long enough to make them writhe with pleasure, but apparently only if they were maids. This, Doña Eulalia knew for sure forty days after Dora was born, when, having endured a hellish pregnancy and a painful birth that made her pay for what was done and what was yet to come, she got out of her bed, took a shower, put on a dress with wide shoulder pads, pulled her hair back with a pretty comb and waited for the sound of the engine in the garage sig-nalling her husband's arrival, then tiptoed across the hallway to surprise him with the sight of her out of bed. In all likelihood, there was another reason why Doña Eulalia stealthily crossed the hallway, because when pressed by Lina, she would admit that she'd been surprised, during those forty days of quaran-tine, to notice that half an hour went by between hearing the sound of the engine and the moment her husband walked into the room to greet her, but—and to Lina this seemed feasible— she had never imagined or even suspected the scene that was to play out before her eyes as she approached the inner door to the garage.

There he was, the husband who had impregnated her unceremoniously and as rapidly as possible, then under the pretext of protecting the baby had refrained from touching her for nine months: Dr. Juan Palos Pérez was on the floor, next to the Ford, on top of the maid—and oh, the disgrace, the shame, the humiliation—caressing her with the treacherous rhythm, the perverse insistence, the irresistible tenacity that a man's hand can possess when he is intent on drawing back the final veil of female modesty, although of course, in Doña Eulalia's opinion that maid had no such modesty. Back and forth he went, on and on, while Doña Eulalia watched the scene in a trance with her stomach in knots, powerless to move a muscle, conscious that, for the first time, she was discovering sin in its original, absolute form, but still rooted to the spot—nailed there, she would tell Lina, between sobs—until the maid gave one final spasm and she, Doña Eulalia, remembering that her surname was Del Valle Álvarez de la Vega for a reason, slowly made her way back to her room, where she burst into tears and swore that she was going to leave (to go where?), to work (how?), to live her life (what life?). But the sequence of thoughts ended in the kind of laments befitting of a tango when, fearing the prospect of threatening her mother with the poorhouse again, she fell to her knees by her baby daughter's crib and swore to sacrifice herself.

Although Lina didn't know the whole story, she was well aware that there had been a sacrifice, since this was the word Doña Eulalia always used whenever she talked about her years of marriage to Dr. Juan Palos Pérez. Lina remembered the doctor, her childhood physician, as a nice man who used to flick her arm to make it go numb when he gave her an injection, and would then hand her a lollipop, reminding her to brush her teeth after eating it. For her grandmother—privy, like everyone else, to his less than orthodox relationships with the local women—Dr. Juan Palos Pérez had simply followed the path mapped out for any man determined to climb the social ladder through study and hard work, and the marriage, from his perspective, had to be considered the crowning glory of his career, the most efficient means of gaining entry to the country club and seats on the boards of the city's most prestigious charitable organizations. On leaving Usiacurí, he had studied at the Pontifical Xaverian University, had specialized at the gringo teaching hospital, built up a respectable client base and had married a woman from a well-to-do family, solving the problems that she and her mother faced. In other words, he had simply followed the rules of a game whose origin and purpose probably escaped him, and his interest in the maids was consistent with a dichotomy that was linked to the same game, a dichotomy that, possibly, he had never questioned either. The city was full of social climbers like him. If anyone had cheated, or rather, been fooled, then in her grandmother's opinion it was actually Doña Eulalia del Valle, because by entering into a loveless marriage and being complicit in the whole social framework, she had demanded from the doctor not only what he could give her— the colonial-style house with the terrace, the garden and the Ford parked out front—but also something no man could give her, at least not without some degree of collaboration. And to add insult to injury, she had disapproved of his erotic inclinations rather than using them to her advantage (everyone knows that a woman will always find what she's looking for if she has the clear-sightedness to recognize it and the courage to accept it when she finds it) or, failing that, if her upbringing prevented her from channelling those inclinations appropriately in the name of modesty or some other idiotic euphemism, then perhaps she should have turned the other cheek or pushed them to the back of her mind. What she absolutely should not have done, however, was make them public knowledge by paying him a surprise visit to his clinic in the 20 de Julio neighbourhood, telling the secretary on duty, right there in front of the patients, one eyebrow raised haughtily in anger, that the doctor would no longer be requiring her services.

Because this is what Doña Eulalia started to do, after replacing the maids with decrepit old women who would have passed unnoticed through the prison cells of fifty men serving life sentences; this, and as Dora would later tell Lina, the sarcasm, the cutting remarks, the outbursts of rage that fed on the boredom of daytime and the unconscious frustrations of nighttime, frustrations that she did not confess or even suspect, provoking a kind of exasperation that slowly took hold of Dr. Juan Palos Pérez. This culminated not in the breakdown of their marriage—even separation was unthinkable in those days, particularly for a man who had sacrificed so much for the sake of convenience—but in an icy silence from the doctor in response to Doña Eulalia's verbal onslaughts, and, perhaps to compensate, it led to his philandering, a continual orgy of clandestine love affairs with secretaries, maids and nurses, raising their status, for increasingly fleeting interludes, to that of lovers. None of this Doña Eulalia knew, because the doctor continued to return home at seven o'clock sharp, and when he left the city for the weekend, it was on the pretext of going to see his mother in Usiacurí, and not even Doña Eulalia could hold that against him.

But a woman who had the whole day to reflect on her misfortune could not be fooled for long: alone, surrounded by those dowdy maids, sitting in a rocking chair facing the trees in her garden—just as her father had for fifteen years—Doña Eulalia managed not so much to discover the truth but rather, and this was even worse, to sense what was happening without ever finding any proof that could free her from her doubts, from the feeling that she was going crazy, she would later tell Lina, crying, because despite all her theories, there was still the mocking, disarming reality of that Ford arriving in the garage at seven in the evening and of the eggs and hens, which he brought back from Usiacurí every Sunday. However, one fact remained, and Doña Eulalia clung to this vehemently not so much to justify her heated insults as to preserve a shred of faith in her mental health: five years into their marriage, Dr. Juan Palos Pérez had decided to partner up with a paediatrician who had recently arrived to the coast. This business decision brazenly defied all logic, prudence and common sense, because by that time not only had his client base shrunk but his financial situation was also visibly beginning to deteriorate—for several months, he had failed to upgrade to the latest Ford, paint their house or pay his country club fees on time—so it stood to reason that either he was spending his money on another woman, or he was planning to take advantage of the new paediatrician being there to spend more time with her, or both of these things at once. The latter was the truth, although Doña Eulalia never knew the whole truth because she never discovered the identity of the other woman. There was, of course, another woman: someone alluring enough to make Dr. Juan Palos Pérez forget about his fickle and ultimately short-lived dalliances to focus on a passion so all-consuming that he was prepared to share his clientele and spend the money that would otherwise have been intended for his family. But although Doña Eulalia sensed what was happening, she was never going to admit it. Even on the day when she told Lina what happened, she chose to refer to the woman as a whore, as did the notes on the police report taken when Dr. Juan Palos Pérez's corpse was found bobbing in the surf at a beach in Puerto Colombia, his mouth full of weeds, very close to the spot where his clothes were discovered alongside an empty whisky bottle. He wasn't really drunk when he died, at least, it wasn't the whisky that caused his death but the fact that he had started making love under the hot sun after eating two portions of mullet rice in a nearby restaurant, the location of which never came to light because no restaurant owner would admit to having prepared or served mullet rice that day, August 11th, when the sea washed Dr. Juan Palos Pérez's body up on the beach, all blue and bloated, spewing seaweed and little sea shells, which is how Doña Eulalia del Valle would see him on a slab at the hospital where the police took him. An hour later, the coroner performed the autopsy and revealed that the cause of death was a blockage caused by sexual intercourse while digesting lunch at one in the afternoon, when as everyone knows, the sun's rays beat down and the only acceptable activity is sleeping through the siesta: in other words, the doctor had departed from this world in the infernal heat of a secluded beach, slumped over the body of a woman who, probably in a fit of panic, had dragged him into the sea to splash his face or revive him with water, and then, realizing the gravity of the situation, chose to let the waves carry him away instead, giving her time to quickly throw on her clothes and return to the city without being seen.

This, at least, was the explanation Lina received from her grandmother when she was speculating about the circumstances surrounding Dr. Juan Palos Pérez's death, a version of events which Dr. Ignacio Agudelo (the paediatrician who had gone into business with Dora's father) would confirm years later, in the days when he became her lover, allowing her to realize the most incestuous of her dreams. But when Doña Eulalia del Valle talked about what happened, Lina realized that she should in no way question her version of the story, in which the heartless prostitute not only caused her husband's death but also dragged him into the sea like a dog, because something told her that despite all her hatred and the time that had passed, she would have been floored by the revelation that she'd been supplanted by a woman with the same social standing and, to cap it all, the same surname.

On that occasion, Lina felt pity for Doña Eulalia. She saw her as an actor, doomed to tirelessly recite the same monologue from the same tragedy so many times that her own life had lost any substance, form or reality, trapped in the role of the pathetic character she was playing or, worse still, limited to the minimum expression of existence that was condensed in her obstinate, feverish monologue: the seconds or minutes in which she related, with the exact same movements and phrases, the woeful tale of her solitary childhood, the younger years reduced to keeping a blind man company and the marriage, which began with her humiliation and ended in the most scandalous indignity. Time already moved differently for Doña Eulalia: it did not pass or fly by, and it did not act as the backdrop against which living things and objects could change; each episode in her life had been permanently fixed in her memory, lacking any chronology or causal relationship but cementing the injustice that not only had these episodes happened, but they had also become her memories. Lina reckoned that the episode had allowed Doña Eulalia at least to express herself, to react, to fight against something which, banal though it seemed, was tangible, like taking a taxi to the clinic in the 20 de Julio neighbourhood and firing her husband's secretaries, one after the other. But later, when she was alone and had no one to confront—Dora was still there but she was like a shadow, and Benito Suárez was not remotely like a shadow but was never around—her memories, spinning around and around, had started to burn out, to dim like certain stars, perhaps shrinking in size but dramatically increasing in density, until they became like ball bearings ricocheting around mercilessly inside a child's head.

Of course, the worst of these memories centred around Dr. Juan Palos Pérez's death, the final vile act that encapsulated all the acts that came before it, starting with the scene in the garage forty days after Dora was born, when Doña Eulalia abruptly discovered not only the meaning of the words 'abstinence' and 'temptation'—terms that, until then, had confused her and were associated exclusively with not being allowed to eat meat during Lent and on the first Friday of every month—but also the true reason for the colour of her husband's skin, which, with a generous instinct of reconciliation and perhaps also recognition, she had initially attributed to the effect of the sun, which beat down like a curse on the city all year round and passed easily through the windows of any Ford. This discovery stunned Doña Eulalia del Valle, serving as further proof of how cruel fate had been to her by mixing her bloodline with that of a race condemned by the Bible, passing on to her sole descendent the dark and lascivious demons, for which religion, vigilance and her own fine example were no match, because they would always be there lying in wait for the first slip-up, ready to slither out and drag Dora to her ruin, erasing the last scrap of honour associated with her surname.

The strange thing—and Lina noticed this more than a few times—was that Doña Eulalia had a fairly ambiguous attitude to what one might call the signs of the devil that lurked inside Dora: in theory she was horrified by what she saw, but sometimes she showed her subject not exactly tolerance but a sort of depleted admiration or even envy, with the words that slipped out of her mouth unintentionally, alluding to the desire Dora would awaken in men with her sensual lips, her curvaceous figure and her abundant mane of hair. Lina never asked herself whether Dora was affected by this ambiguity: for a long time she thought her friend's temperament was indestructible, completely closed off to any influence, like a force that stemmed from the distant past and, fully conscious of its objective, waited not for the first opportunity—as Doña Eulalia feared—but for a specific point in time, a predetermined moment, to take what it wanted, tearing down the fragile barriers established by any form of guidance or surveillance. The thing inside Dora was infinitely tenacious, but more than that, Lina would later discover, it gave her a kind of ingenuity no one would have thought her capable of if they had seen her at school, sitting at her desk, exhausted from the heat and stupefied by the noises that only she seemed to hear.

Lina accepted, with a degree of reservation, her grandmother's claim that it would have been a different story had Doña Eulalia not been so careless as to send Dora to work at the kindergarten that one of her relatives ran, though she also recognized that the kindergarten had played as much of a role as the naivety shown by her relative, a born spinster who, by one of those strange paradoxes of nature, was blessed with an insatiable maternal instinct and, after spending much of her life caring for her sisters' offspring, had decided to convert her house into a kindergarten, not so much for financial reasons as to surrender to the pleasure of cleaning backsides, preparing afternoon snacks and labouring all day long in the midst of utter chaos. The woman, who didn't have a bad bone in her body, had told Lina with surprise that Doña Eulalia had phoned her numerous times, asking if she employed gardeners or servants, whether the children were dropped off by their own mothers, and most importantly, enquiring about the layout of the reception room where her daughter would be working. The spinster relative most definitely understood the underlying meaning of the questions regarding the presence or absence of a gardener whose moral rectitude was by no means assured, but what she seemed to find strange, almost insulting, was Doña Eulalia's insistence on getting her to describe the room for her—a room with pale pink walls, a sofa and a desk—and, since she had been so obliging, to describe the people who drove the children to the kindergarten. As the spinster talked, Lina gradually began to understand the associations that Doña Eulalia made between the reception room (or its contents) and the threats in question; Lina pictured her friend's mother sitting there stiffly in her rocking chair, anxiously trying to list all the dangers that lay in wait for her daughter, whom she had driven, through her own fear, to become the secretary of a kindergarten, one that had no gardeners or servants, thank God, but where the children might still arrive accompanied by their fathers. This minor detail changed everything, taking a place that was essentially untainted, with only an old lady and a handful of children in it, and turning it into a potential stage for the tragedy she so feared—feared and perhaps even yearned for, Lina would later hear her grandmother say, since any excessive dread of something hidden almost always conceals the murky desire from which it stems, first to provide it with an outlet, and then, so that once and for all, the desire can break free from the fear that covers it like a veil whose thickness is determined by the intensity of its violence.

By the time Lina had finished talking to the spinster relative, she had gained a pretty clear idea of the problems she could expect for having agreed to be Dora's accomplice, since Doña Eulalia would stubbornly persist in asking Lina the exact thing that, half an hour earlier, she'd promised Dora she wouldn't tell: yes, there was a desk in that pink-walled room, but she wouldn't mention the sofa she'd been sitting on when she made that promise. At first, Lina agreed that it was necessary to lie to Doña Eulalia about all the creams and powders Dora kept in a drawer of the filing cabinet; in truth she'd enjoyed watching Dora's transformation as she brought out the little containers, even asking her to put a bit of colour on her own cheeks and smearing the orange lipliner over her mouth. But the matter of the sofa disconcerted her. There was something about the way Dora told her, "Close your eyes and describe the room," then interrupted her, saying, "No, remember you never saw any sofa, swear you won't say there's a sofa here if she asks you."

As Lina would later tell her grandmother with admiration, Dora had been cunning enough not to mention the gender of the people who came into the reception room holding their children by the hand and smelling of eau de cologne; hence Lina's astonishment and how easily she made a promise which apparently only involved denying the presence of a single piece of furniture in a room, as absurd as that sounded. But even when she had spoken with the spinster and could see things more clearly, she still found that Dora could not be rattled; when she said to her friend as she sat at her desk, her finger poised with infinite caution over the keys of the typewriter: "I suppose I shouldn't mention the fathers either." "What fathers?" Dora asked, unfazed. "I mean, sometimes it's the fathers who drop the children off at kindergarten," Lina said, noticing a slight smile creeping across Dora's face.

All the same, Lina thought that the place and the presence of a man were almost immaterial. Despite the height of Doña Eulalia's boundary wall, anyone could have climbed over it, and her garden—threshed scarcely twice a year, left to the wine palms and the weeds that shot up ferociously after every downpour—was popular among local maids looking for a hideaway for their nocturnal trysts. As for the man, well, he had noticed Dora when she walked into the country club, and though he hadn't so far dared to approach her, he would do so at his first opportunity, while Catalina and Lina were playing tennis, and Dora was watching from the courtside. If it hadn't been him it would have been someone else, but in all likelihood he would be the first, because few men seemed to have battled their natural urges as hard as he had out of the vaguest sense of respectability. He had a rich but stupid wife, four children and a job as a commercial director for his father's businesses, where his brothers thought of themselves as crusaders of industrial development, and where he, as he'd confided in Dora once, was bored to death. The truth was, Andrés Larosca (Labrowska, originally Slobrowska) did not seem suited to the position he had taken up in the interests of his family— Catholic Slavs with a clan mindset that had survived who knows what foregone dark and forgotten tragedy—and even less suited to the woman he'd been tied to in those same interests. With his handsome face and strong features, he reminded Lina of the Norse kings depicted in her history book: though incredibly courteous, his mannerisms unexpectedly revealed a kind of disgruntled energy, like a wild horse forced to do pirouettes in a circus. Lina had noticed his greedy eyes following Dora and was somewhat surprised when she saw him playing tennis on the court, wielding his racket like a sword and furiously returning ball after ball with the kind of raw power that seemed intended not so much to defeat his opponent as to decapitate him.

The fact that tennis acted as a release for him, or a substitute, was confirmed when he seduced Dora, because for the year and a half that their affair lasted he was no longer seen in the club corridors, his muscular chest straining beneath a white T-shirt, racket in hand, with a wicked look in his eyes. Now was not the time for tennis, because he was busy seeing Dora between midday and one in the afternoon, while the spinster and the children were having their nap, and he usually headed to the country club after six. No, now was the time of the horse running free across the prairie, the alert, frustrated hunter who suddenly discovers the trail of his prey, an awakening, a moment of awareness, an impulse that finally homes in on its target. He remained cautious all the same, arriving at the kindergarten in a taxi or leaving his car at a nearby gas station, and Lina, sitting on the school bus, spotted him several times walking in the hot sun or running along in the rain, holding his bag above his head. Everything would become easier later on, when Dora saw the advert for an experienced secretary in the local newspaper, *El Heraldo*, and read it out loud to her mother, asking for permission to apply, a request which Doña Eulalia immediately denied, but eventually agreed to in light of Dora's pleading and advice from her relatives. But during the

December holidays, between one job and another, Lina would discover the discomfiture of love, the complexity of its power. She would discover this thanks to Dora, not only because Dora and Andrés Larosca were to be the protagonists but because Dora was the one who orchestrated it all, calculating and measuring the whole thing from start to finish: from the advert in *El Heraldo* to the idea of spending the holidays with Catalina and Lina in the big old house that Catalina's mother still owned in Puerto Colombia, or rather the idea of inviting herself to join her two friends, who spent December there every year. The girls were chaperoned by Berenice, who cooked for them and stubbornly took it upon herself to neurotically clean up all the dust that had gathered over the past twelve months, grumbling all day long because of the drum she said was pounding inside her head, which subsided with nightfall, when from her seat on the dilapidated veranda, with a handkerchief soaked in Menticol on her forehead, she began to tell them, in a low voice, the most extraordinary secrets of the families in the city.

Dora had understood that this year Doña Eulalia was not going to argue whether the mere presence of a Black cook, a woman she deemed half-crazy, could truly protect her honour, the same way she hadn't disputed her relatives' assurances of the respectability of the industrialist Larosca family a few days earlier. Because the ingenuity that had crept into Dora as soon as she decided to break free from her mother's protection—nimble and determined, like a bird shaking the water from its feathers by flapping its wings—had allowed her to gauge the extent of this new source of concern for Doña Eulalia del Valle, an anxiety no longer linked to her daughter's virginity but to something perhaps equally as important, namely the standing that she, Dora, was to occupy in Barranquilla's high society, which was already compromised because of her father's dubious origins and that detestable grandmother from

Usiacurí, who was never mentioned and had lived and died so tastelessly, without ever wearing anything on her feet. Not to mention how disreputable it was for a well-bred girl to go out to work like a poor person while her friends were still at school and some of them (the wealthiest ones) were starting to leave for the United States, ostensibly to perfect English skills they had never learned and were never going to learn, but in fact to remove them from any form of temptation in a boarding school run by nuns, and allowing them to return shrouded in an aura of elegance intended to pique the interest of the city's most eligible bachelors. This concern, Dora would confess to Lina, scornfully—she felt no need to climb the social ladder through pride of lineage, and the idea of making a place in society made her laugh back then—was what finally made her mother agree to let her work for Andrés Larosca, thinking (subconsciously, of course) that the high, almost exorbitant salary for the role would allow Dora to save up for her society debut, that is, to buy the ballgown and to host two or three receptions that would be featured in the press, reminding those in the know that behind the dark-skinned Palos was a Del Valle Álvarez de la Vega girl, just waiting to be snapped up by anyone with his sights set on the prestige of her gilded surnames, which, in that world of decay and ruin, had served as the last remaining, albeit sometimes damaged, stronghold of tradition. And this same motivation, the pursuit of maintaining good relations, would prompt Doña Eulalia to let her go to Puerto Colombia with Lina and Catalina, despite her doubts about Berenice's ability to exercise effective control over her.

Those doubts would turn out to be justified. Berenice had spent forty years of her life working for the people of El Prado, and she knew every family's history, their vices, weaknesses, even their crimes, like the back of her hand, but she loved Lina as vehemently as she hated everyone else, and she was willing to extend this same good will to any of Lina's friends, especially Dora. Berenice admired Dora first of all for embracing her womanhood—though she would have never used those words, instead saying, "At least that girl knows what she's got and how to use it"—and, second, for having all the charm of youth with her brazen curves and her golden hair in a mass of curls down to her waist; serene, the central axis of her desire; not heavy or compelling, but motionless and dense, so dense, Lina thought, that she had only to spin round in a circle to make the earth move in a different direction.

Drunk on pleasure and imbuing every word and even silence with sensuality, Dora could calm Berenice's reservations without the slightest bit of effort. There was an instant understanding between the two of them, between the huge Black woman, whose body had developed a layer of blubber on coming into contact with white people, like a seal forced to protect itself against the biting cold, and the girl who joined them for that December holiday. Berenice took Dora under her wing, protecting her then and continuing to do so. She kept quiet about what happened at the big old house in Puerto Colombia, forgetting about the noises coming from the garden at night and the car headlights suddenly piercing the darkness; she forgot about all that, or displaced it in her memory with an absurd story about horses, which she clung to with her usual ability to go over and over the same anecdote, citing an interminable chain of events in which she claimed to be the victim—she and her nerves, which were eternally frayed from Lina and Catalina's irresponsible ways. Intent on tormenting her, the girls had decided to go horse riding, not on any old four-legged beasts trained to tolerate the saddle, bridle, stirrups and a rider, but on the only nags they could get their hands on in Puerto Colombia: two large, ill-tempered beasts that despised the entire human race after ten years of hellish treatment spent moving livestock around the rocky, sunscorched terrain, and suffering cruelty from unscrupulous

farmhands, as demonstrated by their bodies, which were covered in scars, and their bulging eyes, which flashed with distrust and malice.

"Skittish," the owner said with a knowing look when he
brought them to the house for the first time; "Death traps!"
Berenice yelled from the window on the second floor when she
saw them, prompting Lina and Catalina to quickly saddle up
and ride away while Berenice heaved the shapeless, volumi-
nous mass of her body down the stairs to confront that good-
for-nothing who was knowingly putting the lives of two young
girls at risk for the sake of eight lousy pesos, the hourly price
agreed upon the previous day. Because anyone could see that
those two beasts were bound to throw the girls off at the first
fence or wall they encountered, that they would roughly eject
the riders from the saddle, bolt, refuse to respond to the reins,
stop suddenly or nip at their legs. All these things happened,
of course, and were duly noted; in other words, Berenice kept
every detail locked in her memory so that she could criticize
the girls for their actions for the rest of their lives, the way she
did every night while she wiped their knees with iodine or
bandaged their bruised legs with gauzes spritzed with melissa
flower water.

It wasn't that Berenice was wrong: the fact that the girls had
lived to tell the tale of those two horses in Puerto Colombia
was because they were young and well-fed so their bones were
strong, or perhaps because of their swift reflexes, or simply
destiny. But Lina had noticed that Berenice's tears and lamen-
tations increased with Dora's prolonged absences, and that she
also exaggerated the injustice of her situation—it would be just
her luck to one day have to collect the dead body of a girl in her
care—even though the horses themselves posed no great risk,
not because they had lost their bad habits, or become less skittish, to quote the owner, but because the girls had gotten to
know them, and through the slightest movement of the neck,

an almost imperceptible shake of the ears, the contraction of a muscle or a sudden, unexplained change of pace, they could anticipate the horses' intentions and control them or, in the worst-case scenario, leap out of the saddle in time; in other words, they'd managed to establish a modus vivendi with them, particularly since the day they discovered the only place where the beasts were willing to set aside their hatred for humankind: a long, smooth, narrow strip of white sand that appeared out of nowhere and seemed to extend infinitely, plunging into the sea and parting it in two, where the horses cantered along the virgin sand, whipping up the surf, their nostrils flaring as they breathed in the thick scent of salt and iodine carried on the breeze.

None of these arguments, neither subtle human–equine understandings nor special beaches, convinced Berenice. The truth was—and Lina would understand this later—that Berenice was afraid: she was afraid that Dora might get pregnant, afraid that someone would find out or perhaps, most likely, that the affair would end in disaster. Because Berenice knew from experience that when white people fell in love, tragedy was in the air because they were unable to accept the simplest things in life and prone to complicating matters with abstract ideas completely unrelated to the sudden, magical, ephemeral desire to sleep next to someone, to laugh, touch and be touched until their bodies ignited like the flames of a stove and their blood bubbled with relief. That was what she said every night, sitting on the steps to the veranda and dabbing at her brow with a handkerchief that stank of Menticol, as she watched Dora setting off along the path to the beach; rather than talking to the girls, who were hard-pressed to understand her at any rate, she was using them as an intermediary for the ghost she often spoke to in the solitude of the kitchen and who seemed to be advising her, on this occasion, to catch the next bus back to Barranquilla. And though her threats made Lina and Catalina nervous, they only made Dora smile, because nothing seemed to faze her or throw her off course. Nothing could disturb that girl's buddha-like attitude: motionless and content, yet alert, she devoured the nights and slept all day, waking late in the afternoon to have a wash and brush her teeth, then lie on a hammock on the second floor waiting for the car headlights to appear around that final bend in the road, at the top of the slope. Then, she would rise and solemnly walk down the stairs, her eyes shining and already elsewhere, incapable of focusing on anything or noticing anyone, fixed on the memory that guided her footsteps to the beach and quickened her breath, as if her body were preparing to vibrate to a different rhythm, to beat to a different cadence.

In the pale light of the bulb that hung from the living room ceiling, the air filled with a pungent cloud of Flit insecticide that Berenice sprayed from a red atomizer as soon as dusk heralded the arrival of the first swarms of mosquitos; Catalina and Lina silently watched Dora, conscious of the gulf that separated them, with their dirty blue jeans and their hair full of sand, from that immaculate figure currently striding away, her nipples protruding beneath her cotton poplin shirt, and her legs bare, pale and provocative in those shorts; she radiated a musky scent, a mixture of sweat and perfume, having slept and fasted all day, perhaps obeying some instinct, some ritual, some vague preparatory ceremony, the meaning of which Berenice understood every dinnertime when she served her a plate of food and Dora set it down next to the embers of the stove without explanation.

They could have followed Dora, but they didn't. They could have walked alongside her, safe in the knowledge that Dora wouldn't see them, as if they, Catalina and Lina, were part of the landscape, the rocks, clouds, tree trunks and the breeze, as if they were part of the subconscious. And even if they had followed her, Dora wouldn't have minded; not out of shamelessness or exhibitionism, but because right then she existed within a certain orbit and could only harness the world's energy in a given way, which might be classed as love but transcended the concept in the sense that it was a state of complete communication with the universe; because when their bodies joined together, she would tell Lina some years later, she felt connected to everything around her; she felt, she would say, her voice sorrowful as she searched painstakingly for the right words—"That your act was echoed infinitely," Lina suggested—and Dora nodded, relieved, almost happy; "yes," she said, "echoed by the gulls flying across the sky, even the grains of sand that gathered on the beach."

So it was natural for her not to hide or pretend, and natural for her not to feel remorse despite Doña Eulalia's anathemas. Because in those days, Dora could see no resemblance between herself and her mother, and given the disturbance of her bloodline, it would have been impossible for her to identify with that recluse of a mother, who was entrenched in her bitterness and growing old in a rocking chair on the fringes of life, but who still inspired tenderness within her, enough tenderness at least for Dora to have listened to her patiently since the age of nine, to have allowed herself to be possessed, absorbed, dominated by her until the call of her body overpowered her mother's words and she withdrew, brushed her aside, not hurting her mother but simply ignoring her, not listening to her and, perhaps so as not to hurt her, carefully concealing her affairs from her. She did not attempt to hide these relationships from anyone else, because any of the people staying in that big old house could have followed her or led the way and she wouldn't have minded; any one of them could have gone with her when she made her way to the beach, but Catalina and Lina never did, because a voice, a foreboding, told them that following her meant taking the path to the place where childhood died.

So the two girls did not follow her, but they found her, or rather, they saw them, Dora and Andrés Larosca, making love. One Saturday at sunset, a strange sunset when the moon and the sun both shone in the sky and Catalina and Lina were riding along the narrow strip of white sand, following the unexpected tyre tracks of a car that had dared to penetrate that unspoiled place, venturing much farther than normal until they found it, the car, and in the background, two naked figures walking up the beach from the sea. They did not dismount; even on horseback, sixty feet away, they couldn't be seen, but they could still see. They saw: Dora with her head resting on Andrés Larosca's shoulder, his hands roaming all over her body, Dora sliding back onto the sand, Andrés Larosca's penis erect against the golden reflection of the sea. And they saw Dora take that penis between her fingers, play with it, draw it closer to the most secret depths between her legs and hold it there, again and again, following the rhythm of the waves whipped up by the tide, fast, ever faster until her body became taut like a wire, arched like a bowstring, suddenly flopping down onto the sand, emitting the moan of a wounded seagull, of a siren fresh out of the ocean, while that thing she'd held between her fingers entered her, and Lina and Catalina, straight-backed on their horses, looked on speechless, watching the two silhouettes that had now become one, a seamless ebb and flow in the curious light of a sky where the moon rose higher with the darkness and the sun sank below the horizon.

III

It did not begin with the Word, her grandmother used to say, because before the Word came action, and before action came desire. In itself, any desire was and would always be pure, older than language, indifferent to any consideration of moral order, and had a natural ability to balance itself, a precise and reliable mechanism for self-regulation. But since man needed to tolerate community life in order to survive, and since community life implied the existence of convergent and divergent individual desires, that is, desires capable of forming or severing ties, of building or destroying, of creating harmony or causing chaos, an appropriate structure of values had to be invented for every situation. And so desire, losing its primitive innocence, entered into the categories of good and evil. For this reason, man could only inspire pity, because he was the only being that, in order to live, would die twice, because he had the most terrible awareness of one of his deaths, and the most senseless forgetfulness when it came to the other. He began to die before he was born and he knew it, and he was dying when he started to live, but he was unaware of it: he did not know that his shame at the desire he glimpsed, his pain at the desire he repressed, the intolerable feeling of emptiness that accompanied his daily, repetitive, infinite frustration, was a price and nothing more than a price; a simple trade-off, an exchange. It was of no more value than the act of eating or drinking, and like life, it had no meaning, since the meaning of life would never be revealed to us. But if one was determined to go on living despite all this, it would be better to understand that the problems that arise when desire meets social reality could be overcome as long as one did not lose sight of the relative nature of the rules of desire, the advantages that lay in repressing it, and above all, if one managed to glide through forbidden waters without swimming headlong into sanctions or becoming alienated by one's own rebelliousness. In other words, each individual, depending on their drive, their greed, temperament or ability to cope with risks, was forced to find a new balance between the demands of their desires and the imperatives of reality. And that was where everything was at stake. But this was something almost no one knew.

Andrés Larosca probably did not know that if he had eaten the so-called forbidden fruit he would have found within it the knowledge of his own sexuality and, therefore, a first glimmer of himself, cracking the door open for the first time to reveal a part of his personality that had been ignored until then, neglected day after day through the repetitive acts which, although beyond his control, gave him a sense of coherence with the world in which he had been born and lived, even if that meant losing his freedom; then, suddenly glimpsing that freedom, and at the same time the possibility of grasping it, with all the loneliness, conflict and risk this entailed, he would have closed the door. It couldn't have been easier, seeing as everything had been designed to prevent him from opening that door in the first place. It took very little effort for him to step back, to stop seeing Dora as his own reflection, thus ending their affair and making a clean break, or more subtly, accepting the judgement his father and his brothers might make about her: the judgement of men, of the city. From that moment on, Dora was left defenceless: she lacked the analytical skills to understand what was going through Andrés Larosca's mind—presuming that any of this was going through his mind or had made a mark on his conscience in any way—and she would be subjected to his mood swings, his contradictions and whims.

Although Lina did not understand most of her grandmother's explanations at the time, and although she refused to accept that the Norse king, the naked man she'd seen against the reflection of the sea that time when she was out on horseback, would do something as banal as despise a woman just because she had given herself to him, she was aware that the situation between Dora and Andrés Larosca was deteriorating, and she felt helpless when she saw Dora come to her house every evening and sit on the terrace while she waited for her to finish her chores, not saying a word, because suddenly Dora had cut herself off from the world; she had withdrawn into herself and spent hours on the terrace in the dark, in silence, staring out with painful bewilderment at the trees in the garden. One night she finally spoke: she walked into the dining room where Lina was studying, and, opening her hand, dropped a handful of rings and bracelets onto the table: metal, with aquamarines and coral. "Look," she said. "Look what he's started giving me." Then she burst into tears.

Had she known what was happening, Doña Eulalia could have celebrated both her triumph and her defeat right then: everything was going according to plan, and she was right, at least now Dora agreed with her that sex was dirty, and men were despicable, because they were determined to make women commit the act for which they would ultimately despise them, an act which was clearly dirty if it provoked their scorn. There was no way around it. In vain, Lina tried to explain to her that the real problem was essentially the opinion that she, Dora, was forming of herself. Not because Lina discerned the process that links the feeling of being at fault with the need for punishment, nor because she had understood what her grandmother meant when she said how foolish it was to use the gaze of others as a mirror. But because it was the best

argument she could find to convince Dora that she did not
deserve all the humiliation, taunts and contempt, that she
wasn't ruined like she said she was, crying in a corner of the
dining room, and that she may as well give Andrés back his
shoddy rings and his stupid secretary job, probably losing a
few feathers in the process, but not necessarily her dignity.

The word "dignity" would set alarm bells ringing for Lina,
with the realization that she was unable to get through to Dora
using concepts that she seemed to find strange, even disturbing. That was how she discovered that for months she may as
well have been talking to the wind, because Dora, pretending
to understand her, nodding along in agreement with what she
said, had never really listened, not because of any secret ill
intent or duplicity, but out of a simple inability to grasp the
meaning of certain words, which went in one ear and out the
other, the same way that she forgot the lessons she had learned
by heart at school, condensing her vocabulary to the basic
words required only for her immediate environment but making the fewest number of possible connections between those
words, either out of mental idleness or perhaps as a form of
resistance, one she developed initially to escape Doña Eulalia's
voracious ways and then applied automatically, using it as a
kind of conditioned reflex in any conversation, turning any
dialogue into a monologue that created between her and the
person talking an invisible, impalpable wall, built with kindness and passivity, but a wall nonetheless and therefore impenetrable. This, Lina would discover when she tried to make her
see that neither Andrés Larosca's reactions, nor Doña
Eulalia's condemnations, nor the aseptic characters from
those American movies—the Tyrone Powers and John
Waynes, who only touched their even less realistic female
companions with their eyes—should force her to internalize
and project that wretched image of herself to others, since it
was all relative. The word "relative" also made her blink,

although Lina, sensing her friend's bewilderment, told her about old Eskimo men abandoned in the snow, and French peasants who cared more about the death of a cow than that of a child. It was all relative, Lina insisted, aware of how futile her words were, and barely managing not to lose her patience when, in spite of all her examples, Dora's eyes clouded over, first with fear and the refusal to leave the walled confines of her brain, then with tears. Not seeking to inspire solidarity or compassion, Dora's tears expressed her raw grief as she realized that the catastrophe was inevitable, and became more inevitable the longer it went on, and that she, Dora, was sinking, slipping into that situation that had taken a definite humiliating turn since the day they saw Andrés Larosca in the country club and she naively spoke to him of dignity.

It happened one July 20th, a day that would remain etched in Lina's mind for many reasons, not least because that was when she became the owner of Catalina's highly coveted American blue jeans. That was how the morning began, when Catalina turned up at Lina's house with her old faded blue jeans in a paper bag, wearing another pair the same but new, and the two girls set off to call for Isabel and Dora to go and enjoy what seemed to be an Independence Day like any other, one of those parties at the country club that started with races—with donkeys, sacks or obstacles—then continued with a huge lunch of roasted veal that had been slow-cooking over hot coals since the previous night, and ended in a dance at around seven o'clock, when a voice announced over the band's microphone that the youngsters should clear the dancefloor.

Andrés Larosca could have probably guessed that Dora would be at the party, and if it bothered him so much to see her there in the presence of his family, he could have simply stayed at home and sent his wife and children there alone instead of making that face when he saw the girls turn up after lunch, joining their friends at the next table. He greeted Dora with a frosty expression and barely deigned to look at Lina and Catalina. His indifference, it seemed, was a response to a cautious instinct to banish any suspicion from his wife's mind, but as Lina was to discover a few hours later, Andrés Larosca was in fact furious. He simply could not stand to see Dora there, at the next table, so close to his family. Perhaps because he had accepted the judgement of other men, and now, after several months of the relationship he had paid for in kind (the salary was enough to pay three secretaries who would at least have been capable of typing without spelling mistakes), Dora had been reduced to a caged bird, a seduced fifteen-year-old, a fling, a thrill, a risk, a mere lover. And lovers, usually associated with women of colour—the Black-*mulata*-maid-whore—and thus visibly belonging to the lower class, had never held the social status of the *hetaera* or *la maîtresse*, as Lina had heard her grandmother remark several times, especially when she closed one of those weighty novels that regularly arrived in the mail from France and which seemed to make her nostalgic for long-forgotten loves from the distant past.

Lina had noticed that the word "lover" had a different undertone depending on whether it was uttered by her grandmother or by her father, and for some time she had suspected that her father's interpretation was the one most people shared, especially Andrés Larosca, given that he behaved so strangely. But even though she had seen Dora crying in her dining room, she found it impossible to imagine that any feeling, including contempt, could translate into the utter disgust that resounded in Andrés Larosca's voice when he started hurling insults at Dora in the locker room at the country club that July 20th, laying into her for daring to show her face at a party knowing full well that his wife might be there; he wasn't mad at her for running the risk of exposing their relationship, but for insulting his wife with her mere presence, almost as though his wife belonged to another species and had produced their four children by parthenogenesis, Lina thought when she overheard him talking from the hallway. She couldn't see him—the locker room was in darkness, and Andrés Larosca had summoned Dora there with a discreet look as soon as his wife went home—but she could just make out the door, which was slightly ajar. She was dying to throw it open, to stamp her feet, to somehow silence that cruel voice, to shake Dora out of her submissive state, because it seemed Dora could think of nothing else to do but apologize, beg for forgiveness and whimper about her innocence. Finally, Lina could stand it no more and sneaked back into the garden, where she called out to her from behind a palm tree. She waited five or six minutes but heard nothing, and then the shadow of Andrés Larosca cut across in front of the palm tree as he crept stealthily up the pavement outside the main entrance to the country club, leaving the coast clear for her to go and rescue Dora at last. Because that was how it felt to her, that she was saving her, freeing her from humiliation, when she found her huddled on the floor in front of Catalina's locker, wracked with sobs, and tried to tell her that Andrés Larosca had no right to talk to her that way and that she, Dora, had no reason to put up with it, because she was under no obligation to share his opinions. Though the things he said might be hurtful, as they reflected a total lack of love and tenderness, they shouldn't make her feel ashamed, she insisted, wiping away Dora's tears with her handkerchief, because all she needed do if she wanted to regain her sense of dignity was leave the office and never see him again. Dora stared at her then, as if for the first time she was grasping what she was hearing, and her eyes took on an incredulous expression: "Lina," she whispered, "what you're saying is completely immoral."

So in this way, Doña Eulalia could have celebrated her triumph: and for good, if Dora had stopped there and flagellated herself like her grandfather, if she had shut herself away in a convent or looked for some other kind of purification. But despite admitting her fault, Dora seemed incapable of severing ties with Andrés Larosca, and continued to work in his offices until he took it upon himself to fire her. Even then, she had already accepted that she would have to suffer and endure humiliating treatment as atonement, although she would never know for sure whether it was the punishment that made her feel that she was in the wrong, or if her own sense of guilt had caused Andrés Larosca's behaviour, in other words, the punishment he dealt out. In any case, Dora had no problem putting up with all manner of humiliation, because back then, she would tell Lina years later without a trace of cynicism, she needed a man; she needed his hands, his mouth, his caresses, and for this she was willing to pay any price that was asked of her. But every sin had to be redeemed: and that was why, as she celebrated her triumph, Doña Eulalia could have also celebrated her defeat.

Sin was hard to wash away, and it travelled crooked paths seeking atonement. Nobody knew what had gone on between Dora and Andrés Larosca: she, Lina, had told only her grandmother, and her grandmother was as inscrutable as stone, Catalina zealously kept that memory of the beach to herself, and Berenice was still shaken up at the mere thought of those horses. And yet Dora believed that she was the talk of the town, refusing to set foot in the country club because she claimed her reputation was ruined. A reputation she had never thought about before, whose value suddenly took on the dimensions attributed to it by Doña Eulalia del Valle, for whom marriage was life's only salvation and virginity was the only way into marriage. Of course, now that Dora had lost her virginity, she had no hope of marrying any of the boys who frequented the country club, unless she could find a doctor who would be willing to remedy the situation with an operation—either that, or she could wait for some providential gringo to come along. But both these solutions required a certain state of mind, a resolve to face up to the situation and thus to control or momentarily mute the demands of her body by resorting to the outlandish methods recommended by Doña Eulalia, such as mothballs. Approached in this way, the problem seemed to tie in with Dora's version of events, that is, what she told Lina in those days to explain her refusal to return to the country club and her shame at running into Andrés Larosca, into him and all the other men who went there, accepting that contempt from one member of a caste implied and even justified a sense of contempt among the rest of that caste. In other words, Dora appeared to be willing to lose the rights inherent to her sur-name—the Del Valle Álvarez de la Vega name continued to stand her in good stead despite the Palos association, and her status as the orphan daughter of a former member allowed her to attend the country club until she got married—believing, feeling or imagining that being relegated to the middle class, where hundreds of girls enviously followed her privileged life via the society page in the newspaper, was part of the ostracism her transgression deserved. And maybe it was true, maybe Dora sincerely believed it, which explained everything: her decision not to make her debut in society six months later at the grand ball on New Year's Eve, her repeated absences from tea parties and sewing circles, and even her friendship with Annie.

But when Lina began to see things more clearly, believing she could better grasp the implications of the inferiority com-plex, a concept which had become a fashionable way of explaining certain students' aggressive behaviour at school, her grandmother began to devise a different interpretation that astounded her then and would continue to do so for years, because she only managed to pinpoint the precise meaning of her words much later, visualizing them and finding their echo in Paris one spring day in 1978 as she left the Balzac after watching *Looking for Mr. Goodbar*, not because Dora's personality bore the slightest resemblance to that of the female lead, but because they both almost instinctively knew where to find the man they were looking for, or at least where they were never going to find him, since in her grandmother's opinion, Dora's refusal to go to the country club had nothing to do with shame or any kind of inferiority complex, even though she knew that people might think that was the case, but that instead it was down to intuition, a perfect sense of direction, much like the sense that guides animals during the mating season. This intuition led her straight to the middle classes, to those ambitious or resigned men who were brilliant or mediocre but ultimately less refined, less domesticated through acts of courtesy; among those men, she would sooner or later find the only specimen capable of relieving Andrés Larosca of his duties, someone capable of satisfying the needs that her experience with Andrés Larosca had created within her.

Lina vaguely sensed that she could not yet understand the nuances of that reasoning, and whenever her grandmother ventured into the realm of the secret, relentless forces that governed people's behaviour, she lost the ability to think, and stared in anguish at that ineffable figure, tiny as a seven-year-old girl, slowly swaying back and forth in her rocking chair while the future unfolded before her eyes, and six months before Benito Suárez appeared on the scene, his shadow began to loom; his presence was preceded, foretold, implicit in Annie, that friend of Dora's who came out of nowhere. Annie was a meteorite that came into their lives with the light and speed of a rock falling from the sky, and with the same intention to burn out and disintegrate, leaving them with a hazy memory, unclear like everything in her life: three aunts cooped up in a house full of ghosts in a village in Magdalena, and a mysterious father, who apparently lived in the city, and whose protection Annie had sought when she fled from her aunts. There was that, and the memory of her small and fragile body, those two enormous eyes blinking in amazement at the world, and her love for Dr. Jerónimo Vargas, who had just finished his psychiatry studies and was best friends with Benito Suárez.

Doña Eulalia saw Annie show up one day with the same horror she would have felt watching some pest scuttle in through a crack under the door, and immediately turned her out onto the street without letting her unpack her suitcase. That was how Annie ended up staying at Lina's house; her grandmother told Berenice to make up a room for her, and Annie settled in there for a week. She did not eat or sleep there, she just laid her suitcase on the bed and came in two or three times for a shower, bringing chocolates for Berenice to thank her for washing her black toreador pants and her plaid shirts, the outfit she usually wore when she took the bus from Calle 72, and proceeded to wander the streets, stopping here and there to buy colas and ice creams, which was all she ever ate, and waiting for hours in the blazing sun outside Dr. Jerónimo Vargas's office, waiting for him to let her in, to summon her from the window; then she would cross the street, go inside, take her clothes off and make love to him, or if she was lucky, that is if Dr. Jerónimo Vargas felt like it, she would accompany him to the rowdy bars frequented by hookers and hustlers, where Annie, blinking, would suddenly find herself being led off into a room and being thrown down on a bed stinking of semen, sweat and urine, not protesting, not expressing anything other than gratitude, because Dr. Jerónimo Vargas had been Annie's first psychiatrist, her first lover, and she said that she loved him, kept saying that she loved him even when he no longer wanted to see her and Dora tried to pick her up from his house, and perhaps that was what she told him the night when she took all the bottles of sleeping pills and tranquillizers he'd given her, then called him from the pay phone, which was where the police found her the next day still holding the receiver, allowing them to trace the number of the person Annie had been talking to before she fell asleep forever.

So it was through Annie that Dora met Benito Suárez, and she began seeing him in secret, just as she had done with Annie, using various excuses such as going to the country club, visiting Lina or dropping by to see the seamstress. All of this was aided and abetted by a certain Armanda, who was Doña Eulalia's maid at the time and had inherited all the aquamarine and coral rings gifted by Andrés Larosca, whom Dora had since forgotten. Armanda was a beautiful indigenous woman with yellow eyes, a lover to several soldiers, and probably in love with Dora too. Because back then, Dora was more than a woman: she was soft, lithe and languid; her eyes seemed to caress everything they touched; there was something about her body that screamed out to be taken, a carefree abandon, something that was sensed by men and woman, even animals, and Lina had seen it when Dora walked into her house, only to find herself immediately assailed by one of the setters trying to hump her leg. This sensuality, combined with Doña Eulalia's strict control and how difficult she made it for Dora to step outside the house, made it easy to understand how a man like Benito Suárez could be so fascinated by her, because he'd never had the chance to meet any of those women who'd inherited the old-established surnames and were always shrouded in the mystery of the forbidden, the inaccessible; the sisters and future wives of his university classmates, those aloof men who could afford to study less and didn't have to work so hard, safe in the knowledge that upon their return they would find the connections and support they needed to secure a position that he, Benito Suárez, could never aspire to, not even with years and years of hard work.

What he did aspire to was finding a virgin, a woman who

had been faithful to him since before she was born so his name would never be dragged through the mud, he would never be mocked by other men, or become a laughing stock in the city, and he aspired to this despite having devoured Nietzsche since the age of twenty and being convinced that he was separated from the rest of mankind because he, Benito Suárez, was far superior in strength, nobility of spirit and contempt.

But he did not seem too perturbed by his own contradictions: he simply made sure he lived them separately, splitting himself into endless conflicting personalities, and that was how, after having exhausted Dora for two months talking about his theory that a higher being is inherently sceptical, not bound by morals or ideologies, he ended up beating her with a belt when he found out that she had already lost her virginity. Lina was the one who was most surprised by the change, because, as Dora's confidante, Lina had been aware of all Benito Suárez's speeches about the idiocy typical of women and of the masses, those imbeciles who need to cling to a religion, to find an absolute, to define themselves in terms of a yes or no. Every time she came home in a daze after spending an hour listening to Benito Suárez holding forth at some ice-cream parlour or other, Lina had achieved the impossible by translating that language to her; she realized that her efforts were probably in vain, but told herself that he might be the providential man, the only one prepared to laugh in the face of Barranquilla's prejudices. As soon as Lina read the two Nietzsche books that her grandmother swiftly lent her on discovering what was behind Benito Suárez's theories, she was certain that an individual with such contempt for society, who was so above scruples and conventions, could indeed love Dora just as she was, the way she ended up after Andrés Larosca had finished with her, and so Lina began to hope for the best possible outcome. She paid no attention to the reservations expressed by her grandmother, who insisted, from the placid rhythm of her rocking chair, that Benito Suárez's references to Nietzsche served the same purpose as her walking stick, that he was not being supercilious but using those theories as a crutch, probably clinging onto them out of desperation. Because Benito Suárez was the son of Doña Giovanna Mantini, and she (Lina's grandmother) had met Giovanna Mantini, who was married by proxy to José Vicente Suárez, when she arrived from Turin in the days when Mussolini was organizing the March on Rome and Giovanna's brother was running the first fascist newspaper in Turin.

Years after her grandmother's death, Lina would frequently cross paths with that Italian lady who, despite her age, still had the furious energy of a tyrant hell-bent on changing the world, and remained convinced of the need to educate the youth under the motto, "believe, obey, fight," reciting from memory the speeches of Il Duce, that genius who was capable of conceiving the creation of a new man by taking him from the cradle and only giving him back to the Pope after his death. Doña Giovanna Mantini had followed these instructions to the letter, applying them to her only son, Benito Suárez, applying them with vigour, because Doña Giovanna had understood from the outset that she would not only have to fight against man's natural perversions, but also against the genetic inferiority that her son had inherited from his father, which continued to develop in the breeding ground of the city's moral laxity. Doña Giovanna's fascist ideology partly explained her pedagogical methods—she'd had a whip and a pair of leather handcuffs made, for example, and she used them to restrain her son, at the age of four, flogging him until he bled whenever he did something wrong—but it shed no light on her decision to go against her family's wishes and marry the lawyer José Vicente Suárez, bearing in mind that José Vicente Suárez was a *mulato* and Doña Giovanna's racism seemed to be imprinted in her genes; in short, she did not even question the inferiority of the

Black race, seeing it as a given, as an obvious fact. To ask her what led her to that decision would have meant forcing her to revisit the memory of the Turin she knew when she was twenty-five, when, through her brothers, she met José Vicente Suárez, an exotic Latin American who had moved to Europe to specialize in international law and was seduced by fascism, wore a black shirt like her brothers, and loudly proclaimed his support for Il Duce at rallies. Why had she, Doña Giovanna, someone so blonde and blue-eyed, agreed to join her life to that *mulato*'s; what defiance did her decision hide, what revenge or disillusionment? Because the only explanation she provided, her belief that all Latin Americans were like that, was by no means convincing, and it would have been incongruous to talk to her about love. No, there was never any love between her and José Vicente Suárez. Passion perhaps, in the form of a sudden sexual desire that was shamefully acknowledged and therefore more easily directed towards a man she considered inferior. But if this was the case, that feeling did not persist once Doña Giovanna Mantini arrived in Barranquilla. Because when her ship came into port and Doña Giovanna saw José Vicente Suárez's relatives waiting for her on the dock, forty-five of them, a drunken rabble, and next to them, other men and women with white skin and straight hair—not flat-nosed, not thick-lipped and, above all, not drunk, not cackling with laughter and waving at her fellow travellers—Doña Giovanni was horrified: she had left behind a Turin shrouded in autumn mists and a house of austere marble on the right bank of the Po, and now, stretching out before her eyes was an immense river the colour of mud, emanating the rotten stench of alligator, of dead animal, of mangroves that had been decaying since the dawn of time. She thought that there, on those banks, the walls of a palace or the spires of a cathedral could never stand. She thought the swallows would never again fly in that sky of molten glass, only the dusty-winged predators that seemed to exist solely on what died and decomposed beneath the sun.

But she did not cry, she would tell Lina as she furiously wiped away a rare tear that afternoon when she told her about her arrival in the city. Not then, not as she crossed Barranquilla's main street in the boiling glare of the morning, surrounded by a throng of street vendors and beggars, nor during the eight-hour drive to Sabanalarga, the town where her husband lived, in the six cars hired for the occasion, which bumped over the unforgiving potholes along the dusty main road in a landscape of ploughed fields and limp-looking cows overwhelmed by the heat, and which pulled over every ten minutes because of the urinary urges of their occupants, who became increasingly drunk and rowdy as the bottles of white rum were passed around, along with *arepas, chicharrones* and iguana eggs, foods Doña Giovanna found barbaric, just as she found Sabanalarga barbaric, with its bahareque houses lit by kerosene lamps, and its dark streets, the air still stiflingly hot and seething with mosquitos. Just as they came into town, Doña Giovanna saw something she would describe to Lina years later, and though she laughed raucously as she spoke, there was something in the minute detail she recalled that conveyed to Lina how much the sight had affected her: a procession, a procession of the Virgin. Though Doña Giovanna was the daughter of a socialist, her mother had instilled in her the age-old Italian reverence for religious symbols, and the Virgin—whether as a representation of an idea, an object of worship for the illiterate or inspiration for the great masters— was an image that stirred Giovanna's heart despite her will. So to suddenly find, in the dusty streets and the constant, visceral, inescapable heat of Sabanalarga, drunkards carrying a float that seemed like it might topple over at any moment, and the Virgin sitting atop it with make-up smeared over her face, wearing a low-cut crimson satin dress and a sort of sash across her chest that read *"Égalité de Jouissance,"* which had appeared from who knows where, and which the poor village priest took for a pious invocation in Latin—well, that was more than she could bear, she would later tell Lina. It was a point of no return, an ending to something that would never really begin, because she flatly refused to sleep with her husband as long as they stayed in Sabanalarga, and so José Vicente Suárez reluctantly settled in Barranquilla, abandoning his relatives and saying goodbye to a prominent political career, and all for a woman whose blue eyes flashed with contempt for him, for his family and the privileges he enjoyed as the son of a cacique; he was forced to make his way in a city where he would always be considered a hick, a second-rate lawyer who would find it impossible to rise through the ranks given his lack of connections and the colour of his skin; all simply for the dubious privilege of making love to the woman who logically belonged to him much like a mule or a calf, but who was afflicted with insolence and defied his wishes, and not in the way women usually do—that is, with tears, pleas or sanctimonious behaviour—but with insults and blows. Because from the very beginning, and with the passing of the years, things between José Vicente Suárez and Doña Giovanna Mantini were like a pitched battle, in which they both hurled chairs, vases and pictures, and José Vicente Suárez did not always emerge victorious: twice he suffered head wounds, and on another occasion, he had to urgently have his stomach pumped, when Doña Giovanna—having received a beating that left her bed-bound for four days—suddenly remembered the methods one of her friends back home had used, and decided to pour rat poison into the coffee that the maid served her husband in the morning, an action that did not kill him but at least scared some sense into him, because from then on— Giovanna would tell Lina, her blue eyes gleaming wickedly— the poor fool refrained from hitting her, insulting her, breaking her furniture and other loutish behaviour, leaving her in peace so that she could raise their children: a girl and Benito Suárez.

Lina never learned why Doña Giovanna had not tried to go back to Turin. The Italy evoked by her memories had the hopeless and elusive nostalgia of a postcard: there were churches and palaces, dark winding streets and fields bathed in pale pink light. Sometimes, hearing her speak, Lina thought that her ideology helped her stay closer to that past, that perhaps it was a way of surviving in a city where she never even tried to adapt. Doña Giovanna did not seem to have hung on to many of the ephemeral socialist principles of fascism, nor to any of her mother's religious principles. For her, men were divided into the strong and the weak; this was a distinction created by nature, she noted, and something every society had to accept to achieve order and civilization, even, she said to an astonished Lina, to have something as pleasant to look at as her hands. This comment about the hands came after a long argument Lina had had with her about the injustice implicit in Mussolini's politics: backed into a corner and forced to concede that fascism had betrayed the workers' hopes and expectations, Doña Giovanna calmly said that social injustice was a condition of art, science and beauty, since millions of men had been sacrificed to build the Great Pyramid, to provide the leisure time that was so crucial for writers and philosophers, and also for those hands of hers, which for centuries had been protected from manual labour, from the heat and the cold. This argument would not only make Lina look uneasily at her hands until the end of her days, but also convinced her that it would be impossible for her to discuss politics with Doña Giovanna ever again. Because given her complete lack of scruples, it was juvenile to attempt to find any common ground with that woman or to try to make her change her mind; but also because deep down, Lina's own scruples prevented her from doing so: Doña Giovanna was very old by then, and at her age, when every hand had already been played, won or lost, it was not the best time to question the principles that had shaped a life. Indeed, her life had been conceived as a merciless battle ever since Doña Giovanna arrived in Barranquilla and decided to be strong, to fight and win by accepting the marriage and everything that went with it: the anonymity she was thrust into when her brother continued to run the most important neofascist newspaper in Turin despite Mussolini's lamentable demise; the intellectual impoverishment she endured in a continent that had never come up with a single original idea, simply copying, imitating and chaotically applying the theories devised by European thinkers; and the indignity of having to accept her son, that son, Benito Suárez, who was white at least, but, like his father, had been born into a race whose defects would have to leave the body the same way they entered it, by blood, and which she, Doña Giovanna, would go to any lengths to eradicate, even if her life depended on it. She was forced to accept that her entire life would become a battle against her son's nature, whipping him, cursing him, day after day, year after year—for stealing a piece of fruit, insulting a teacher or groping the maid—until she could make him into the closest thing there was to an Italian in Barranquilla, a man who could appreciate the operas of Scarlatti and Monteverdi, achieve a surgeon's degree in the capital and return buoyed by the praise of his professors and with the idea in his head that the feeling of power—the will to power, power itself—was the only form of nobility to which any human being should aspire.

And yet Benito Suárez fell in love with Dora of all people, or rather became interested in her or was subjugated by her, or something to that effect. After making love to her in the back seat of his Studebaker and discovering that another man had defiled her, as he put it, instead of breaking up with her and never seeing her again, he beat her to make her repent and tell him the name of that man, his behaviour therefore in keeping with those theories of strength of character and contempt for women, theories he held so dear. Benito Suárez continued to desperately seek Dora out, giving her pleasure amid explosive scenes, and starting to display signs of what Lina already referred to as his mental imbalance, since it would only occur to a madman to stake his honour not only on a woman's vagina—which was already common currency among the men of Barranquilla—but on what that vagina had done six months before he saw it, penetrated it or even imagined it; only a madman would resolve to wash away the sin by going to confront Andrés Larosca with the gun he kept in the glovebox of his Studebaker, essentially implying that a person can be insulted six months before the fact, without being known by the person who has insulted him, and without that person having the slightest intention of insulting him.

Untenable though it was, this reasoning had been cementing itself in Benito Suárez's mind as his interrogations made Dora reveal the details of her love affair with Andrés Larosca. Dora was incapable of shirking his questions, because to do so risked triggering a brutal reaction from him: at the slightest hint of avoidance or imprecision, Benito Suárez's anger would erupt in the form of a beating, like the time Lina saw the blue Studebaker pulling up abruptly on the corner by her house and Dora fleeing the car with her face all bloody. By that time, Dora had nothing more to say, she told Lina: she had no recollection, no secret left in the privacy of her memory that had not been revealed, exposed and subjected to Benito's meticulous analysis, having surrendered to his morbid curiosity as passively as she had given in to Doña Eulalia's morbid curiosity in her childhood, and perhaps for the same reason: to please, gaining peace and quiet in one case, and in the other, for the pleasure her husband gave her. Dora never questioned the motives for his interrogations or where his questions might lead, because at no point did she believe that Benito Suárez was capable of carrying out his threats, and she was surprised—terrified, she would say to Lina—when one night, while sitting beside him in the car, she heard him boldly declare that he was going to kill Andrés Larosca. Dora had heard him say this many times before, but in a different way, not with the furious determination that was in his voice this time when he looked at her, and then, certain that he had seen a flicker of disbelief in her eyes, started shouting that he was going to kill the man that very night, yelling it over and over, as if he was trying to tell himself he had to do it, while Dora—who found the only way to calm him down was by simply promising that she believed what he said—cowered in the passenger seat as she watched him drive over to Andrés Larosca's house then start speeding around the block, taking the corners on two wheels, until at last he brought the Studebaker to a screeching halt, grabbed the gun from the glovebox and strode up the garden calling out Andrés Larosca's name. Trembling with fear and shame, Dora watched him walk away from the car: that head of tightly combed curls, slightly flattened at the back; his body, broad and strong but not fat, with those rower's shoulders straining beneath his spotless white jacket, making him look like he'd been stuffed into a suit a size too small for him. She heard him yelling and expected to see Andrés Larosca suddenly appear at the door, but when the door opened, what she saw was a tiny fox terrier, just as agitated as Benito Suárez, and behind him, a figure wrapped in a pink bathrobe, with her hair in curlers: it was Andrés Larosca's startled wife, who, as she would later explain, thought that someone had come to deliver some bad news because her husband had only left for Cartagena half an hour ago. Dora could not hear what they were saying: all she could see was Benito Suárez gesticulating and waving the gun around, and Larosca's wife ducking from left to right, out of the way of the gun as the lights in the neighbouring houses came on one by one. Those lights were the eyes of the city, always alert and active, focusing in on the details of the scene like the lens of a camera: there was Benito Suárez, in the process of revealing Andrés Larosca's escapades to his wife, swearing to chase him to the ends of the earth if necessary and to riddle him with bullets for corrupting minors; then, the wife in tears, falling to her knees in front of him and begging him for mercy in the name of her four children, and suddenly Benito—magnanimously, with a solemn, almost theatrical air, as if behind the woman there wasn't just a tiny dog barking but a vast audience watching with baited breath—telling her, "Get up, Señora, that bastard doesn't deserve a woman like you, but for the sake of you and your children, I'll spare his life."

The lights stayed on after Benito Suárez, flushed with satisfaction, returned to his Studebaker and drove away as fast as he had come. The doors of the neighbouring houses opened and closed, and curious onlookers came and went, unsure whether to stop and comment on the incident or rush straight home to their phones. It was late, almost midnight. But the story was already fanning out like the ripples on a pond disturbed by a pebble thrown into its centre, and by dawn, when the streetlamps languished in the pale light of morning and the milk floats began their rounds, everyone knew that for a year and a half Dora had been Andrés Larosca's lover.

In a city that needed so little fuel to start the gossip mill, Benito Suárez had given them a gift. Everyone knew everything in that place. Always. Or almost always. They knew what happened in the privacy of people's homes or in the secrecy of their hearts, what was said or left unspoken, even what was whispered in the confessionals. Everyone found reasons to talk, since disapproving of other people was a form of exorcism or revenge, and above all, because people found it palliative. It was like Lina's grandmother used to say: gossip always started when a person found out that someone else had done something they themselves had always wanted to do (without admitting it) or were afraid they wanted to do (without knowing it), which meant that any accuser was judging their own reflection in that person, and any inquisitor was blindly persecuting himself. This explanation made it possible to understand many people, especially Doña Eulalia del Valle, who had spent her life fiercely disapproving of others: she barely saw a soul and only roamed the neighbourhood at night, but used the phone and her relatives to divulge other people's secrets, interpreting them in her own way, unfairly, and vindictively, with all the vindictiveness of a lonely old recluse who, sitting in a rocking chair, felt the days slipping away, inventing fantasies in her mind that were most likely unmentionable. Grim, bitter and capable only of self-pity, she had more than one ruined reputation to her name, having granted herself the right to judge as if it were some divine prerogative associated with her age-old family name and that terrible, unwavering virtue from which she drew much of her pride and all (or almost all) of her frustration, even if she did not realize that everything she did was a form of frustration: reading romance novels on the veranda, suffering constant headaches and going out at night with a rosary in her hand to walk the streets of El Prado, her distrustful gaze falling on the darkened facades, her ear attuned to rumours, even to the conversations going on between maids from one garden to another. Then suddenly this stranger—a certain Benito Suárez, whose name she, Doña Eulalia del Valle, had never heard before—was telling all and sundry that her daughter was a loose woman, loose like those women she had criticized so often and who now, like a swarm of vengeful wasps, were attacking her with anonymous phone calls.

The anonymous phone calls were the first thing Lina heard Armanda mention when she arrived to pick her up, saying that Doña Eulalia wanted to see her immediately. On the way,

Armanda told her that Dora had left around ten o'clock, half an hour before the phone started ringing off the hook. Lina found Doña Eulalia in her room, sobbing, her head buried in a pillow. The windows were shut, and it smelled like mothballs in there; like a sick, sweaty animal. Groping around in the darkness, Lina felt as if she was treading on piles of paper; as she cautiously drew the curtain, the light filtering through the window slats revealed a staggering number of photos of Dora torn to pieces, and all the newspaper clippings containing her name or her portrait had been torn up or crumpled by some wrathful, most definitely crazed hand; she was picking up the only photograph of Dora that appeared to have survived the massacre when suddenly Doña Eulalia leapt out of bed and shoved her against the wall. The violent blow to the head made Lina dizzy; for a moment she thought she might faint from the pain and from the stale smell, the damp and rancid scent that emanated from Doña Eulalia's body. She looked at her and instantly knew that she was in danger: that pale, sharp-boned woman, her eyes calm and glittering with madness, seemed prepared to kill her. Before she was thrown against the wall again, Lina managed to say, "We have to save Dora," and as she slipped to the floor in a daze, she saw Doña Eulalia slowly turn around, staring at her own scrawny figure in the dressing-table mirror as she broke into sobs once more.

When Armanda came into the room to announce that Dora and Benito Suárez had arrived, Doña Eulalia had already come to her senses and was sitting on the edge of the bed, crying bitter tears. Dishevelled and wrapped in a musty old bathrobe covered in cigarette burns, she had apologized to Lina, begging her to pick up the photos and clippings of Dora that had not been destroyed or could be mended with sticky tape. But when she heard Armanda's voice, she jumped up, and her expression clouded over with delirium again. Lina saw her walk resolutely toward the door, where she found Benito

Suárez dragging Dora by the arm, already crossing the hall and making his way towards her, his face contorted in a sort of icy fury.

They both stopped at the same time, standing five feet away from one another like a couple of animals setting the imaginary battle line from which to launch into mortal combat. But Benito Suárez's determination, the wrathful demon that inhabited him, seemed more powerful than all of Doña Eulalia's feelings. It was he who took the first step forward, he was the first to speak. And when he spoke, he said, "I've come for your daughter because you're clearly incapable of looking after her for me." That was all.

When Lina experienced what happened next, it was as if she had been propelled out of reality into a world that was parallel but different, hard to grasp with words, or even with thought. Because everyday logic, the kind that allows us to understand and articulate things, had simply disappeared. It had been nullified, suffocated by a will that not only offered no other system of explanation but did not even try to find one: the terse, rabid will of Benito Suárez. What alarmed Lina the most was not so much that this man acted on impulses that were beyond any known form of reasoning; after all, there had always been madmen in her family, and Lina and been taught to respect them. No. What disturbed her more than anything was his magnetic personality, that strange ability he had to subject others to his delirium, because everyone—Doña Eulalia and Dora, and later, the people who had been arriving at the house as Benito Suárez called them on the phone, Doña Giovanna Mantini, her daughter and her son-in-law, the red-bearded psychiatrist Lina was seeing there for the first time, Jerónimo Vargas—had been following his nonsensical orders with no qualms, without the slightest hint of astonishment or opposition. Starting with Doña Eulalia, who seemed to lose the power of speech when Benito Suárez angrily berated her—the one who had been ridiculed and offended—for not having taken proper care of her daughter. Wide-eyed and with her hair in disarray, clutching to her chest the folds of her bathrobe pockmarked by countless cigarettes, she agreed to follow him to the living room, where she shut herself away to talk to him, or rather, to listen as he talked, while Dora fielded questions from Benito Suárez's relatives about the scandal that had taken place the night before. When they came out into the hallway, Doña Eulalia in tears but looking vindicated, and Benito Suárez pompously proclaiming, "Just so you know, Dora's going to be my wife, and from now on her mother will protect her from everyone, including me," Lina calmly told herself that she had to expose the parameters that would allow her to understand this man's behaviour, or investigate if she couldn't find any. It was only later, while driving in a convoy of three cars to Puerto Colombia—where Benito Suárez knew a priest he wanted him and Dora to take confession with—that Lina was suddenly reminded of her grandmother's words.

Because her grandmother had already got the measure of Benito Suárez: she had seen him once, not long after that Saturday during Carnival when he burst into her house chasing Dora and calling Lina a little fucking bitch. On that occasion, her grandmother had called in a carpenter to give her a quote to repair the furniture that Benito Suárez had kicked and damaged, and then she sent him a letter inviting him to come and see her on Thursday at six o'clock so that he could apologize, she wrote, and so that he could settle things with the carpenter himself. Written on the beautiful white paper her grandmother had had sent over from England, with her initials embossed in gold, the tone of that letter was fairly terse, and the controlled politeness of its phrasing hinted at an order rather than an invitation. All the same, Benito Suárez turned up on time on the appointed day.

From the dining-room table where she sat doing her homework, Lina saw a huge bouquet of gladioli, roses, carnations and immortelles approaching from the pavement, and beneath it an immaculate pair of white trousers and a pair of white shoes with thick rubber soles. As Lina's grandmother opened the door wide to make way for the gift, she saw Benito Suárez's beaming face peeking through the flowers. Without giving her time to utter a word, he greeted her with a vigorous handshake, bowed to her in apology, barely glanced at the bill and wrote out a cheque to the carpenter, then sat down in a rocking chair to chat with them. He gave the impression that he was happy. Looked clean shaven and smelled of cologne. In his handsome face with its strong jawline, his eyes glittered with intelligence. For two hours he spoke passionately about his work as a surgeon, and the novels of D'Annunzio. He also talked about politics, philosophy and music. He frequently spoke of "earning respect." Her grandmother simply listened to him, occasionally asking him one of those casual questions which seemed harmless but which nevertheless, by some mechanism known only to her, helped her to weigh up a person's character. Lina saw him to the door when he got up to leave, and when she returned, her grandmother was deep in thought. "Intelligent, isn't he?" Lina remarked. Her grandmother took her time to answer. She seemed to be somewhere very far away, and then, as if returning from that distant place, she finally said, "Intelligent? Yes. But above all, he's a killer."

IV

Although none of the definitions known to her grand-mother could express the true essence of instinct or the various stages through which it set about transforming perception, awareness and behaviour into action, it seemed reasonable to assume that those urges came from far away, performing the simple mission of sustaining life, which explained their power, the secret energy that caused them to erupt violently when they no longer served a purpose in the social context and could inspire only terror or perplexity. Her grandmother believed in the existence of opposing instincts, shared out unequally among people and either accentuated or inhibited by circumstances or experience. But although everyone had a right to assess these instincts on a scale of values, disapproving of those they deemed asocial or favouring those that formed the basis of altruistic behaviour, it did not make sense to judge oneself based on the moral values one happened to inherit, since they did not correspond to any personal merit or to God's design, but instead to the most arbitrary whim of chance. The corollary followed effortlessly: it was frivolous and even juvenile to look down on a person when, following their urges, they behaved contrary to how our own instincts of sociability and human solidarity told us to react, because the tasks of judgement and punishment fell to the bodies of repression that society had established, but not to individuals, at least not to her, Lina's grandmother, who apparently had not been conditioned to persecute anyone or to take on the role of an inquisitor, and had a healthy dose of pessimism that made her believe that reason almost always served instinct, awailing itself of a whole array of ideas intended to justify its satisfaction. She did feel entitled to observe people, however, to listen to them talking and to anticipate their behaviour, even going so far as to call Benito Suárez a killer, albeit without insulting him, because there was no moral undertone in that statement, just the simple recognition of a fact that was visible to her, the discernment of a series of signs which, together with her memories, allowed her to recognize in Benito Suárez not someone who was prepared to kill if circumstances obliged him to do so, but someone who was unconsciously predisposed to murder. Based on that impression, which transcended mere supposition despite its lack of certainty—which was why Lina preferred to exercise caution when referring to the vague concept of a premonition—Lina's grandmother intuited the path that Benito Suárez was going to take based on what she called the rooting instinct, or more simply, the hunting response whose mechanism could be understood by observing the setters' behaviour: though they ran riot on the beach and barked vociferously as soon as the car door opened and they sniffed the sea, the dogs behaved differently when they were out in the countryside, on Uncle Miguel's ranch for example, where they arrived quivering with excitement, sneaking stealthily between the shrubs, noses to the ground, tails stiff, searching for the tracks, the trail, the urine that would awaken their prey drive, even though they knew from experience that Uncle Miguel's ranch was a desert and there was not a single rabbit or game bird that hadn't already succumbed, in its boredom, to the bullets from his rifle.

So Benito Suárez was eventually going to find the reasons he needed to kill a man, but in the meantime, like the setters, he would keep chasing, provoking, tracking the spur that would allow him to commit that act, the one that was foreshadowed in the uncouth display he put on when he set out with his gun to cause a scene in Andrés Larosca's garden. Not only did Lina's grandmother never forget that recklessness or refuse to accept it as an isolated act determined by specific circumstances, but for the twelve years that Dora's marriage lasted, she often brought it up when she remarked on Benito Suárez, using it as an enduring reference, a sort of *Ceterum censeo Carthaginem esse delendam* that made Lina's explanations melt away to nothing whenever she found out about a new issue Dora was having and returned home, confused, to tell her grandmother about what had happened, attempting to whittle the incident down to its immediate causes, the ones that seemed to have triggered it, until finally she trailed off, still as confused as when she started, and her grandmother set about patiently unravelling the thread of her interpretations. This invariably led her back to what happened in Andrés Larosca's garden, not to dwell on the fact per se, but to highlight the apparent ease with which Benito Suárez had rid himself of any inhibitions when he had something to prove to himself, whether it was honour, courage, contempt or something else; that ease suggested the existence of an uncontrollable instinct, and the perception of that instinct, not exactly having knowledge of it but rather the act of noticing it, of taking it into account or relying on it, was the closest thing to a pattern that could explain the kind of behaviour which could not simply be classed as cruel, as Doña Eulalia del Valle described it, nor as sadistic, Lina would eventually understand, because sadism implied taking pleasure in someone else's pain, and it was clear that Benito Suárez gained no pleasure from making Dora suffer, even though he accepted that she suffered.

In fact, he did not seem to ascribe any emotion or substance to Dora, if anything, likening her to a plastic doll that cries at the press of a button or closes its eyes when it lies down to sleep. Perhaps at the beginning of their marriage this had been another incentive for him, and perhaps it was why he had married her, because her having slept with another man was the

perfect affront to his dignity: a living, permanent, visible insult
that justified any angry remark or outburst. But marriage, with
its pregnancies and family parties, made everything holy, and
Benito Suárez had stubbornly reduced Dora to a lifeless body,
as if the arousal she personified was too much for him or enervated him, or perhaps because he had unwittingly fallen into the
great contradiction of the man who cannot respect the woman
he desires and does not even dare to lust after the woman he
loves, or more precisely, the woman other people see as his
wife and the mother of his children. The first evidence of the
process aimed at suppressing Dora's eroticism or sexual urges
came with the dramatic confession the two of them endured
with the priest in Puerto Colombia, an incident that was witnessed by a dumbstruck Lina, who had been in a state of shock
since the people who gathered at Doña Eulalia del Valle's
house got into three cars parked out front, Benito Suárez taking the lead in his blue Studebaker with Doña Eulalia and
Dora, followed by Jerónimo Vargas, the psychiatrist with the
flame-coloured beard, and Lina, then closely behind them,
Doña Giovanna Mantini and the rest of her family, all heading
for the main road at breakneck speed while nannies and gardeners turned to look at them just as the workers harvesting
vegetables along the roadside looked up from their hoes, perplexed at the sight of that convoy led by a raven-haired man
driving a blue Studebaker with ferocious determination, and
behind him, in another Studebaker, this time a green one,
another driver with a fiery beard and the same look of irate
obstinacy on his face, neither man appearing to grasp that they
were simply headed for a small fishing village where they
would find nothing that merited such effort and determination—apart from the priest, that is, the gang member assigned
to the seminary for some mysterious reason, whose nasty temperament, known to all, had probably earned him that miserable parish and the friendship of those two men, who were

speeding along the dusty main road that afternoon, not heeding the scant traffic signs, and honking furiously at every bend
in the road, as though their horns were Joshua's trumpets outside the walls of Jericho.

Lina, who spent a month's holiday in Puerto Colombia
every year, knew more than a thing or two about that priest
and his tempestuous sermons, but it was only when she saw
him in the town square next to Benito Suárez and Jerónimo
Vargas that she understood the relationship between them, or
more precisely, it occurred to her that they belonged to the
same species of man, because the three of them were handsome and strong—not burly, but broad-shouldered and muscular—and apparently prepared to commit any outlandish act
that crossed their minds, regardless of the destruction they
wreaked in the process. Since they could all see themselves in
each other, the men seemed to need few words to understand
one another, back each other up or agree on something; so
without further ado, the priest agreed to let them inside the
church, closing the door behind them and subjecting Dora and
Benito Suárez to a public confession, or rather, making Dora
disclose the secrets of her sex life, revealing to those present—
or at least to her, Lina—that the humiliation of an individual is
above all the humiliation of others, of those who cause it or
stand by and watch it, or, as Doña Giovanna Mantini put it
when she interrupted the masquerade, of those who are somehow part of it. Because it was Doña Giovanna Mantini who put
a stop to the scene when she walked towards Dora, the priest
and Benito Suárez—who were standing to the right of the altar,
not far from the confessional—and threatened to report the
priest to the bishop for violating the principles of Christian confession, if confession was the right term for forcing someone to
divulge the contents of their private life to nine people, barely
one of whom had the right to hear it, and if they did, only in the
strictest of confidence. It was then that Lina discovered that

this plump little woman with piercing blue eyes, whom she had never seen before, had not once been intimidated by her son's erratic behaviour and did not appear to think particularly highly of the priest either, calling him by his first name and telling him that, priesthood or no priesthood, he was still the same good-for-nothing she had met ten years earlier.

And so that confession was a failure for Benito Suárez, ending with neither absolution nor penance; but there would be others, especially during the first year of the marriage, because once he was her husband, Benito Suárez started to have qualms about giving Dora sexual pleasure, and began taking her to Puerto Colombia every two months so that she could confess to the priest, whose warnings—based on the conviction that a wife's body was not intended for lust but for reproduction, and at most, to stifle male temptations—proved futile; in fact, Dora would tell Lina, his warnings seemed to serve as a stimulus, because afterwards, on their way back to the city, the couple could not resist the urge to make love and so they left the Studebaker parked on the roadside, ventured into the scrubland and groped each other excitedly in the bushes, up against a tree trunk or at the edge of the *ciénaga*.

The problems came with the birth of their son, Renato, who was named after Doña Giovanna Mantini's brother, the one who ran Turin's most influential neofascist newspaper. Because from the moment the child was born, Benito Suárez, with the erratic tenacity that characterized all his decisions, refused to give Dora pleasure, claiming that her means of arousal—using his penis to stimulate her clitoris—was fundamentally perverse, quite aside from the fact that the mother of his child should not take pleasure in the marital bed like some hooker. This was a particular dilemma for Dora, because that decision took away the only thing that made her nightmare marriage bearable: not only was she forbidden to challenge even the smallest order from her husband, answer the phone or look out of the window—and to put her to the test, Benito Suárez called several times a day and honked his horn before driving into the garage—but she was not allowed go to the cinema or visit her friends; she could not even go to see Doña Eulalia del Valle, who lived three blocks away, unless she was chaperoned by an elderly maid.

Perhaps because they simply duplicated the pattern of surveillance she had experienced from her mother, the restrictions Benito Suárez imposed out of mistrust did not particularly bother Dora. It was even possible that she viewed these restrictions as a reflection of her surrender, of her status as seized property, part of the continuation and prelude to her pleasure. But even when pleasure was ruled out for her, Dora still never complained about her confinement and solitude, though she did speak to Lina of an emptiness and how she felt like she was sleepwalking in a house where all she was allowed to do was take care of the baby. Her anxiety appeared to stem not so much from being ostracized as from the loss of all hope, in other words, losing the ability to imagine that circumstances would lead her to the man who, overcoming the obstacles that stood in the way of her freedom—the nuns, Doña Eulalia and so on—would make her quiver, because she was subconsciously waiting for him, for any man, a lawyer, gardener or truck driver, someone who could exist as a potential or as a reality but vanished without trace when a priest uttered a few words in Latin; phrases which, everyone knew, bound them in marriage for eternity. Dora resigned herself to that loss of hope, but something inside of her died. Though initially she was conscious that she had become a zombie confined to grappling with a baby, as time went by she seemed to adjust to her situation without seeking definitions or answers, her senses began to grow duller, her interests and curiosity waned, and in the space of a few years she had become a shapeless, withered woman who ate very little, slept a lot and lived in a daze of tranquillizers and migraines.

The migraines began shortly after Renato was born and

Benito Suárez made her abstain from pleasure. Dora believed the headaches were linked to a pain she felt in her groin caused by some strange lumps or polyps that twice required surgery and which, according to the gynaecologist, could be attributed to arousal that had been repressed and not released through orgasm. The lumps did not come back, but the migraines persisted, and the doctors always found a way to explain them, whether it was the syphilis she contracted from Benito Suárez, leaving her bedbound for almost a year only to emerge infertile, or the nasal surgery he made her have, claiming that she was keeping him awake with her snoring, or the menstrual problems, the profuse bleeding, the intermittent rhinitis, the late-afternoon fevers and so on; in short, from one specialist to the next, from one treatment to the next, Dora's body was analyzed, cut open, amputated, injected, drugged, and still the migraines would not go away. Most importantly, Dora never asked herself why they were happening. And Lina did not hazard to offer any interpretation, because as far as she knew, the headaches had a first and last name, and no one, least of all Dora, was capable of confronting Benito Suárez; better put, it was possible to stand up to him as long as one was prepared to declare all-out war by giving him a dose of his own medicine, using fists or a gun, or by inhibiting his aggression and gaining his respect like Lina's grandmother. Because ever since that time when her grandmother sent him a note ordering him to call by her house that Thursday evening in order to apologize and pay the carpenter's bill, Benito Suárez had been impressed by her—by her level of culture and elegance, he told Lina—and every birthday he would go to see her, arriving with huge bouquets of flowers and ensconcing himself on the terrace until dinnertime to discuss the subjects that interested him and to listen to her grandmother's opinions, respectfully, not daring to question them. This same consideration was partly extended to Lina, because she was Doña Jimena's granddaughter, of course, but also because Benito Suárez, a hot-tempered man who made foolish assertions, also appreciated culture, in other words people who possessed or were interested in culture, and since Lina read whatever fell into her lap, he had a degree of regard for her, just enough to accept her as a conversation partner, and then later, as someone with whom he would share his most intimate and embarrassing secret: his ambitions of becoming a poet. Yes, Benito Suárez wrote verses in the style of Julio Flórez, and every stanza was a painstaking labour of tension and emotion, a struggle against a language that distorted or limited the expression of his feelings. This was where Lina came in, suggesting adjectives and metaphors he could use, but never mocking his inability to put rhyme to his ideas, not even internally, perhaps because Benito Suárez's interest in poetry was one of his few likeable traits. All the same, given his treatment of Dora, he and Lina would argue many times, openly and with hostility, trading insults and threats that created rifts between them for months, and though Lina continued to call round at their house out of solidarity with Dora, during those intervals she acted as though Benito Suárez did not exist, walking past him without saying hello or leaving as soon as she saw him arriving home. Always, and this minor detail touched Lina, he was the one to hold out the olive branch: inexplicably, his reaction was to take Dora to Sears and buy her whatever she wanted, whether it was dresses or trinkets, a new living-room suite or ornaments for her room.

However, not because he'd stripped Dora of her status as a stimulus—and she might even be described as a counter-stimulus, because as well as losing her primitive sensuality, she had also lost any trace of gracefulness since her hair had started thinning from the drugs and her nose had been numbed and permanently disfigured by the operation—Benito Suárez had given up hunting for living beings and objects to take his aggression out on. Or, as Lina sometimes thought, he'd given up training for the act her grandmother believed he was destined to commit, that he had pursued with the perseverance of an athlete who spends whole years preparing to compete for one hour or less, knowing his triumph or defeat will depend on strengthening his muscles and reflexes, but unlike the athlete, unaware of his goal and simply heading towards it in complete darkness. Because Benito Suárez was not one for taking stock in any way, nor did he seem to realize that his behaviour was characterized by repetition, continuity and increasingly serious acts of pent-up aggression. Out of pride or fear, he refused to acknowledge the irrational elements of this violence, perhaps offering up some half-fantastical explanation, one he did not completely believe in at first but ended up accepting unreservedly and defending pig-headedly, in other words, trying to back up his explanation with incomprehensible and sometimes esoteric arguments related to supposedly scientific theories, which he only told himself were true so as to justify his behaviour. Lina never agreed to follow him into this terrain, choosing instead to observe his atrocious dialectics from a distance, right on the boundary where good judgement helped to curb such gibberish, exposing his act, whatever it was, stripping it bare, leaving it intact and holding back the logic that would have allowed it to be plotted like coordinates, measuring the intensity of violence on the x-axis and, along the y-axis, the force that drove Benito Suárez to lose himself and ruin the educated, respectable surgeon who was perfectly adapted to society, with his house in El Prado, his blue Studebaker and his submissive wife who was languishing in frustration and swollen from migraines. From this boundary, Lina realized that there was an apparently inevitable progression in the course of his outbursts, and though she accepted this with the fatalism of someone who witnesses the succession of the clouds, the thunder, the rain and the lightning, she felt real fear for Dora; not for what Dora had to put up with every day from that man, being insulted, slapped and kicked in the stomach—all things she seemed to have become used to—but for what might happen the day when Benito Suárez finally deflected his aggression and directed it towards her, making her the target of his hatred and, of course, finding the pretexts he needed to justify it with very little effort.

Because that was the problem, or rather, that was what Lina perceived to be the biggest problem at that time: Benito Suárez's unwavering ability to bury the meaning of his reactions in that brand of delusional verbiage to which Lina listened intently despite her mistrust, trying to commit to memory certain phrases, slips of the tongue and associations, already fascinated by the deceptive intentions concealed by the things people said, and conscious that Benito Suárez was the best example she had of a man who runs away from himself in his words, or disowns himself, disguises himself, ultimately producing an absurd, shameful feeling of compassion within her, Lina, even though her solidarity initially and instinctively shifted towards Benito Suárez's victims, as it did the time she saw him attacking an old farmer with a machete in the countryside near Sabanalarga. Lina was there when it happened: she was with Dora, Renato and Benito Suárez in the Jeep he had bought so as not to ruin his Studebaker on the dusty trail to the ranch he'd recently inherited from one of his uncles, and as they turned a corner the farmer appeared out of nowhere, riding an ancient mule, leading an emaciated cow that was tied behind him and besieged by flies. It was clear that the Jeep should have the right of way because it would be easier for the mule to move aside into the brush, and so, understanding the situation, the farmer started to pull on the reins to turn right, hitting the mule's flanks and coaxing it with his voice. When the beast refused to deviate from the familiar path, the farmer jumped to the ground to gain better control, right at the point when Benito Suárez started insulting him completely out of the blue, yelling that he, his mule and his cow had been birthed by the same whore and if they didn't get off the trail that instant, he was going to run them over with his Jeep. The farmer dropped the reins and turned to look at them: he was a bony little man, his brow furrowed with dark wrinkles beneath his Panama hat, and though he probably could not read or write, there was a sort of dignity in his eyes; not pride, but the calm sobriety of the old, of those who have had time to reflect on things and put them all into perspective. He looked at Benito Suárez, unfazed, and told him: "Be patient, kid, the mule is a bit skittish." That was all the farmer said, but his nonchalance and his lack of deference was enough to make Benito Suárez attack him with the machete he was taking to the ranch foreman, jumping out of the Jeep so fast that Lina didn't even see him take the machete out of its sheath; she only saw it a second later, wielded in the air and then descending on the farmer, then back in the air again, dripping with blood, while Dora screamed and Lina searched frantically for some kind of blunt object, until she had thought to lift the lid of the tool box she had been sitting on in the Jeep, found the jack, then ran back over to where Benito Suárez was still hacking away at the farmer, and bashed him over the head with it. After that, everything seemed like a nightmare to Lina: forcing Dora to help her heave the two bodies into the Jeep; trying to control Renato, who was running about and shaking like someone possessed; then reversing to the main road and driving the Jeep to Barranquilla, to the main hospital where the city's top specialists—emergency doctors, anaesthetists, surgeons and cardiologists—rushed to fix the old farmer up in the operating room, helping Benito Suárez to dodge prison and a scandal in the process. When they got back to Dora's house, Renato drowsy from an injection and Benito Suárez with a bandage around his head, Lina felt like she was on the verge of a nervous breakdown. She took a shower to wash off the blood and the dust, told Berenice to fetch her some clean clothes, and then for the first time ever, she asked Dora for one of those tablets that helped her survive.

But in the meantime Benito Suárez, who was brooding on the living-room sofa with a kind of sombre focus, had realized that the farmer, given his age, must hold considerable sway over the poor people of Sabanalarga, in other words, over the world of dispossessed people who were just waiting for the first opportunity to seize a piece of land, justifying themselves as squatters in collusion with some demagogic or would-be liberalist priest, and he, Benito Suárez, who was planning to turn his ranch into a huge breeding farm for pedigree dogs, would have found himself exposed to repeated abuses and trespassing had he not responded forcefully when the farmer had the audacity to treat him as his equal, because even though the farmer did not report his assailant thanks to his offer of compensation (which indeed he did generously pay) he would go on to tell his relatives what happened, thus inspiring respect for his assailant's name. Benito Suárez completely disassociated himself from the barbarous impulse that had made him jump out of the Jeep and start hacking away with a machete at a helpless old man, as if he thought this was just one of a range of possible human responses, or perhaps one of those virile attributes his mother had taught him to admire ever since he was a boy, when she flogged him until he bled, demanding he adopt a stoic attitude—no crying or begging, but instead the courage and hardened spirit of those fierce warriors in Rome, Naples and Turin, who poured castor oil down their opponents' throats while singing the fascist anthem amid a sea of black banners. Furthermore, and as if coming full circle, two hours after he had been sitting deep in thought on the sofa in the living room—the farmer was still in surgery and would remain there until the following day—Benito Suárez had come up with his theory of emanations, according to which, his body must have sensed a wave of animosity coming from that man who, by blocking his path to the ranch, was simply intuiting, grasping and channelling the resistance that he, Benito Suárez, would face from the residents of Sabanalarga, who would never be able to forgive him for having climbed the social ladder when they shared the same origins as him, and who, condemned to poverty due to their idleness, cowardice or malice, would be inclined to believe that he, like them, was prone to weakness and incapable of defending his interests.

This idea of bodily emanations transmitted by the collective unconscious was something Lina would hear Benito Suárez talking about for almost a year, the whole time the farmer was in the hospital, and also the time during which the beautiful boxer bitch that arrived from Medellín with all kinds of certificates attesting to her noble origins, destined to be the reproductive mould for Benito Suárez's projects, would enter her second season, so she could be mated with the only animal in the city that matched her pedigree, a burly boxer without much of a libido, who stubbornly insisted on hiding underneath Dora's bed while the bitch (Penélope was her name) eagerly padded around the yard scratching and pushing at the service door, until one afternoon she managed to push open the latch, trotted out into the street and mated with the first mongrel that came along.

Lina and Dora were talking in the living room when they heard the Studebaker screeching to a halt and, almost instantaneously, the shouts from Benito Suárez as he called out for Antonia, the neighbour who owned the pharmacy next door. The mongrel in question belonged to her, and Benito Suárez was berating her for a thousand things at once, or rather he was trying to berate her but all that came out of his throat was a jumble of sounds and words, interrupted by something resembling hiccups, while he ran around in circles kicking at them in an attempt to separate the two animals—which had already mated but were still joined together, sullen-eyed, almost embarrassed by all the yelling—while Antonia stood guard, inserting herself between the dogs and Benito Suárez's white shoes with their thick rubber soles, as the curious bystanders—neighbours, gardeners, a few taxi drivers—gathered to enjoy the scene, roaring with laughter and muttering obscenities, which Benito Suárez seemed oblivious to because he was immersed in a fit of rage that only allowed him to spew insults at Antonia. He abruptly stopped and looked around, and, seeing his jaw suddenly clench, Lina got the feeling that the story was going to end with some cruel act aimed at silencing the laughter and jeering. So she was not surprised when she saw him heading for the Studebaker, where he took out his gun and, wielding it, began to turn slowly, his eyes squinting, scanning the crowd, who suddenly fell silent and started to retreat three feet, six feet, until they quietly scattered and the only ones left on the pavement were Antonia, Lina and the bitch, who was no longer attached to the mongrel: Lina wondering whom he was going to shoot, because she knew that only a gunshot could deliver him from ridicule, and the bitch, looking happy to see him, too highborn and well-fed to know any better, shifting her hip to the left and lifting her paws in one last movement before she fell onto the pavement when a bullet tore straight through her muzzle and buried itself in the boundary wall, shattering one of the stones into pieces.

This incident would be the source, or rather, it would be at the root of Benito Suárez's latest theory, that of impregnation, which he elaborated in depth to demonstrate to Lina, and anyone else who would listen, that the sperm cells of a given male left an indelible mark on the female; in other words, this female only had to be impregnated once to keep giving birth to offspring with the same genetic traits, even if they had different fathers. The theory was pure invention and tended to justify an illogical act, much like his theory of emanations, but it set alarm bells ringing for Lina because at that time Benito Suárez's poems had already exposed his affair with a woman who was married and apparently pregnant, to whom he had dedicated an ode entitled "Impossible Love," which alluded to her husband—a man full of regrets and memories, who spent a sombre youth in morgues among dead people—and hinted at an old friendship between colleagues, a poem with no bearing on reality because the husband turned out to be a law student who had never set foot in a morgue or seen a single dead person and had already been operated on twice for ulcers at Las Tres Marías hospital, where Benito Suárez was a partner with nine other doctors.

So it was this nonsense about impregnation that troubled Lina first of all. She knew Benito Suárez was in love, seriously in love: she would never forget the way he looked that afternoon when she found him in tears beside the record player, listening to a pitiful recording of Rubén Darío verses, or rather, she would associate that moment in her memory with the line, "Do you remember that time, Margarita, when you wanted to be another Marguerite Gautier?" Benito Suárez in tears, telling her, "There's someone else," his voice choked with emotion while the record player, Lina would recall years later, seemed to repeat the same line over and over, "Do you remember that time, Margarita, when you wanted to be another Marguerite Gautier?" Days later, he had sent her a letter full of empty words in the form of poems, all consisting of short lines, each with four syllables and of a highly dubious musicality, which Lina corrected and commented on without ever referring to the content, and without attaching too much importance to it. But it was another thing to suddenly discover that his lover, the Enriqueta from his anagrams, was carrying his child—otherwise he would not have laboured the subject of impregnation to such a degree—because Benito Suárez wanted a child, another one: a true descendant of his own, who would not cry like Renato when he took him to the municipal abattoir to see the cows being slaughtered in an attempt to toughen him up, a child who would not have a nervous breakdown if he felt like kicking Dora, hacking at a farmer with his machete or gunning down a dog. One way or another, Lina was counting on the lover's husband, whom she figured was a doctor and, at least in theory, must have enjoyed the same share of power that society had granted to Benito Suárez, and she hoped that the difficulty of dissolving two marriages or choosing between two children would make him see some sense while time took care of matters; she didn't have the slightest inkling that Benito Suárez had already decided to sort things out in his own way, with brutality, it seemed, in the husband's case, and more subtly when it came to Dora, having subjected her to analysis with Jerónimo Vargas, the red-bearded psychiatrist, around the same time he started writing the poems inspired by Enriqueta. The psychoanalysis she was made to undergo could not be taken seriously, first of all because Jerónimo Vargas was not a psychoanalyst, but also—and Dora seemed to be aware of this—because a half-baked reading of Reich was to blame for his lack of good sense, assuming he'd ever had any, and because ever since he'd married some unknown girl from the Colombian interior—a tall, skeletal thing with a milky complexion, made up like Juliette Gréco in the 1950s—Jerónimo Vargas had started to put into practice a vague notion of the orgasm as a form of release, or rather, the perpetual orgasm. In his opinion, this practice helped a man to tap into the creative forces of the universe and required, among other things, the unconditional involvement of a woman, which is why his wife, a hungry-looking girl with green eye shadow, was made to spend all day at home in the nude, submitting to her so-called marital duties every three or four hours, which he, Jerónimo Vargas, completed like clockwork, even if that meant cutting his sessions with Dora short and excusing himself to go and make love to his wife, then returning a little later with his shirt drenched in sweat, sometimes with a smudge of green very close to the line where his red beard began.

In other words, Dora's psychoanalysis sessions (where most of the time, all she did was listen to Jerónimo Vargas's chaotic interpretations) could have been cause for amusement had they not coincided with Benito Suárez's affair, and above all, had they not been accompanied by enormous doses of tranquillizers which, around the time when Enriqueta must have been about to give birth, suddenly turned into a prescription for drugs usually reserved for serious mental disorders, which Lina cautiously kept hold of when she began to suspect, not the truth—although she knew Benito Suárez, the thought of him being involved in something so melodramatic appalled her—but more simply an intention to weaken Dora's will so that she would be forced to give up Renato or something along those lines.

That prescription would end up forming part of the enormous case record presented in court by Dora's lawyer when Benito Suárez was trying to evade justice after hiding Renato at his sister's house, but at that time it ceased to be of any particular use because Benito Suárez beat a hasty retreat as soon as his intention to lock Dora up in an asylum was discovered, at the very moment when Dora's cook overheard him talking about the matter with Jerónimo Vargas and told Berenice, who in turn went roaming the streets as usual later that day, picking up the latest gossip from the wagging tongues of gardeners and maids so she could keep up with the changing fortunes of the people of El Prado. Ordinarily, Berenice would delight in any turn of events that supported her dismal opinion of white people, but she was fond of Dora, and the news horrified her, and so she set off to the house at a run, kicking off her flip-flops to balance her considerable weight better. That was how she looked when Lina saw her arrive: barefoot and panting, her breasts as big as melons, heaving beneath her shirt

covered in little flowers, and in her eyes—not in her pupils but
in the whites of the eyes, which were swivelling and darting
around in fear—a terrified expression that clouded over with
tears as soon as she managed to regain her voice and started
gabbling to Lina about mad people, asylums and ambulances,
with much weeping and wailing, which Lina's grandmother
put a stop to when she walked into the living room and asked
her to take a deep breath and explain herself calmly. From
what she was saying, apparently Jerónimo Vargas had already
made a request for Dora be admitted to the El Reposo clinic at
nine o'clock the following morning, when Renato would be at
school. Her grandmother listened to Berenice without interrupting, gently waving a hand in the air to calm her down, then
with a similar gesture, and still without making the slightest
comment on the matter, she shooed her off into the kitchen.
When they were alone, Lina noticed that her grandmother
looked thoughtful: as she stood there, diminutive and tenacious, so small that she barely reached Lina's shoulder, she
seemed to be meditating, contemplating the top of her walking
stick, lost in thought. Perhaps she had started to analyze
Berenice's words in spite of the irrepressible, age-old suspicion
she had towards gossip among maids. Or perhaps—and just as
the thought struck her, Lina once again felt her childhood anxiety of being unable to access a certain kind of understanding—her grandmother was secretly beginning to break the pattern of thought that had enabled her to analyze Benito Suárez's
reactions until then, adopting instead a more complex level of
reflection, tracking the metamorphosis that Benito Suárez
himself must have undergone, and leaving behind the pre-
dictably irascible, primitive and ultimately tyrannical husband, that attacker of old people, killer of dogs, writer of bad
verse, and venturing into the maze of a scheming man who
orchestrated his violence with all the treachery of a Florentine
courtier. Alternatively, no such pattern had ever existed, and

having discovered that the order of things had changed, her grandmother was taking the time to think about it while she, Lina, waited patiently to hear her conclusions despite the thousand or so plans that were running through her mind, from hiding Dora in her house to threatening Jerónimo Vargas with a media scandal. All the while, she was confused, because even in those moments, and stemming from an unutterable affection for an individual she trusted about as much as she would a scorpion, she was unwittingly seeking out the grey areas of the whole business—a glitch, a crack, something to cling on to— and starting to wonder whether Berenice, given her inclination for drama, might have in fact exaggerated or distorted the meaning of some harmless conversation or other which, in turn, had been misinterpreted by Dora's cook, when she heard her grandmother say, in a calm yet commanding tone: "You should tell your father straight away."

Her father was the last person in the world Lina would have thought to tell that Benito Suárez was planning to lock Dora up in a mental asylum. Not because her father was indifferent to Dora's fate: even though he never spoke about it, the subject usually made him tense and silent, or to excuse himself from after-dinner conversation. Lina had noticed that he even managed to get home late from the office when Benito Suárez was celebrating the anniversary of his first meeting with her grandmother by showing up at the house uninvited behind an over-the-top bouquet of flowers. But given her father's disposition and his most extraordinary indifference to life's calamities, Lina usually chose to keep him out of her problems, as if that carefree, cheerful giant, who watched unblinkingly as things came crashing down around him, and serenely drove his beat-up Dodge at six miles per hour, was many different characters at once—a friend, an erudite man, a history teacher— everyone except someone who might offer her just one valuable piece of advice if, say, her clothing was on fire or if any

other disaster should happen to her. So, while she was on her
way downtown on a bus she had hastily caught on the corner
of Calle 72, oblivious to the heat and the din of the passengers,
with Jerónimo Vargas's prescription in her purse, glancing at it
obsessively from time to time to check she hadn't lost it, Lina
was trying to find the words to tell her father about Dora's situation in all its seriousness without giving him time to cut in
with one of his usual jokes or some sarcastic remark about
Berenice's silly ways. Lina pictured his scepticism approach,
do a pirouette, then sweep everything aside as she mulled over
the different ways to express such a shocking tale, one based on
a series of signs that would never wash with her father—psychoanalysis, a few meagre verses, gossip between maids—telling
herself the story over and over amid the din of the bus and the
smell of burnt petrol, and then again while she waited for her
father in his office on Calle San Blas, which he had left open as
usual, risking losing his only asset, if that was the right word
for his old black Remington with stiff keys, on which he typed
up reports and briefs with astonishing speed. It was here that
Dora's future would be decided, and in a way, Benito Suárez's
fate too, in that dusty office where, years later, torn between
astonishment and tenderness, Lina would remember: the typewriter, and on the wall, next to the framed photograph of her
hands which she had cut into pieces and thrown in the trash
one day, the oil painting of that great-grandfather—who was
the son of a rabbi-cum-diplomat, and according to her father,
the ninth pretender to Israel's throne (had there been a monar-
chy in Israel) and the one to blame for Cartagena de Indias
almost being destroyed by the Dutch fleet. Waiting by the window in that office, which no man with more than a hundred
pesos in his wallet had ever set foot in, Lina would see her
father making his way up Calle San Blas in his white linen suit,
looking miraculously clean, miraculously fresh in the leaden
heat that melted the asphalt; he smiled at beggars, shoe shiners

and candy vendors as he walked past, no doubt calling all of them Lucho because there were too many names for him to remember them all. She would hear the wheezing of the old elevator that took him up to the office, the upbeat tone of his voice as he greeted her, the squeaking of the swivel chair when he sat down at his desk beneath the plaintive flapping of the ceiling fan; and then, surprised, almost perplexed, she would register the grave look that crept onto his face when she told him what she knew, reaching into her purse for the prescription from Jerónimo Vargas. This time there were no jokes, no glib remarks, not even the slightest hint of scepticism. Her father's face was fixed in an expression that Lina would see only three times in her life, and always with fear: a kind of hardness, his muscles tense and his eyes shrinking alarmingly until they turned into pure flashes of rage. Without saying a word or stopping to look at the prescription that Lina had laid in front of him on the desk, her father slowly started to dial a number on the telephone. When Benito Suárez's voice appeared on the end of the line, Lina heard her father say, his voice quiet with rage: "Listen, Benito Suárez, if you put Dora in the madhouse, I'll put you in prison. You know I can do it." And that was that: her father hung up without bothering to wait for a response. Lina was simply lost for words. For one thing, she got the impression that she had all of a sudden discovered the meaning, importance and consequences of the word "law," that concept in whose name a mild-mannered man like her father, who had never felt the weight of a gun in his hands, took it upon himself to challenge Benito Suárez from his humble office on Calle San Blas. For another thing, she'd detected an irrevocable threat in the words he used, an allusion to something that she did not know, and that apparently her own story had confirmed. But knowing her father's reservations about anything that remotely concerned the practice of his profession, she refrained from asking any questions and even left his office with a sense of relief. Not a sense of triumph—because it seemed that Benito Suárez was on a winning streak and this truce, like so many others, would be over in a matter of months—but the calm feeling of being able to picture Dora in her house, stuffed full of tranquillizers, yes, but with her mind out of harm's way, distracting herself from her boredom by looking after Renato and the two boxer puppies that had been brought over from Medellín to replace Penélope.

The worries came later, when Lina told Berenice about the meeting with her father and Berenice was struck dumb with terror, as if she could hear the horses of the apocalypse galloping towards her. Because she really was speechless: not only did she keep her thoughts to herself in that moment, sensing how futile it was to express them, but for a week she remained in a distraught silence, which probably harked back to another time, to those dark nights when the rustling of the rainforest was pierced by cries, when the metallic sounds of chains answered the crashing of the waves, and whips hissed through the air in the sudden, bright light of some mysterious port. All that week, Lina would catch Berenice anxiously peering out of the windows as soon as night began to fall, her hands—so tiny in proportion to her large, rounded body—clutching the folds of the curtain, and her back shaking as she stifled sobs, no doubt trying to avoid attracting Lina's grandmother's attention. She would see Berenice's bloodshot eyes when, dressed all in black except for a white organza apron, she served dinner with a look on her face that revealed the most hopeless fatalism. She would hear her bolting the doors at night and sighing all day long in the kitchen, and eventually, by contagion—or perhaps, Lina thought to herself, because of the unidentified share of Black blood that was coursing through her own veins—she, Lina, would also find herself staring onto the street furtively, more or less waiting to see the cars driving by, and more or less convinced that Benito Suárez was bound to show signs of life sooner or later.

Which of course he did: he appeared one night when Lina was having dinner with her grandmother and her father, and as was to be expected, Berenice was the first to spot him. Before his ominous blue Studebaker turned the corner, Berenice was already rushing into the dining room in a tizzy, yelling "He's here, Miss Jimena, that lunatic's here." There was no point in Lina's grandmother telling her to show him in, because Berenice was in no state to carry out that order, or any other. So it was down to Lina to open the door. Standing there was Benito Suárez puffed up with self-satisfaction, holding a large crate of champagne, and, next to him, Dora, looking more lacklustre than ever, in her trusty old blouse and skirt from Sears and with a white purse she was probably debuting for the occasion. Lina led them down the hall and into the dining room, where her father and her grandmother were still eating dinner, unperturbed, and Berenice was pressing herself against the sideboard that she, Lina, had hidden Dora behind years ago, after seeing her cross the garden with her face all bloody. And while Berenice daringly reached a wary hand across the table, slyly removing the knives one by one, Benito Suárez launched into one of his pompous speeches, the kind that seemed to have been rehearsed in front of the mirror, or rather, on a podium lit up by spotlights; and, watched by Lina's grandmother and her father, whose eyes hardened into the same neutral gaze, devoid of expression, he attempted to defend his honour, which had been trampled by the vilest aspersions and the envy his personality inspired in miserable souls. For, here was his wife, safe and sound: the thoroughly respectable mother to his son, his lady wife who had received medical treatment for those common depressive episodes that regularly attacked the fragile female nature. "Look, she's cured now," he said, pointing at Dora, as if he were addressing interns in a hospital seminar room. "So to celebrate that, and to celebrate clearing up these horrible misunderstandings, I've taken the liberty of bringing you this champagne. You," he continued, turning to Berenice who was hiding the knives beneath her apron and staring, startled, at the huge crate of bottles decorated with colourful ribbons, "bring us four glasses—no, make it five," he said, glancing at Dora, who he seemed to have forgotten was there.

Because for him, Dora had the curious quality of half existing, or sometimes not existing at all. Rather than being someone, she was something that appeared or disappeared depending on his mood, receiving his blows and yells passively, following his orders like a robot, never putting up the slightest resistance. Perhaps, Lina thought back then, that was because resisting involved actually having to think, or at least having to tell herself that the values imposed by society could be discussed or rejected, and this was something that never occurred to Dora. She had agreed to the marriage with the same bewildered resignation with which her mother, Doña Eulalia del Valle, had agreed to her own marriage, but for different reasons to Dora, imbuing it with the sacred quality espoused by the catechism, recognized by society and emphatically affirmed by the priest in Puerto Colombia, Benito Suárez's friend, who officiated the ceremony. Based on that premise, any act of rejection or refusal was impossible for Dora, as was any form of questioning, scrutiny or hesitation, because any argument she could present would invariably cast doubt over the foundations of a union conceived a priori to be eternal and inviolable. Her situation, evoked in hundreds of turn-of-the-century novels, was similar to that of almost all the married women Lina knew, but Dora had not ended up in that situation for the same reasons, because she had no interest in social standing or money; moreover, she was an atheist, not exactly a devout atheist but irreligious out of indifference, in the sense that she had never been concerned with understanding why day followed night, how good and evil existed or where the miracle of life and the indignity of death came from. Lina was convinced that her friend's thoughts revolved only around the here and now, and did not go beyond the level of immediate sensations, with the lassitude of a plant that shrivels in the heat of the sun and quivers in the wind. After eleven years of living with Benito Suárez, Dora's capacity to react had weakened and she even lacked the instinct to defend herself, that blind, chemical, primitive mechanism that makes a simple cat bristle and fold back its ears in the presence of danger. Dora accepted, gave in, let him ride roughshod over her like someone who knows their will is broken and gone forever, or even less, because such an awareness implied that it was possible to think about that loss, and therefore, to put a name to Benito Suárez's control, to define it as something that worked against her but that existed outside of her and could be limited, whittled down to a single word. But Dora immersed herself in that control as if it was part of the air, part of the people and things she saw around her, not so much out of fear—though naturally fear must have played a part in her docility—as out of a kind of puerile gratitude to the man who had married her, giving her a house, a son and a surname, despite her being damaged goods when he met her. She was damaged goods, not because of how society might perceive her, but in fact because of the contempt she felt for herself. Yes, Dora had renounced her youth over time, that vital impulse which had allowed her to open her body to desire and surrender her sensuality without any reward or simply in exchange for the pleasure she got from giving; she had shrunk back into an intractable sense of shame which Lina believed had developed as a conditioned reflex, seeing as the blows, shouting and kicks from Benito Suárez were always accompanied by references to her perverse relationship with Andrés Larosca and the equally brazen sexuality she'd exhibited when they first met. Added to this was the constant nagging from her mother, Doña Eulalia del Valle, who saw Dora's original sin as the justification for her own cowardice towards

Benito Suárez; her protest was limited to a long litany of woes
about the misfortune of having a daughter who had lost her
way, ignored her warnings, disregarded the example she set
and sullied her surname, thus turning any pain or humiliation
on Dora's part into yet another reason to feel sorry for herself.
And then there was the environment Dora had grown up in, all
the things she had seen and heard, the things she learned in
school, the religious teachings, the things she read in novels,
the things insinuated in films; all those repressive morals,
momentarily overpowered by the heat of her adolescent body,
ideas that had fought their way into her head and settled there
once and for all, evolving over time until they created not a
sludge of maxims tinged with religion, superstition or philosophy, but instead the most tremendous agglomeration of platitudes, truisms and clichés that left her absolutely wide open to
Benito Suárez's tirades, which seemed to echo her own self-
condemnation. Nevertheless, by marrying Dora, Benito Suárez
had salvaged her dignity, acting both as her protector and her
link to reality, because apart from her mother, Doña Eulalia del
Valle, that querulous shadow, ageing by the trees in her yard,
and Lina, who ultimately did not have much to offer her, Benito
Suárez was the only person Dora could rely on. This depend-
ency (and fear, too) was at the root of a feeling Lina never managed to define, something that resembled respect, the propitiatory veneration shown by men crouching in a cave, souls
crushed by terror, who tried to appease their ferocious gods, or
like them, primitive men, intimidated and fearful, who fumbled
around in the dark, trying to behave in a way that did not provoke God's wrath, or in a way that earned his favour or his forgiveness. That devotion was also the point of reference in a hostile, incomprehensible world known only to Benito Suárez and
ruled by him alone: his voice was the North Star in the nighttime, the position of the sun in the daytime, a beacon, a sign, a
memory, a guide. Any doubt, even the simplest question, threw

her completely off course. And so that is why, perhaps, Dora listened to his speeches without reservations and was not wary of his intentions; and that is why, perhaps, it was too much to ask of her to doubt the man who completely controlled her, accepting, even in theory, that this same man had been underhandedly plotting to lock her up in an asylum.

If it had been up to Lina, Dora would never have found out. The few people who visited her—Doña Eulalia del Valle, Antonia, her neighbour, her mother-in-law, her sister-in-law and her maids—had the same instinctive reflex to silence or distort the truth so that everything was reduced to a misunderstanding between Benito Suárez and Jerónimo Vargas. Curiously, that narrative drove a wedge between the two friends, as if the need to feign discord had spurred them on to create it, or maybe because once they had crossed that line, that is to say, once they stopped behaving amicably, in a way that allowed them to appease each other, they would find that they were quite capable of attacking one another and could see no reason to hold back. They had met as schoolboys in the Colegio de los Hermanos Cristianos, and by the end of the first week they had come to blows at recess, under the smug gaze of the prefect—a grim-faced Spaniard, as large and stocky as one would expect a campesino to be, entrusted with keeping the students in check by hitting them round the head—who must have sniffed the danger as soon as he saw them get off the bus on the first day back at school, even though they were only ten years old and had turned up at Biffi College with a confused look on their faces, like two puppies unceremoniously dumped in a cage full of adult dogs. All week long the Spaniard kept a keen eye on them from the hallway, Benito Suárez recalled, and still neither of them realized that they were the sole focus of his attention, because they themselves were busy gauging, weighing up and testing the mental fortitude of the teachers who came into the classroom; they caused mayhem with slingshots and darts, name-calling, face-pulling, hurling insults and all the other uncouth habits he and Jerónimo Vargas had picked up as the leaders of their respective neighbourhood gangs, the two of them bound by the perfect complicity of people who know they are equals and are programmed for the exact same purpose. Until the morning when the Spaniard spurred them on to fight in the schoolyard, trying to put an end to their partnership in crime, but to no avail: at the first exchange of blows the puppies understood that they would do better to turn against their common enemy when the time was right, which could not be then, as they would risk being expelled from school, but later on, with their diplomas in their pockets as they left the theatre where their graduation ceremony was held, when they ran into the Spaniard in an alleyway and gave him the beating he'd feared ever since he saw them step off the bus six years earlier.

So, together they had passed the test of high school, and together they had visited a brothel for the first time, and they had even taken the same plane to Bogotá to study medicine. They were two feral animals who were aware of what it was that made them alike and set them apart from everyone else, Lina thought, and for this same reason they were willing to help each other out whenever one of them was in difficulty, but their alliance became vulnerable if fate put them on opposing sides, causing them to lose the subtle mechanism of mutual recognition and solidarity that had stopped them turning on one other.

Because only by thinking about the two men in terms as inadequate as scent, colour, plumage or ritual behaviour, could one explain how they could be getting along fine one moment and then suddenly start quarrelling over any old thing, particularly when it came to their ideas about the best way to treat a woman. Granted, Nietzsche and Reich did not share the same opinion on the matter, and Jerónimo Vargas seemed to be truly in love with the skeletal girl who drifted around the house all day in the nude. But after months of confinement, of heat, solitude and living behind permanently drawn curtains so as not to scandalize the neighbours, the girl began to grow bored, even though few women in the city could boast of being so well looked after, and became eager for a more balanced life, threatening to pack her bags and return to Tunja, Sogamoso, Ramiriquí or wherever it was she came from. This prospect terrified Jerónimo Vargas and prompted him to seek advice from Benito Suárez, a man who believed that a woman ought to be trained like a dog, none of this taking her opinions into account, heeding her threats or bending to her whims, but rather imposing one's will upon her in accordance with the laws of mankind and religion. Emboldened by his advice, Jerónimo Vargas insisted on indulging in his daily marital orgy until the girl, losing patience, found a way to fend him off: getting pregnant and refusing any kind of sexual contact for those nine months. He was frustrated, irascible and ill-disposed to Benito Suárez as a result, tearing into him the night when he found out about the situation, in such a strange way that even Dora found herself questioning his mental state later on: because that night, she and Benito Suárez had been invited to his house for the first time, and when they arrived, Jerónimo Vargas opened the door, and, before slamming it again in their faces, he snapped at them, asking what the hell they were doing there, thus renewing the hostilities that the school prefect had unsuccessfully tried to provoke years before, which culminated in a grand finale two months later at Dora's house with Benito Suárez and Jerónimo Vargas fighting with their bare fists, shattering all the porcelain in the living room and spilling blood on the brand-new rug.

It happened on a Monday or Tuesday during Carnival. A day earlier, Benito Suárez had blacked up his face by smearing shoe polish over it, and then, after drinking all afternoon, he headed over to Jerónimo Vargas's house, supposedly to make peace with him. But when he arrived, the only person home was his emaciated wife, bonier and more haggard now, two months into her pregnancy, and afraid: afraid of the carnival her husband and his maid had rushed off to earlier, leaving her all alone; afraid of the men and women she'd seen at the Batalla de las Flores parade with their faces all painted, throwing corn starch and swigging out of bottles; afraid of the noise and confusion, the dances, the complete pandemonium which, for four days, dispelled the listlessness of the city that she, the girl from Tunja or Sogamoso, had thus far thought to be sleepy and sun-scorched—at least on the few occasions when her husband had allowed her to put on some clothes and take a walk around the streets. So when she opened the door and saw Benito Suárez standing there with his face blacked up, she was scared. Perhaps she had always feared him and he either knew it all along or realized in that very moment, and with his eyes locked on her, he started imitating a madman, or rather, making the kinds of faces and voices he had observed in mad people, lumbering toward her menacingly as she edged backward and started scrabbling up the stairs, slipped and fell, finally breaking into screams that turned to groans as the pains of miscarriage set in. Benito Suárez managed to call an ambulance, but by then she had lost the baby. This was the reason why he and Jerónimo Vargas went at each other, exposing their respective secrets while Dora, who had hidden herself away in the bathroom with Renato, found out about Enriqueta and the true purpose of her psychoanalysis. Then she went to pieces: shot down, defeated, she let herself sink into her intrinsic inertia, like an animal withdrawing and surrendering the weight of its body to the darkness of the refuge it has sought out to die.

V

If Lina had asked how best to control an instinct, her grandmother would probably have told her that human impulses operated in uncharted regions, advising her to be wary of any attempt to interfere with them. Because her grandmother believed that human instinct was self-regulating and could encounter opposing tendencies within one person, tendencies that could temper the violence of that instinct or divert it from its objective, thus allowing it to readjust in accordance with the laws laid down by society. To her grandmother's mind, passing judgement or imposing moral imperatives linked to some utopian idea of freedom of choice only served to aggravate man's feeling of guilt and, consequently, to vilify an aggressiveness that perhaps only needed to be expressed fleetingly before falling dormant again. Above all, this morality confined a man to his own singularity, breaking the bridges that were meant to identify him with all other men so that he could see himself reflected in them, be it in happiness or misfortune, in greatness or wretchedness. Once he was cut off from other men, he either became demoralized, losing all self-respect, or hid behind a delusional pride that sought to affirm its legitimacy through a new series of blunders. But the instinct never disappeared: it was always there, lurking, more incoercible than ever, and if it had been severely repressed for some time, the smallest stimulus would cause it to be unleashed.

Guided by this notion, Lina's grandmother was perhaps the only person who observed Benito Suárez's behaviour without optimism over the eight months that followed his thunderous quarrel with Jerónimo Vargas that day during Carnival. Because in those eight months, Benito Suárez's personality seemed to change unexpectedly: no longer irritable and overbearing, he became an obliging individual who sought the company of others and wrote verse after verse of poetry, expressing his philosophical disillusionment with the twists of fate. In fact, and as he stated in his poems at the time, probably influenced by reading the Greek authors, destiny mocked human endeavours like a merciless deity, grinding their hopes to dust and imprisoning their existence in a maze of unfathomable plans. That sense of impotence stemmed from very distinct causes: Enriqueta's child had been stillborn a month after her husband, the law student Antonio Hidalgo, mysteriously passed away at Las Tres Marías hospital. Meanwhile, Jerónimo Vargas—who, drawing on his newly acquired psychoanalytical knowledge, had diagnosed Benito Suárez with the unconscious desire to make his wife miscarry because his own hopes of becoming a father had been dashed by the death of Enriqueta's baby—insidiously spread rumours which, if confirmed, would call into question Benito Suárez's very right to practise his profession. And then there was Dora, the problem of Dora. Actually, in one way or another, she had always been a problem for him, but he had been able to display her as his wife all the same: a subdued woman who performed her marital duties to perfection, taking care of their home and staying in her husband's shadow every step of the way. Suddenly, this plasticine object refused to be moulded the way his hands wanted, ceasing to be exhibitable, showable—not through some act of decisiveness, will or rebellion, but quite the opposite: by being so excessively pliable that, paradoxically, it perverted her malleable nature. Dora was nothing: ever since that day when she discovered Benito Suárez's machinations to lock her up in a mental asylum, she seemed to stop living. Withdrawing into herself, refusing to take the drugs to which her body had become accustomed, she fell into a state of absolute despondency, the aim of which, if there was one, was to escape into silence and inertia, or perhaps death. Lina went to her house every day at about noon, accompanied by Berenice. The two of them would get her out of bed, take her to the bathroom, sit her on a wooden stool beneath the shower, and wash her skinny, slightly contorted body, which they could move around like a doll's. Then they would settle her into a rocking chair, tucking a red blanket over her legs, and patiently, spoonful by spoonful, they would get her to eat a little mashed potato and ground meat, setting a glass of sugary *aguapanela* beside her before they left. In the evening, Lina would return to take her to the toilet then put her back to bed, where it seemed she did not sleep, dream or think about anything at all.

Of course, in a state like that, she could not make the kind of public appearance Benito Suárez wanted, one which would allow him to vindicate himself to those who insisted he'd locked her away in an asylum or completely alienated her (which was closer to the truth) so that he could marry a woman whose husband he'd murdered while he lay asleep in a room at the Las Tres Marías hospital recovering from a minor operation. As far as Lina knew, there was nothing conclusive to support these claims, and the investigation that later sparked the drama had not even been opened yet, but people were talking and whispering about it, excitedly spreading the word, and that was just as bad, if not worse. All Benito Suárez's attempts to coax Dora out of that state of inertia had failed: he tried reasoning, promises and gifts; he used truth and lies, seduction and threats. But nothing worked. One day, maybe out of exasperation, he tried to force her to swallow some pills, and when he saw that she had spat them out, he punched her, splitting her lip, then tied her to the rocking chair and injected her with a drug that was supposed to induce euphoria but only served to make her faint and render her unconscious for fifteen hours. That time, Lina reacted with the same hatred, the same calm yet irrepressible resolve that had compelled her to creep through the corridors of her house years earlier, out to the yard where the nameless mutt was tied up and waiting silently for the chance to tear apart the first man that came near it, then, taking it by the collar, set it upon Benito Suárez, who tried to run, but the dog was hot on his heels, shredding his trousers, tearing the skin off his arms and sinking its teeth into his buttocks, knocking him to the ground and mauling him despite the punches and kicks, even ramming against the door of the Studebaker when Benito Suárez finally reached safety.

Perhaps Benito Suárez was reminded of that incident with the dog when Lina entered the room where he was trying to revive Dora, and pointed the gun at him, his own gun, the one he always kept in the glovebox of his blue Studebaker. Lina came up with the idea of taking the gun as soon as she made it to Dora's house, when Antonia, the neighbour, beckoned her over to tell her that Benito Suárez had come to her to buy a concoction of drugs used for resuscitation. Even before Antonia started speaking, perhaps by the look on her face, Lina had connected the gun and the Studebaker she'd seen parked in the garage. But she wasn't sure exactly when she'd taken it out of the glovebox, or how she'd made her way through the service door with her index finger resting on the trigger, while Dora's cook watched in horror. She would remember making this connection and noticing that look of horror, like fireflies glowing in the darkness. The lapse of time between hearing Antonia speak and the moment she entered Dora's room vanished from her mind. And it would never return to her memory, not even years later. Yet what she did remember later, when Benito Suárez had fled the scene and she'd taken Dora back to her house, was that she was holding the gun when she entered the room. Benito Suárez turned to look at her. She saw Dora lying on the bed with a split lip, her mouth busted up like a boxer's after a knockout, and four trickles of blood already congealed on her chin. Lina thought she was dead. Suddenly she noticed Benito Suárez and remembered how she'd once read that women always missed their target when they shot because they aimed for the head instead of the stomach, and so that's what she said to him. She lowered the gun and said, "I'm going to shoot you in the stomach, not the head." That was when Benito Suárez started running.

Lina would often ask herself, petrified, if she would have been able to fire the shot, to destroy a life. Life, the only thing in the world that she definitely revered, that inexplicable principle her grandmother had taught her to respect in men and in animals, even in plants. Perhaps she wouldn't have killed Benito Suárez, because, seconds before she saw him flee, she decided it would be better to shoot him in the leg. But the fact that she had threatened to kill him was a revelation of a dark aspect of herself, as well as a dreadful lesson in humility. In any case, that outburst allowed Lina to take Dora to her house and leave her in the care of Dr. Ignacio Agudelo, while she braced herself for a visit from Benito Suárez and tried to imagine his reaction—or rather, the attitude that would convey his reaction—convinced that on this occasion there would be no display of submission from him, simply because the fact that he'd fled from a woman who, to add insult to injury, was wielding his own gun, must have been the ultimate humiliation. So she waited calmly, or at least relatively calmly compared to Berenice, who stood guard day and night at Dora's bedside with a kitchen knife concealed in the folds of her starched apron. But she kept thinking about it quietly, eventually tracing the outline of the figure who would help him keep his self-respect intact—Benito Suárez, a man who had been offended but was willing to forgive, because his aggressor, Lina, had acted impulsively at the sight of Dora lying there unconscious. She also guessed that Benito Suárez would choose to speak to her father, partly to get back at him for the phone call which no doubt absolutely mortified him, but also to lend a particularly formal tone to his defence. So when he finally showed up at the house and Lina answered the front door, it didn't surprise her in the slightest to see him nod in greeting and then hurry down the hall to the room where her father was reading, enjoying the cool of the evening next to the large iron grille overlooking the yard. What disturbed her was his appearance, but not his look of wounded dignity, which was to be expected, nor his paleness or the three-day beard, which hinted at sleepless nights and, based on what Dora's cook had told Berenice, a complete lack of appetite and excessive whiskey consumption. No, it was more the difference in his expression, something that emerged from farce and transcended it, morphing into an irreverent fatalism, a desperate determination, as if he had at last come to terms with the demon that slumbered inside him. And yet the change in his mindset—recognizing, adjusting and surrendering to that demon—was not related to Dora in any way, Lina thought as she followed him down the hall and watched him walk right into the tie that her father had left hanging in the doorway of his room to deter bats: at that moment, Dora merely served as a pretext for another performance, one that was momentarily interrupted by the implausible tie fluttering in front of his eyes, which he dodged abruptly, as if he were the very bat it was designed to confuse and he didn't even know it. And Dora remained a pretext throughout the scene that unfolded as he approached Lina's father, who, without moving from his rocking chair, had laid the half-open book on the table and rested his glasses on top of it, glancing at Benito Suárez to assess what state he was in, and tilting his head back expecting to better hear, perhaps, some pompous speech about a husband's rights or some other such nonsense (since the only thing that her father knew about Dora's presence in the house was that Lina had brought her there, unconscious, so that Dr. Agudelo could treat her). But he definitely did not expect the sentence that Benito Suárez uttered with his jaw clenched so hard that his voice was barely audible: "I've got something important to tell you, Dr. Insignares. I'm going to report your daughter for attempted murder." Her father blinked twice and said, "What in God's name are you talking about, Benito Suárez?" "About me," Lina interjected, "I pointed his gun at him so he wouldn't kill Dora." Benito Suárez's face became even more contorted, and his nostrils began to flare to the rhythm of his breathing. "You see, Dr. Insignares, she admits she's guilty: she tried to kill me, and she kidnapped my wife." Lina saw her father's eyes light up with a glimmer of laughter, which instantly gave way to the kind of indulgent calmness normally reserved for regarding someone unhinged. "Well, Benito Suárez," he said, "I doubt it's as serious that." And then within herself she felt Benito Suárez's bewilderment, his furious impotence. She couldn't have called it perception; she didn't even need to look at him. For an instant as brief as the shadow of a cloud at high noon, she felt like she was inside him, inside that outraged mind that had come in search of some sort of redress, certain that for the first time, he would be able to command respect, a two-way conversation or perhaps an apology, only to find himself confronted with a calm and collected man who didn't take the dressing-down seriously but still allowed himself to be treated with condescension. He, Benito Suárez, didn't have a gun or any kind of weapon, and her father was not some poor old man from Sabanalarga. So he hesitated, and Lina could also sense his hesitation. Then she lost him. In fact, it seemed like Benito Suárez was losing touch with reality altogether. As he backed away from her, she saw him stumble again into the tie that was meant to trick the bats, and then look at it in fright for a second, as if it were a curse upon him. Then, without moving or taking his eyes off the tie, his expression began to change: although the tie must have seemed like a deliberate affront, he probably realized in a flash of lucidity that no one, not even Lina's father, that wily old fox, could have guessed that he was intending to come and see him that day, at that time and in that place. So the tie became something else entirely, perhaps a symbol of the persecution he either felt he was suffering or was in fact suffering, and so, he swiped it from the door jamb, flung it onto the floor and proceeded to stamp on it with the thick rubber soles of his white shoes. Her father looked on from his rocking chair, unfazed by what was happening, and at the other end of the passage, Berenice opened the door onto the street. Benito Suárez looked back and forth between them, rabid, nervous, like a cornered animal, and his breathing quickened again. He stammered the word "kidnap" and then repeated it several more times until he was finally able to come out with the words, "They've kidnapped my wife." In his mind, that idea served as a foothold, or rather, as the justification that allowed him to regain a little balance: suddenly calm, he strode over to the phone and called the police, or more accurately, he picked up the receiver and began talking to an imaginary person on the other end of the line and accusing her, Lina, of having abducted his wife, also saying that he, too, was being held against his will at Dr. Insignares's house—all this without having dialled a single number, and seeming completely oblivious to that fact.

Lina watched him, torn between distrust and pity. She knew that Benito Suárez had slipped up, or to put it another way, he had crossed the line that winds its way between reason and the irrational, but she did not how he would react when he came to his senses and found himself talking on a phone without dialling a number. Fortunately, her grandmother took charge of the situation: appearing though a side door, she greeted Benito Suárez calmly and passed by in front of him with her walking stick, saying, "When you've finished talking, come out onto the terrace with me for some lemon tea." What they talked about, Lina never knew. She simply took the tray with the two cups of tea from Berenice's hands and carried it out to the terrace, where Benito Suárez was kneeling on the floor with his head buried in her grandmother's lap, sobbing like a child. The look on her grandmother's face told her she should make herself scarce at once, and so she went to her room. Then three hours later, at around midnight, she heard the front door opening, the blue Studebaker starting up, and her grandmother's tiny, almost furtive footsteps as she made her way around the house, turning off all the lights one by one before bed. That was the last time her grandmother talked to him on the terrace.

For eight months after that, Benito Suárez behaved impeccably: he treated Dora nicely, took her to the cinema to see premieres, and even took her out dancing at the Patio Andaluz one Saturday night. This sudden gallantry threw into relief his vague expression of self-acceptance, of malevolent satisfaction with that alter ego, perhaps his innermost self, his authentic self, which appeared sporadically with a barbarism he had always tried to justify. Seeing the new, hardened look on his face, those wary eyes that glazed over without showing the slightest sign of emotion, Lina anxiously recalled her grandmother's theories about repressed instincts, and though she rejected or didn't completely share her grandmother's ruthlessly fatalistic outlook, she was nevertheless waiting for the outburst that would restore the natural order of things. Because she knew Benito Suárez too well to believe he had changed overnight, and because she knew that he was dealing with a serious problem at that time, a real problem: the investigation into the death of the law student Antonio Hidalgo, which was secretly being conducted by his colleagues at Las

Tres Marías Hospital. As had happened so many times with the crimes committed in the city, the investigation could have been stalled at any moment, or rather, it could have been reduced to a pantomime had it not been led by the hospital director himself, Dr. Vesga, a Santander man who had taken refuge in Barranquilla with his wife and six children, fleeing the civil war. In fact, perhaps fleeing was not the best choice of verb to describe whatever course of action Dr. Vesga might have taken, pursued or pulled off, because it was easier to picture him squaring up to a whole mob of *chulavitas* than abandoning his ancestral home, even if that house had been burned to the ground, his mother raped and his two brothers beheaded with machetes. He was specializing in France when it happened, Dr. Agudelo would tell Lina, and apparently—at least according to him—he had left his wife and children there and returned with an arsenal of grenades and rifles that he smuggled across the Venezuelan border and distributed among the labourers on his hacienda, who had escaped the massacre and who spent a year helping him chase down one by one the people responsible for the destruction of his family. Perhaps he killed them all, because he was from Santander. Or perhaps he only killed a few of them, because he was a doctor. In any case, what he saw (if he saw anything) or what he did (if he did anything) forged or reinforced an irreducible consciousness within him, where good and evil were concrete and, in any case, identifiable entities. So he arrived in Barranquilla with his wife and children, his Templar principles and his reputation as one of the finest surgeons in the country. Which he was, according to the doctors who gathered around him when he did pro bono operations in the city's major hospital; the ones who followed him at a respectful distance through the corridors and fought amongst themselves for the privilege of assisting him in the operating room.

As the hospital's only female OR nurse, Lina worked on his

team three times; three times she helped him into the green gown, helped him slip on the rubber gloves and, trembling at the thought of making the slightest mistake, passed him the forceps that closed blood vessels, extracted fat and isolated the tumour meticulously, with a precision so exact it was almost inhuman. For major operations, which she, of course, was not invited to work on, the older doctors attended as observers or assistants, and the younger ones gladly agreed to serve as nurses or gathered outside the door, craning to see something through the round glass windows. A man like that was bound to make an impression on Benito Suárez because he was the kind of man he would have wanted to be: a renowned surgeon, descended from nobility, a man who was said to have boldly avenged his family; not a showoff or a thug, simply a man, and an honest one at that, always capable of speaking his mind and performing what he saw as his duties.

His exacting nature, or rather, his scruples or professional integrity, led him to believe the rumour that Benito Suárez was responsible for the death of the law student Antonio Hidalgo. He himself had performed the operation and judged his patient to be out of the woods on the night he died. But although, in principle, the haemorrhagic complications could be attributed to random, unforeseeable factors—all the more so since Hidalgo had forgotten to inform him, out of carelessness or ignorance, that he had been ill with hepatitis a year earlier—two apparently inexplicable facts still required investigation: the sister who was on the ward that night swore she had seen Benito Suárez leaving Antonio Hidalgo's room, and that same day, the pharmacist had discovered that a box of heparin was missing. Anyone could have stolen the box in question—well, not exactly anyone, since doctors or nurses with a prescription were the only ones who came into the pharmacy, and when they did, they signed a receipt before leaving with their medicines. Benito Suárez had been there at around six o'clock that evening (his signature appeared on the register) to pick up a new anaesthetic, wanting to know the side effects before allowing it to be used on the patient he was operating on the following day. This in itself did not prove he had committed the theft; however, it was puzzling and even suspicious that Benito Suárez should be in the room with Antonio Hidalgo, who was not his patient, just at the moment when the ward sister was called away from her post by a false alarm, since the patient in the room where it sounded was resting under the effects of a strong sedative. That was where the mystery began: the ward sister had heard the bell in room 20 ring, which in itself she thought was strange, then she scurried all the way down the corridor, went into the room, and saw that the patient was sleeping, which made her think he must have woken with a start and rung the bell in an unconscious reflex before falling back to sleep. When she stepped back out into the corridor, she saw Benito Suárez closing the door to Antonio Hidalgo's room, leaving in such a hurry that she thought—and this she stated in the course of the investigation—that something serious must have happened to the patient for a doctor to be examining him at that time of night. She rushed over to Hidalgo's bedside, and was quite surprised to find him sleeping soundly. It was six hours later, when she was making her final rounds, that she discovered him dead, his body covered in bruises, eyes red, nose bleeding. The autopsy revealed major haemorrhagic complications in a young man who had developed phlebitis after undergoing surgery on an ulcer and was being treated with a heparin infusion as a result. But he had been Dr. Vesga's patient, and Dr. Vesga did not like it when his patients died; in fact, he wouldn't tolerate it. If, as Dr. Agudelo had explained to Lina on so many occasions, a good doctor was one who made death his personal enemy and fought against it fiercely, almost pathologically, then Dr. Vesga was a doctor right down to the marrow. He detested death: he had learned to see through its guises, its lies, its ruses, to detect its lurking presence months, maybe years before it appeared, and he met it head-on like a bull, but a bull that had already been duped by the cape, going after it with his relentlessly enquiring mind, an excellent clinical eye and a merciless scalpel. Hidalgo's untimely death had been a blow to him. More than that, considering his rigorous ethics, it was an accusation of negligence on his part: by prescribing that medication, he had condemned Hidalgo to death because the hepatitis had most probably caused problems with his blood circulation. He was responsible. So was Hidalgo's family, for not having informed him of a disease whose aftereffects could prove fatal during an operation. And so too were the hospital staff, if someone had drastically increased the dosage of heparin. For this reason, after following the autopsy step by step, Dr. Vesga began to tirelessly investigate every detail connected to Hidalgo's death from the moment he left the operating room. Not just the medical records that kept track of how he was responding to treatment, which he'd already examined every night and every morning, but also the analyses performed in the laboratories, the electrocardiograms and the equipment installed in his room. Like a prosecutor, he grilled the various nurses who'd been caring for Hidalgo for three days, checking whether the patient had been given the drugs he'd prescribed, in the quantities indicated. Finally, he turned his attention to the ward sister, who revealed, quite innocently, that Benito Suárez had emerged from Hidalgo's room a few hours before she found him dead. It was around that time that Antonio Hidalgo's father had gone to see Dr. Vesga, waving an anonymous letter that he didn't even bother to read to the end. An anonymous letter seemed underhanded, a jilted nurse seeking her revenge, perhaps—and Dr. Vesga took a strict stance on relationships between doctors and staff—but there was a disturbing coincidence there. Why had Benito Suárez gone

into Hidalgo's room if he wasn't his patient, and, most importantly, why, when questioned, had he heatedly denied the sister's claims? When it came to believing the word of a woman
who devoted herself to voluntarily caring for others, or that of
an arrogant bully, there was no doubt in Dr. Vesga's mind. All
the same, in the name of diligence or objectivity, he made the
ward sister undergo an eye examination that revealed no
anomalies, and he himself reconstructed the scene at the time
of night that Hidalgo had died, meaning he went into room 20,
came back out into the corridor and verified that from there,
she could perfectly identify any person leaving the room where
Hidalgo had died. From that point on, all that remained for
him to unearth were the motives of a crime he was starting to
picture in his mind with horror, but since he lived in a bubble
and was known for his aversion to gossip, he had not yet heard
the rumours Jerónimo Vargas was spreading.

Meanwhile, Benito Suárez was doing anything and everything in his power to improve his image by suppressing a violent side that, in other circumstances, would surely have made
short work of all the partners at Las Tres Marías Hospital,
starting with Jerónimo Vargas. The allegation made against
him was too serious for him to react impulsively, and too conclusive to be treated recklessly. Suddenly, he discovered that
his role as a gun-toting bully no longer worked in his favour,
no longer created the much sought-after respect from those
around him, no longer stopped a tenacious man who, it was
said, had risked his life years earlier when he confronted a
horde of *chulavitas*. All his acts of violence, all the brutishness
that had enabled him to assert himself in the world with
impunity, now sprung forth in the memories of those who had
been his victims, accomplices or witnesses, people who had
stepped forward to accuse him—without giving him the benefit of the doubt—of a crime that he may not have committed.
That, at least, was what Lina chose to tell herself at the time,

knowing the proud satisfaction Benito Suárez derived from doing his job, and it was probably the same thing he confided to Lina's grandmother the night they sat on the terrace talking. An echo of that doubt would reach Lina years later, in the most curious way, when she was living in Paris and Benito Suárez was nothing more than one of her many increasingly hazy memories.

It happened one afternoon in an interminable summer that reminded her of the scorching Barranquilla heat, while she, Lina, was packing her old paperwork into a cardboard Contrex box to take to the new chambre de bonne she had rented very close to the Place Maubert; suddenly she stumbled upon a sealed envelope, a letter to her grandmother, which had arrived two weeks after her funeral, and which she had completely forgotten existed. In that letter—a jumble of demented gibberish in which oaths mingled with Nietzsche quotes and lines of poetry, with no apparent regard for logic, written in a seemingly unsteady hand, each word rising and falling, violating the horizontal line like a child's script—Benito Suárez tried to explain to Lina's grandmother what had happened, alluding to a conversation they once had, when he told her how he'd been the victim of a vile accusation. He would have been quite capable of challenging Enriqueta's husband to a duel, he wrote, but never of brutally increasing the dose of a medicine to kill him, knowing that he was lying helpless in his own hospital, and knowing, too, that he was doomed to develop a new ulcer and would not withstand the shock of another operation. And further down, nestled among the chaotic, tortured handwriting, Lina found a surprisingly clear sentence that summarized the conclusion she herself had reached: "I'm a killer, but I'm a doctor first. I would never bring shame on the profession that has allowed me to show the best of myself."

Reading that letter, Lina was instantly transported back to the times when she'd discussed Benito Suárez's behaviour with

Dr. Agudelo, who did not believe he was responsible for the crime his colleagues were accusing him of, and had even advocated on his behalf to Dr. Vesga. Because there was no proof of his guilt, in other words, there was no overwhelming, irrefutable evidence, and even his relationship with Enriqueta, which made him a so-called killer, could also be used, paradoxically, to speculate on his innocence. Antonio Hidalgo was, in effect, doomed: he'd been operated on three times in two years for duodenal ulcers, and Dr. Vesga's scientific knowledge, his scalpel, his treatments and his recommendations, were no match for that young man's inability to adapt to life. He was a young man with frenzied eyes, and Lina had often seen him haranguing students at a table on the university campus. Back then, he was known to the police as an agitator whom the other young men carefully avoided, the ones who studied Marx and Engels in search of a revolutionary strategy, young men who, months or years later, having tired of their leaders' rhetoric and indecision, would go and sacrifice themselves in the mass murder of the guerrillas. Hidalgo didn't seem to have time to think it over: he wanted to change society overnight, relying on simple student protests as a way to magically spark a revolution. Over the years, Lina would retain just one image of him, as a skinny and pale young man leading the demonstrations, his voice hoarse from shouting, waving a placard, first in line to receive the blows from the police. She, Lina, never knew him personally, but her father did because he had gone to get him out of jail on two occasions: once for breaking the windows of the shops on Calle Cuartel, and another time for setting a car on fire. Her father thought Hidalgo was quite the visionary, an individual possessed by faith, consumed by passion, blinded by utopia. There was no point trying to talk sense into the man or even trying to reason with him; he simply needed to be freed so that he could go away and lick his wounds, only to be found a week later back at the university causing a stir, organizing another demonstration over the smallest matter, and so on, until another ulcer eventually ended his life. Lina's father helped Hidalgo, who was the son of one of his less influential colleagues, initially taking an interest in him out of curiosity, although not without sympathy, recognizing in him a small-scale model or, alternatively, the embryo of one of those whirlwinds that wreak havoc on the world from time to time: the Genghis Khans, the Alexanders, Napoleons, Lenins and Hitlers, whose biographies he knew by heart, people he believed reflected and facilitated human foolishness, taking it to its extremes. However, in the end, Hidalgo had come to seem more like an abortion than an embryo to him, since his fanaticism operated in overly black and white terms and even directly referenced psychiatry. This, Lina would hear her father say the first (and only) time he spoke to her about Enriqueta's husband, not so much to justify his actions as to defend Enriqueta, although Lina hadn't really attacked her; rather, she'd referred to her using an expression that her father perhaps thought pejorative or unfair enough to require clarification from him about Enriqueta's role in that whole story, the role of a birdbrained, dreamlike creature, oblivious to any manipulation and caught between a fanatical husband, who still hadn't managed to take her virginity a year into their marriage, and a lover who was equally hot-headed but with the fieriness of a man who, having passed the age of forty, is forced to caracole his virility. Both men were raving mad, beyond comprehension for that girl born in the San José neighbourhood, in a pink-fronted house with two smallish rooms and a kitchen blackened by smoke from the stove, with only her mother for company: a widow, employed out of charity at a notary's office, who took the bus at six in the morning and came home at nightfall. A woman who, like her daughter, had never understood all that much: she never understood her parasite son-in-law, who was incapable of studying, working or providing even bread for breakfast and was always banging on about revolution in the name of some guy named Marx; nor did she understand her daughter's troubled lover, Benito Suárez, whom she must have looked at with a confusing combination of dread and fascination, and cursed the fact that her daughter had met him when she was already married, slightly ashamed of the gossip that his showy blue Studebaker stirred up in the neighbourhood, but at the same time proud, because for years, she and Enriqueta had known what it was like to go to bed on an empty stomach, the shame of begging the corner grocer for a new tab or more time to pay, and what it was like to smile humbly on receiving hand-me-downs from a relative. But they had their principles. At any rate, Enriqueta's mother was never willing to prostitute herself, even though she could still make men lust after her when her husband died; she brought up her beautiful daughter, who looked like something out of a Botticelli painting, in this same spirit of integrity. Benito Suárez had been allowed into their lives with some reluctance, and not because of his money—the heater, the refrigerator, those things arrived over time but could not be described as prostitution—but because he was a man, and Enriqueta wanted a man. Perhaps Enriqueta's mother had dreamed of the kind of husband worthy of her daughter's beauty while stoically enduring all those years of poverty. It would have to be someone not too demanding, given what she knew about life, but not someone overly humble either: just a man who could take them both out of that sweltering little pink house in the San José neighbourhood and move them to the outskirts of El Prado, forever erasing that shopkeeper's face and that relative's faded hand-me-downs. Later, that practical side of hers, which she must have gained from working in a notary's office, would allow her to accept that Benito Suárez was the best possible substitute while waiting for the promised divorce, and, perhaps secretly, without even admitting it to herself, while waiting for the death of that unruly son-in-law, who had learned nothing other than how to get himself beaten up at demonstrations, later developing the ulcers that were operated on by Dr. Vesga at Las Tres Marías hospital.

As Lina would discover listening to her father's circumspect explanation, everyone was more or less aware that Antonio Hidalgo was heading for ruin, and Benito Suárez understood this better than anyone, because he knew that Dr. Vesga's prescriptions never made it to the pharmacy and Hidalgo's exploits as an agitator, which were probably connected to the home-made bombs that had suddenly started going off around the city, had triggered a kind of persecution complex that kept him in a state of perpetual alarm, encouraging the formation of new ulcers, for which Dr. Vesga's scalpel would be no match. The operation that took his life was not as minor as people made out: before it, Hidalgo had been coughing up blood and was in such a weak condition that an ambulance had to take him to the hospital. Lina could well imagine Benito Suárez ringing the bell from room 20, both to distract the ward sister and to see for himself how Hidalgo was doing, and when his doctor's eye no doubt recognized that he wasn't going to make it through the night, he hurried away, afraid of being accused of negligence later on. The fact that the ward sister saw him leaving Hidalgo's room on the same day that the box of heparin disappeared was something that, in a nod to Nietzsche and his interpretation of Greek mythology, she put down to those unpredictable forces of nature that entered people's lives on a whim to wreak havoc, and lead them to ruin. Perhaps the Nietzsche explanation disappeared altogether to make way for the little boy who was beaten by his mother as a child while his playmates were punished with a simple scolding. Or perhaps his reference to the capricious Olympian gods masked a memory of darker forces, repressed for centuries, which bounded through the jungle with the leopard, caused the skin to erupt in pustules, made the rivers rage, and emerged bellowing from the depths of the earth. For whatever reason, Benito Suárez did not seem cut out to face that kind of adversity. He did not have the patience of a man who has discovered his own endurance through pain, learning to detect the direction of the wind while others are burning in the fire that they themselves have lit. He knew how to storm a fortress but not how to resist a siege, how to respond to an attack but not how to diffuse it, how to run like a dog after a hare, but not how to wait for hours with the stillness of a cat in front of a hole from which, sooner or later, a mouse will emerge. Even in those eight months when he tried to behave reasonably, his true nature betrayed him, revealing—at the most inopportune moment— the violence he seemed to have come to terms with since the day when his professional integrity had been called into question. As if the fact of being a doctor, of fighting against the misery of the human condition, had allowed him to join society, striking a precarious yet effective balance, considering that in spite of everything, he lived in a house (in El Prado), drove a car (a Studebaker) and earned an honest living (practising his profession). He was not yet the outcast, the fugitive the police would chase along the scorching sands of La Guajira, the expatriate who would treat starving *indios* in a shantytown in the Amazon rainforest in exchange for a handful of food. Not yet. He could still introduce himself as Dr. Benito Suárez: surgeon, co-owner of the best hospital in the city, related by way of marriage to a respectable family with noble titles. He became all these things to ward off any mishap that might lead to his to ruin, but his nature, temperament, instinct, call it what you may, betrayed him.

It betrayed him the night he was planning a final flourish for his burgeoning social life—if that was the right term for the string of random invitations intended to instantly secure the friendship of people he'd known until then only in a strictly professional capacity—who suddenly, awkward or shocked, heard Benito Suárez's voice on the phone inviting them over for lunch that day, or the next, or whenever they liked, while Dora—who, for the first time, had a big enough budget to buy linen tablecloths, silver cutlery, crockery and contraband French crystal—busied herself with the duties of being a reluctant hostess, taking pointers from Lina and assisted by Berenice, whose reputation as a Cordon Bleu chef allowed her to lord it over the kitchen, giving Dora directions as to how to serve the cakes, sauces, fillings and all the delicacies she'd learned to make by watching the French chef at the Hotel del Prado forty years earlier. Despite Dora's pleas, Lina had always refrained from participating in those get-togethers because of her apprehensions about seeing the tight-lipped Benito Suárez—whose intentions she couldn't guess, but feared because of the effort he made to conceal them—and her friend Dora, smiling blissfully like a convalescent discharged after a lengthy illness. On that occasion, however, the reception was being held in honour of Dr. Vesga, and, according to Benito Suárez, it required the presence of a woman of the world, as he so graciously described to Lina when he invited her. It required someone who was accustomed to frequenting the country club, livening up a conversation and entertaining people; basically, someone capable of guiding the timid Dora, who barely opened her mouth and went completely unnoticed all evening.

Believing she was attending a conventional soiree, Lina accepted the invitation, after having approved Berenice's menu and helping to set the table, arranging vases of flowers and laying out ashtrays and appetizers. Everything seemed to be in place, including Benito Suárez, who welcomed the guests at the door as they walked in looking somewhat bewildered and then greeted each other with obvious relief, while the waiter hired for the occasion hurried to serve them some stiff whiskeys that helped to ease their suspicions and even the

uncomfortable feeling that they were merely passive partici-
pants in a farce designed to win them over. The only one there
who was not at all uncomfortable was the guest of honour, Dr.
Vesga, because he was not attending out of a fear of snubbing
Benito Suárez, nor out of some subconscious intention to give
into the flattery of an invitation—Dr. Agudelo explained this
to Lina as they stood in a corner of the room—but more precisely, because he wanted to see for himself how this man lived,
this individual he'd decided to expose once and for all.
Although he hadn't been convinced by the accusations before,
believing that impulsive men like Benito Suárez tended to be
driven by emotions, the story that Jerónimo Vargas told him a
few days earlier had plunged him into confusion. Not because
he fully believed the melodramatic version of the story, the one
in which the psychiatrist was suddenly confronted by his
patient's husband, who showed up demanding that the psychiatrist lock his wife away in an asylum, and found himself facing a barrage of insults directed at his wife—but because that
story would reveal a capacity for manipulation that he never
knew Benito Suárez had in him. So Dr. Vesga stood there,
lucid and detached, observing without satisfaction the people
and things around him. His eyes roamed over the cheap white
lacquered furniture, the garish coloured armchairs and the
fake Persian rug, while Lina, who did not lose sight of him for
a second, congratulated herself on managing to replace Benito
Suárez's chinaware with vases brought from her own house on
the pretext of decorating the living room with roses and gladioli. From time to time, his penetrating, clinical gaze lingered
on Dora, evaluating her gestures and mannerisms to detect the
possible pathological traits of her personality and perhaps
sensing, in the blankness of her expression, in her puffy face,
the desperate weariness of twelve years of marriage to Benito
Suárez. His attention was also drawn to Renato, the spoiled
little boy whom Lina had never once seen smile, and who was

running around all over the place, jostling the guests and shoving his hands into the trays of appetizers. Suddenly Renato did something Lina had seen him do once before, while his father looked on impassively: he kicked the muzzle of a little fox terrier bitch and, indifferent to its howls of pain, kicked it again until the animal managed to escape underneath a table. Benito Suárez had watched the scene without trying to prevent it or even telling Renato off; in a split second, Dr. Vesga's pupils dilated, a computer-like eye capturing, fixing and logging the information for eternity. Then, slowly, his gaze swivelled towards Lina, sized her up and pierced her, exposing the instinctive reaction of horror that Renato's actions had provoked in her.

From that moment on, Lina began to feel annoyed with herself, or rather, with the ambiguity of the situation: Benito Suárez had unenthusiastically asked her for help, and he had unenthusiastically agreed, arranging the get-together and demonstrating, with her mere presence, the friendship that in principle existed between them and how little importance she attached to the allegations made against him. And surprisingly, a current of understanding took hold in the space between her and Dr. Vesga, for no plausible reason, because the little Lina knew about him—his inflexibility, his penchant for authority, his tendency to see the world in black and white, and finally, the presumptuous right he had granted himself to pry into Benito Suárez's private life, like an inquisitor—was enough to make her dislike him intensely. But that current continued to flow between them, warm and contradictory, and it persisted throughout the evening—until the party took an unconventional turn due to Benito Suárez's strange notion of how to entertain people—allowing her to figure out, understand or share Dr. Vesga's reactions with an uncomfortable sense of impotence, perhaps because the things he was logging with his watchful eye corresponded to reality but did not take the whole reality into account, and she, Lina, couldn't explain it: Benito Suárez was not well-versed in the subtleties of high-society life, and although his mother, Doña Giovanna Mantini, had beaten the tendency towards laziness, irresponsibility and frivolity out of him, instilling him with the ethics and stu-diousness of the European haute bourgeoisie, she had never attempted to turn him into a nice person, someone who was sensitive to the nuances of courtesy that facilitate human rela-tions, perhaps because she thought that to do so would be impossible. So at that get-together, attended mostly by doctors from middle-class backgrounds who had more or less adjusted to the ways of the local bourgeoisie, Benito Suárez was like an elephant in a field of daisies: his voice dominated conversa-tions, he opened his mouth too wide as he munched the appe-tizers, his movements seemed as brusque as the tone he adopted to address the waiter, and his treatment of Dora, the way he ordered her about and criticized her for the pettiest things, would have offended even the most misogynistic men there. On top of this, Benito Suárez did not know that the pri-mary duty of a host is to minimize the attention he bestows on his guests, and so he circulated among them, pointing out the quality of his whiskey or the origin of his glassware or, and this beggared belief, gracelessly asking them to thank him for the invitation. Seeing that display of bad taste through Dr. Vesga's eyes, and realizing the aggression it ultimately revealed, Lina had decided to call everyone to the table earlier than planned, claiming that Berenice's soufflé couldn't remain in the oven a minute longer, when suddenly Benito Suárez announced in a loud voice that he was going to show them a film recorded in the city's major hospital. The murmuring died down, the lights went out, and everyone gathered around Benito Suárez and the gleaming projector that had appeared by his side. The purpose of the film was to demonstrate an operation he'd performed to remove a tumour that had spread from an old woman's belly down to her knees, a tumour so gigantic that in order to get around, the poor woman had needed a kind of purpose-built trolley with two wheels and a wooden board to support the protrusion, and two bars at the top to put the apparatus into motion. The operating room appeared on the wall, followed by a close-up of the tumour and Benito Suárez in full swing, surrounded by assistants who were handing him instruments and wiping the beads of sweat from his forehead. Not a single detail of the operation was left out, and within an hour, most of the women had left the room, some of them sobbing, others rushing to the bathroom to throw up. Everyone else watched the projection in stunned silence, and Lina hovered in the living room, unsure what to do, nipping to the kitchen from time to time to calm down Berenice who, on the verge of hysteria, had watched her soufflé collapse and her turkey in prune sauce turn to charcoal. Benito Suárez, on the other hand, was beaming: he had the city's finest doctors around him, most notably Dr. Vesga, all of them observing every step of the biggest operation of his life, performed and filmed in secret in order to impress them. His state of euphoria, and all the whiskeys he'd consumed, made it impossible for him to notice the bewilderment of his audience, who were exchanging disapproving glances. Apart from Dr. Vesga, who didn't look at anyone. His face was frozen in shock. To film in an operating room without aseptic precautions must have struck him as unbelievably irresponsible; to boast publicly without modesty was a reprehensible weakness; and to subject a group of guests to a screening like that was a serious insult to the most rudimentary sense of courtesy. But what made him snap out of his incensed stupor was the final part of the film—which really should have been at the beginning—when the image of the poor old woman appeared on the wall, showing her a few days before the operation, naked and ashamed, trying to cover her flaccid breasts with one hand and hiding her face from the camera that mercilessly pursued her until it managed to capture her eyes brimming with tears, already defeated and humiliated. Setting down his glass of whiskey on a table without even taking a sip, Dr. Vesga said in a voice so thick with contempt that it sounded metallic: "This is like something out of Auschwitz. Dr. Suárez, you have no right to exploit human misfortune. You're discrediting your profession, you're discrediting all of us." Someone flicked the light on and Lina saw Benito Suárez standing beside the projector, looking taken aback. Gradually, his face twisted with anger and his lips parted as if he wanted to speak, but no sound came out, not even the desperate stuttering that Lina had heard from him on other occasions. With one swipe he knocked the projector to the floor and strode over to Dr. Vesga, who was standing there motionless, waiting, without even flinching; he neither moved sideways nor stepped backwards, he simply raised his left arm to shield his face and, with his right arm, responded to the blow from Benito Suárez by shoving him across the room, where Lina saw him fall half-stunned, taking one of her grandmother's best vases down with him. And as Benito Suárez lay on the carpet, soaked in the water from the vase, and with seven gladioli scattered around him, Dr. Vesga made his excuses and said goodbye to Dora, then left the house, followed by the other guests.

But that incident was not the reason why Dr. Vesga agreed to preside over the board of partners a month later to discuss Benito Suárez's conduct and eventually fire him from Las Tres Marías hospital. It was not that, nor the scandal he caused in the city after that party, when he threw Dora out of the house in the middle of the night, waking the neighbours, who saw him open the front door and kick her out, leaving her semiconscious in the garden where Lina (alerted by Antonia, who owned the pharmacy next door) went to find her with Doña Eulalia del Valle, her lawyer friend from church and two other friends, who would act as witnesses to the fact that Dora had been violently forced to leave the marital home. No, both these things had only cemented Dr. Vesga's contempt for Benito Suárez, prompting him to continue his investigation into the death of the law student Antonio Hidalgo, even though he knew he would never be able to say for sure whether his death was a near-perfect crime or the result of a combination of indeterminable circumstances. Perhaps Dr. Vesga was venturing into lion's territory under the pretence of following a rabbit's trail—all the while conscious that the lion was watching him—and intentionally provoking it by hacking at the bushes with a machete, crushing the undergrowth beneath his boots, letting the wind carry his scent, while the lion, hiding behind a bush with its belly pressed to the ground, its body hot and its heart beating fast, felt the growing suicidal urge to pounce on the man who so insolently defied him. It was Dr. Vesga's fearlessness that drove him to attempt such an undertaking—that, and his scruples—but more than anything, he was spurred on by the existence of doubt. Lina, who had assisted him in the operating room three times, knew that he had a surgeon's character through and through: the need to explore with his own eyes, and with his own eyes measure the extent, nature and depth of the problem. By provoking Benito Suárez, Dr. Vesga seemed to be following that same impulse—his desire to find the truth, his inability to accept, acknowledge or tolerate doubt—by deploying the strategy that had served him so well in his profession, but using a different tactic, because tactic was the right word for that kind of continuous harassment, which involved endlessly interrogating all the people who had attended to Hidalgo in the three days leading up to his death. Apparently—Dr. Agudelo had told Lina—he'd been interested in one detail alone: establishing whether or not Benito Suárez was carrying his doctor's bag when he was seen entering the pharmacy and leaving the room where Hidalgo had died. Neither the statements from the two ward sisters, which changed each time they were interrogated, nor those of the other doctors and nurses, who suddenly, with implausible precision, recalled having bumped into Benito Suárez in a corridor that day, bag in hand, were of much use to Dr. Vesga, because logically, he must have realized that a visual testimony was needed to establish if there had been a crime. No, he wanted only to aggravate the lion, to force it out of its hiding place. And Benito Suárez fell straight into the trap, or rather, he swiped at the partners of Las Tres Marías with his claws a few times, outraging the partners to such an extent that they decided to call the meeting, which Dr. Vesga in his capacity as hospital director agreed to preside over. The charges that had stacked up against Benito Suárez—threatening the ward sisters, attempting to bribe the nurses, a bumbling ploy to make it look like another doctor had stolen the box of heparin— were enough to get him dismissed from Las Tres Marías without overly tainting his professional reputation. But he did not know this. He showed up at the hospital that day in his blue Studebaker, with his starched doctor's coat and his thick rubber-soled white shoes. He was carrying the bag that was the subject of such controversy, and his face was so strained and pale that he could have been wearing a plaster mask. As he entered the stark white room, where the only sound was the purring of two air-conditioning units, he looked haughtily at the doctors already seated round the table, and, placing his bag half-open on a chair, he refused to sit down, saying: "I've come to defend my honour, and I'll defend my honour standing up." It was very likely that, as Dr. Agudelo suggested to Lina, Benito Suárez was convinced that he was about to be accused of the death of the law student Antonio Hidalgo. At any rate, he was not in his right mind: aware of Dr. Vesga's investigations, he believed that Dr. Vesga thought he was guilty and even imagined, perhaps, that he had discovered the way to ruin his life; so, during his last few days in Barranquilla, especially in the week leading up to the meeting, he had lapsed into an almost paranoid state and refused to leave his house, making hourly phone calls to a nurse from Las Tres Marías, an ex-lover who kept him abreast of the latest rumours about the situation, and meeting with a dodgy lawyer, the same woman who would later act as his defence and help with his plans to escape and take Renato away from Dora forever. If he had been able to analyze the situation lucidly—not to mention exercise a little self-control—he would have realized that Dr. Vesga was not planning to try to pin an unprovable crime on him, running the risk of being sued for defamation and slander, but that his only intention was to incriminate him for intimidating the hospital staff and trying to corrupt a nurse to make her testify that she had caught another doctor stealing a box of heparin.

But he, Benito Suárez, was already swimming in other waters, and this Lina would discover in Paris, when she read the letter he wrote to her grandmother, not knowing that her grandmother had already died. He scribbled about how he felt he was facing a kind of final judgement before a merciless god who remembered all the sins he had committed since before he was born. Perhaps he was referring to the sins of hating the man who had fathered him, of disowning the bloodline that his father had passed down to him, of justifying as an adult the lashes that had scarred his back as a child, a justification that would force him to go through life as a bully until finally he destroyed his wife and warped his son's personality. Or perhaps he was alluding to the sin of being an extreme embodiment of the model he had been shown by society—the example of the aggressive, violent, domineering man—all the while unwittingly rejecting a different notion of human relationships, a suggested example, a forgotten message, an ideal or some sense of yearning. God might never have existed, but now Nietzsche was on his deathbed.

Even without reading that letter, Lina could already imagine

the hell Benito Suárez had gone through after he'd kicked
Dora out of the house, as he burst through the final dam that
stood between him and the hostility of a world which had
encouraged him to be the way he was and even rewarded him
for it, but which would turn against him like a viper at the
slightest betrayal: by testing the extent of his power as a doctor and a husband, Benito Suárez had betrayed that power, like
the father-killer who discovers his hatred for his father, or the
adulterous woman who reveals her feminine sexuality. And for
this indiscretion, he would have to pay. He began to pay for it
with loneliness, because he was left alone, taking advice from
two women who, unbeknown to him, wanted to see him
ruined: the jilted nurse, who was unexpectedly presented with
an opportunity to take revenge by terrorizing him, and the
devious lawyer whose struggle to achieve the same privileges as
her male counterparts (having to put up with problems at university, patronizing contempt from certain professors, and a
misogynistic code of behaviour) had probably led to her hatred
of men and her contempt for women. No one ever knew how
he'd met that lawyer, or the nature of their relationship, but
Lina only had to talk to her once to realize that she had hastened his demise: not by pushing him or even showing him the
way, but simply by bending him to her own logic with the perversity of a doctor who might listen to a depressed patient's
rationale and then leave a suicide pill within easy reach.
Because she was the one who told him about all the legal loopholes that would help him avoid prison if it came to trial. If
Benito Suárez had not been convinced that he would have to
justify his actions in front of a court of law one day by giving
the most tremendous performance of his life, then perhaps his
attitude, his state of mind when he entered the room where the
partners of Las Tres Marías had gathered, might have been different. Heeding the woman's advice, he believed he could
choose between two possible alternatives: he could do what he

did, fleeing until circumstances allowed him to face a court of law that was predisposed in his favour, with his name splashed all over the headlines and his actions being debated by the country's top lawyers; or, he could respond to Dr. Vesga's accusation by reading out a pre-prepared speech, which he thought would win him the respect of the doctors present and restore his dignity. In the doctor's bag, along with the four-page speech, was the gun: Dr. Vesga did not realize that the trap had not completely closed on the lion. Hence, when Benito Suárez pompously declared, "I've come to defend my honour, and I'll defend my honour standing up," Dr. Vesga had the temerity to say to him, in a sarcastic tone: "You'd better sit down, Dr. Suárez, if a stool is honourable enough for you." Someone in the room laughed. A second later, as he saw Benito Suárez taking the stubby, black, brutal object out of his bag, Dr. Vesga realized that he'd dangerously wounded the lion. That object was familiar to him, and ill-fated: he had sensed as much ever since he was a child, seeing it on the belts of the muleteers who travelled across the wild crags of the province where he was born and, later, in the tragic dawn brawls in the cantinas and bars of the capital where he studied. "You're not going to kill me," Dr. Vesga managed to say, in a voice tinged not with panic but perhaps with astonishment, just before the first blast took his colleagues by surprise, and, as the glass tumbler shattered on the table, they saw him slump to the ground, blood blooming on his shirt. The five shots that followed were unnecessary: by then he was just firing like a madman. And so it was that Benito Suárez finally performed the act which Lina's grandmother had always believed he was pre-destined to commit.

PART TWO

Y ou must not eat fruit from the tree that is in the middle of the garden, and you must not touch it, or you will die."

"You will not certainly die," the serpent said to the woman. "For God knows that when you eat from it your eyes will be opened, and you will be like God, knowing good and evil."

So from the very beginning, as soon as they started to invent their story, men showed cowardice: implicitly recognizing woman as the origin of rebellion, they set forth the formidable message of power inscribed in those sentences, only to diminish it to a sense of loss. Because men never escaped the law of the father, and if, compelled by a kind of feminine intelligence, they revolted against their father in one moment, they would return full of remorse the next, anxious to bow to his authority. This is what Aunt Eloísa said from her deep blue velvet easy chair, surrounded by her Birman cats, while the fans whirred, chasing away the heat, the sultry air, the sticky humidity of the street, as if once inside her house the city did not exist, or it became a dream or an illusion as soon as she, Lina, opened the enormous cast-iron gate, walked across the garden full of centuries-old ceiba trees and climbed the granite steps to that silent world, where the light was dim and every room, every part of the house, glistened with fascinating objects brought from far away, cloaked in the perfume of rose, jasmine or sandalwood essence. Lina usually went there once a week, holding her grandmother's hand when she was a child or driving her grandmother there when she was older, or simply going alone for the pleasure of seeing her smiling aunt, to whom the years had been kind, with her dyed hair and clear eyes that flashed with mischief as she shattered concepts, religions, ideologies and all the other ruses men had come up with to justify their ravings and dominate women. Because this had been the aim of all discourse since the dawn of time: to find an explanation consistent with the story of blood and fury which the male of a defective, maladjusted species—whose evolution had been halted due to an error of nature—had woven as he made his way around the planet, destroying life gratuitously, in other words, not so much to feed himself, protect himself or defend his offspring, but rather to satisfy his mad urges, and all this despite having at his disposal a tool which, in principle, could control them. But this tool had done nothing but allow him to excuse his behaviour with a condensate of childish beliefs and foolish interpretations, which Aunt Eloísa recounted with a chuckle as she showed Lina which books to take out from the library, open to a certain page and start reading from a specific line to back up those claims that amused her so, despite observing how subversive they were and the infinite uncertainty they gradually sowed in her consciousness; even though she'd been fascinated by the story as a child and had toyed with it in her imagination, even going so far, for example, as to picture Adam as a pitiful individual, standing there covering his modesty with his pathetic fig leaf, and to blaspheme and deny that Eve had also taken the fruit from the tree of life before the cruel cherubim bearing flaming swords barred them from the garden. At the age of twelve, Lina told herself that things would have turned out differently if Aunt Eloísa had been in the Garden of Eden instead of Eve.

For a start, her aunt would have convinced Adam that no matter what the wrathful God of Genesis said, his sexuality was a fantastic discovery and he would be better advised to take pleasure in it than to curse it in shame. She would have told him that to emerge from the white void of nothingness, only to then fall into the dark nothingness of death, had nothing to do with any divine punishment and everything to do with the laws of organic matter; she would have told him that any action taken against a woman would treacherously come back on man himself, and that anyone who, like Hesiod, called her a curse, the ruin of men, cruelty of desires and longing, would end up spending his days in sad, cold limbo. Or perhaps Aunt Eloísa would not have needed to explain anything to anyone, Lina thought in awe, because her sheer beauty, nimble mind and infinite capacity for seduction surely could have calmed the aggressions of Adam and his God. Lina could well imagine her aunt debating with the wrathful God, ultimately grinding his vanity to dust or throwing down the gauntlet to the people who had invented that belligerent character, trying to make them see that the sorrows of life were implicit in the dialectics of life itself, and so if they wished to gain a little wisdom, they ought to join in. But it was precisely in the name of wisdom that Aunt Eloísa had stopped trying to reason with men from a very young age. Because they, men, were different: they were rough round the edges, burly, scruffy; their nervous systems caused them to act rashly, the adrenaline their bodies produced made them pathologically aggressive, and the regularity of their hormones meant they would never be able to appreciate all the nuances of feeling. To one extreme or another, men had deviated from the norm: woman, the being who gave, protected and continued to affirm life amid the constant chaos wreaked by man's mere existence. Full of frustration, men had succeeded in creating a situation that allowed them to ignore the reality of their own insignificance and claim that they had been created in the image and likeness of God (an idea that could surely only make the universe quake with laughter). Putting their physical strength to use, they had taken their revenge on female fertility at every opportunity as part of what they referred to as culture, which ultimately boiled down to a series of pretexts for barbarity itself. This barbarity was exposed in all its glory among the primitive peoples who sewed up the vaginal opening only to force it open again with a knife, or who tore off the clitoris with a tool resembling a picklock, and it had become more elaborate or camouflaged in the society that she, Aunt Eloísa, had chosen to adapt to without ever losing her sense of self—in other words, where she always occupied the role she naturally deserved, that of a queen surrounded by lovers and servants—but while maintaining exemplary relationships with members of the inferior sex, because despite all their flaws, Aunt Eloísa still loved them, those hairy, self-satisfied, conceited men who had given her so much pleasure in her life.

Forever faithful to that view of things, Aunt Eloísa had her own set of guidelines for passing judgements, albeit without the indulgence of her sister Jimena, Lina's grandmother, who, despite her lucidity, could hold the whole world in her heart. She, Aunt Eloísa, never had time for mediocre people, and she wouldn't have tolerated the presence of someone like Benito Suárez in her home, not even for a second. Vulgarity horrified her; violence filled her with contempt. She had gone through life forcing fate's hand every step of the way, constantly struggling against the society that had tried in vain to reduce her to immanence, stifle her sexuality and condemn her to resignation; all this had given her a rather elitist understanding of human beings and made her believe that freedom was possible for those who had attained a certain level of consciousness, as long as they had the courage to embrace it. Of course, to be more exact, Aunt Eloísa was referring exclusively to women when she spoke about human beings, and even then, they fell into two categories based on their behaviour. First, there were women who accepted male dominance in the name of love, children or security, despite having managed to wriggle out from under the weight of an ideology or religion. Then there were the others, those strange, vulnerable, fugitive women, who flew through life with their wings outstretched—full of buckshot, perhaps, but free—soaring up into the sky, higher and higher until, struck down like Icarus, they plummeted down in a swirl of flames and sank to the bottom of the sea. Men feared these women, fascinated, and desired them, tormented; to know them meant to discover the fragility of the conventions they had created in the pursuit of power. Because women had challenged the order of things when they offered a piece of fruit, and they'd sowed doubt by opening a box. They wryly danced with the severed head of a prophet or emerged from the desert sands to taunt the eremites. They were elusive; they seemed so close but were always at a distance.

Aunt Eloísa had known only a few women like that, and in the city, only one: Divina Arriaga, Catalina's mother. Divina Arriaga had made an impression ever since the day she first set eyes on her in Paris, gliding into the Sonia Delaunay exhibition with two white greyhounds leading the way. She told Lina, not without admiration, how the other guests had sensed her coming even before she arrived, perhaps because they could hear the engine of her Bugatti, or the pitter-patter of the greyhounds' paws, which seemed not so much to touch the ground as to scrape against it with the tips of their claws. She told her how everyone had stood there silently, drink in hand, eyes fixed on the doorway where she finally appeared, looking disdainful and magnificent in her white satin gown with gold embroidery and her boa of feathers plucked from some fabulous bird. She was beautiful, Aunt Eloísa repeated, her beauty was blinding like an insult; her hair was black, her eyes a dazzling green. She'd made her way through the gallery with the deceptive indifference of a feline, and big cats were exactly what her aloof sensuality brought to mind, giving nothing away, nor showing off or seeking to seduce. Divina Arriaga seemed to be above the desire to possess, and when she took something—an object, a horse or a man—she did so not in order to call it her own, but to let it into her life for a moment, just to gaze at it a while, ride through a forest, or make love between the silver satin sheets she took with her on her travels, along with her greyhounds and her maids.

Lina was surprised to hear Divina Arriaga being talked about in this way, and as she grew older, she found it harder to associate the image of that bedazzling character with the pale-skinned woman she saw languishing in a dark room with a far-away look in her eyes, in the care of an equally distant maid. Sometimes, when Lina was playing with Catalina in one of the large rooms in their old villa, the maid would come looking for them and summon them to the bedroom where Divina Arriaga—less pale, perhaps, more present—offered them a cup of tea, following an exact ritual that hinted at an ancient ceremony in which each movement was transcended, symbolizing something that Lina could not and did not want to grasp, for the same reason she lowered her voice when she entered the room: the fear of breaking the spell cast by the presence of that quiet figure, whose white, almost transparent fingers flapped like ungainly butterflies over the silver samovar and the Limoges teacups. The other Divina Arriaga, the one people talked about, seemed to emerge from the half-light of the room like an ironic ghost, the same way the woman falling asleep between the silk cushions became wrapped up in Aunt Eloísa's words and the murmur of the fans as they took her back to the golden longing of those wild years, dining at Le Dôme and La Rotonde, and the tango and the foxtrot resounding until the early hours in Le Bal Nègre, where Divina Arriaga's beauty shone, fully ablaze. Both images of her would remain etched in Lina's mind, superimposed at first, but drifting further and further apart as the years passed and she slowly realized what aim her aunt was pursuing when she suggested piecing together the life of a woman whose name alone was synonymous with scandal in the city.

However, Aunt Eloísa had never tried to hide the fact that she wanted to pulverize the influence Lina's grandmother had over her, and since her grandmother didn't raise the slightest objection, Lina had listened contentedly to the siren song that had been slipped into her ears ever since she was a child, encouraging her to rebel against the crude fatalism of imagining that the future contained in the past ruled out the possibility of ever changing one's life through conscious action. Even though she knew that Aunt Eloísa was disingenuously belittling her grandmother's worldview, Lina, amid the whirring fans and the purring Birmans that wandered over and rubbed against her legs, would listen to the two women debating the subject countless times, and yet she would never be able to arrive at any definitive conclusion, because she thought their arguments were both valid, especially when they spoke about Divina Arriaga and tried to analyze the factors that had shaped her personality. Her grandmother always cited the privileged circumstances in which Divina Arriaga was born: as the twelfth daughter of a married millionaire couple whose eleven previous heirs had died before the age of one, her parents thought it made sense to protect her from Barranquilla's ferocious heat—which was only fit for the cows that had forced their owners to settle in that hell three centuries earlier, having fled from a drought—and they sent her to Europe when she was still a very young girl, accompanied by governesses whose mission was to educate her without denying even her smallest whim. Aunt Eloísa chose to brush those facts aside: she did not refute what it meant for someone to come into the world with the finest fairy godmothers watching over their crib, but she had seen many a pampered, blue-eyed heiress crushed by life just like any maid; more easily, even, because their narcissism kept their gaze turned firmly inward, and the indulgences they'd received throughout their childhood made them unfit for the struggle, dulling any critical awareness. Aunt Eloísa was willing to concede, at most, that the circumstances Lina's grandmother was referring to might have been a prerequisite for Divina Arriaga's personality, but as far as she was concerned, they in no way sufficed to explain that perspicacity, the determination that already shone through when, at the age of five, she chose her own governess from twenty applicants, ultimately settling on an Englishwoman so passionate about freedom that the first decision she made was to take her to Berlin and enrol her in a dance school led by Isadora Duncan. Because it was Divina Arriaga who chose her, having rejected all the other candidates and offering no explanation when met with the look of surprise on her mother's face, that woman who was incapable of reacting, exhausted from twelve successive births and her deep conviction that this child of spine-tingling beauty had been born by the power of the Devil, carrying inside her not a variety of chromosomes from her two biological parents, but only those belonging to the father, the demon who had whisked Divina Arriaga's mother away in his chariot, snatching her from the monastic serenity of her house, her prayerbook and daily mass, then proceeded to rail against the whole world in a whirlwind of energy until he became the richest man in the city, viciously attacking his rivals and any fool who happened to cross his path, but also attacking what she had confusingly been taught to think of as her virtue: a certain composure, a kind of modesty that all the women in her family shared, and which he would wickedly demolish on their wedding day when he ignited an insatiable fire in her belly, one that was immune to the passing of the years and impervious to the threats from the priests, who made her shudder and him laugh. A fire that was rekindled every night in the silence of luxury hotels and sumptuous bedrooms aboard the ocean liners the two of them rushed on to—he in search of business opportunities, clients and contracts, and she tailing him like his nocturnal shadow, his pleasure ground, his poisoned flower, contaminated by those sensual pleasures, which heaven would punish by depriving her of eleven children, and hell would reward with a child of such brazen beauty that she could only be called Divina.

Her mother was afraid of her and would never have dreamed of opposing her daughter's will, and in return she, Divina Arriaga, ignored her mother, thinking of her perhaps as a mere extension of her father, with whom she identified wholeheartedly; he was the master and lord of that beautiful house in which she spent the first five years of her life surrounded by obliging nannies, waiting for him, expecting to suddenly spot him strolling among the linden trees in the garden, through the light that seemed to etch its iridescent silver opacity in her memory from then on. He always came from somewhere very far away, full of life and jovial, laden with gifts he might have given to any of Divina Arriaga's eleven dead siblings: a miniature model of a car; a pony with a golden mane; a tiny rifle, which she carried on her shoulder when they went out together at the crack of dawn to hunt rabbits in the forests where, seventy or eighty years later, Lina would only see the sad, identical façades of the Parisian suburbs, and in the deserted street of that Sunday in springtime, the house that Aunt Eloísa described, which cut a stately figure even in its devastation; the tall pillars of the portico on the veranda were almost in ruins, and the linden trees in the garden were indifferent to the passage of time and as if transfigured by that same silver light trickling through their leaves. Lina did not go inside the house, but she saw the weed-ridden lawn, the fountain covered in disgusting slime and the green, indefinitely still water of the pond. She made her way along a well-worn path lined with trees, trying in vain to recall long-gone memories, circling the garden until she stumbled upon that marble head nestled in the grass, which she lifted up, contemplated and patted in a doleful stupor, the way blind people feel their way around. It was the head of a girl with a grave stare and flowing locks, who looked eerily like Catalina did when she, Lina, had met her: the girl Divina Arriaga had been not long before she followed her parents to one of the large rooms in the Ritz to study the procession of carefully selected governesses—from whom she chose the only candidate capable of catapulting her to freedom—with the same alert, inflexible spirit which, five years later, would prompt her to replace this first governess with a female anthropologist, less affable than her predecessor perhaps, but like Pygmalion, willing to move heaven and earth to breathe life into the fledgling woman that Divina Arriaga was back then. Travelling the world at the anthropologist's side, Divina Arriaga learned about the events of the past in situ: she read Aristotle beneath the columns of the Parthenon, translated Virgil in a house in Mantua, discovered the Middle Ages in ruins, castles and monasteries, and methodologically reconstructed the march of Hannibal, Timur, Caesar and Napoleon's armies. All this, Aunt Eloísa said, gave her a decent cultural grounding, as well as fluency in several languages, which prevented her from rolling the Spanish 'r' correctly. It also made her strong: although she was thin and looked dainty, she could spend the entire day on horseback, as if the energy of those eleven dead siblings was pulsing inside her. She loved foxhunting, fencing and trekking across remote regions of the world, always followed closely by the anthropologist who was surely in love with her but didn't realize it, in love with that girl who would turn around to glance at her after walking a hundred miles with a bag slung over her shoulder, still looking as fresh as a rose out of water. The anthropologist followed her until one day she could follow her no more. And so she died— of a heart attack, Divina Arriaga would later tell Aunt Eloísa as they sat drinking pastis on the terrace at La Coupole. She, a woman so reluctant to confide in people, so cagey about her past, chose that particular anecdote to sum up her younger years. She did not say how the anthropologist had turned her, an heiress who was intended to become a docile butterfly beautifying the house of some husband or other, into the young woman who would eventually discover the pleasure of reading the classics in the original language, or observing the customs of an order of Tibetan monks; nor did she talk about the difficulties they encountered during their travels: the exhaustion, the filth, sometimes the hunger, the weird and wonderful food. No. She simply mentioned an incident that synthesized all the experiences she had gone through with the anthropologist by her side, particularly the things the woman had taught her about men and how to react to their violence: an incident that involved a rifle. Although a handgun or a knife would have done the trick too, Aunt Eloísa said, but the rifle certainly seemed to be the most effective solution when it came to confronting three brutes intent on raping her. She, Divina Arriaga, had helped to dig a grave for the anthropologist in the sands of the African desert, which they had been crossing dressed as male explorers from England when she had the heart attack. And she had stood guard for the whole night at the foot of the grave, sensing that the guide and the two porters did not make any particular distinction between the woman she really was and the boy they saw in front of them, devastated by the death of his teacher. She said that she had been watchful of their movements for hours, catching the glint of their lustful eyes in the darkness, and, when she felt them lunge toward her, she slowly raised the rifle and pulled the trigger three times. Then she went quiet and stayed that way as she watched the trail of smoke rise from her cigarette in its mother-of-pearl holder, while passers-by slowed their steps to look at her as she stood on that terrace in Montparnasse.

Aunt Eloísa did not recall hearing her mention the anthropologist's name even once, and Lina would only find it out much later, by chance—even though by then she had already given up believing that chance had played any part in her relations with Divina Arriaga, or more precisely, in the subtle link that Divina Arriaga had established between the two of them as soon as she returned to the city and sent a card to Lina's grandmother, asking her to send Lina to her villa in El Prado so that she could introduce her to Catalina. Because here, again, she had a choice, that same ability to bet lucidly on a person's behaviour and anticipate how they would react in the long run, not because of who Lina was at that time, when she was barely eight years old, but because of who Divina Arriaga imagined she would become under the influence of her grandmother, Jimena. And once again, she was not wrong: like her governesses and lovers, she, Lina, always served her, and continued to serve her even after she'd died, in complete ignorance for years, then knowingly, once she'd understood the role she'd been cast in by that woman who had vanished among the silk cushions, the same woman who one night, not long before she sank into the long oblivion of her illness, would summon her up to her room, and while they were alone—her eyes suddenly aglow, momentarily torn from their dream of seaweed, willow and wilting lily—would say to her: "Help Catalina. Your father will tell you what to do and when."

Lina, in her adolescence tempered with rationalism, would refuse to hear anything other than the ravings of a sick woman in that plea. Catalina did not need to be helped, and in those days, she was so intent on avoiding Lina that she refused to come to the telephone: she'd decided, in the end, to marry Álvaro Espinoza, a taciturn, gaunt-faced man who seemed to be driven by an incomprehensible contempt for humanity. For months Catalina had mercilessly made fun of him, systematically rejecting him and telling Lina her impressions of him: she thought his *mulato* face had a greasy sheen to it, she said; his hands were always sweaty, and the collar of his shirt, which was not particularly clean, gave off the same smell as the black cassocks worn by priests. While all of this was true, in Lina's opinion it paled into insignificance compared to Álvaro Espinoza's ideas and his perverse insistence on marrying Catalina. Because there was a touch of madness and something very troubling about his indifference to her repeated rebuffs and, later, the way he seduced her by corrupting her, in other words, by offering up his contacts and his sway to integrate her into the society that had viciously humiliated her, punishing the daughter of Divina Arriaga within her.

At the time when this happened—the affront, the public grievance—Catalina didn't know who her mother was or what people said about her in the city. In fact, she was oblivious to anything that might make her sad or affect her self-confidence because, like those heiresses Aunt Eloísa spoke of, Catalina had been paradoxically protected and disarmed by her own beauty: doors opened automatically as she walked by, and if they remained closed, she either failed to notice or refused to give it a second thought, always looking for the easy route. Lina attributed her lack of inhibitions to the admiration people felt for her, creating a kind of halo around her which acted as a filter: everything that reached her was more echo than noise, more foam than wave, more reflection than light, keeping Catalina detached from her surroundings like a doll wrapped in cellophane. There was that, but also her capacity to sidestep obstacles, invariably finding an easier route, albeit not necessarily the best shortcut; this was one of the traits that made such an impression on Lina when they first met, an aspect of her character that her grandmother tried to put her on guard against, advising her against any attempt at imitation. However, there was no one in the world who could imitate Catalina or look like her, with those luminous green eyes, that ebony hair and that skin, pink like the inside of a large seashell, someone beautiful enough to be brazen, yet elegant enough to get away with it. But above all, it was impossible to copy that charm of hers in any way.

Perhaps because Catalina knew that she was loved instantly and unreservedly, her heart only harboured kind feelings that were expressed in the smile of a goddess to her admirers or the gaze of a child who has never encountered evil. During the years they studied together at La Enseñanza, Lina would never see Catalina argue with anyone or fall victim to the nuns' spiteful ways. In fact, she was their favourite: if she was part of the group causing trouble, the nuns would simply smile, and the punishment would be minimal. And Catalina was almost always involved: she planned the disturbance, and Lina executed it. Because her excellent memory—which allowed her to learn an entire page after reading it just once—and her instinctive understanding of mathematics, were combined with a mischievous spirit, always on the lookout for an opportunity to disturb the ant-like submission the nuns tried to impose on them with those twenty little blue cards, known as *notas*, which had the number of each student printed on them; if one of those little cards was taken away, it lowered the grade of conduct that was read out to everyone and in front of the prioress at the end of each week, in a ceremony that opened with hymns to the Virgin and ended when the two or three pupils who had managed to keep hold of all their *notas* proudly marched into the garden to hoist the national flag. Catalina lost as many of them as Lina, but at least once a month she would still be among the classmates who hoisted the flag. Although that puzzle surprised Lina, it didn't particularly bother her because by that point she had already developed a soft spot for Catalina that would stay with her all her life; she wasn't even shocked the day she discovered that it was the Mother Superior herself who stealthily slipped her the little cards that the other nuns had taken away—if those same nuns had not secretly given them back already, perhaps so that they could

see her walking along the corridor in the line of students, looking so beautiful, her green eyes reflecting an intangible purity,
beyond any form of pain or knowledge, which is how she
appeared before a dazzled audience at the school's solemn ses-
sion every year, playing Jeanne de Lestonnac, the founder of
the religious order to which the nuns at La Enseñanza
belonged.

Because Catalina was pure and impervious to evil, like a
bird that could let all the dirt in the world glide over its feathers without leaving the slightest trace. And paradoxically or
not, she retained some of this purity for the rest of her life,
even when she cheated on Álvaro Espinoza with any man who
awakened her desire, and then later, when she knowingly
drove him to suicide, because by that time, Catalina had
already devised a moral code she would always abide by, the
rules of which were never to lie to herself and never to seek justification for her reprehensible acts. Perhaps the nuns weren't
wrong to give her back her *notas*, conveying a kind of faith in
who she really was and casting a little doubt over Divina
Arriaga's supposed ruin. After all, things might have been different if Catalina had simply been the orphan of a stranger, if
no one even knew whether her father had been married as God
intended to the woman who had instigated the city's most reprehensible scandal, in other words, if there wasn't a sliver of
truth in the story that was barely whispered about that man—
a Polish aristocrat who had been persecuted by the Nazis and
was an active member of the French Resistance and was tortured to death in an old house in Brittany—and if Divina
Arriaga had really been ruined when she boarded the ship
which, like a coffin, took her to Barranquilla forever. If none of
that were true, Catalina wouldn't have recouped those little
blue cards so easily, and in all likelihood, she would never have
been accepted into the school in the first place. La Enseñanza
only admitted girls from well-heeled families or the daughters

of major landowners from the coast, who sent their future heiresses to board at the school until it was time to find them a suitable husband, and they were only allowed in on the condition that they were born nine months after their parents' Catholic wedding and their parents—or rather, their mothers—had always behaved in an exemplary manner. All conditions that Catalina, according to all and sundry, did not satisfy: she was already ten years old when she arrived in the city barely stammering Spanish, and her mother, Divina Arriaga, had her registered as a Colombian, born in Saint Malo on August 21st, 1937, the legitimate child of a man named Stanislas Czartoryski. Not that she'd provided any papers or documents to confirm any of this, because the city hall where such documents were kept had been burned down in a bombing by Allied aircraft. All anyone knew was that Divina Arriaga had returned to Barranquilla with a little girl who was her spitting image and whose surname was impossible to pronounce. They also knew that she had taken over her parents' old villa and was drip-feeding the money needed to bring the building out of the neglect slowly eating away at it, but not receiving any visitors or accepting invitations, nor making any attempt to revive that fantastic lifestyle that had taken the city by storm twenty years earlier. That was when the talk of ruin started. With glee. With relief.

They had talked of ruin when she arrived for the first time, or more precisely, when she returned to Europe, while Barranquilla's bourgeoisie was still shaking from the immense pandemonium she had been attributed with creating, organizing and promoting, for various reasons that from her proclivity for immoral behaviour to blatant complicity with the devil, who had ordered her to spread chaos not only to lead their souls to perdition, but also to smear the reputation of the members of the ruling classes to better facilitate the penetration of atheist materialism. As the years went by, all that speculation was forgotten, but not the scandal that gave rise to it, turning Divina Arriaga into a symbol of everything that well-bred people ought to condemn—on moral grounds, indubitably, but also because her outright defiance of conventions seemed to have brought misfortune upon her. Because when she left Barranquilla, Divina Arriaga no longer had any tangible assets to her name. Nothing remained of her father's river transportation company or the import and export business that controlled most of the trade with Germany throughout the country and which Aunt Eloísa had bought stocks in. At any rate, none of this remained in her hands, and no one in their right mind believed that the money from those transactions would be left in her hands after the orgies she had hosted, plunging the city into turmoil. Only Aunt Eloísa, who had paid for her stocks in cold, hard cash, was foolish enough to believe it, even saying that those orgies had simply helped Divina Arriaga get rid of a few pesos that might have caused her problems with the taxman had she converted them into gold or another currency. But Aunt Eloísa usually only spoke to very few people, and Divina Arriaga's financial ruin fixed everyone else's lives, calming the indignation of those who declared it was unacceptable for a woman to dare to behave so disrespectfully and get off scot-free. Her ruin also served as a warning for other women, those who dared to have any capricious dream of emancipation, or those who, not daring to dream, meekly carried out their work, chasing away their bitterness with household chores. But in the long run it would serve, above all, as an example: various generations of young girls would hear Divina Arriaga's story and shrink back in fear at the punishment she received for challenging the male order: born with a silver spoon in her mouth, she was welcomed into the city like a goddess, and after squandering her inheritance on all that indecent revelry, she vanished amid the general air of outrage, abandoned by her friends and spat out by her lover, Ricardo Montes de Trajuela, who, after winning three houses from her in a game of poker one night, had gone looking for her the next day along with witnesses and a notary, demanding the transfer of the deeds. Ricardo Montes de Trajuela, an elegant, handsome descendant of a blue-blood family, had studied at Oxford, where he learnt everything there was to know about how to wear a dinner jacket, talk to servants or assess a fortune. Committing such a reproachable act not only implied outright contempt for the woman who had been his lover for five months, but also showed that, convinced of her misfortune, he'd cast aside the precepts of good manners he'd been taught at Oxford or wherever it was, in order to strip her of the last remaining crumbs of her inheritance. Of course, Aunt Eloísa had her own version of events: that gold digger, who was handsome, granted, but not the brightest spark, had been chosen by Divina Arriaga in full awareness, following the old adage, "Better a small fish than an empty dish." And the notorious game of poker that she, Aunt Eloísa, witnessed, had allowed Divina Arriaga to dismiss him with pay and a redundancy package, as well as forcing him to reveal his true colours. This was her one last victorious move in the strange game she had been playing throughout her stay in the city, or more precisely, ever since she had gauged the degree of hypocrisy to which the individuals in its elite could stoop.

There was no way this outcome could have been predicted when Divina Arriaga first arrived in Barranquilla to take on her inheritance, when the men and women who had served her father in the most wretched adulation fell at her feet, dumbstruck by her fabulous jewels, her splendid attire and the self-assured way in which she expressed a few ideas that exploded like firecrackers in the face of the city's blind puritanism. Such admiration had surprised Divina Arriaga more than anyone, but as the student of an anthropologist, she set about studying the customs of this indigenous bourgeoisie, and not without curiosity, quickly discovering that the city's racist, smug and prodigiously uncultured society was sleepwalking in a swamp of frustrations, which bubbled to the surface in the form of backbiting among women—when, sitting at a canasta table, they laboriously digested lunchtime feasts in which every *arepa*, every extra helping of rice with meat eased the shame of nocturnal failures—and in the form of obscene vulgarity among men, who competed for the paltry privileges of a provincial city and noisily sought their reward in brothels full of girls who could make the whores of Saint-Denis look like princesses. Following the rules she had learned from the anthropologist, Divina Arriaga simply observed them the same way she might have observed a tribe of African pygmies: analyzing their behaviour from a distance, keeping her conclusions to herself. But insofar as the middle classes of the city were not African pygmies, that is to say, they had not lost all capacity for evolution and could react to the stimuli of a more advanced culture (should Divina Arriaga evoke such things merely with her presence) they began to imitate the outward signs of her personality, failing to consider that this personality had gone through the filter of twenty-four years of experience and perfect education before it was fully formed. So, Aunt Eloísa said, they began making clumsy attempts to copy her: hemlines got higher and hair was cropped as the local women fell for the charms of the garçonne haircut; coloured tights and pointy shoes suddenly came into vogue, as well as fringed dresses, accessorized with long beaded necklaces and headbands, and everyone was singing a little ditty about Tutankhamun fashion; women decided to smoke in public and developed a taste for whiskey, and the men, for the first (and last) time in the history of the city, spent time with their wives at parties instead of sitting in a corner discussing politics and brothels.

Everyone fell at Divina Arriaga's feet. Soirees and dances were held every night in her honour, and she reciprocated by taking fifteen or twenty couples to her house in Puerto

Colombia for the weekend, not suspecting that these most sophisticated gatherings, complete with bonfires on the beach, pavilions in the gardens and endless food and free-flowing drink, would turn into complete and utter orgies when the guests found themselves in such circumstances, which were rather conducive to depravity. And so honest partners, fathers or mothers who were suffocated by a tangled web of repression gave free rein to their desires with the frenzy typical of any violation of prohibitions, and with persistence, the murky, vague, unspoken intention to delay the consequences of an act by repeating it. They even shocked Aunt Eloísa, who, despite having seen more than her fair share of things in her life, had been struck dumb by such debauchery. Through her aunt, and from the elaborate accounts provided by Berenice, Lina would learn what went on in that house in Puerto Colombia during the five months Divina Arriaga spent in the city, shattering taboos and conventions, not so much with her behaviour— ultimately, she always stayed on the sidelines of any form of excess, and only at the eleventh hour could anyone say for sure that she had been Ricardo Montes de Trajuela's lover—but because of the upheaval caused by her attitude of wry indulgence toward the weaknesses and contradictions of the people who had rushed to seduce her, hoping to get a piece of the enormous fortune she had inherited from her father, only to find themselves falling prey, one after the other, to her disquietingly seductive schemes. And they fell hard, which Aunt Eloísa insisted was what they deserved and how Divina Arriaga no doubt put it when she was back in Europe and relayed the tale to future friends or anyone who was familiar with the work of Dürrenmatt, reminding them of the characters from the small city of Gullen, whose reactions (caricatured, of course) could be compared with those of the Barranquilla's bourgeoisie when it came to their talent for neglecting all their principles to shelter under the wing of an immensely rich woman.

But that was all; in other words, that was as far as the analogy could go, because the woman herself, Divina Arriaga, was barely twenty-four years old and harboured no resentment towards the city. Resentment never came into it, not even later, when she discovered that the friends who turned up at her house an hour before the parties to help her get ready, and the men who were always happy to flatter her if it meant they could keep or land a cushy job in her father's businesses, made fun of her behind her back, accusing her of base acts or nefarious intentions. No. A more accurate description was the feeling that Aunt Eloísa respectfully classed as wickedness. If Lina had understood correctly, wickedness implied refinement and a certain sense of humour. Similarly to the lawyer who had used Benito Suárez's own logic against him to bring him down, Divina Arriaga simply created the conditions in which the people who called themselves her friends would fall into temptation. It wasn't just a matter of giving them free run of a house with more than twenty bedrooms, surrounded by a dense garden and looking out over a vast beach where, from six in the evening, couples could slip off without anyone noticing: it was her tolerance, the ease with which she welcomed women's secrets and men's intrigues, leaving them to get caught up in the web spun by their own passions. Deep in her eyes she carried the astonished disdain of the first conquistadors, but she held no cross in her hand. Without seeking it or asking for it, purely because of her wealth, she had been granted the power to judge. But rather than choosing to repress people, she liberated them. Anyone who set foot in her house in Puerto Colombia felt they were escaping the city; following their whims, they ventured into the labyrinth of an unknown self, toing and froing until they found their deepest truth, which could make them euphoric or suicidal, lead them to gamble away their fortune at a poker table or their life in a ridiculous bet, or to discover their desire for a friend's wife, or even for the friend himself.

So, over the course of five months, the scandals played out while the city pretended not to notice, partly because at least one member of each family attended Divina Arriaga's parties or depended on her for their livelihood, then later on, because the brazen display of her wealth inspired an almost sacred respect that either stifled the rumours or rendered them inaudible. But people knew: many of them took the train to Puerto Colombia at the end of the week and got off at the dusty station without really knowing where to go, searching in vain for a room in the village's only spa resort—which was already filled with far-sighted summer holiday-makers who had suddenly discovered the benefits of bathing in hot springs. People of good stock, but whose modest lifestyle denied them access to Divina Arriaga, sneaked into the gardens surrounding her house as soon as the sun began to set; crouching behind the palm trees and shrubs, they spied on the guests, who laughed and danced to the sound of trios, orchestras and Cuban ensembles while the scent of veal and suckling pig wafted over from the beach, where the meat was being slow-roasted over the coals and drizzled with sauces mysteriously seasoned by an equally enigmatic Frenchman, who had absconded from Cayenne and had been promoted to chef by Divina Arriaga, and would start working at the Hotel del Prado months later with Berenice (his student and lover) in tow. Lina would learn from Berenice herself how the guests had resolved to put an end to that importunity one night by releasing some hunting dogs brought along for the occasion, forcing the intruders to stampede through the dark streets of the village in a daze of shame and humiliation. Still, there were no complaints from the locals. But when Carnival season came around and Divina Arriaga aided and abetted a troupe that would be talked about for years, the sight of that group of eighty ambiguously dressed individuals entering the country club incited so much rage that it was impossible to keep hiding the truth. For it was no ordinary troupe of Carnival revellers all dressed alike, that is to say, with a fairly inoffensive theme that each participant had to interpret. No. It was an irreverent amalgam that had a little of everything: nuns pushing strollers with men dozing in them, wearing only a simple diaper and with their hairy legs in the air as they glugged whiskey from a baby's bottle; women dressed as Catholic schoolgirls pursued by old men who were pulling on their braids with mischievous grins on their faces; tarted-up men in drag brazenly making eyes at the onlookers; four Catholic Mothers dressed as *mamasantas*. In short, an abomination. As far as the people were concerned, the worst thing was that Divina Arriaga— from whose mansion the troupe had emerged—appeared at midnight dressed in a sumptuous black dress, more breathtaking than ever, aloof and seemingly separate from the racket her friends were making, barely even glancing over at them from the table where she started drinking champagne in the company of a unknown man in an evening jacket. Meanwhile, some of the debauchery had rubbed off on the members of the country club: on the dancefloor, couples were locked in embraces based on desires rather than marital ties; the lights had been switched off and gasps of surprise and satisfaction could be heard from the darker corners; after locking the president of the club in his office, the tipsy guests who usually left or were made to leave at midnight had organized a competition by the pool to see who had the longest and strongest stream of urine; others were beating each other up and destroying the exquisite plants in the garden in the process, and a few distraught women were running back and forth, pleading with the staff to put a stop to all the madness. Despite their shock, the staff were the only ones to remain calm: not only did they free the president of the club and keep the bottles of alcohol under lock and key, but they also put out a fire that was started when someone threw a flaming coat at the curtains in the billiards room. It was thanks to them that there was no need to call the police, which would have smeared the club's reputation irretrievably. But the next day the people were overwhelmed by the most profound feeling of dismay. Faced with the sheer scale of the disaster, the priests who had screamed blue murder soon gave up threatening them with excommunication, because the idea of casting the city's entire ruling class out of the church was preposterous. As was to be expected, there was no mention of the incident in the press, the women ended up running to the confessional, the men suddenly remembered the duties that came with the exercise of power, and the poor staff lost their jobs at the country club, leaving with plenty of cash in their pockets to help them forget all about it. So in the end, Divina Arriaga would have to be the scapegoat, the fall guy, the one held responsible, just at the point when the consensus was that nothing remained of her father's fortune. Then certain people, emboldened, started saying that her behaviour brought shame on the city and decided to take the matter to the president of the Catholic Mothers, who requested an audience with the bishop, once she had expelled the lost sheep from the congregation, her aim being to appoint a committee of dignitaries whose mission it would be to boldly confront Divina Arriaga and deliver a few home truths. No one could agree on the substance of those truths: not the Mother President, nor the people who went with her to the Curia and were granted the bishop's permission to form the committee. It was already difficult enough to convene fifteen public figures without a blot on their reputation—in other words, without any relatives who had visited Divina Arriaga or benefited from the privileges of her friendship in one way or another. But after much deliberation, the chosen dignitaries resolved to accuse her of corruption and demanded that she sell her share in the country club. In a city where membership of the club was seen as the ultimate mark of distinction, this was the most

severe punishment, one comparable to the demotion of a soldier or the excommunication of a priest forbidden from taking
communion. In the notice they sent her setting a date for a *ren-
dezvous* (which they wrote in French after checking in the dictionary) there was no mention of this, only a series of vague
remarks about wanting to find out who had been behind the
troupe that had infamously broken with Barranquilla's whole-
some Carnival traditions. Since Divina Arriaga failed to
acknowledge it, the members of the committee turned up at
her house in Puerto Colombia on the allotted day, egging each
other on with memories of all the chaos that had occurred
since she arrived five months earlier and the bad example her
waywardness was going to set for the youngsters. The door was
opened by a huge, smiling, completely disorientated Black
man, who had just arrived on a boat from Haiti and could not
speak a single word of Spanish. It was only then that the dignitaries noticed that the blinds were drawn and the piano in
the living room was covered in a blue oilcloth. The room did
not seem fit to welcome anyone, neither gentlemen nor simple
street sweepers. There were no paintings on the walls, and the
furniture was preparing for a long sleep beneath Holland
cloths. Feeling their blood boiling with indignation, the visitors started asking the man for Divina Arriaga's whereabouts,
but he simply smiled and shook his head from side to side with
an air of amusement. Suddenly seeming to understand, he
showed his large, very white teeth in a big guffaw. "Madame?"
he asked. And opening the window, he pointed to the boat
drifting away across the ocean, golden in the dimming light of
dusk, its plaintive horn announcing that Divina Arriaga had
spread her wings once again and was flying far away, like an
enormous bird soaring to new heights, beyond good and evil.

II

Lina could not fathom the dialectics that had led Aunt
Eloísa to devise the set of values that she used to place
herself above the contingencies of ordinary women
while at the same time rejecting the mystifications of men.
Perhaps because her logic was based on a paradox that Aunt
Eloísa never intended to let her in on, barely letting her
glimpse, by way of explanation, that behind the apparent flip-
pancy of her reasoning and the cheerful nonchalance of her
conclusions was an iron will with which she faced all the problems inherent to the male condition until, curiously, she finally
earned the privilege of embracing her womanhood. As far as
Aunt Eloísa was concerned, being a woman implied a certain
harmony with nature, a certain integration into its rhythms:
women had never seen nature as an enemy to be defeated or
destroyed, but as a double, an ally, a mirror that reflected their
cycles and their fertility. Nature gave them the strength they
needed to keep the species alive despite the devastation
wreaked by men's madness, but it also gave them the weakness
that had enslaved them to men. So, femininity had to be disowned in the beginning and then won back later, fighting with
the masculine parameters and emerging victorious, like a
reward that could be possessed without humiliation or servitude, turning an asset earned at the moment of birth into
something deliberately lost and then regained in complete
lucidity. Divina Arriaga had always known this. And in time,
Catalina would discover it for herself: in time, because it was

not simply a matter of becoming wise to all the seductions, traps and lies that had to be circumvented with the cunning of Ulysses on his voyage. No. The journey of trial and initiation had to be relatively short in order to return with the strength and enthusiasm required for life; and turning back did not imply resignation—in other words, reaching a state of mind which could alter reality—but instead a kind of withdrawal, an attitude of indifference towards power, accompanied, like the break of a new dawn, by a triumphant reconciliation with the deep drive for love and sensuality that nature, in her wisdom, had given to womankind.

Whether or not Catalina ever reached that state, Lina never knew. Every time she met her in Paris, she felt she could detect the disquieting coldness of a hunter on the prowl in those green eyes. One day, for example, she went with her to an exhibition where the main exhibit was a magnificent portrait of Catalina's mother, Divina Arriaga, looking very pale, with a string of pearls draped around her long neck. And as the visitors glanced from the painting to Catalina in disbelief, Lina heard her casually say, "I knew it existed, but it's part of a private collection and there's no way it can be sold." That image, which to her was as heartrending as the memory of Dora being hit by Benito Suárez, or of Beatriz's face twisted in despair, would stay with Lina for a long time: Catalina looking triumphant and domineering as she descended the museum steps and, with a haughty flick of the wrist, summoned the driver of the Rolls Royce she hired whenever she was in Paris, while she, Lina, repeated to herself: So that's that, there's no way it can be bought or sold. But when, nearing the end of her life, she found out that Catalina was living with an American millionaire out of love, purely for love, she preferred to picture her regaining the mischievous sweetness she'd had as a child and the charms of her youth, growing old in some sumptuous New York apartment with her heart at peace, having understood that all the time she'd spent struggling relentlessly against the world in order to defend her integrity, she had simply been wandering in the wilderness.

It was a struggle she'd been thrust into when she was barely seventeen years old and had no weapons to defend herself. Blindly, because she was oblivious to the grudge that the people of the city harboured against her mother and the hatred that she herself was bound to provoke for being such an infinitely beautiful woman. A well-mannered girl, she lived in a world devoid of sharp edges or anything resembling an obstacle, with silks and tulles laid out for her to wander along without ever coming up against any limits or boundaries, a world where everything was designed to protect her and yield to her touch. Then there was her recluse of a mother, who would send for her from her death-chamber once a week, perhaps to find out how many inches she'd grown or if anything about her body was beginning to defy the opaque austerity of her uniform, spotting some flicker of curiosity or rebellion in her eyes, and perhaps expertly gauging the levity of her spirit, checking how her environment encouraged her to avoid the conflicts that would sooner or later overwhelm her. And nevertheless trusting in the unpredictable forces of succession, secretly convinced that dozing somewhere behind her innocuous appearance was a fighting animal, one programmed to flex its muscles and pounce with its claws in the air when the signal woke it from its slumber. Divina Arriaga was counting on that wild awakening for the plan she had devised before returning to Barranquilla, which was to be implemented as soon as Catalina decided to react, that is, once it dawned on her that going into battle with feminine weapons was about as ineffective as confronting a tank with a slingshot and three pebbles. She'd even predicted how long it was going to take: roughly thirty years. No time at all, or at least very little for a woman who had been rendered powerless by an incurable disease with no known name, a woman who, in her rare lucid moments, could imagine her daughter clumsily struggling against an order—one she herself had defeated and conquered—but then gradually gaining the knowledge she needed for that victory. The patient, calculating mother, who, on recovering her dormant faculties, coming to her senses for an instant, was suddenly able to grasp eternity and tell herself that thirty years were barely a heartbeat in the long, pounding pulse of life, and the same woman who would observe the groom she had chosen without batting an eye: the ugly *mulato* with the pockmarked face, which was already starting to mortify, as if his hatred for women, Black people, the dispossessed and the weak made his glands function differently, so that instead of secreting the substances needed by the organism, they produced acids that could alter the texture of the face, making it old and blotchy, like a shrunken head. She, the woman whose strange disease had kept her youthful beauty intact—refining it, even, making her skin clearer and intensifying the feverish glow of her green eyes—would stare unblinkingly at the fiancé Catalina brought home to meet her; for two hours, she would make him present his Jesuitical rationale for believing he could escape the curse of being *mulato* and misogynistic in a society that, come hell or high water, held up the macho white man as its ideal, in other words, the man who was least likely to reveal the contamination of his lineage and most likely to repress his homosexual side in order to marry a woman of his social standing and start a family.

Divina Arriaga would agree to see him three months before the wedding and then again on the day they got married, but never again after that. The first meeting doubtless gave her everything she needed to get the measure of Álvaro Espinoza, to scrutinize him under a magnifying glass and then, after identifying all his idiosyncrasies, to leave him to Catalina, already knowing what kind of hell her relationship with him would lead her to in time. She said nothing. Lina, who witnessed the encounter, watched Divina Arriaga staring intensely at her daughter, trying perhaps to work out how resilient she could be, the way she had done two months earlier, when Catalina announced that she was planning to enter the newspaper beauty pageant. And Lina understood, or at least she thought she understood: Divina Arriaga had anticipated the disaster without trying to prevent it, not because she felt little or no tenderness toward the daughter who was hurtling toward her ruin, but because she had to think in terms of her own logic, so lucid it was relentless, and so similar to Aunt Eloísa's belief that the bigger the mistake, the quicker the lesson learned. She had not been able to give Catalina the chance to learn from anthropologists or trips that unfurled the past before her eyes, nor through constant exposure to different customs and beliefs capable of lambasting uncertainty, nor by visiting museums, watching operas or listening to concerts and symphonies. She had seen nothing but that dusty city, where meditation was impossible and inner reflection was useless, beneath a harsh sun that appeared suddenly in the dead of night and moved across the sky mercilessly, brutally slowly, until night fell again. Barranquilla's art scene, which amounted to an illusory music academy, sweltering theatres that had been turned into cinemas, and hungry poets celebrating industrial progress or writing playlets to flatter the vanity of the local nobility, was much more disturbing than a parody: it was the sentimental babble of a forgotten culture, the disjointed recollection of an irretrievable past, the mechanical movements of a ritual whose meaning was already lost in the meanderings of memory. And yet, this was the place Divina Arriaga took Catalina to live in the final stage of her long illness, the strange disease that had scrambled her mind, causing all her mistakes, Aunt Eloísa said, the first of which came when, disrupting the magnificent equilibrium of her flight, she agreed to descend and join a world that was not her own, where all she had to do was to exalt the things that world spurned—beauty, irony, eroticism—and unearth its vices so that, in the lifetime allotted to her, she could play a part in speeding up the process that would hasten its ruin. But, debilitated by ill health, she had accepted that world to the point where she was trapped in the horror of it. A horror inspired by the war and its long series of atrocities, by something comparable to infinite desolation.

She, Divina Arriaga, had listened a hundred times to the anthropologist explaining how the system which had ruled the social life of human beings for six thousand years could only bring disaster: whatever guise it came in, whether it was expressed through different ideologies, whether it was masked by seemingly conflicting principles, the outcome would always be the same. But in her sickness, with her wings singed and no compass to guide her, she had foolishly attributed sufficient validity to the male rule of law to believe in an intelligent evolution based on the culture that was flourishing on the most civilized continent on the planet. And lo and behold, that continent had ended up as the breeding ground for those aberrant ideologies, the first echoes of the apocalypse: in the country that produced Beethoven, Goethe and Kant, the hordes of automatons marching leadenly to the cries of a deranged clown; in Italy, the land of palaces and cathedrals, the stupefied mobs deliriously obeying orders from that clown's jester. With Spain disillusioned and the dream of communism dying in Russia, Divina Arriaga gave up imagining there was any hope and retreated into her own life. Hiding somewhere in militarized Europe was the man she had loved enough to make him the father of her daughter, and she began anxiously searching for him, accompanied always by her maid and a couple of white greyhounds, until she found him in London, where he was involved in an espionage network and working as a liaison officer for the French Resistance. No one ever knew for sure if she worked alongside him, and Aunt Eloísa was outraged at the very suggestion. A friend of hers had simply found Divina Arriaga in her *hôtel particulier* in Neuilly, with a map of France spread out on a desk in the only heated room in the house during the winter of 1942. Next to the map dotted with red arrows marking the advance of the armies of the Third Reich, was a pile of clandestine newspapers and the radio, turned down low, transmitting the news from London. And waiting for her downstairs in the freezing living room filled with Gobelin tapestries was a handsome German officer, who was related to a certain Stanislas and abhorred Nazism as much as she did, and who provided her with all sorts of safe-conducts so that she could follow her lover's footsteps (or his instructions) across the country. That officer would give her the final clue: a manor house that the Gestapo had requisitioned twenty minutes from Saint-Malo, where people were tortured to death in the cellar. Divina Arriaga went to see the house just after the Germans had abandoned it. As did Lina, years later, posing as a photographer. The owners of the house only stayed there in August, and an old peasant couple were taking care of it at the time. The man walked with a limp and seemed standoffish, but his wife agreed to let Lina take photographs of the large house, apologizing, as they made their way down a poorly lit staircase to the cellar, for the strong odour that stung their eyes; all flustered, she explained that she cleaned the floor and walls with ammonia every week so that she would never again have to see the stains she'd cleaned up years before. It was down in that cellar that Divina Arriaga felt the first tangible symptoms of her illness. Rising from the grotto at the end of the garden, which had been used as a mass grave, came the stench of rotting flesh. The last man who had succumbed to torture lay on the ground, his body, puppet-like, twisted in pain. There were fresh blood stains still on the floor, and congealed blood on hooks hanging from the wall. Divina Arriaga took all this in, and suddenly her mind clouded over; it could not exactly be said that she passed out, because she stayed on her feet and, with those same feet, climbed the stairs, went out into the street and headed to Lausanne to look for Catalina. But she couldn't remember any of this, or rather, she only remembered it by fits and starts. She even forgot the elaborate steps she'd swiftly taken to safeguard her fortune until Catalina reached adulthood. Divina Arriaga's mind flicked on and off intermittently: one day it would work perfectly, and then she would fall into the reverie of emptiness. She would come back to reality for a few hours and then fade away unexpectedly when things got too real; on the occasions when the image of the cellar did return to her memory, she could not quite manage to place it exactly. Perhaps because in that cellar, her consciousness had shattered like a crystal vase struck by a stone. From that moment on, she could piece together the shards and remember even the things she had forgotten, but those lucid moments became increasingly fleeting as Catalina grew older, as if, in an attempt to completely lose herself in oblivion, Divina Arriaga had secretly given herself a time frame to protect Catalina with her presence until Catalina could do without her, always giving her the freedom to choose, but not showing her the way. In other words, she never expressed any opinion intended to interfere with the influence of her environment, leaving her to fend for herself instead, like an adult abandoning a child in front of an immense desert, with enough water and food to last the crossing and animals to carry the water and food, but nothing else: the child would have to decide whether to walk by day or by night, whether to expose their eyes to the sun until they went blind or to use the stars in the night sky as a guide. Hence, Divina Arriaga's presence in her daughter's life was more like an absence, and nobody could hold it against her, Aunt Eloísa said, because to do so would have been as preposterous as criticizing a dead man for not being alive: when she boarded the boat that took her to the city for good, along with Catalina, her maid and the last two white greyhounds she ever had, Divina Arriaga took many possessions with her, including books, furniture, crockery and porcelain, but most importantly, in the manner of Dracula, her own coffin, and inside it, herself, because Barranquilla had always seemed like an enormous cemetery to her, a place of desolation and ruin.

Left to her own devices, Catalina had never really known authority; she did not even find going to school a chore; in fact, she enjoyed playing with mathematics or picking languages apart, and history—the sacred and the secular—struck her as a succession of fairly interesting anecdotes, while drawing maps or memorizing the names of mountains and rivers allowed her to escape into dreams of travelling to exotic countries. Besides, school gave her an opportunity to make friends and assert her influence over them, to break the rules and have some fun, because her innate sense of supremacy gave her a cheerful rebelliousness that paradoxically endeared her to the nuns and the pupils alike: she was the one who came up with the best systems for passing answers in exams, and it was her idea to offer lower prices to her poorer classmates for the sodas and candies that one of the nuns made them sell at recess, or which, to be more exact, they had volunteered to sell in order to get out of having to play in the blazing sun and so that they could gossip with total impunity from behind the little counter, feeling against their legs the coolness of the large ice tubs of ice where the colas and orange sodas were chilling. When the time came to cash up, Catalina would make up the missing pesos from her own pocket, without wanting any reward in return, because apart from Lina, nobody would ever find out about her generosity. This aloof attitude toward money would remain with her throughout her life, not just when money became her obsession because of Álvaro Espinoza's insidious pettiness, but also in the days when she traded in art, buying and selling paintings all over the United States. Whether she earned it through effort and shrewdness, or whether it was lavished on her as a child by Divina Arriaga's maid, having money, in her case, was not so much a way to obtain the finer things in life, but rather it gave her the warm feeling of knowing that she was living up to the image she liked to project.

For years Catalina searched for love: not the love of one person in particular, but the love of anyone who had the privilege of seeing her, of contemplating her and adoring her as the child-goddess she secretly knew she was; too intelligent to be content with rudimentary narcissism, she had learned at a young age to play down the admiration her beauty inspired, developing an accommodating persona which, using the subtlest signs of complicity, captivated anyone who spoke to her. This covert work on herself—for it was work, trying to understand others, their actions and motivations, to the point where an attitude of tolerance took over from the initial impression of rejection—would leave her with a distinct inclination for analysis, which would prove so useful to her later, and a fairly unstructured consciousness, undermined by the need to reason, and always yielding to leniency so she didn't feel obliged to judge or criticize. Like her mother, Catalina accepted everything. But whereas Divina Arriaga's indulgent gaze concealed a good dose of wry, almost contemptuous curiosity, Catalina was only asking to be loved. Perhaps, despite her true motivations, her disposition was something akin to kindness, and this is what Lina believed for a long time. What neither she nor Catalina knew back then was that if beauty, with its fatal power of seduction, was combined with a more or less unsuspecting benevolence, the desire for destruction provoked by the former would be spurred on by the latter, the same way that the sight of the small, innocent animal at play excites the child who is about to torture it. The two of them would learn this one night at the country club, just when circumstances had led

Catalina to leave her adolescence behind; led and almost forced, because until then she had shown no desire to join adult life, and although she had already achieved her high-school diploma, she still had the air of a schoolgirl about her, with her fresh, bare-faced looks and her easy manner. The only things she liked were the ocean, the cinema and horse-riding. On weekends, she and Lina would head to the country club or watch six films in a row, starting at the Rex cinema then moving on to the Murillo, and to any other double bill being shown at an open-air cinema at night. They would eat whatever they were given, they wore jeans and supported Atlético Junior football team. But there were two of Lina's interests that Catalina did not share: her passion for reading, and her fascination with men. Lina had felt like a woman from very early on, whereas Catalina seemed to be oblivious to sexuality, and she kept away from men, as if deep down inside she was afraid of discovering that, as well as being able to seduce them, she could drive them to despair. That subversive beauty of hers was countered back then, not just by her jeans and her pony-tail, but because Catalina disowned it, appearing not to be conscious of her femininity, in other words, appearing not to make any particular distinction between herself and members of the opposite sex. Which, in a way, was true. One night when Catalina was thirteen years old, Divina Arriaga's maid had walked into her room holding a box of Kotex and started telling her, in a matter-of-fact way, about the changes that would soon be happening in her body, and showing her how to use the cotton rectangles in the box she was holding. And so Catalina accepted the fact of her menstruation with indifference, simply deciding that she would go horse-riding at her relative's farm on the weekends when she got her period, instead of swimming in the pool at the country house. That was the extent of her adolescent crisis. She did not suffer from menstrual cramps, her breasts were a couple of hard, barely noticeable bee stings that developed slowly, and the skin on her face, unaffected by the sun and wind, would always keep the texture it had when she was a child. A picture of health, she channelled her energy into her studies and sport, and put the best of her intelligence into her games of chess. Because Catalina played chess almost every night with Divina Arriaga's maid, an odd, slightly Asian-looking woman who could speak several languages without an accent but chose not to express herself in any of them. No one knew where she came from, and any attempt to work out her age would have been in vain. Aunt Eloísa, who had met the woman in Paris in the 1920s, said that she'd had the same impenetrable appearance even then, that same stony muteness: she'd followed Divina Arriaga around like a shadow, completely devoted to serving her, for reasons that had been lost in the haze of time, perhaps connected to some debt incurred long ago, a debt so significant that it could only be paid off with a lifetime of loyalty. She didn't pay much attention to Catalina, simply giving orders to the maids entrusted with her care. Yet, at some point she must have taken an interest in the fate of that little girl who had been left to fend for herself in the desert, as Aunt Eloísa used to say, and so she set about teaching her to sit and deliberate in front of a magnificent chessboard and thirty-two ivory pieces inlaid with lapis lazuli, albeit without dropping her stony silence for a moment, that is, using only the words required to indicate that she had won or was about to win the game. Watching them play, Lina would assess the subtle extremes of Catalina's capacity for concentration, and likewise, that tendency of hers—which would right itself over the years—to choose the quickest solution off the cuff, at the risk of sacrificing a vital piece or dismantling a perfectly well-thought-out strategy. If Divina Arriaga's maid ever noticed, and it was impossible for her not to, she carried on playing with no change to her imperturbable expression, the same look she had when she watched Catalina roller-skating along the pavement despite having a bandaged knee, probably following Divina Arriaga's advice, the tactic that Aunt Eloísa claimed she employed: since circumstances prevented her daughter from knowing anything other than that city, a place that cowed beneath its unyielding climate, and where any thought—relegated to the few minutes of the day when the body took a break from its fierce unconscious struggle to acclimatize to the sun, the heat and the humidity—was met with a mocking if not downright suspicious apathy from other people, and since there was no anthropologist around to inspire her curiosity and critical mind, and since her mother was aware that she herself had been dead inside for a long time, it was better to patiently let life do its work: any experience was welcome, from falling off a bicycle to simply losing a queen in chess, if it showed Catalina which path to never take again. And so, in the presence of a man like Álvaro Espinoza, whose misogynistic ways would soon put paid to any naïve dreams of marital bliss, Divina Arriaga must have felt the same sense of wry, tender resignation of three months earlier, when she saw Catalina come into her room, flushed with pleasure, announcing that she had just been invited to represent one of the local newspapers in some second-rate newspaper beauty pageant. She didn't say anything then either, even though she had predicted how society would react: from the impassable half-light of her room, where most of the echoes of the world faded away, she'd noticed how the people of El Prado discriminated against Catalina; she knew that she was never invited to her classmates' homes, except on Dora, Lina or Isabel's birthdays, and that no Carnival Queen had ever invited her to be part of her entourage. And she must have known how Catalina, succumbing to her tendency to look past anything that might upset her, didn't seem to resent being snubbed, contenting herself with the solidarity of her close friends as a child, then prolonging her adolescence so as not to be forced to define her place within a social context that insidiously rejected her. But with all the malevolence the contest entailed, it was the perfect springboard to launch Catalina into the world of adults; it didn't matter whether she entered a beauty pageant, a coconut-throwing contest or any other competition.

And so Divina Arriaga decided to tell the silent figure that followed her around—the woman born somewhere beyond the line stretching from the North Pole to the Persian Gulf— that from then on her door would be open to her first cousin, Pura de Altamirano, who couldn't accept that she was ruined and had been trying in vain to get an invitation to her home for a long time. Divina Arriaga wasn't suggesting that she would welcome her face to face, which she never did. But since her cousin was a widow with very little in the way of money and six daughters to support, she thought she could at least give Catalina some pointers and take advantage of the buzz surrounding the pageant to push her eldest daughter Adelaida— who was the right age to get married but had no suitors on the horizon—into the limelight. After her first conversation with the maid, Pura paid a quick visit to Miami and returned laden with outfits for Catalina and Adelaida, transforming them into two dazzlingly elegant ladies, as one of the passionate journalists who was rooting for Catalina described them a week later. By then, that newspaper beauty pageant had become an all-out war, dividing the two candidates' supporters into fiercely opposed camps. On one side was Catalina, who had not only the entire staff of the *Diario del Caribe* flocking around her, from the editor to the most anonymous linotype operator, but also the middle classes, who were fascinated by the legend of her mother, and the poor people who were used to welcoming, along with four days' holiday and plenty of rum, their annual Carnival Queen: an untouchable messenger who was graciously displayed to them and offered up for their admiration, like a magic mirror that dispelled all misery, reflecting the illusion that she was permeating the world of the people who had chosen her, believing for the first time that they had a real queen in Catalina, with her strange, unpronounceable surname, which conjured up images of royal courts, not festivals or tacky imitations, but scenes from Metro-Goldwyn-Mayer swashbuckler films; someone so beloved that charities asked her to visit hospitals and asylums because the mere sight of her eased the pain of the afflicted and even seemed to calm the delirium of the disturbed; someone so beautiful that her portrait was displayed next to the Virgin in the brothels, and the murderers in Calle del Crimen fought in her name. On the other was Rosario Gómez, representing *El Heraldo*, a nice girl, but nothing special to look at, who was supported by all those people who thought the brilliant ascent of Catalina, with her diabolical resemblance to Divina Arriaga, made a mockery of the city's traditional morals. They had been happy to turn the other cheek to the little girl who used to play on the swings at the country club or scamper around the gardens, just as they had chosen not to notice the young girl in jeans and moccasins they saw sitting at a table next to Lina, sipping on Coke floats. But they were forced to react differently when they noticed the turn that things were taking: all of a sudden, the newspaper beauty pageant, which had passed them by to begin with because it was being held for the first time and seemed to be just another ploy by the geniuses on the Cartagena tourist board, was turning into a real event, as journalists and radio broadcasters mobilized the people, interrupting their programming every ten minutes to report on the new support the candidates were gaining. Likewise, Catalina had been transformed into a woman overnight: a woman of mind-blowing beauty whose photograph appeared every day on the front page of the *Diario del Caribe*. Dozens of curious onlookers flocked to the pavement outside her house, waiting in the sun to see her emerge onto the street, hop into the convertible provided by the newspaper's editor and drive through the city followed by fans in their cars, shouting her name in time to the honking of their horns and stopping traffic with riotous scenes: "Ca-ta-li-na, Ca-ta-li-na." Everyone stopped what they were doing and rushed out to see her: shopkeepers left their shops unattended at the risk of being robbed, secretaries got up from their typewriters and crowded at the windows, the furious yells from the foremen fell on deaf ears as workers downed tools and scrambled to find any small crack where they might catch a glimpse of the most beautiful creature that human eyes had ever seen. That was what the journalists proclaimed: the journalists who followed her, pursued her, hounded her, madly in love, a love expressed in verses, anagrams and reports so lyrical that the words made people laugh and cry at the same time, evoking the smell of old books and seemingly pulled from the dustiest, most romantic corners of memory, talked about by everyone, going from mouth to mouth, from the enlightened to the illiterate, making them all buzz with the same passion for Catalina, all the more so since they knew that the people of El Prado scorned her and increasingly snubbed her with parties held in Rosario Gómez's honour and signatures backing her candidacy (sometimes resorting to force, blackmail and threats) which *El Heraldo* highlighted with a loud banging of drums, trying to beat out the apathy of its editors and the evident malice of its linotype operators.

But Catalina did not read that newspaper. There was no point in Divina Arriaga's maid leaving it on her nightstand when she brought her breakfast in bed, just as there was no use in Lina pointing out to her how the people who had supported her in the early days (including former classmates and tennis partners) had switched to her rival's camp, leaving only coarse-mannered supporters whose names were completely unknown to them. Catalina did not pay any attention to such minor details; she did not even register them. Lost in rapture, she could only contemplate the world from the golden heights of a goddess. She had always known she was the prettiest, and sure enough, her beauty plunged a whole city into ecstasy and was endlessly reflected in the hundreds of eyes that followed her in wonder wherever she went; inclined to kindness, that character trait was now recognized by the admiration she received from the ever-growing crowds that came out to meet her, holding out hands, documents and even sick children to her, for they were starting to believe that she was capable of performing miracles. She was called to the poor neighbourhoods where committees were formed in support of her candidacy; people would wait for her for hours on end, rhythmically chanting her name like a religious incantation, pausing only for a few seconds to listen, on a transistor brought along by some thief or privileged person, to the developments of her procession being transmitted by the radio link truck that accompanied it. "Catalina, Catalina," they shouted, and suddenly a cheer would erupt in the crowd, and there she was, her black hair shining with a thousand reflections in the midday sun, those green eyes glittering like emeralds in her perfectly formed face, her white hands waving back at those other dark, calloused, dry hands, while the convertible tried to make its way through the roiling sea of impassioned supporters. Back at the villa in El Prado, Catalina barely had time to take a quick shower before she collapsed into bed and fell straight to sleep with a serene expression on her face, her lips parted ever so slightly in a smile.

She was happy. So happy that it felt wrong to tell her about the rumours that were spreading among the people of El Prado, to tell her that they called her mother a prostitute and her an illegitimate child, either that, or a foreigner who had come to stir up the masses. Wrong, Lina thought, and as cruel as cutting the vocal chords of a canary intoxicated by the harmony, purity and resonance of its own song, something very small and fragile, obliviously absorbed in the joy of achieving its wonderful raison d'être. Even though she was familiar with Divina Arriaga's story and her calamitous dealings with the city, Lina could not fathom all this resentment; back then, she could not suspect how unbearably subversive it was for society to have to acknowledge a woman who was not only free in her own eyes and in the eyes of others but also, and most importantly, capable of sweeping away any illusions with just one glance, stripping the king of his finery and going even further, to the realm where the king had never existed and would never exist. Understanding this meant having fully assimilated Aunt Eloísa's reasoning, crediting Divina Arriaga's rebellion (at least before her illness began to blunt her intellect) with the metaphysical character her aunt ascribed to it, comparing it to a battle that aimed to violently expose the hypocrisy of society's traditions and its false sentiments by kicking the male order in its Achilles heel so that a new morality could be built on its ruins. Lina could only take this assertion as a theory, telling herself, though not with any real conviction, that at the least it could serve to explain why everyone flinched at the memory of Divina Arriaga, sensing a danger they could not name, with an apprehension that strangely morphed into respect, overriding any desire for aggression; even when she was ill and apparently ruined, her enemies still chose to leave her alone, like an evil deity who was best avoided but whose power they tried to exorcize by constantly slandering her. She did not have her mother's wealth or her arrogance, but she did have the naivety to believe that she could expose herself to slander without any consequences, or that she could show up at a country-club ball when most of its members supported Rosario Gómez purely because she was her rival.

The ball was not officially part of the schedule, and the local organizers of the pageant had planned to select the winner at the Hotel del Prado the next day, when the candidates were to parade in front of a jury composed of lecherous old men, following the model of traditional beauty pageants. But the owner of the *Diario del Caribe*, outraged by the contempt the country club had shown to the girl representing his newspaper, had demanded that the club's board of directors host a reception in honour of both candidates so as to demonstrate his impartiality, and Catalina decided not only to attend—ignoring the warnings from Pura de Altamirano, whose former experience as a woman of the world and her more recent troubles as an impoverished widow had sharpened her sense of social awareness—but to wear her most sumptuous dress for the occasion, a white chiffon gown embroidered all over with tiny ivory beads, and to pair it with a magnificent pearl necklace from her mother's jewellery box, the same one Divina Arriaga had worn so often on her nights of splendour, when she emerged from her cloud of worshippers like the eye of a goddess reflecting the light.

Lina turned up at the villa in El Prado early in the morning. Catalina had learned how to do her own make-up by then, letting Angélica, a Spanish woman with magic hands, style her hair, brushing and curling it to make it even fuller. But that night Angélica, inspired by the style of the dress or perhaps taking her cue from some mischievous sprite, decided to pull Catalina's hair down to her earlobes and fasten it in a bun at the back, so that, from the front at least, it was curiously reminiscent of a garçonne hairstyle. When Catalina appeared in the living room, where her friends were waiting for her, Lina felt like she'd stepped back in time and Divina Arriaga was standing right in front of her: she had the same dazzling beauty, the same defiantly elegant posture, the same hint of sensuality in the lustful green of her eyes. She was a perfect replica of her mother, who was dozing on the upper floor, letting her consciousness drift between flashes of lucidity and infinitely long, suffocating hours of oblivion. But only a physical replica, because Catalina's appearance did not match her personality in any way. Watching her cross the room, Lina remembered that a few days earlier the same comment had provoked a scathing response from Aunt Eloísa, who thought that a person's personality did not equate to their nature, because in her view one of those things was formed on the basis of the other, which in turn was its innate, unchangeable, probably hereditary essence. Then Lina realized that Catalina evaded all definition. While Dora struck her as being amorphous, and she, Lina, tended to have a gloomy view of herself, Catalina defied all definition, as if the thing that set her apart had been out of view until then, concealed behind a stubborn and perhaps unconscious desire to adapt; despite having known her since childhood and growing up and studying alongside her, Lina had never managed to break through the barrier of politeness and self-assurance she had built around herself. Suddenly she was caught off-guard by Catalina's affability, her tendency to go around ignoring the harsh realities of life, always finding the most immediate solution. And although Aunt Eloísa claimed she could detect the presence of a latent force in all this, something like an embryo deliberately delaying the moment to reveal itself while waiting for circumstances it had already foreseen, Lina told herself that, whatever her aunt had to say on the matter, Catalina's practicality—which made her inclined to adapt to anything without being discouraged by adversity—was part of her nature, and as such, her nature had caused her to make a false move that night. After all, Catalina had decided to go to the country-club ball not in an attempt to challenge her critics (which she did not even know she had) or to humiliate her rival by wearing that outfit which, lending her magnificent poise, made a mockery of the idea that she was competing with her for a crown or anything of the sort. But being pulled in two separate directions, with Pura de Altamirano warning her not to go to the ball and the *Diario del Caribe*'s owner determined to see her at the club at any cost, Catalina had taken the easier route, bowing to the stronger will without stopping to consider the repercussions of her decision.

Not that she or anyone else would have been able to consider the consequences. Even Lina hadn't seen it coming, and she had given plenty of thought en route to all the different ways in which they might be snubbed when they arrived at the country club: an icy welcome, impromptu applause, aloof greetings. In fact, the country-club members had been taken aback by the news of the ball, because they were accustomed by now to seeing Rosario Gómez appear with her entourage every Saturday night and were convinced that, despite her being only modestly attractive, the jury would have the decency to make sure she won. The more intelligent men among them thought that the scandal caused by the matter was excessive, secretly likening it to an outburst of collective hysteria. Cautiously, they chose to keep quiet, not only to avoid fuelling their wives' bitterness but to temporarily redirect those resentments towards another target, as well as giving them the illusion that they were exercising a moral power, one that in no way contradicted their husbands' power, but instead reinforced it. But when it came to Catalina, most men reacted passionately: she was the child-bride of tempting beauty, but she was out of bounds because of her age. Most importantly, she was the daughter of Divina Arriaga, whom the gossipmongers had turned into a lustful fantasy for those men, with their domesticated wives and their banal, ever-predictable prostitutes, conjuring the image of the all-consuming sensuality they had divined at some point in their childhood and been looking for in vain throughout their life: unrecognizable, disjointed, mortal desire, crying out its frustration in the underworlds of the unconscious. Suddenly, that image had come back to earth and was sashaying up the steps of the country club like a mischievous nymph, her green eyes sparkling; once again those men felt the same yearning and involuntarily began to clap, loudly, louder and louder, repeating her name, the same way they'd called for Divina Arriaga so many times before, from the dark depths of their bodies. Radiant, Catalina walked down the hallway and smiled at them. She was smiling at them as the first tomato burst against her shoulder and, like a bloody tumour, rolled down her beautiful white chiffon dress. A hand reached out to grab her necklace, someone cut the power, and then everything descended into chaos. By the light of the matches anxiously flaring here and there in the darkness, Lina saw chairs flying and people running; she saw men punching each other, women chasing the beads of the necklace that were rolling across the floor, and the orchestra's musicians holding their instruments in the air to protect them. They were all beside themselves, everyone except Catalina: she had been showered with rubbish, her mother's necklace had been ripped off, her dress was torn and there were fingernail marks embedded in her back. Yet her face showed no pain or humiliation. Only shock. Icy shock. As she helped Catalina make her way to the door, Lina, who had also been attacked and was struggling to hold back her tears, was struck by the thought that perhaps, slowly and with great difficulty, having gradually given up on her own body, Divina Arriaga had begun to inhabit Catalina's instead.

That fantastic, almost esoteric supposition would come back to haunt her again and again over the days that followed; instead of being discouraged, retreating or somehow evading people's curiosity, Catalina immediately accepted support from the most Machiavellian person she could count on: a certain Álvaro Espinoza, who had been pursuing her in vain for six months, calling her on the phone and going to see her at the country club at all hours of the afternoon, abandoning his patients at the psychiatric clinic where he reigned supreme as emperor. Álvaro Espinoza had the double advantage of

serving on the board of directors at the country club and
being one of the spoiled children of Cartagena's bourgeoisie,
as he had been born and brought up there before his parents
decided to move to Barranquilla for mysterious reasons.
Catalina had never been able to stand him, his pedantry, his
stubbornness, or the smug way he once assured her that
sooner or later she would be his wife because no other man
would be able to defy society by marrying Divina Arriaga's
daughter. Even without grasping the true meaning of what he
said, and although the interest she was being shown by the
most eligible bachelor of the moment secretly massaged her
ego, Catalina began to hate him from that instant, suddenly
discovering that she found his physical appearance repellent:
his greasy nose with its dilated pores, his constantly wet
mouth, the rancid smell of sweat that clung to his shirts; it
was an aversion so violent that it suggested an obscure attraction that Lina could never fathom. In her naivety, Lina had
agreed to hop over the walls of the country club or run across
the golf course as soon as his Cadillac appeared, black,
imposing and hearse-like, not just to please Catalina, but also
to frolic again with the spirits of chaos, the ones that had
been there when she played hide-and-seek with her cousins at
night or amused herself flouting the nuns' rules. She, Isabel
and Catalina had passed messages to and from the boarders
many times, at the risk of being expelled from school; they
would also escape from sewing class, sneaking into the yard
full of fruit trees, where the nuns forbade them to go,
quenching their thirst on the Spanish limes and plums or
cooling off by spraying their faces with water from the hose.
The fact that Álvaro Espinoza had come to replace the
Mother Prefect did not make any big difference in her eyes,
and the tricks they used to escape kept alive the playful spirit
that Lina would miss so terribly later on, when her childhood
was gone for good. But Catalina's reaction was much more

complex: although her rejection of Álvaro Espinoza was not the work of an adolescent tease, that man's persistence awakened a vague sense of confusion within her, one linked—she would tell Lina years later—to her memory of Andrés Larosca penetrating Dora on the beach in the smouldering dusk; it was not the man himself, his body, or the touch of his hands she desired, but the desire he seemed to feel for her, since he would cross the city at all hours of the evening to see her and was completely unshaken by her rebuffs; nor did she fully believe what he said about it being impossible to find a single man who would be willing to marry Divina Arriaga's daughter, but as she allowed the doubts to creep into her mind, she prepared herself to accept the help he was quick to offer when the members of the country club humiliated her: it was his idea to approach the organizers of the pageant in Cartagena, his friends and even his relatives, asking them to make Rosario Gómez the candidate for Atlántico and Catalina the representative of La Guajira. La Guajira, no less, Aunt Eloisa remarked in dismay, a region that was inhabited at that time by illiterate *indios* who had never laid eyes on a newspaper—and if they had, they would have surely have taken it for a piece of paper that wasn't even worth wrapping their coloured fabrics in. In any case, Catalina arrived in Cartagena bearing that dubious title, trailing four motorcyclists that had been sent there by the mayor, making her way through the streets amid a din of horns, and whipping up the same delirium among the people of that city as she had done in Barranquilla, also attracting a respectful fascination from the members of the upper class, who were more inclined to pay attention to prestigious surnames and skin colour than any wild story of debauchery, as people who had seen and tolerated so much for the sake of class solidarity since the troubled colonial era. Of course, they could not take that defiance to the extreme of awarding her the crown, and, in order to appease tempers, they opted to consecrate their own representative. But Catalina had won: while Rosario Gómez and her entourage were biting their nails with rage in their rooms at the Hotel Caribe, she was receiving all the privileges and distinctions bestowed on the queen: she was invited everywhere, parties were held in her honour, and she was greeted with adoring applause when she swanned into gala balls dressed in increasingly sumptuous outfits, decked out in her mother's jewels and radiating sheer splendour, just like her mother.

As a naïve fifteen-year-old, Lina watched in astonishment as her friend discovered the complicated mechanisms of social success one by one: it wasn't enough to be pretty, to have money or to know how to dress; she had to transform herself mentally by subjecting herself to a kind of self-censorship which, like the creams that smoothed her skin, served to conceal any impurities, any thought that might warp the image she projected of a doll programmed to respond with exquisite stupidity to people who didn't doubt that stupidity for a second, eliminating the most miniscule trace of personality from herself, any look, word or gesture that might reveal a conscious mind, and therefore breaking the spell of those who could only (and only wanted to) adore her as an object. Álvaro Espinoza was no stranger to the new seduction techniques Catalina had started using: he was the one who provided the subtle explanations and the wise advice, not to mention the abrasive response at the slightest hint of hesitation or rebellion. Catalina either had to think like him or not at all; she had to accept that, for the time being, triumphing in society was her sole interest and hearsay her only concern; she had to believe that her cousin Adelaida encouraged her to seek the company of young boys out of a fear of incest, and that when she, Lina, warned her that he was being controlling, she was trying to possess her and thus revealing lesbian tendencies. Álvaro Espinoza defined most people in terms of their supposed pathological traits, apart from his small group of friends, and any men or women who came anywhere near Catalina fell into the category of being impotent or homosexual.

Since she had never heard such words before and could barely grasp their meaning, Catalina listened to him speak, feeling somewhat perplexed. She didn't know whether to see him as a sick person or some sort of sorcerer who was initiating her into the secrets of life, with the same supercilious astuteness he had shown when he decided to debut her in Barranquilla society. His psychoanalytical theories intrigued her without entirely convincing her: she had never met her father nor had she met any men at her boarding school in Lausanne, so incest was a foreign concept to her, and she hadn't seen a man naked until she was fifteen, so the idea that she'd been suffering from a complex since childhood because she lacked a male organ was implausible. As confusing as his theories were, Álvaro Espinoza's words were slowly stirring a sexuality within Catalina, one that had lain dormant until then— partly involuntarily, given her experience as an only child and as a student of cloistered nuns, but also because she had allowed her uncertainty about her first encounter with love to hover in the distance, picturing it as something remote, yet predictable and even inevitable, in other words, as something that was inscribed in her destiny as a woman and that would come along to complete her, putting an end to any possibility she had to project herself into the future. Just like in the films she watched, love was the culmination of the story, where life ended. The curtain came down with that final kiss, and so began the blur of lifelong happiness onto which vague images of children, parties and trips were projected without ever altering the disconcerting vision of a man who, immune to the passing of the years and the ups and downs of existence, eagerly sought the touch of her lips on a beach. That man of her dreams had always been blond, stylish and handsome, with a lively expression, a feline gait and unnerving strength—basically, all the attributes that could make him resemble Andrés Larosca and set him apart from Álvaro Espinoza, that gaunt-faced man with a soggy cigarette permanently wedged between his nicotine-stained fingers. But Álvaro Espinoza was there, he was available and attentive, and he made people respect her simply by leading her into ballrooms on his arm, and it would take Catalina a long time to forget the humiliation she had suffered at the country club. In fact, she never forgot it.

III

If there was any doubt left in Aunt Eloísa's mind that mankind was a species condemned to disappear from the planet, that doubt vanished on August 7th, 1945, while she was still in bed, half asleep, surrounded by her Birmans and drinking her first tamarind juice of the day, and she read in a local newspaper that an atomic bomb had been dropped over Hiroshima. She thought, not that human insanity had reached fever pitch—this had already happened infinite times throughout history—but that it seemed the process that was driving the species to suicide could no longer be contained; in other words, there was no time left to radically change the structure of a society which was unwittingly paving the way for its own ruin by consecrating violence as its mode of action. Folding the newspaper, she thought she could hear the sound of bells tolling for the end of hope, announcing that the nefarious forces from which the patriarchy had emerged were adding the final flourish to their project of desolation, and that the same devil who had impelled mankind to fight for power had ironically given him the power to destroy himself. Until then, attributing a temporary nature to the patriarchy, Aunt Eloísa thought it was a dead-end road where thousands of generations had crashed and burned, one that humanity would turn away from sooner or later to establish a different order, where love triumphed over fear and life ultimately won the battle against death. But in light of such a disaster, there was no point imagining there were better days ahead; one had to accept that salvation began at an individual level, that each person had to break their own chains and tackle repression wherever it might be, using the weapons within their reach, and not allowing any kind of remorse to stand in their way. Men had invented an aberrant organization whose principle and aim were to dominate women: whether she was an innocent or guilty accomplice, woman's victimhood cleansed her of any responsibility because if her intelligence did not succumb to prejudices and her courage resisted the pressures of her environment, all her energy would be used up liberating herself through a slow, painstaking apprenticeship, one crisscrossed with woes and exacerbated by solitude, a journey which culminated with her imposing her human dignity upon the world and began with her stealing language from man, the same language he had cunningly used to make her bend to his will, thus creating the template on whose basis this atrocious relationship—in which every man turned into a wolf in the face of other men—had been devised and executed. In the beginning there was the Word, the Bible said, and at least in this respect, the Bible was telling the truth.

Catalina definitely did not know the power of language, whereas Álvaro Espinoza was familiar with its darkest meanders, having made words his favourite instrument, spending years mastering it while studying at a Jesuit university, and then, when he was confident that the Jesuits had taught him everything they knew about the art of concealing oneself and exposing everyone else, working in a mental hospital in Paris, remaining discreet and seemingly inoffensive but on the alert, with all his tentacles outstretched, ready to capture every last secret of that formidable invention which betrayed the soul, allowing anyone who knew how to use it to uncover feelings, anticipate reactions and break a person's will. The practice of psychiatry or, to be more precise, the relationships formed with his patients, had confirmed his belief that man was a

beast, tyrannized by his most base instincts and unscrupulously seeking the means to satisfy them. As for woman, Freud
had provided the key to her behaviour: castrated and resentful,
her actions had a tendency to lessen the power of the opposite
sex by taking advantage of man's inclination for lust, hence she
had to be confined to the role of simply perpetuating the
species, and provisionally at that, because some day man
would finally be able to do away with her by making children
in test tubes in a laboratory instead. In the meantime, she
would have to be forced to resign herself to her circumstances,
because woman's animosity—like that of Black people, Jews,
the sick and the weak—stemmed from her resentment towards
the power of those who naturally oppressed her, and this was
what caused those foolish conflicts that society tried to resolve
through psychiatry.

He, Álvaro Espinoza, loved order. Not even the ontology
he'd been taught at the Jesuit college had made him any less
repulsed by the abominable chaos that was life: in the infinite
coldness of eternity, in the metallic beauty of the heavenly bodies and the perfect harmony of the Absolute, a deranged will
had come along and introduced this greedy, dribbling, tenacious thing, which began to deteriorate as soon as it came into
existence and had to cause death in order to exist. The idea
that creation had a diabolical origin—with all the doubt this
cast over the power and goodness of God—had put paid to his
ambitions of entering the Order of San Ignacio and prompted
his third suicide attempt. Aunt Eloísa, one of the few people
that his mother used to visit in the city, had seen him that day,
slumped in a rocking chair while his father was crying out in
pain in the next room, in the death throes of delirium tremens.
It was then that Álvaro Espinoza decided to specialize in psychiatry: in order to possess the word and conquer the world
with it, escaping from the doctors who wanted to put him in an
asylum, not to mention the taunts of his fellow students, who

had always despised him, and the indifference of a mother who felt the irresistible need to retreat to a spa in Puerto Colombia on pain of falling into the torment of allergies whenever he was at home. His mother, Doña Clotilde del Real, was classed by Aunt Eloísa as odd, which basically meant she didn't understand her. During the sixties, Lina would laugh to herself, thinking how her aunt would have used the expression "prone to somatization," she had been alive in those times, describing the case of a person who, maintaining the strictest composure, rabidly turned the traumas of their emotional life into illness. But at that time, Doña Clotilde, who had settled in a luxurious apartment on Rue du Faubourg Saint-Honoré in Paris with a toy dog so spoilt it was unsufferable, had overcome all her health problems and spent her time attending editorial board meetings for the feminist magazine that she was largely responsible for financing, or on cruises in the company of her current lover, a ninety-year-old former playboy, who was infatuated with her and as capricious as the little dog. Not a single memory of Barranquilla seemed to graze her recollection, and as for her son, well, Lina decided it was better not to speak to her about him, considering that even he had been so gracious as to walk out of her life for good. In fact, Álvaro Espinoza never truly managed to enter her life, and it was impossible for Doña Clotilde del Real to hide this fact. As far as Aunt Eloísa could remember, no one had ever seen the woman touch her son, not to change his nappy, give him his bottle, take him out for a walk or even just hold him. An overwhelming disgust prevented her from putting her hands anywhere near that viscous, intensely dark creature, pulled out of her by a midwife after forty-eight hours of pain, only to spend the first three months of his life crying desperately day and night, not letting her get a wink of sleep, until, on the verge of madness, she ordered her maid to take him to the servants' quarters, in the Bahareque huts formerly used as dwellings for slaves. When the baby

grew tired of bawling, she gave him the room furthest away
from her own in her house for the sake of convenience, but she
could never bring herself to touch him.

Doña Clotilde del Real had been brought up with the fear
of God—that is to say, with the fear of a particularly dull-witted father, whose reactionary opinions shocked even the most
conservative members of the Club Cartagena: a man who, after
killing his wife by making her endure so many pregnancies, tyrannized his fifteen offspring, demanding that they exhibit an
exacting discipline and the most servile obedience to his will:
none of them had the right to address him by the informal *tú*,
look him in the eyes, speak to him, talk at the table, answer him
back or step out into the street without his permission, and the
slightest offence was brutally reprimanded with one of the
leather whips that hung from the wall in every room of the
house for that purpose. His offspring reacted to this oppressive treatment in different ways depending on their health and
their temperament: the weakest ones never made it to adolescence after succumbing to pox, the common cold, fever or
tuberculosis; two of the survivors stowed away on a boat that
was leaving for Jamaica, and no one ever heard what happened
to them; one of his sons committed suicide, another became an
alcoholic, and then there was the one who spent his youth in
brothels until he caught syphilis and went blind. Nevertheless,
Don Cipriano del Real never doubted his pedagogical methods, because, by the grace of God, one of his heirs went on to
take holy orders and eventually become a bishop, and the
other, the one who was most similar to him, served as the
leader of the conservative party of Cartagena for a while and
even became senator of the Republic. His daughters didn't
cause him any serious trouble either, although the eldest two
sought refuge from his despotism behind the bars of a cloister,
thwarting his mission to marry the eldest off to Genaro
Espinoza, the shrewd businessman who had gone from being

204 · MARVEL MORENO

his estate manager to his associate and later his creditor, ruthless but inclined to compromise if it meant he could elevate himself to the ranks of Cartagena's aristocracy. Last but not least, there to rectify the situation was Doña Clotilde: a rather sickly girl, certainly, but docile enough to have never warranted punishment with the leather whip, and in love with a wealthy relative, sadly too young to make use of his fortune to pay off Don Cipriano's debts.

His name was Cristian, and he was handsome. He was sixteen and could not bear the betrothal. His pride of lineage, the fire in his blood and the naivety of his heart would not allow it. As fate would have it, his father bought a horse from an *indio* around that time, a thoroughbred that, having been born in a respectable stable, had fled to the bush as a colt, fiercely gaining its freedom: a jet-black horse that had become a legend, which the hunters said they'd seen running with the wind in the desolate savannahs of the Sinú Valley, its prowess attested to by several pumas with broken necks and the bloody remains of all the dogs set upon it in the hope of capturing it. The *indio* had been more astute: he dug up his grandfather's bow and arrows, then he asked his wife to prepare a concoction of hypnotic herbs, and, after tying a mare on heat to a saman tree, crouched amid the foliage. When the horse awoke in Cristian's father's hacienda, it was in a state of complete despair: it was tied at the neck by a rope, and all around were the barriers of the manège it had been unconsciously fleeing since it was a colt, as it galloped freely, breathing in the wild air, sometimes hungry, worn out by the sun and the insects, flaring its nostrils to follow a trail of water; but without a halter; risking its life at every moment, learning to distinguish the snake from the branch, the smooth bush from the sly puma, the nighttime breeze from the flapping of the vampire bat; but running at its whim with its jet-black mane, kicking up all the dust and the courage and the solitude of the savannah. The horse didn't fear man; it hated him. It had not been stupefied: through its struggle for life, it had regained all the intelligence its breed must have possessed at one time. So when the first farmhand entered the manège, it let him approach; then when he was within reach, it trampled him to death. On the morning of Doña Clotilde del Real's wedding, Cristian had the animal restrained by his farmhands, and once he had mounted it, seeing his father running toward him, he shouted out, a second before he cut the ropes with his machete, that if the horse killed him, he should give it back its freedom. And that was how the rebellious thoroughbred returned to the savannah, and how, when Lina was visiting an aunt's hacienda on the banks of the Sinú River many years later, she would hear talk of a phantom horse that galloped among clouds of dust, crushing those unfortunate enough to cross its path. And how Clotilde del Real would sense it prancing about beneath her window during her seven-month pregnancy with Álvaro Espinoza, feeling an ice-cold liquid trickling between her legs, her body contorted as it tried to expel the foetus that had been planted in her womb by a stranger while she lay unconscious in a bed, still wearing her white wedding dress, deathly pale, just as she had been when she fell to the floor, surrounded by the wedding guests sipping their first glass of champagne, when someone rushed in announcing that Cristian was dead.

Such an incident was relatively insignificant given the social order of things, and Doña Clotilde could have accepted the boredom of a sexless married life if her body hadn't played the nasty trick of mercilessly rejecting her husband's semen and bringing her out in rashes and eczema every time she slept with him. The case, which all the doctors, shamans and charlatans in the city studied closely, was quite unheard-of: as soon as Genaro Espinoza so much as masturbated on the inert, highly virtuous Doña Clotilde, she began to feel a terrible burning sensation in her sexual organs, which swelled up and turned

red, even making her skin flake and leaving her flesh raw, while
the rest of her body, in the same allergic reaction, started stinging as it erupted into blisters much like chickenpox. This torment ceased when their spiritual advisor intervened—in
exchange for Doña Clotilde del Real's jewels being offered to
their church's Virgin—explaining to the couple how such a
phenomenon of repulsion, in its complex Latin meaning of
repellere, indicated that not even the Christian sacrament had
been able to violate the pristine purity of someone who, perhaps as part of some divine plan, was destined for chastity. By
imposing the marriage on Doña Clotilde and making her stray
from the path her elder sisters had forged, her father had likely
committed a detestable impiety, not just by having contradicted the supreme will, but moreover, and most importantly,
because he had handed an innocent girl over to the lustful
ways of someone who frequented the worst brothels in town, a
man whose perversions had been recounted by more than one
horrified prostitute in the confessional. Don Cipriano del Real,
who could allow himself the luxury of regaining his sense of
dignity after rectifying his financial stalemate, immediately
started beating his chest and raising hell against his son-in-law,
accusing him of corrupting his daughter and poisoning her
with a substance putrefied by sin; after all, only certain practices in his private life could possibly explain that vile itching,
so similar in appearance to the blisters that bubbled up after
eating bad seafood. Convinced that he was in the right, he
ended up brandishing the threat of divorce, a prospect that
would not only stub out Genaro Espinoza's social ambitions
but that could also lead to serious questions about his virility,
stirring up the venom of everyone who refused to forget the
scandal his wife had caused when she fainted in the middle of
their wedding on hearing that a youngster thirty years his junior had died, and then later, to add insult to injury, when she
gave birth to a seven-month-old baby, calling his paternity into

question and prompting the snide glances he was sure he could see on the faces of the members of the Club Cartagena when they saw him working the room. Either excessively obliging or overly reserved, Aunt Eloísa used to say, he always somehow managed to disturb the blend of indifference and courtesy that made for polite behaviour. And so he found himself forced to tolerate a *mariage blanc* to a wife he could hold nothing against, because she appeared to feel no attraction to men and ran the house with matronly virtues. He took revenge in his own way, with flagrant nightly binges in brothels and by only taking her out to social receptions; only then would he increase the paltry monthly allowance that meant she could only drink a glass of *aguapanela* for her meal. She accepted her unhappiness with the kind of resignation that was going to earn her the love of her father, subdued by the years and anguished at being unable to pass the glory of his surname on to posterity, since his only daughter-in-law not only hated him but had brought four girls into the world before becoming infertile as the result of a miscarriage.

Gradually, Doña Clotilde's father got into the habit of visiting her every afternoon. Appearing behind a Black woman carrying a basket of provisions, he would sit down on the porch to catch a breath of fresh air, endlessly lamenting, in his senile obstinacy, how that Creole, Simon Bolívar, had ended Spanish rule and allowed slavery to be abolished, shattering the established order that kept each person in their place and sowing the chaos they were made to endure in that wretched country, where even the illiterate could vote in the name of the pernicious democracy. At the time, Doña Clotilde was beginning to read Voltaire and Diderot in secret, and she nodded with a smile, just as she lowered her eyes in disapproval—having cried all day, following the adventures of Iphigenia—if her father declared, flushed with rage, that the liberalists would end up taking women to the polling booths one day.

Meanwhile, the basket of provisions had given way to moro-cota coins, followed by donations of land in Barranquilla, until finally, when her father died, she owned the best part of his assets. So, between incomprehensible outbursts and with quiet cunning, pitting her father against her detested husband and her husband against her dispossessed brothers, she got every-one involved on the pretext of safeguarding her son's fortune, a son she didn't love and whom she would never give a cent of his inheritance. As far as Lina knew, Doña Clotilde would eventually spend that money on psychoanalysis in Spain, as well as two rounds of plastic surgery in the United States and a rejuvenation treatment in Romania, before settling for life with her pampered little dog in the apartment on Rue du Faubourg Saint-Honoré, taking a new lover every six months, depending on where the cruise liners took her. All the men who had made her life so very bitter ended up well and truly dead and buried in Colombia, but hanging on the ivory silk-upholstered walls between two Berthe Morisot paintings was a small oil painting with creases that suggested it had been kept for a long while, depicting a very beautiful young man with passionate eyes standing proud outside the Walls of Cartagena. He had such graceful poise, and such innocent eyes that Lina instantly understood why his ghost had tormented Álvaro Espinoza, contributing in no small way toward his suicide. He, staking everything on the power of the word, had forgotten that the very power of the dead lies in the fact that they do not speak.

His mother did not speak, either. She never spoke. At least not to him. When he went home for the holidays from San Pedro Claver school, where he had boarded since a very young age, he was met with a distinguished, absent woman whose only comment was to enquire about whether his asthma attacks had bothered him much during the school year. He remembered all the nights he'd spent gasping for breath in the nurse's office, clutching the bars of a bed and desperately trying to get a little air into his lungs in that stark bedroom, while a priest held a wooden crucifix in front of his eyes and urged him to call upon the grace of God; the cold showers at five in the morning after a sleepless night, just as exhaustion turned his eyelids to lead curtains; the intense gymnastic exercises, which used to make him wobble at the knees sometimes and, much to his classmates' amusement, sent him tumbling to the floor, completely sapped of strength. But he didn't say anything; he couldn't bring himself to utter a single word. Not because of the fear she struck in him with her indifference—that woman who had already turned away to ask the maid for some cold compresses—but because the only response he could have mustered would have been to wail with all his might, and he had been taught that men didn't cry. Especially not a man who could boast of being both a Jesuit student and the son of a conservative, but above all—and this he barely intuited at the time—not someone whose paternal grandfather had foolishly married a *mestiza* despite the fact that he belonged to the white race, making him one of the chosen few who commanded and ruled the roost. In the beginning he had not noticed that flaw, shielded as he was from the world in the arms of the Black woman who cared for him with ferocious tenderness; there was very little to set him apart from his foster brother, the son of a Dutch explorer, who had a lighter complexion than his own and was blessed with regular features. But everything changed when that Black woman died and the explorer sent for Henk, and he, Álvaro Espinoza, started at a school where the smiling indulgence of the Black people was in stark contrast with the pride and competitive spirit of the white people, where the frail constitution he had inherited from his mother came up against the coarseness of the young boys who had been educated by the Soldiers of Christ; brutally, he was forced to adjust to a different model, and perhaps because the model had no place for him, he stubbornly adopted its values; the more he internalized these values, the more debilitating the asthma attacks became, but there was no other way to join this world of power and win the affection of his father, who was the only person who was willing to love him, albeit not without certain conditions, that is to say, not unless he made an effort to give his surname a respectability it had only possessed by proxy until then, climbing to the ranks that his father had been cheated out of despite marrying a Del Real woman. He, Álvaro Espinoza, did not know this. He was now entering his house through the front door behind a Black boy who was carrying his belongings and climbing the staircase, his back very straight, following the carpet that led, like a red streamer, to the second floor, where his mother was relaxing, sipping on herbal tea with her friends; he pulled back a glass bead curtain and bowed before her, gently kissing the tip of her elusive fingers and heard her asking yet again whether his asthma attacks might have prevented him from getting good grades at school. He felt that familiar cry choking his throat, but instead of staring at her in disbelief, distressed by her terrible aloofness, he managed to greet her friends and then leave in silence, hearing the jingling of the bead curtain behind him on his way out. He had three months of solitude still to go. People saw him accompanying his parents to Sunday mass in a white suit stained with crescent moons of sweat at the armpits, his face covered in purulent zits that he attempted to hide beneath the straw boater hat worn long ago by one of his stylish uncles; sometimes he could be seen on the street, looking skinny, with odd mannerisms and a pensive air about him, as if immersed in profound thoughts that made him oblivious to his surroundings, above all doing his best not to look at or say a word to anyone with darker skin: even then, he was already demonstrating his disdain for Black people, and at social gatherings he never missed an opportunity to expound his arguments against the sons of Ham, declaring that they had never created a true civ-ilization or anything worthy of such a name, and that they had not contributed any scientific discovery, religion, morals or philosophy to the progress of humanity. In Cartagena they called him *farto*, pretentious, believing that his pretensions would fade over time like those juvenile pimples, because in that ancient city of inquisitors and slave traffickers, people were much more discreet and hypocrisy slithered around in baroque subtleties, which the children learned by listening intently as their elders spoke until they discovered the cruel nuances of racial discrimination hidden in the tucks and folds of everyday language, with the same perceptiveness that they employed to distinguish a *mulato*, no longer by reading signs as obvious as the shade of their skin or the waves in their hair, but something more subtle than that—a certain shade of violet in their gums, a dark hue around the nails—thus exposing some affair that had happened fifty or a hundred years earlier, to the delight of a society that was stifled by the weight of hatreds as old as the city walls, where everyone bragged that they knew the life and travels of their ancestors by heart, back to when the first member of their bloodline disembarked in the city for God and the King, sporting a shining breastplate and a helmet adorned with plumes. They were all *mestizos*, of course, try as they might to ignore it—racist, too, even though racism was a concept that could not even be expressed yet, and even though many years later, when that word had become commonplace and Lina was arguing with the most refined member of her class in a Parisian restaurant, she would see that handsome but overly pale face fall, insulted at the mere suggestion of it, because they had never beaten or lynched their Blacks: they loved them, they had integrated them and allowed them to lead a decent life outside of the colonial town of Cartagena; their Blacks could go fishing, clean shoes or sell lottery tickets, and if they were very old or poor, they could beg outside church doors; they were addressed by the informal *tú* with derisive ease but not the slightest hint of contempt; and they, unlike the crack-brained Gringos, tolerated their defects, knowing from the outset that no religion or ideology was going to make them any less roguish, idle or cowardly. It followed that an attitude like Álvaro Espinoza's would aggravate the people of Cartagena and make them wonder whether the Jesuits might have been overestimating his intelligence: though he could achieve excellent grades at school and finish each year armed with prizes and awards, he seemed incapable of adjusting to the most basic rules of coexistence, and to top it all, he had adopted his maternal grandfather's pigheadedness, forgetting just who his paternal grandfather had married. Only his actions as a notorious snitch at the San Pedro Claver school had prevented anyone from refreshing his memory about that, even though by then his classmates had already started indulging in the hateful prank of touching his genitals when there were no Jesuits around to see; in fact, as soon as the coast was clear, they would set upon him, yelling, "Ten bucks to anyone who grabs Álvaro Espinoza's ass," and he would go running for his life along the corridors until he made it to safety or one of them achieved their aim. It was partly because of this game that the truth about his miscegenation was thrown in his face later on, in a way that everyone including Álvaro Espinoza himself would rather forget, except for one of Lina's future friends, who had committed the scene to memory, to pinpoint the onset of his own paedophilia, he said, the indescribable pleasure he felt when he saw any young boy, coarse like sandpaper, lose all sense of arrogance when he discovered the abyss of passivity that lurked in an organ he'd regarded as an object of action until then, looking at it with the same expression of ashamed lasciviousness that flashed in Álvaro Espinoza's eyes when one of the Ribon twins touched his penis and his penis hardened, dampening his school trousers, to the astonishment of the boys who had been following from the soccer pitch, while the other twin, horrified, loudly declared that only a fucking half-breed could be such a faggot.

From that moment on it was impossible for him to offset his misfortunes with the pride of belonging to an elite race. Still, he, Álvaro Espinoza, must have noticed that his father's family tree neglected to mention the ancestors on the maternal side, as if one generation of boys in his family had been born by some divine breath, and yet he had never tried to get to the bottom of the enigma, perhaps because he was afraid it might confirm that his grandmother had really been a beautiful *mulata* of unknown descent who had walked into the city one day barefoot, accompanied by a mangy-looking dog and carrying her flip-flops in a bundle with the steamed corn rolls her godmother had given her before she waved her off and told her to go to look for honest work in Cartagena, warning her to keep her legs well and truly closed no matter what promises they made, advice that this wide-eyed little lady with golden skin would follow to the letter, securing a job as a maid in the Espinoza household and tenaciously resisting the pressures, threats, flattery and attentions of the only single boy in the family until she finally drove him wild with desire and got him down the aisle; nine months later, when she died in childbirth, the boy, Genaro Espinoza, was entrusted to the care of one of her father's sisters, who was married but infertile and incredibly neurotic; though she thought of him as a son, she could never forgive him for having been born from the womb of a commoner, and she was plagued by confusing and probably incestuous feelings, either covering him with kisses in unexpected fits of tenderness or flogging him if some whim or act of disobedience happened to remind her of the detested *mulata* who had discredited her family with her cunning ways, which she cursed and secretly envied, while Genaro Espinoza struggled with a dreadful restlessness that he had nipped in the bud with his first visit to a brothel—where he discovered the comfort of being able to treat women like cattle—but which would return to him forty-six years later when he married Clotilde del Real and found himself thrust back into the confusion of his childhood, in other words, at the mercy of an impulsive woman who was wild and unfathomable, or at least far more complicated than any animal.

All these experiences had given him a deep-rooted conviction that women existed to pervert a man's character, stripping him of his dignity in brothels, or infuriating him when they took refuge behind the devious veils of marriage and used a thousand subterfuges to evade his control. There were certain things in life that he, Genaro Espinoza, did not really understand, and as he would repeat tirelessly years later in his alcohol-induced ravings, he believed that women had always betrayed him. Perhaps what he was alluding to—even though his consciousness, wisely, did not bear the slightest recollection of the fact— was the ancient betrayal that had befallen his Jewish ancestors, who, renouncing their beliefs to escape the Inquisition, had been harassed to such an extent that they ended up seeking anonymity in Cartagena. But the real treachery began in the mists of time, and it seemed that it had no name and could not be explained: he knew (because he had been told, and because everything he saw around him confirmed it) that there were differences between men, establishing a hierarchy in which the most able men occupied the best posts and, consequently, had the right to demand the submission of their subordinates. The problem lay precisely at the level of this subjugation, which was too elusive and devoid of substance, as if the people who endured it were under the impression that they were performing a comedy where the roles could be reversed without them realizing. Observing the behaviour of the poor on his business trips to the Colombian interior—the way they tipped their hats, looked at the ground, and mumbled a *su merced* as they shrank down into their ponchos—he'd concluded, perhaps hastily, that the self-confidence of the people from the coast could be explained by geography or was somehow linked to the humidity of the climate, the strength of the sun or the intensity of the light. These theories kept the drunkards at Club Cartagena entertained and eventually bored them to sleep, and then later, when his intellectual faculties started to dull from all the drinking, they escalated into bare-faced rants against the trade winds, which he blamed for the slovenliness of decent people and the lack of respect shown by commoners. But although he was obsessed with the social phenomenon of how, on the Atlantic coast, the subalterns didn't internalize the inferiority of their circumstances by resorting to a wall of amusing nonchalance that made them hard to fathom, Genaro Espinoza never stopped blaming women for all his sorrows, because it was through them that misfortune had befallen him, ever since he came out of the belly of the scheming *mulata* who regrettably seduced his father, until he married that elusive woman whose body broke out in rashes at the slightest contact with him, turning him into the laughing stock of Cartagena. The whores, too, would eventually destroy his self-confidence, when he grew older and they started appearing in his dreams, sardonic and smiling, emerging from the depths of his recollection clothed in the luxurious robes of courtesans and odalisques; those women, the filthy dregs of society whom he'd whipped as he pleased, not to mention urinating over their bodies and ejaculating in their mouths, had etched their image into the backs of his eyes when they watched him pull on his trousers and toss a few coins onto the canvas cot. And that image would stay there as long as they lived, perhaps even when they died, reflected in an eternal eye from whose retina no image would ever disappear.

But still, a whorehouse was where he took his son as soon as he found out about the disgraceful turn of events at San

Pedro Claver: terrified of adding to his long list of troubles the prospect of being the father to a homosexual, he threatened to report the madam, Doña Ofilia, to the police, the priests and the Catholic Ladies unless she managed to make his son copulate in the proper way, vowing to stay there, in a hammock in the yard, until someone came to tell him the good news, for which he was willing to pay one hundred times the price of all the girls in the brothel, or rather, the equivalent of a cow in perfect health. He waited for three days. Three days of anguish for Madame Ofilia, who, after locking the sombre young man in a bedroom she could see into from a conveniently located slit in the wooden wall, started to parade her whores one after the other: the beautiful Black women with shiny skin, the big *mulatas* with ripe breasts, the pale white women with bleached hair, and her collection of young girls, dwarves, albinos and Down's syndrome girls; in short, all the different kinds of females that could arouse male desire—but still the stupid boy did not show the slightest sign of virility. He continued to crouch there in a corner, anxiously fiddling with his rosary beads, choking from asthma if they came anywhere near him, while she, Madame Ofilia, called upon Shango on the one hand and Saint Anthony on the other, appealing to them for the right combination, for mercy, for the spark that finally lit up her mind when she heard a student from San Pedro Claver talking. Since she was also aware of the young rogue's hatred for people of colour, she sent out a distress call to her colleagues, asking them to send her a firm-buttocked black girl, even if they had to drag her out of hell itself: one who looked as much like a young boy as possible, and accustomed to having sex in the wrong hole. That was how she saved her brothel, and it was also the beginning of Álvaro Espinoza's sex life. For years, his sexual preferences did not cause him any real issues, because he lied in the confessional and an extra dollar or two in the brothels overcame any kind of resistance, but Aunt

Eloísa believed that by the time he got to Paris, his studies in psychiatry must have taught him that sodomy was perverse and a sign of latent homosexuality, which he would have to fight against with his strength of character if he wanted to dominate in the world of men. Because he returned from Europe a changed man. And, much to the astonishment of the prostitutes in Barranquilla, who had known all about his little quirks ever since his family settled in the city, he came back making love as God intended, between doling out hateful insults and imbibing the equivalent of two bottles of whiskey, slowly, sitting at a table in the company of his friends, where he appeared to be focused on the conversation but was following the comings and goings of the girls with a keen eye, aiming to choose the one who had done the rounds the most times that night: hence his nickname Morning Rooster, which a drunkard blurted out on the day of his wedding to Catalina. Puzzled to see him still at the party late into the night, when he really ought to have left after they had cut the cake, prompting knowing looks or wistful grins from the guests, instead of the bewilderment on their faces when they realized he was there with them, caught up in a political debate, impenetrable as ever, barely blinking as he stared his conversation partner not in the eyes but right between his eyebrows to disconcert him and gain the upper hand. Even Catalina was baffled: she'd tried to understand Álvaro Espinoza's indifference during their three months of courtship by telling herself that a man of his age and standing couldn't be so irresponsible as to take her for a drive to the hills of El Prado for a kiss and a cuddle, because someone might find them and then tongues would be wagging with rumours that could tar a psychiatrist's respectable image. Since the day she'd introduced him to her mother, making their engagement official, Álvaro Espinoza had gone no further than to invite her to dinner every night at the country club or the Hotel del Prado, where she devoured

218 - MARVEL MORENO

Chateaubriands, French fries and various desserts under his obliging eye, and so she'd come to accept that their romantic relationship boiled down to a kind of endless feast—a substitute, Aunt Eloísa explained when Lina told her how, invited by him and some friend or other of his, she had spent the night watching a procession of dishes long enough to curb even the appetite of a castaway.

And yet, Catalina dreamed. Though not one for reading, she had started making forays into Divina Arriaga's library, an Ali Baba's cave of thought containing most of the books ever written—the religious, the cursed, the scholarly, the banned— almost always in their original versions if they were printed from the fifteenth century onwards, or in lavishly illustrated manuscripts if they came from the more remote past, each one categorized by subject in rectangular glass cases and lovingly safeguarded by Divina Arriaga's maid, who spent much of the day inspecting them under a magnifying glass to determine the toll that the years had taken on the ink, paper or wood, and using an array of little brushes and mysterious, strange-smelling products to repair them, as if in one of her former lives she'd inhabited the body of a Benedictine monk from whom she'd inherited the proverbial patience that allowed her to lock herself away for hours in that sanctuary, with the curtains drawn and a kind of alchemist's air furnace designed to combat humidity. It must have been the maid who showed Catalina where to direct her investigations, perhaps with the same laconism and the same kind of concise, impersonal explanation she gave her when she came into her room with the Kotex box four years earlier; otherwise, Catalina would have got lost in the labyrinth of that dark room, where tiers of glass rectangles kept those words embalmed like pharaohs in their tombs, preserving them for eternity, but in the meantime fostering the curiosity of a girl who had never really questioned anything until the day when Lina found her sitting at a table studying the great oriental erotic guides in the faint glow of a table lamp, from the *Kama Sutra* to the *Gita Govinda*, from the dialogue between the Plain Girl and the Yellow Emperor to the Japanese shunga images in their intense blacks and blues; all the sexual magic and poetry of civilizations untainted by the unhealthy frustrations of Christianity, where, blissfully, gods made love, teaching men about the pleasures of the flesh, and, perhaps, the possibility to transcend the limits of their condition on discovering, through the vertigo of love, that the many is one, and that hiding behind the diverse is the whole. No one in Barranquilla knew the first thing about this kind of concept of love, least of all Álvaro Espinoza, Aunt Eloísa repeated, her fingers plunging luxuriously into the fur of one of her Birmans and her eyes flashing with fascination as she stumbled upon the trail of Divina Arriaga once again, this time issuing a challenge from her gloomy grave to the man who intended to reduce her daughter to the role of wife, even though Catalina entered into marriage with no experience whatsoever and with the innocence to be expected of a girl who had studied at a convent and who, owing to her circumstances or temperament, had spent her younger years not knowing the first pangs of desire, the unsettling images that suddenly jumped out from between the pages of a book or which slipped away as fast as a snake on waking from a dream, the stifling anxiety as dusk fell, and that angry, incomprehensible sadness when the sky went dark, announcing the imminent arrival of rain, living in an empty house where no man would ease her worries or dispel her fear with a word. She, Catalina, was more naïve than a twelve-year-old girl, but still she'd been willing to grasp the deeper nature of sexuality ever since she was a child—out of ignorance, because no one had introduced the ghosts of repression to her mind back then, and her flippant nature made her view the nuns' religion absent-mindedly, not really internalizing it or analyzing its concepts in any depth, truly believing that the loss of Paradise had been caused by the simple act of eating an apple, and surprised that such a triviality had caused men so many heartaches, forcing the best of them to be nailed to the cross for their redemption.

Perhaps Divina Arriaga also had this in mind when she'd enrolled Catalina in a religious institution: her imperviousness, her tendency to make light of human discourse, evading any attempt to steal her soul or to do anything to change the feeling she had deep down (but had yet to express) that the only way to find balance was by loving herself; although such subtle foresightedness seemed highly debatable, Aunt Eloísa was convinced that Divina Arriaga had chosen to send her daughter to La Enseñanza with the deliberate intention of stopping Catalina being accepted into a group of female friends, thus conforming to a defeatist ideology due to the renunciations required for this integration. In fact, none of Catalina's classmates had ever dared to defy popular opinion by inviting her to their house and allowing her to join the circle of girls who were destined to eventually make their societal debut together, frequenting the country club until they got married, and finding various excuses to meet up during the holidays until then, from playing cards to embroidering all kinds of useless rags for the poor; their conversations, which consisted of little more than repeating gossip, spouting clichés and swapping ridiculous ideas of what the sexual act entailed, prepared them to reproduce the species in ignorance and disillusionment, just as the social order dictated. Spared from all that nonsense thanks to the discrimination she experienced, Catalina had preserved the purity so highly prized by the moralists, giving her the perfect ability to hear the call of sex, that distant, eternal cry which was echoed fully by the books she found in Divina Arriaga's library, and which helped her to discover the hidden springs of eroticism in her body and to imagine any man, including Álvaro Espinoza, determined to lose himself with her in that lustfulness she sensed when they were dancing and their cheeks brushed, or when he gently kissed her lips each time he said goodnight to her in the darkness of his black Cadillac, never suspecting the fires that his feeble caresses ignited within her, the longing and heat that rose to her cheeks as she waited for the ceremony that society required for the two of them to tear down the thin walls standing in the way of desire.

This ceremony was finally held at the country club, with hundreds of guests and a level of sophistication that harked back to those parties held years earlier by Divina Arriaga, represented this time by Aunt Eloísa. Álvaro Espinoza stood there unfazed, impervious to a situation that made him the envy of most of the men in attendance, while Catalina saw the intense blue light of dawn appearing outside the windows and hazily discovered the shadow of disappointment, although she wasn't quite sure where it was coming from, the nebulous rage that pricked at her soul like the sting of an animal which had lain dormant until then—not inside her but around her, because it existed in her environment—and which she had always chosen to ignore, all the while still believing, blind butterfly, that she was escaping her fate thanks to the protection of the goddesses, entities or fairies that had granted her so many favours by making her so beautiful from birth, and quietly telling Lina that maybe Álvaro Espinoza behaved so oddly because he was trying not to alarm her by taking things too fast and offending her sensibilities. Those scruples were going to last much longer than expected: a week, to be precise. In the seven days they spent together in Santa Marta, Álvaro Espinoza set about strengthening Catalina's religious sentiments, which he deemed too half-baked and superficial, taking her to pray before an image of Our Lady of Sorrow every afternoon to make her see that, contrary to what she might think, a woman's purpose was not to laugh, enjoy herself or love, but to bear the pain of humanity, following the example set by that Virgin who, when the torn sky cried for the death of the Son of God, had stood alone next to the cross, alone and carrying on her fragile shoulders the weight of the sins committed by men. Catalina was dumbfounded. She would later tell Lina that she had initially wondered why Álvaro Espinoza insisted on driving her to a church when he himself, given his psychoanalytical understanding of the facts of life, was clearly completely sceptical of religion: she seemed to be deliberately at sea, caught between two opposing discourses that in fact pursued one and the same aim, namely to dispossess her of something, although she could not pinpoint where exactly this something was, and although, in a complete state of confusion, she not only began to question everything that Divina Arriaga's erotic manuals had taught her, but to tell herself that if it weren't for seeing Dora and Andrés Larosca making love on that beach, she would have been able to accept that the sexual act simply involved contemplating the suffering face of a Virgin and then going to bed after dining sumptuously, while Álvaro Espinoza wished her goodnight and headed out on the pretext of going for a few drinks in the hotel bar, tiptoeing back into their room at daybreak.

She told Lina this in the living room of her new apartment the day after she returned from their honeymoon, carefully analyzing each fact as if trying to reconstruct the moves of an opponent who had put her into checkmate and beaten her in a game of chess. By that point there was no doubt left in her mind that she had unwittingly come up against a man of calculating intelligence, who had decided to behave in a particular way toward her, predicting her reactions and tenaciously seeking to humiliate her until finally he defeated her and could inflict his schemes upon her. It was a subtle manoeuvre. She recalled how the first comment she made about how abnormal their situation was prompted such a barrage of insults that she had cried all night long: because the Álvaro Espinoza she knew, severe and opinionated, yes, but always polite, had used obscene language, telling her that subjects of that sort could only be of interest to a slut—or to Divina Arriaga's daughter, which was the same thing. This insult, despite traumatizing her by alerting her awareness to a conflict that had been judiciously suppressed, interested her with hindsight in the sense that it helped her to recognize a form of manipulation that was designed to diminish her self-confidence, leaving her wounded and with no will of her own—in other words, incapable of making the only sensible decision in the circumstances, which would be to put all the embroidered silk lingerie and dresses that Divina Arriaga's maid had ordered for her from Europe into a suitcase and to return to Barranquilla, at the risk of creating an enormous scandal; because while Álvaro Espinoza launched into long-winded speeches as they stood there before a painting of Our Lady of Sorrows, the local journalists continued to comment on their marriage, and a photographer had been sent to snap the happy couple on their honeymoon. Ultimately, there was no way she could flee: she didn't want to find herself being cast out of society again or to somehow end up in a situation like the one she'd been in before that awful experience at the country club, even though by this point she was already beginning to work out that Álvaro Espinoza was relying on her fear in order to subject her to a humiliation whose purpose she could not understand, no matter how much she thought about it night after night, eating less and discovering insomnia, lying in the solitude of their hotel bed, sometimes picturing herself as the victim of some kind of physical defect that only a doctor could perceive, but swiftly dispelling those speculations when she noticed the covetous or admiring gaze of a man on the beach, then hating Álvaro Espinoza with an aversion so intense that it caught her off-guard, bringing strange thoughts to the surface of her mind—thoughts that rose to the surface, she would explain to Lina, still mystified, as if they had always been there, though they were veiled and hard for her conscious mind to grasp, like the flickers of an ancient dormant memory, the creaking of a statue, murmurs from a grave. Hence, almost without realizing it, she'd started to pull at the yarns that, years later, would lead her to untangle the skein and toss the jumble of crumpled wool into the rubbish.

For the time being, however, the yarn that caught her eye was the one which helped her understand that Álvaro Espinoza not only intended to hurt her and plunge her into perplexity with his nocturnal absences, but most importantly, that he was waiting for her body to be ready to be fertilized. And while this conclusion did not exactly explain anything— in fact, it aggravated her bitterness, knowing that she had been reduced to the value of her reproductive organs and nothing more—it at least allowed her to more or less pinpoint when they were going to surrender to the voluptuousness of that eagerly awaited pleasure, believing in her gullibility—this word she herself would use—that love was one thing and all men experienced it in the same way, without making the slightest connection between the way it was approached and the prejudices people might have towards it—in other words, as if someone pressed an invisible button and their bodies entered a kind of ecstasy that chased away resentments and memories, giving way to the fires of passion. And so her own indifference surprised her the day when, just as she predicted, Álvaro Espinoza invited her to join him at the bar after the meal and announced in a sombre tone that they would be sleeping together that night.

She would tell Lina how she spent hours keeping watch for any sign of emotion inside herself, following the slow progress of the pale moon across the night sky while he sat there drinking and drinking, indifferent to her presence, silent and seemingly absorbed by his resentment, as if a furious battle raged in his heart. But she felt nothing, she would say; she did not discover the magic spring of desire. She stayed by his side, pervaded by a feeling of emptiness, until he finished drinking the bottle of whiskey and summoned her into the bedroom. As they were getting ready for bed and she heard him moving around in the bathroom, she noticed his silhouette in the glow of the lamp, and she still felt that same emptiness, the ice-cold sensation of being conscious and nothing more. Afterwards it was different. It was the shock she felt when he yanked up her delicate lace nightgown from Brussels and threw himself on top of her, where he stayed for several minutes, motionless, his eyes closed and his face twisted in steely concentration again, like an athlete grimacing in one last effort to reach his goal, then suddenly she felt something hard between her legs, something blindly and brutally forcing its way through, causing her unimaginable pain, a pain so violent that she started to cry, and then Álvaro Espinoza's hand was over her mouth, and she heard him mumble spitefully: "This is what you wanted, bitch: now you've got it."

IV

It must have taken a lot of contemplation for Aunt Eloísa to understand the phenomenon of subjugation, because having never been bound to anyone, it was hard for her to imagine that a sound-minded individual would willingly submit to another person's whim. She said she'd taken the right path when, ceasing to look outward, she began to take an interest in the exceptional case she formed with her sisters and her cousins, all of whom shared an innate revulsion toward any form of authority and belonged to a family where, for at least five hundred years, women had mostly given birth to girls and became widows early on, always falling in love with two types of men, who were complete opposites but fundamentally the same, or at least controlled by the same obsession with self-destruction: the melancholic men who let themselves die, enervated by sadness, and the troubled men who spent their whole lives trying to get themselves killed until finally they succeeded. The fact was, the women in the family were left alone at a very young age and forced to run the family business in order to support their daughters, unknowingly replicating, on a smaller scale, a social structure that appeared and renewed itself with every generation, representing the antithesis to the patriarchy, since no hierarchy was established among its members, and not only was property naturally regarded as a common good, but profits were distributed irrespective of individual performance. When Aunt Eloísa's mother became a widow, there was even a time when all her aunts and relatives occupied two blocks near San Nicolás square and the back yards of their houses were connected by doors that were always left open so that the children could come and go, and were free to play, eat or sleep wherever they wanted. Structured in this way, the community allowed the women to pass on their legacy but not the cultural values that they all viewed with distrust—apart from a few stray sheep who had happened to find a particularly strong or curiously level-headed husband—having learned as young girls to regard these values as a direct emanation of the Law of the Father, which in no way concerned them but rather posed a threat to the unusual, fragile, yet resilient family structure that allowed them to find their balance, because any time they deviated or took a wrong turn, they found the community poised not to exclude but to embrace them, to understand their predicament with the calm generosity of spirit of women who had accepted themselves, could tolerate difference and found the desire to control others juvenile. Everything was permitted among these women, and while the family was large and the city remained small, no serious conflict came between them. But later, as the city grew like an immense ivy, it began to suffocate them, and they had to pretend to adapt to its practices in order to survive, losing themselves in the pretence at times, but secretly retaining the solidarity of the old clan, where problems were resolved amid soft voices and smiles.

Everything was allowed, even sexuality. Neither Engels, Freud nor Reich had been conceived in the mind of the Almighty when Doña Adela Portal y Saavedra, the revered genetrix of the family, arrived in Cartagena de Indias to run the plantation that had belonged to her third husband, a Spanish admiral who had died at sea; she disembarked with her daughter and her granddaughter in tow and the strong conviction that only an error in the natural order of things could explain the predominance of men and their foolish habit of debilitating women by imposing chastity on them from childhood.

How such a distinguished lady had come up with ideas like these, no one ever knew, but from that point on, in every generation there was always someone who would come along to stoke the subversive embers of feminism, and when the torch passed into Aunt Eloísa's hands, that liberal way of thinking had already made its mark and Doña Adela Portal y Saavedra's brilliant intuition, the link she made between sexual repression and the exercise of power, could be thought of in simple terms and tackled within the terrain of male ideology. And of course, Aunt Eloísa was not going to let this opportunity pass her by. She, a woman whose love affairs and business dealings often took her to Europe, had followed the babble of psychoanalytical theory step by step: from its horror at discovering the importance of sexuality, to what one might call its lamentable surrender, in other words, the way in which—out of ignorance, cowardice or ill intent—the subject had refrained from deriving logical conclusions from its own discourse, getting caught up in assumptions whose purpose was to subdue the uproar and preserve the established order. This inevitable outcome wouldn't wash with Aunt Eloísa: she didn't believe that the pleasure of love was at odds with the effort of work, she flatly rejected the patriarchal model of civilization, and whereas Freud maintained that sexual repression was its corollary, she was able to argue that, curiously, the restraint in question had always been applied to women and never to men, not even as an afterthought. However, the very essence of the theory suited her down to the ground in the sense that it provided a structure for an understanding which had always been overshadowed by the weight of traditions but could suddenly be labelled, forcing people not only to acknowledge that repression existed and was at the heart of all neuroses, but most importantly, that its existence was the *sine qua non* for power. Hence Aunt Eloísa's enduring refrain: since chastity was imposed on women in order to control them, rendering them infantile, dependent and faint of heart, any woman who wanted to assert herself would have to claim her sexuality first.

This lengthy analysis was not presented to Lina in any order; rather she would hear it in snippets over the course of many years, following her Aunt Eloísa's musings when she talked to her sisters in the quiet half-light of her living room, while the fans cooled the air and the Birmans slumbered, waiting for the sun to flee the horizon so that they could disrupt the peace of the night garden with their love affairs, while somewhere in the house incense burned and scented the air replete with words spoken by other men and women at the ends of the earth, whose echo could only resonate there. Lina listened to her relatives speak, not asking them anything or understanding all that much, vaguely intuiting that these splintered ideas would eventually arrange themselves in her mind when circumstances plucked her from the cottony uncertainty of her adolescence. And yet, she recognized that what Aunt Eloísa said articulated an understanding of something that Catalina was trying to uncover blindly, like symbols carved in an ancient stone, which she could trace with her fingers but could not see or decipher as she hopelessly scrambled to find her way out of the predicament she had been cast into by a seemingly harmless marriage, assimilating it into a barb-covered maze where she could barely move because any expression, word or silence from her immediately prompted the scathing criticisms of her husband, who was hell-bent on convincing her that she was his inferior and had to conform unconditionally to his view.

Initially, during her pregnancy, Catalina had been overwhelmed by her experience of marital life, like a rat in a laboratory learning to recognize, either through pain or fear, the levers not to approach—or perhaps worse, because rats in a laboratory were likely given reward stimuli or moments of rest, whereas she found herself at the complete mercy of Álvaro Espinoza's animosity without any mercy or recompense, and in a state of total confusion, incapable of arguing with his methodical rhetoric aimed at diminishing her value, treating her like an imbecile whenever she dared to offer an opinion, or like someone depraved if, taking many precautions and overcoming her reserve, she attempted to rebel against a concept of sexuality that oppressed her. However, what truly set her apart from the rat was not so much the desperate desire to run away as the will to comprehend the validity of the logic that Álvaro Espinoza used to torment her, because while the nuns had not succeeded in instilling their precepts into her at school, Catalina had learned from mathematics that every hypothesis had to be strictly verified. Álvaro Espinoza's behaviour was incomprehensible to her, even though she'd gradually managed to distinguish between the ways in which he expressed himself, scrutinizing his behaviour with the formidable capacity for concentration that Lina had seen her employ so many times when faced with a chess problem: on the one hand, he had that obsessive need to insult Catalina over the slightest thing, and without rhyme or reason, because any given action and its opposite triggered the same aggression from him; then there was his strange reaction to the allowance he gave her to cover the household costs, which, when it came to balancing the books, triggered miserly disputes about how the money ought to be spent and the liberties, real or supposed, she had taken for her own ends. But very quickly and almost instinctively, Catalina had turned her attention to what was in fact the crux of the conflict, even though she didn't know it at the time: Álvaro Espinoza's fierce refusal to entertain any conversation that remotely touched on the subject of sexuality. And although she was tempted to regard his refusal as legitimate for a while, telling herself that her frustrations and fantasies were signs of abnormality, as soon as her daughter was born she began systematically searching for anything that had ever been said or written about the subject, sparking a dialogue with the books in Divina Arriaga's library until she grasped the sheer scale of the problem, its countless ramifications and its almost metaphysical nature—not to get closer to the sphere of reflection from which her mother had serenely contemplated the world, discerning everything (including sexuality) in its exact dimensions, but to argue with Álvaro Espinoza and force him into a discussion, despite the hunch she had that nothing would make him change his attitude and that he took refuge in language, a territory where he seemed unassailable and could dodge her questions with his verbal pirouettes, which he had learned from the Jesuits and whose secret mechanism he was unwittingly going to teach her. It was the right move: the gods, as everyone knows, never explain themselves, never answer.

Just like Benito Suárez, and possibly repeating the same mistake, Álvaro Espinoza had married the antithesis of the kind of woman who would have logically suited him, setting the scene for his own downfall. A man so cold and calculating, who claimed to understand the innermost secrets of the soul, might have been expected to exercise greater caution, or at best, to behave in a way that was better aligned with the system in which the world, stripped of all its sharp edges, surrendered to him. A wife who was not particularly bright and used to bowing to others would have agreed to live by his side like a shadow. But not Catalina: she flouted respect and, with the nimbleness of a water snake, had always evaded authority. Álvaro Espinoza would have to perform a lobotomy on her if he wanted to control her, because there was one fact that none of his concepts could disguise: if nature had really wanted to confine her to reproduction, she would exist as an entity with the ability to perpetuate the species and nothing more, something like a womb hanging from the trees or floating on the water. So after marrying a woman who lacked what he referred to in his own jargon as a superego, he eventually gave in to vanity and began to unfurl the brilliant logic of his reasoning in her presence, like an army general intoxicated by his powerful weapons, skilled officers and proud insignia, making his soldiers march, day by day, before a tiny, insignificant opponent, one struck dumb with anxiety and admiration but nevertheless forced, by that display of power, to assess its own weakness and gradually imagine ways to fight it.

Declaring war on him would be suicide given the circumstances, whereas the guerrilla warfare of interminable debates posed the dual benefit of exasperating him and keeping her in a state of constant combativeness, and this, given her sporting spirit—horse-riding would be the first activity she took to as soon as her daughter was born—would swiftly prompt her to progress from the ideas she found in Divina Arriaga's library to a desire to tread on more concrete ground, where sex existed not so much in words as in reality. And since Catalina came to the conclusion that no one could know more about this aspect of reality than a prostitute, Petulia furtively entered into their lives.

Before she started practising her trade, Petulia had been quite the lady, leading a dull existence with her elderly husband, Jewish by religion and a jeweller by profession, whom her mother had forced her to marry so that she would never have to want for anything. Her mother had acted reasonably, bearing in mind that so many of her relatives had died in a concentration camp and nothing, not even her arrival in Barranquilla, where the expatriate communities could go forth and multiply in peace, had altered her conviction that the goyim could go crazy and massacre the Jews at any moment, accusing them of eating their children raw or some other such aberration. Petulia did not see things in the same way: from her father, a Greek man who was indifferent to religious matters and in whose fishing boat she had spent the best years of her childhood, she had inherited the taste for adventure and an exuberant sexuality, which did not sit well with her mother's litanies of woe, or the tedium she endured with her husband, who showered her with jewellery but rarely made love to her.

For years she remained faithful to him. Lina used to see her walking past her house, pushing a stroller along the pavement, and later, when the child was big enough to join his father at religious services, she and Catalina would stand there, in the garden where they used to play, admiring the swaying step of that woman, beautiful and glowing like a ripe orange, who, swathed in silk dresses, roamed the streets of El Prado in the evening as cars tailed her almost stealthily, headlights off, with a silence that expressed the anxiety of the men behind the wheel. One afternoon she walked over to them and came straight into their garden, where, lazily swaying back and forth in the old swing, she would tell them about the scent of sea bass fresh out of the water, about the islands with strange names, and about her father, who was so strong that he could lift her from the dock onto his boat with just one hand. Her first lover would be strong too, the Italian she ran away with naively believing that he was going to marry her, and this vigour and burliness, if nothing more, was also evident in the last man Lina saw her with before she left Barranquilla: a hideous truck driver who lewdly clutched her against his body beneath the coloured bulbs hanging from a carnival booth, while Petulia, slightly drunk, her face weary, told him, smiling, that he mustn't grab hold of her like that in front of so many people; Lina remembered her fondly, as she once was.

There was something about Petulia that inspired Lina's respect: she had enough fire and subversiveness about her to embody the legend of Doña Barbara on a local level, and she could have almost gained mythical status herself—in fact, for years she reluctantly became almost a legend among the rich men in the city, who fought over her and displayed her like a hunting trophy. But her steadfast nature made her uncompromising, and, paradoxically, out of the pride she took in staying true to herself, she fell deep into the inner workings of prostitution, doing the rounds in El Prado before moving on to Las Delicias, and then, to the tiny house in Barrio Abajo, where she was living when Catalina found her in a clairvoyant's parlour. Even though by that time, Petulia's disdain for men told her it was wiser to keep them at a distance, she was touched by Catalina's confusion and immediately resolved to take her under her wing, teaching her how to defend herself; or perhaps, tucked away in the folds of some obscure desire for revenge, she wanted to make her see the truth of romantic relationships, helping her to approach them while dodging the traps that had been her own undoing. She was not cultured, and her language lacked nuance, but that didn't bother Catalina: hearing her speak, she realized that the male order had sealed women's fate arbitrarily, condemning some to prostitution and others to the frustrations of chastity. Her instincts—or rather, a kind of belated ability to spot the rare men who, not stricken by a fear of nature, were willing to accept their sexuality without prejudice—would do the rest in the future. Without further ado, and always following Petulia's instructions, she set herself one sole objective: to find out where Álvaro Espinoza drove to on those Friday evenings, when he vanished until dawn and came back reeking of a mixture of alcohol, sex and cheap perfume. Imagining him out on a binge wasn't enough for Catalina: she wanted to see him with her own eyes, leaving that little yellow house with his black Cadillac parked outside, while Lina, at the wheel of her most puritanical cousin's car, listened in the darkness as her friend repeated not only the full list of grievances she had endured since her marriage, but also the various possible explanations for each one of them, her analysis ice-cold but not free from hatred, like an arachnologist examining the attributes of the scorpion that killed her child with its sting, contemplating the strange creature pinned out on her lab bench before performing a vivisection on it; her voice, sure enough, had the impersonal tone of an expert, and her irises, which lit up from time to time with the flare of a match, reflected the irascible shade of green that the ocean turns when a storm is approaching. She hated him, there was no doubt about that, but when she saw him appear on the doorstep, swaying and clinging onto the arm of a sorry-looking girl in gold heels with dyed-red hair, Catalina did not make a scene, as Lina had secretly feared she would: she merely looked at him fiercely, and her face became fixed in heartless concentration, trying, perhaps, to commit to memory the image of that drunk man with his fly undone, staggering as he tried to fish his car keys out of his pocket. That was all she wanted: to creep up on him in the wretchedness of his private life; when the Cadillac drove away along the dimly lit street, she simply said to Lina: "We can go now."

She never discussed the incident with Álvaro Espinoza, and from then on she ceased from challenging his opinions: whether he insulted her or bombarded her with sarcastic comments, Catalina remained impassive, beyond his reach but still attentive to his monologue, catching the mistakes, lies or moments of hesitation here and there which, with help from Divina Arriaga's books, allowed her to follow his train of thought like Kubrick's astronaut who, on taking apart the pieces of the killer computer, discovered the various stages of its programming until he found it learning to babble like a child.

Her hatred, nevertheless, kept her tied to him. As did conventions: thanks to her marriage—and the money that Divina Arriaga's maid discreetly passed on—Catalina sparkled in the ballrooms, becoming a vision of fashion and elegance, a queen whose presence or absence at a party was the main source of concern for the host. The women who had jeered at her at the country club two years earlier now explicitly sought her company and invited her to join the various religious or civic associations in the city; she could often be seen in the street, sporting uniforms of different colours, leading a group of ladies badgering passers-by, trying to sell them little flags, insignia or raffle tickets in the name of altruistic and completely ineffective causes. Serving as more than compensation, in the long run this mundane activity would reveal itself to be a kind of unconscious strategy that allowed Catalina to lose her inhibitions towards Barranquilla's society when, one by one, she discovered the different sides of a world that seemed dull at first, and then threatening, but which now, as the wife of Álvaro Espinoza and a secret friend of Petulia, she could examine in depth and learn how to manipulate. Her initial feelings of bewilderment and indignation at the hand she had been dealt as a woman had given way to a stony selfishness; not without disdain for those who adapted or chose to resign themselves to their fate, she remained cool in her belief that any project of social transformation was out of reach and that she already had enough on her plate trying to make herself secure. Because for years her real objective would be this: to find a way to escape Álvaro Espinoza's control by mercilessly crushing the image he had constructed around himself, a fortress built from the inside out, seemingly impenetrable in the absence of any battlements, embrasures or anything resembling an opening. Eventually, under Catalina's watchful eye, the cracks would show, revealing a vulnerability and allowing the fortress to be breached; the greater his need to protect himself, and the less attention he paid to his opponent—who felt that demolishing those walls was the only way to break free from the oppression—the more gravely he would be wounded. Feeling that way, gradually perceiving a terrible manifestation of anguish lurking under that carapace of power, Catalina waited for the right moment with the calm certainty that she was holding a fan of cards which time had dealt in her favour, while he, a man who liked to pontificate about the mysteries of

the soul, basked in his authority, convinced that he had succeeded in taming a living being, one who was now conscious of
her own intelligence and locked away in a silence so persistent
that, if it did not alarm him, should have made him sense that
a subtle but definite change had taken hold within her.
Catalina's muteness—far from being a fleeting reaction of rage
or contempt—sustained since that morning at dawn when she
caught sight of Álvaro Espinoza leaving the brothel with its
yellow-painted walls, had become a tool that allowed her to
evade the shrewdness of that psychiatrist, whose only means of
understanding her was through language. Everything else—the
things he supposed or imagined that went on inside her
head—was mere conjecture based on theories, and Catalina
derisively let it all wash over her, not feeling the slightest need
to look for arguments to refute his claims; sometimes, in a
game that very closely resembled perversity, she behaved in a
way that allowed Álvaro Espinoza to define her in light of his
own assumptions, in other words, to assimilate her into the
intellectual structure that not only justified his confidence in
himself but also his curious contempt for women: if Catalina
deliberately indulged herself in extravagant whims, he could
be satisfied of the immaturity of the female nature; when she
feigned affection in the presence of her daughter, he had the
proof he needed that motherhood served as a substitute for the
phallus women so yearned for, and, of course, in her systematic
refusal to sleep with him, he believed he was discovering the
frigidity inherent to her sex. Protected by appearances,
Catalina forged her personality, secretly sharpening the ban-
derillas she would thrust into him one day. It seemed Aunt
Eloísa was not wrong when she intuited that Divina Arriaga's
daughter had the ability to defy time: what took other women
a whole lifetime to understand after a long string of hopes and
disappointments, she had learned in just two years of marriage,
getting the exact measure of things and coolly preparing to

embark on a journey of initiation and trials that would culminate in Álvaro Espinoza's death and her own liberation, both of which were prefigured as soon as Catalina became aware that as long as she continued to deny her femininity, she would never be able to regain any kind of dignity.

It happened on a day like any other in Divina Arriaga's beautiful library, which Álvaro Espinoza didn't even know existed: a flash of inspiration, a fortuitous association, or just the right combination of sentences set the mental process in motion that would allow her to defy her husband's rule by taking her first lover, whom she paradoxically chose not based on detached calculations but in a moment of emotion that only related to her original reasoning in the sense that it had been preordained. But she did not reflect on or assess the consequences of her actions, just as at no point did she try to avoid her fascination for the *indio* with the golden eyes, who had met them from Montería airport and, by way of a greeting, with a cheeky glint in his eye, had simply looked the Barranquillan women up and down as they stood there next to the airplane steps, burdened by their puffed-out crinoline dresses, unsure whether to turn back immediately or stay and face the fierce wind in that god-forsaken place, where the humidity in the air was almost tangible, oozing like a thick mist, and the men had never bothered to wear more clothes than strictly necessary to cover up their modesty, with the exception of the *vueltiao* hat, which he himself did not wear, and the three-strap leather sandals he had on his strong, very long, weather-beaten feet—which he was wearing not as a sign of deference, Lina would later learn, but because he put them on every time he went to the city. He usually preferred not to wear shoes, just as, barefoot and without stirrups, he rode the most spirited horse from his aunt's hacienda, a sorrel he had trained up to be muscular and burly, gently encouraging it in a strange language when he worked it in the corral, and taking it out at dawn to gallop

through the dew-sprinkled pastures. Nor did the leather sandals suggest any kind of submission to the city's conventions;
in fact, he wore them to avoid contamination, he said, thus
demonstrating his contempt for the most glaring symbol of the
white man's civilization, which had destroyed his race by
flooding it with diseases imported from other worlds, before
filling the survivors' minds with aberrant concepts intended to
make them feel ashamed of themselves, smashing their identity
to pieces. They, his forebears, had killed and plundered, conquered and defended their land in all-out battles, but they had
never been so bold as to conceive of personal property: they
were already committing a grave crime as it was by helping
themselves to the land's resources, and as atonement they had
to perform very precise rituals, which they had tried to accom-
modate, groping around in the dark as they sought to maintain
balance in the natural order of life, until eventually they
slipped up, and their punishment came when they saw those
men appearing in the grasslands one day, their skin giving off
the scent of death: men who spread death and procreated in
the name of death inasmuch as their rule inevitably sowed discord. And so they had been defeated—defeated but not van-
quished, at least not as long as one member of their race was
still drawing breath, his grandfather had told him, with the
same serene conviction that Lina would hear from one of his
sisters when she told her the same story.

Because he did not speak unless it was to give orders to the
farmhands in his role as ranch foreman. He lived on the other
side of the river, in the back country, and he had turned up at
the house after mounting his sorrel to meet Lina's aunt for
breakfast and to tell her about the problems related to the
running of the property. He glided through the hall with an
assured, stealthy step, barely disturbing the air around him;
then he sat at the table, his head of copper-hued skin,
scorched by many a sun, held high in stubborn, insuperable

indifference. He did not make a single sound; he slowly devoured the various dishes prepared with his big-cat appetite in mind, the fried banana slices and cassava, the chunks of meat and the cheese *arepas*, which her aunt merely picked at out of courtesy to him, still amazed that she had been able to hang on to the best foreman in the region: the *indio* loved by animals and feared by men, whose *güipirreo* call resounded in the solitude of the savannah, guiding some lost calf or lovesick horse; the shamanic man with calm, illicit eyes who ran around at nighttime with an equally agile puma in tow, performing rituals from ceremonies of times gone by; there was something bewitching about him even as a child, when his grandfather made him run barefoot alongside the hunting dogs, faster than them, swifter, pursuing the deer whose trail the dogs sometimes lost but he never did, gently weaving his way among rocky hills and splashing through muddy waters while the pack of hounds hurtled along behind him, with no scent in their nostrils other than the distinctive odour of his tireless body. He was still just a boy the day his legend began to take shape in the square in Cereté—where a hysterical priest, who had arrived from the Colombian interior as the harbinger of La Violencia, was inciting his congregation to turn against the liberals in the area—and he showed up in the company of a former Partido Liberal leader who used to hunt with his grandfather; the two of them, the furious grey-haired man and the twelve-year-old boy, perhaps too small for his age, armed with a riding crop and showing no trace of emotion in his face, where his eyes were the only thing that hadn't been scorched by the sun. He looked at nothing and no one, as if he was entranced. Then the man said: "Go." And that was the last thing anyone heard in the square, or rather, it was the last articulated sound, because like the crack of the riding crop, there was nothing human about the cries of the priest.

From then on people began to fear the *indio*. Even though

he never picked a fight and remained indifferent to everything
that was going on around him, people chose to avoid his yellow gaze, which was not defiant or even insolent but, when it
came to rest on a man, seemed to instantaneously calculate the
exact way to kill him before idly drifting off again toward the
immense savannah, as if drawn to mirages only he could see.
That landscape of perfectly still bushland, where the air was
vitrified by the heat, was the world he had known since childhood, when he learned to find his way among the rocks and
trees, venturing far beyond the river, where the savannah
ceased to resemble an infinite sea of grass and the rainforest
emerged, bristling and ominous, in an anachronism of eternal
rainfall. He could move around that whole area blindfolded.
And in a way, that was what he did every night when he ran
around the grasslands in the darkness searching for the women
he was courting in the local villages. And during the civil war,
while he was leading a band of fighters descended from run-
away slaves, he had sown panic among passing military patrols
when they crossed a line he had established, an imaginary and
completely arbitrary line, as the terrified little soldiers were to
discover as they watched their officers fall to the ground, their
throats slashed by a knife that came from out of nowhere or
killed by a bullet none of them could remember hearing being
fired when, on returning to the camp, soaked in sweat, their
faces covered in nasty mosquito bites, their eardrums exasperated by the incessant whirr of cicadas, they were asked to
explain how they had forfeited their superiors without finding
the shadow of a man in the oppressive solitude of the savannah. It was the work of ghosts, they said, inwardly cursing their
fate, the army and even the Partido Conservador. Meanwhile,
the ghost in question started to feature in the songs they
hummed in the cattle ranches and the authorities wasted their
time detaining campesinos who would apparently rather be
flayed alive than give them a tip-off about the golden-eyed

indio, not only to escape civil unrest, but because they were convinced of the complete ineptitude of those military men who seemed to be bent on catching a devil in his own hell.

When the military had left and the *indio*'s band of Black fighters had scattered, he was spotted in the area again, around the time when Lina's aunt's very conservative husband had been so careless as to die, leaving behind twenty-eight illegitimate children, all of them professed conservatives to be more like their father, and all of them quarrelsome and emboldened against this poor woman who had the look of a papier-mâché figurine about her after ten years of marriage and giving birth to five daughters, but who, on being widowed, was forced to summon from within if not the strength, then at least the skill required to win over the most bellicose foreman in the region, instantly protecting her from any rogue who might conspire to ruin her, even if the *indio* came at a high price, demanding a third of the net monthly earnings from her by way of a salary. Money he spent helping his relatives and acquiring the land that bordered on his own farm, a kind of animal sanctuary where there lived, along with the legendary puma, all manner of monkeys, cats and reptiles mesmerized by his magnetism, creatures he usually addressed in the same language he used to speak to his sorrel, using a very soft, calm tone of voice and staring into their eyes while his hands traced gentle movements in the air, movements presumably aimed at calming the animal's fears until rendering it fascinated, its pupils dilating and contracting as if lost in a rush of pleasure.

In the depths of her soul, Lina's aunt believed that he had worked similar black magic on Catalina, but a curious trepidation to the hands of fate stopped her cutting his stay on the hacienda short under any pretence: there, more than anywhere, one could hear the ghost of the horse that Doña Clotilde del Real's boyfriend had used as the instrument of his own death many years ago, and it was that same man's grandfather who had sold the horse to Cristian's father after catching it using his concoction of magical herbs, thus setting the scene for one of his descendants, an *indio* with inexplicably golden eyes, to join Divina Arriaga's daughter in the realization of plans that defied human comprehension.

Out of superstition or from experience, her aunt claimed that she'd seen that love affair coming the moment they climbed out of the Jeep he'd picked them up in from the airport. He, the unrelenting lothario, whose passions were immortalized in songs warning boyfriends and husbands to hide their sweethearts in his presence, had never met anyone so beautiful, so exciting with her unruly sensuality: a strong woman, like her mother before her, who could gallop along beside him for hours on end, her only sign of fatigue being the lustful pink hue that rose to her face below her sparkling green eyes. In a vague attempt at keeping up appearances, Aunt Eloísa suggested that she, Lina, accompany them on their unholy rides, which would end with her slumped over the horse in exhaustion with her lungs full of dust, longing for the bathtub back at the hacienda, with its fancy solid-gold taps and even for the water, carried from the river by a procession of maids, a slimy, strange-smelling liquid, concealing tiny toads that jumped up to her knees unexpectedly. Either the bathtub, or spending the day shooing away flies as she lounged in a hammock, Lina would tell her aunt unequivocally one afternoon: anything but following two riders who were apparently versed in all the most sophisticated aspects of horsemanship apart from the very simple art of making their animals keep pace.

Love had made them extreme and reckless. At night, when the farmhands gathered to talk outside the house, the *indio* would suddenly appear and the voices would start to trail off, giving way to the sounds of the savannah while his eyes twinkled like nuggets of topaz floating in the darkness. He had come looking for Catalina, that much everyone in the hacienda knew: from Lina's aunt to every last one of her employees, all of whom were used to imagining him running through the grasslands—with his brooding puma leading the way or following along behind—on his way to woo some local woman or to perform the pagan ceremonies his grandfather had taught him. But no one said a thing. From the living room, Lina listened to the silence that lingered in the absence of laughter and voices, and she watched Catalina get up, feigning a sudden desire to go to sleep, then later, while she lay there in bed and her aunt cautiously asked from the hallway if she was okay, she responded that yes, she was, as she glanced over at the empty bed beneath the mosquito net and the window that a shadow would creep back through at daybreak. This would be Catalina's most authentic love—the only love she had no need to protect herself against, she would tell Lina later on, a love that allowed her to go to the very depths of herself without fear of being hurt or disappointed, because the man who loved her knew instinctively what she wanted, and he had no qualms about satisfying this desire. He was too much at one with the earth to recoil from sexuality and had been raised by an irrepressible grandfather, the incarnation of his ancient roots, who had taught him not so much to defend himself against nature as to join with it, distilling in his spirit—which had nothing remotely frenzied about it, only the calm resolve to tackle whatever came his way—an energy that was linked to his being perfectly adapted to the rhythms of life and knowing his exact place in the universe. Catalina was a woman, perhaps the most beautiful woman he would ever have the privilege to call his own, but he barely had to ask her for the thing she yearned to surrender to him: something indefinable and more ancient than any form of thought, which palpitated faintly in her body and could only be expressed when she was with a man. And he waited for her there in the sprawling savannah, where their horses galloped freely on a boundless horizon, beneath a harsh sun that seemed to have given birth to them both, with their fierce, indomitable will to breathe life deep into their lungs. Because those impassioned days were short, and they sought each other out with the feverishness of condemned lovers; day and night, in the hideouts he knew from childhood or between the coarse folds of the hammock on his ranch, they tried to make the most of every moment of a passion that they knew, from the very beginning, was closed off to any kind of hope. Refusing to take precautions, Catalina got mad when anything got in the way of their love, which served no purpose other than to exist in and of itself, or perhaps, without her knowing it, to give life to the girl she was to conceive just when she could no longer extend her stay in the hacienda with that man, who would remain etched in her memory for years, forcing her to seek in other men, anxiously and perhaps in vain, the same completeness he had given her. But the plan, if indeed there was a plan, seemingly came to fruition in the form of Aurora, who was identical to Catalina and born, like Divina Arriaga, under the sign that would determine her fortune or misfortune depending on whether she could impose the secret scandal of her beauty on the world. Aurora's eyes were golden instead of green, and when Lina left Barranquilla she still had the guileless look of a kitten about her; later she found out that the girl had followed Catalina to New York, where she graduated as both a sociologist and an anthropologist, with excellent grades. It was as if Divina Arriaga's spirit lived on inside of her, the same curiosity that had inspired her grandmother to study the classic authors and travel the roads taken by the armies of the great conquerors, whose ambition she understood but surely scorned, accompanied by the anthropologist who died from loving her so much, and could have no idea, when she collapsed from a heart attack on the scorching sands of an African desert, that the granddaughter of that girl of hieratical beauty, who stood like the statue of an ancient goddess, would learn her discipline at an American university, reading the books she herself had written. Lina realized this when she asked Catalina to send her Aurora's study programme and list of recommended authors from New York. She had asked for them because she wanted to check once again that coincidence always led her back to Divina Arriaga, as if the fact of having known her implied that it would be impossible to forget her or escape the influence she wielded like a wry yet stubborn ghost, gently clawing at the doors of worlds she was secretly seeking. Her name was the common thread that led to the crazed mind of the man who was going to alter Lina's perception of life most of all, an English poet based in Mallorca whom she asked, one summer night, what she had been like, the Divina Arriaga he had met in his youth, to which he stammered, "She was, she was," falling into a plaintive silence as he struggled to define her sheer beauty, then suddenly looking up with an expression of rekindled awe: "like that," he mumbled, pointing at the star-studded sky.

By then Lina was a long way from her father's office on Calle San Blas, where the solemn portrait of that Jewish ancestor hung on the wall and the ceiling fan grumbled, powerless to shift the unyielding air of the September afternoon when the existence of Divina Arriaga's fortune was revealed to her and she glimpsed, for the first time, the change that was about to come about in her destiny. It was a surreal day, one which transported her back to a childhood full of stories in which fairies and magicians scandalously introduced excitement to her life. It had been surprising enough to wake up and find a note from her father asking her to stop by his office, in a formal tone as if addressing one of his clients, but it was even more surprising when she noticed the circumspect way in which he told her to take a seat opposite him then pulled an old document out of his desk drawer, asking her (not without scepticism) if she had ever heard of Utrillo, Degas, Picasso or Modigliani, and, if she had, whether she had any idea what these gentlemen had done for a living. Lina would have cracked a joke were it not for the hint of seriousness she noticed in her father's tiny eyes, putting her on guard. Then she found out: she found out that although Divina Arriaga had died ten months earlier and her slightly Asian-looking maid had absconded to some corner of the planet with all the books she had bequeathed to her, and with her house in El Prado designated as the sole property in the will, at that precise time, she was setting the wheels in motion to pass on her entire fortune to Catalina. Every detail had been planned: Lina's father was a simple executor, the pawn in the game of chess, and she, Lina, was the first knight, moved with the purpose of initiating a relentless offensive, the logic of which was intended to completely crush Álvaro Espinoza or any other man who might have dared to marry her daughter. In other parts of the world, in London, Paris and New York, a number of men went about their work, silently following instructions issued twenty years earlier: bankers and lawyers who had been engaged in an enigmatic correspondence with Lina's father; owners of art galleries whom Divina Arriaga had advised to wait for this date to see more than two hundred works by the great masters appearing on the market; antiquarians who had occasionally passed down, from father to son, the secret of magnificent objects stored in various banks and safes until the heiress had learned to get a feel for life. Divina Arriaga had calculated the time with relative accuracy: Catalina was an adult woman now, overly hardened perhaps, but impervious to whatever mirages society might stir up to deceive her; ideologies, feelings and clichés perished as they passed through the filter of her lucidity, yet the fact that she was living in the world devoid of dreams did not seem to bother her all that much: God did not exist, and the world could be absurd, but all she had to do was fight her own corner. When Lina, unable to understand how the most unyielding fighting spirit could be combined with such embittered scepticism, tried to convince her that in her case hope existed in the form of individual liberation, Catalina just smiled. As teenagers, it was Lina who introduced matters for reflection into their conversations, but then the roles became almost inverted: the compelling questions came from Catalina, as did the pressing desire to explore each issue until it was broken down to its truth, or to whatever there was to be known of its truth. They had been like two rockets programmed to reach a set point together, from which one of them had to gather momentum and soar far away, to places where the other could never follow. Lina had felt the blast of the launch, and for a time she had observed Catalina in awe as she rapidly fired off arguments like a computer, her face strained in concentration, slightly exasperated by Lina's comments, which she perhaps found ridiculous. Later she learned to stay quiet, secretly proud to be able to call a woman of such exceptional intelligence her friend.

At least that was what she always thought while she lived in Barranquilla, and then later in Paris, when she received letters from Catalina providing shrewd instructions on how to sell a painting or approach a client, even when she was the victim of her friend's sharp tongue, as happened the last time they saw each other and spoke for a while, sitting on the terrace at a café: she, Lina, poorly expressing her chronic indignation at the absurdities of the world, and Catalina listening quietly, with the condescendence of someone hearing the echo of a delusion, until she finally checked her watch, tired, and by way of a farewell, said to her: "There's something hopelessly naïve about you, Lina." And once again Lina, bewildered, found herself thinking that she must be very intelligent, even though she did not understand her. So Divina Arriaga's mission would go without a hitch: had she waited a few more years, her daughter—either out of pride or impetuousness—would have told Álvaro Espinoza about the existence of that fortune, allowing him to take possession of it; a few years later and perhaps it would have been impossible for Catalina to find the energy to start a new life, making a clean sweep of the past. But when she received Divina Arriaga's inheritance, she was still young and dynamic, and her detached, reflective mind gave her an almost fiendish capacity for weighing things up. Very little remained of the diaphanous young woman who used to play the part of Jeanne de Lestonnac at the end-of-year ceremony: only the loyalty to her friends and a certain kind of purity, conveyed by her will to fully accept herself, without ever lying to herself. That was all; she was too familiar with the puppeteer pulling the strings behind each person, tightening resentments or shaking their pride, to abstain from using this knowledge in her own interests—particularly given that her relentless struggle against Álvaro Espinoza also made her think of the world as an immense battlefield where only the best and the strongest prevailed. Truth be told, it was hard to imagine her thinking of human relationships in any other way, as someone who had to contend day after day with the hotheaded aggressions of a man who was intent on breaking down her defences so that he could regain a position of dominance which he refused to accept he had lost; a man who, in the fury of his impotence, blindly tried to hurt her with insults, which over the years, and encouraged by inertia, became a monologue consisting purely of words brimming with hatred but stripped of all efficacy. Álvaro Espinoza, too, had become a victim of circumstances of his own making: his personal ambitions—manifested in a political career whose crowning glory was a short-lived appointment as governor, combined with a preposterous mission to reconcile psychoanalytical theory with Catholic doctrine in a book he never got round to writing a word of—had died a death in the firepit of his rage toward

Catalina, as if the possibility to transcend himself had been overridden by something that ultimately boiled down to a simple marital problem which his own neurosis had blown out of all proportion. He'd made the mistake of justifying his power with the authority that society allowed him to exert over his wife, and on this basis he asserted himself in the world, unceremoniously suppressing anyone who was thrust under his authority by circumstance. And lo and behold, that child-bride had surreptitiously devised a wicked system that allowed her to rebel and left him with an alternative whose only two solutions caused the social scandal that extinguished his ambition: either he could agree to a separation, implicitly acknowledging that for years he had been a cuckold, echoing the whispers of all those gossiping tongues, or he could continue to feign a harmonious marital life, reaping the benefits this presented for his career and enjoying the pride of being able to step out with the most beautiful woman in the city on his arm. He had made full use of Catalina's charms in his political campaigns and at the parties hosted in honour of the conservative leaders visiting from the Colombian interior. She knew how to host and seduce, how to dazzle while still appearing reserved, and how to spark conversation or break up a dispute. She was the perfect companion, even though she wouldn't let him set foot inside her room and she led a secret life he suspected existed but never dared acknowledge. Constantly reminded of the lie he had to endure because he lived by her side, his self-confidence had started to wane: in conversation, he no longer stared at the point between the other man's eyebrows to disconcert him, nor did he insolently express contempt for opinions that contradicted his own; his eyes had become shifty, and his thirst for whiskey had grown stronger, yet he continued to try to get a rise out of Catalina even though his insults fell on deaf ears, and he used his power over their money to humiliate her, making her argue cent after cent with him in woeful scenes that showed his bitterness. Catalina embraced these scenes with an unshakeable cynicism. Although at first it embarrassed her to see him scrimping on the essentials that he himself demanded, over the years she learned to use all kinds of ploys to trick him: from emptying his pockets when he came home drunk at dawn with no recollection of the whorehouses he had frequented, where he could well have been robbed, to asking sympathetic shopkeepers to issue her bills for two or three times the price of a product. Then Divina Arriaga's fortune came along to sever the final tie that bound her to him.

It would also sever any ties between Divina Arriaga and the city, and for good, because Aurora, the granddaughter into whose spirit she seemed to have transmigrated, would leave Barranquilla never to come back. Lina heard from her while she was working as Catalina's agent in Europe; she learned of her studies and her journeys, she read her thesis and occasionally heard her name mentioned by people who moved in the circles of cosmopolitan high society. But she never met her as an adult, and she tried in vain to imagine what she might be like. She would eventually see her photograph when the illness had taken hold, not long before she died: when leaving the metro one rainy day in autumn, she was caught off-guard by the face staring out at her from the cover of a glossy magazine; for a second she thought she was looking at the image of Divina Arriaga and her indescribable beauty; then, in the fog of fever, smiling for the first time in a long while, she realized that the yellow eyes staring back at her had a murderous glint in them: murderous and serene.

V

Paradise did indeed exist, Aunt Eloísa would sometimes say, impassive in her royal blue velvet armchair, although Lina was not sure whether her comment concluded a thought or a dream, because it always followed one of those detached silences she withdrew into at the close of the day, when her sisters were leaving and the fans carried scents of fading essences into the living room. An Eden recalled with nostalgia, she insisted, smiling at Lina when she noticed her bewilderment; an Eden located not in space but in the times of an ancient consciousness that had not yet begun to distinguish between the individual and the whole. Perhaps back then, pain and fear were shared, self-love was extended to others, and the end of an individual life was suffered as death by everyone else. No longer animals but not yet men, the beings who possessed this pulsating consciousness moved around unwittingly, searching for the knowledge that would allow them to prevail over the land, but that would also bring them solitude. And difference. And the estrangements required so that, based on some hierarchy or other, a chosen few would rule, and others would obey. At that time, human beings had been wretched: not only because of their blind longing for a past so lost that it would become a legend, but also because when they achieved that level of intelligence, they found themselves in the terrible contradiction of being free individuals who were capable of reflecting on their freedom but forced to bend to the will of others, always torn between the pride of rebelling with their lucidity and the carelessness of losing themselves in the dizziness of derangement. Many times they tried to find a way out of this conflict by inventing forms of society in which the exercise of power was concentrated or watered down based on momentary needs, like the last flickering glow of that primitive wisdom, finally culminating in the patriarchy that cemented the specific pathology of the man who, forgetting his mortal condition, chased after illusory honours while sowing pain and suffering in his wake. This was how Aunt Eloísa spoke sometimes, addressing only Lina in the silence of the villa surrounded by ceiba trees and shrouded in darkness, where the lustre of buddhas, jewellery boxes and incense burners was reflected in her Birmans' blue irises.

The subject matter changed when she spoke with her sisters; she no longer talked about the curse that mankind had put on all of humanity, threatening to wipe it out in the deranged fires of a collective suicide, but about women, whose resignation plunged Aunt Eloísa into a kind of appalled astonishment, which her sisters shared to a greater or lesser degree, their voices soft like the fluttering of tiny birds' wings as they meticulously analyzed the possible process through which the oppression had established and then consolidated itself, drawing upon a set of morals intended to justify it. But although they all agreed that liberation was undoubtedly at odds with the principles of the male system, Aunt Eloísa was the only one among them who believed that only an implacable battle could contend with the ferocity of male violence. And in that battle, there would naturally be a winner and a loser.

Aunt Eloísa's sisters were amused to hear her speak with such conviction about the battle between the sexes, knowing that she'd been loved completely by the men in her life. But then again, they were used to expecting the unexpected with her. To begin with, they told Lina, she departed from the norm when she was born five months after being conceived, leaving her mother's womb without causing her any pain, like a fully formed doll so tiny she could fit in the palm of a hand. Fortunately, her mother had come up with the brilliant idea of wrapping her up in cotton and keeping her close to her breast—so that she could listen to her heart beating—using a kind of sling that she would wear on her chest for four months. Several goats were hurriedly brought to her yard and milked so that the baby would receive a drop of milk every hour, day and night. And to make sure her mother got some sleep, the older sisters took turns in the delicate operation of opening her blouse, finding the tiny Aunt Eloísa and making her drink that droplet of milk on which her life depended. Lina's grandmother told her how she'd occasionally noticed, terrified, that the little baby, who still wouldn't take to the breast, was watching her from the depths of her cotton nest with those grey eyes open wide; Aunt Eloísa didn't cry or make a single sound, she said, and she simply gazed around her intensely each time they fed her. Later, and for ten whole years, the child would have the same attitude: she noticed everything because she was heeding her mother's instructions—provided they didn't displease her too much—and she diligently studied the courses that tutors delivered to the sisters and cousins who were roughly her age; in other words, she completed grammar exercises, solved arithmetic problems and wrote down the correct answers to the questions they asked. But whatever she did, it was always in the most intractable silence. Things might have continued this way were it not for the distant relative who turned up at the house one day from Mompós with her fifteen-year-old son in tow: a beautiful, shy boy who, following bad advice from a priest, had got it into his head that he wanted to become a clergyman. It was a Sunday, and they had all gathered on the terrace overlooking the yard: the older girls; the boy not daring to glance up from the ground; Aunt Eloísa looking very pretty with her golden ringlets and her organza smock dress, greedily contemplating him from her wicker rocking chair like a puppy eyeing up a saucer of milk. When the distant relative finished recounting her woes, amid the sympathetic murmurings of that assembly of women who had gathered in order to support each other through adversity, Aunt Eloísa's voice suddenly piped up, saying "What a waste." The rocking chairs, the needles, the hands reaching out to take glasses of juice or sesame-seed brittle from the table all froze on the spot in utter amazement: that pampered little girl—who was coddled and showered with affection and gifts wherever she went, could always be found sitting on one of her aunts' laps and always got the best sweets because of her muteness— had spoken. And not only had she spoken in a mocking, res- olute little voice, but she'd summed up in three words what all the women there had been thinking, suggesting an extremely advanced precociousness.

That was when Aunt Eloísa's love life began, because the boy, fascinated, abandoned his dreary plans and married her two years later. But like all the young men who came into the family in one way or another, he died young, leaving her with four daughters and an export business that took her all over the world, earning her plenty of money and letting her take her fair share of lovers along the way. And so as far as her sisters were concerned, there was nothing she could complain about in a system she'd always known how to work, transcending the female condition and its procession of woes thanks to her wealth and her intelligence; moreover, Aunt Eloísa was elitist, so much so that she regarded man's existence as an error of nature, and it was entirely conceivable that deep down she lamented the absence of parthenogenesis in the branch of superior mammals from which humanity had emerged. Only Lina, who listened instead of arguing with her, believed she could detect a note of profound moral conviction in her wry remarks, a belief she chose to keep to herself out of a sense of

shame, and, perhaps, because she thought it was absurd to suggest a way of life that involved mutations similar to those that
had enabled human consciousness to form. At heart, Aunt
Eloísa never stopped being the little girl who attentively
observed the world in silence for ten years. And if she ever suggested some of her ideas to Lina, her aim, among other things,
was to involve her in the plans laid by Divina Arriaga, who,
before arriving in Barranquilla in ill health, had decided to give
her daughter the means to spread her wings and fly far away.

Because Lina was destined to support Catalina unconditionally, abstaining from judging her acts in the name of any
principle, and she was destined to serve as her scout almost as
soon as her father spoke to her about the inheritance and told
her to protect it from any swindlers, charlatans or thieves in the
art market—in other words, anyone who was remotely
involved in the art trade; having only studied economics and
with no experience to speak of, Lina was going to be thrust
into a world of complete and utter fraudulence, where every
movement had to be calculated like a game of chess and executed with the self-control of a poker player. She would lose
more than a little hope from all the treachery she would face,
but little by little she would earn her stripes in the challenging
apprenticeship of patience. And while she, Lina, travelled back
and forth to the United States to assess the fair value of a painting or a client's moral rectitude, Catalina put into action the plan
that was destined to free her, creating a kind of theatre play in
which the actors did not realize they were performing before
an audience of one, Álvaro Espinoza, who, in turn, could not
establish any relationship between them or imagine the purpose of their unexpected entrances, because he knew nothing
of Catalina's intentions or the tenacious intelligence with
which she had observed him for years until, finally, she understood every single one of his fears and desires. Arrogance
would be his Achilles heel. If it had occurred to him, for

example, to associate his loathed foster brother Henk's presence in the city with the gun Catalina had bought, feigning a sudden fear of thieves, he would have dismissed the idea immediately—not only in the belief that a woman would be incapable of such premeditation, but because of the questions this would prompt about his own mental health: this, in his professional jargon, was called paranoia, and nothing horrified Álvaro Espinoza more than madness. He wasn't going to be suspicious of the tempting bottle of whiskey either, which was always on the coffee table with a glass next to it, day and night, no matter how much alcohol he'd already imbibed; even when he smashed the bottle against the wall in his desperation, another one would be put there just as soon as the maid finished sweeping up the shards of broken glass; at any rate, the boxes of whiskey were stacking up in cabinets and sideboards. He believed he reigned supreme in the brothels, unaware that Catalina's gaze followed him there too, unblinking and lying in wait, having discovered the benefits of occupying a vantage point in a place where men revealed their true selves, believing that they were safe from any indiscretion because their common vice guaranteed them solidarity and the women they used for sex inspired less fear in them than a pet. Through her long-time friend Petulia, Catalina had observed Álvaro Espinoza's evolution over the years: his initial promiscuity had given way to a series of more or less enduring relationships with girls from the Colombian interior whom he met in whorehouses and made his mistresses, giving them just enough money to rent a tiny apartment and buy the essentials they needed to survive. Whenever a mistress grew tired of his miserly ways and started looking like she wanted to leave him, Catalina would give the mistress money via Petulia to secure herself a degree of tranquillity, and, most importantly, so that she could arrange to see her own lover without risking getting caught. If the girl had any inkling of where that money came from, she went to great lengths to make sure Álvaro Espinoza did not find out, afraid that if he did, she might lose the goose that laid the golden eggs. Petulia also proved to be extremely cautious in this respect and was completely loyal to Catalina: she, a woman known for rigidly sticking to her fees, would help her friend at no cost for years, and only when she was older would she accept the gift of two small houses in Siape when Catalina travelled to Barranquilla for the last time.

Álvaro Espinoza was long-dead by then, and Lina, who had since settled in Paris, was still trying to understand how Catalina had managed to drive him to suicide. She did not doubt Catalina's involvement in the slightest because, following her friend's instructions, Lina herself had bought the gun in California, and she'd invited Henk from Boston when, in a happy coincidence, Catalina learned of his reputation as an art connoisseur and an advisor to major collectors. And Henk, who was reticent at first but then became interested, had agreed to travel to Barranquilla, where he would fall hopelessly in love with Catalina (or her paintings). But even if he'd been a docker or a dancer, it wouldn't have made any difference: Henk's destiny was going to change as soon as Catalina did some digging around and found out that there had been a foster brother in Álvaro Espinoza's past—not by asking Doña Clotilde del Real, who could flare up with a terrible allergic reaction at the mere mention of her married life, but by quizzing Flores the cook, who had been a shoulder for her to cry on back in Cartagena and shared the same aversions: she truly detested Álvaro Espinoza, the wretch who looked down on her for the colour of her skin, on her, the woman whose sister had nursed him as an infant.

All her life Flores had harboured that bitterness in her heart, holding back the urge to express it so as not to inflame Doña Clotilde's sensibilities, and suddenly she had found someone who was willing to listen to her, someone to speak to openly, telling the truth in her own way, slowly, with spellbinding circumlocutions in which her memory conjured up outrageous acts and nostalgias, but also the conflict around which Álvaro Espinoza's personality had structured itself. Listening to her speak, Catalina could see it all: the boy conceived in horror and rejected by his mother; the awkward, ugly youngster, ashamed of his homosexuality; his father, the brothels, the firm-buttocked Black girls with unusual penchants, and everything else. Perhaps that was when Catalina came up with the idea of plunging him into an abyss of temptation; she just needed to find the right character for the role, someone who could resist the man's will and outwit the psychiatrist's intelligence; in fact, she just needed to hear about María Fernanda Valenzuela, a well-born lesbian, who turned tricks in Cali and whose main eccentricity consisted of her refusal to engage in any contact that conformed to the accepted norms, even if she had a knife to her throat or a sack of gold at her feet.

There was nothing left for María Fernanda to learn about male violence when she was fifteen years old and a nun helped her to escape the asylum, hiding her in the Buen Pastor women's correctional facility. There, washing sheets and scrubbing floors, María Fernanda started to recover her mental health when it dawned on her that perhaps she'd never lost it in the first place, and finally, she could put a name to the abomination: being raped by her own grandfather at the age of ten was a tough trauma to overcome, even more so given how her father reacted when he found her covered in blood; he decided to shut her in a room away from the rest of the family to hide the truth and expunge the disgrace, attacking not the guilty party—the respectable patriarch, owner of the finest hacienda in the province—but the victim, that girl who had embodied temptation and had to hide away in a room, left almost in complete darkness with no one allowed anywhere near her, not even if she cried day and night; the girl who would survive on the basket of food hoisted up to her window every evening. Alone in her room, without hearing a single voice and in complete confusion, she held out for two years. When she got her first period, she stopped eating. Then they declared her insane and sent her to an asylum in another city with a false identity, leaving it to psychiatrists, drugs and mistreatment to finish her off. And in a way they succeeded, because as soon as she managed to escape from the Buen Pastor prison, she threw herself into prostitution, saving up every measly cent to pay a lawyer to legally reinstate her surname when she reached the age of majority; she didn't want to file a lawsuit against her parents or demand any kind of compensation, her only wish was to work as a prostitute under her real name, throwing her family into disrepute.

Soon enough, word spread among the wealthy men in the region that the favours of a sister or cousin of the aristocratic Valenzuela family could be procured in a brothel in Cali, at least for those who were willing to spend a lot of money and conform to a strange way of making love, one more exciting than any other because of its thoroughly perverse nature, representing the very height of sin and, consequently, the irresistible desire to commit it. Thus, María Fernanda started not only to take her revenge on her friends and family, but also to acquaint herself with the fantastic power of the pesos that were stacking up in her bank account, allowing her to choose clients and lovers as she pleased. And just at the point when she had finished setting up on her own and creating a lucrative network of telephone services, she received an unusual proposal from Barranquilla, inviting her to travel to that city to seduce a psychiatrist in exchange for half a million pesos in hard cash, completely tax-free, the only condition being that she remain true to her sexual practices, which in itself was an unnecessary request since María Fernanda was willing to do anything except repeat the act that had brought her such unhappiness.

Perhaps what appealed to her more than the money was the challenge of snaring a man who, as a former governor of the province and a psychiatrist, personified the two powers in whose name she'd suffered her torments. So she immediately accepted Petulia's proposal, and, after launching a successful campaign to advertise her services, she took to frequenting the bars where Álvaro Espinoza usually met up with friends, and started sleeping with people left and right, always for a considerable fee, while the rumour of that quirk of hers prompted jokes, obscenities and wagers but no particularly lurid excitement among those men of the coast, who were generally inclined to be understanding of certain curiosities of extramarital sex. Only Álvaro Espinoza reacted to her presence with secret horror: he'd fought so hard against his sodomite tendencies, knowing that the dormant demon of homosexuality lurked behind them, that resisting his desire for María Fernanda was going to be his obsession for months. The forbidden fruit was not hanging motionless from a tree, it was everywhere: in bars and brothels, in cabarets and restaurants, looking androgenous and standing proud with that body of an adolescent boy, wearing a silk shirt and tie. María Fernanda usually kept her hair short and slicked back, she refused to wear jewellery or perfume, and when it came to make-up, she simply painted her long nails scarlet red. Her whole attitude oozed a similar ambiguity: she had refined manners—an indelible mark of her upbringing—and yet she was completely unfazed by any display of vulgarity; an autodidact of not inconsiderable culture, she started reading intensively as soon as she escaped from the Buen Pastor prison, having understood that knowledge was part of power, and she affected a simple way of talking in order to defuse the rivalry of other women and the distrust of men, always choosing to listen politely rather than expressing her own opinion. The truth was, in those five years of solitude, pain and fear, María Fernanda had learned to reflect; to reflect and hold her tongue: no one knew anything about her past or the circumstances that had driven her into prostitution despite coming from an aristocratic family. Her experiences with psychiatry—when, head shaven, barefoot and wearing the humiliating gown from the mental asylum, she appeared before an insincerely friendly man who, from his position of superiority, tried to make out that her tragic memories and her reality as a victim were nothing more than delusions—had left her with a hatred so intense it was invisible, intangible like the frozen, motionless air of the Antarctic. Like Catalina, Fernanda believed that psychiatry appealed to those who, afraid of falling prey to a latent madness, built their own lives around other people's obsessions so as to minimalize the significance of their own deliriums. Following this logic, she had quickly understood the object of the game: to fatally wound Álvaro Espinoza, forcing him to face up to his homosexuality. And since she knew all about the models of reasoning that kept psychiatrists on the right track, allowing them to stay in control of any situation, she withdrew into a silence aimed at arousing his curiosity without letting him understand her, barely insinuating that she only managed to achieve pleasure through the methods for which she was known. Leading questions and deliberate silences were of no use, because María Fernanda knew every trick in the book. She could spend hours sitting at a table, looking around without letting the slightest expression appear on her face; she said she'd forgotten about her childhood and smiled calmly when he classed her behaviour as abnormal. In the face of such controlled madness, Álvaro Espinoza was lost for words: as far as he was concerned, the idea that a woman who had been born with a silver spoon in her mouth should declare herself a lesbian, agree to prostitute herself and delight in the aberration, revealed a complete mental imbalance; but this particular disorder was not expressed by any symptoms he was familiar with from his medical experience: there were no striking defects in the coherence of her language, nor in the apparent logic of her behaviour; furthermore, María Fernanda, who did not drink or smoke, gave the impression of being at peace with herself, accepting her own truth and the reality of things, albeit without making the slightest moral judgement. What he did not know, and this she refrained from telling him, was that in order to live she needed to sleep twelve hours uninterrupted, which she did with the help of strong sleeping pills, going to bed at six in the morning and getting up at nightfall; she also kept her fears from him, such as the panic she felt when she walked into a room without having the key in her pocket, or her compulsion to carry tiny tools that could open any lock and hide them in wallets and the heels of her shoes. But the less María Fernanda revealed of herself, the more Álvaro Espinoza tried to understand her, feigning a strictly professional interest even though his friends never asked him for an explanation and at best were surprised to see him so infatuated with a woman, a complicated woman, yes, but one who was ultimately willing to sell herself, just like the other prostitutes he frequented.

He, however, found himself in a state of complete agitation. Perhaps it was true that initially he took an interest in María Fernanda's case because it represented a formidable provocation to his activity as a righter of wrongs and guardian of the all-important order required for the proper functioning of society. Behind that calm appearance, he must have intuited the implacable irony of madness, more threatening than the kind he encountered daily in his mental-health clinic, where men and woman made a mockery of any pretence of rationality but he could take his revenge by administering drugs and electric shocks, turning them into stupefied or terrified animals. Whereas María Fernanda represented a triumphant kind of madness that prevailed over the systems invented to repress it and even over the knowledge employed to detect it. Veiled challenge, invisible intimation, nameless soldier, Álvaro Espinoza could not rid himself of his fascination; he could escape it by trivializing it; in other words, he could agree to sleep with her, but then the ghosts he'd been running from since his youth would come back to haunt him in droves. Perhaps he thought of himself like a former alcoholic who could be pushed back into alcoholism by a single drop of whiskey, regarding sodomy as the act he must never commit if he wanted to keep his psychic structure intact. Not because the unspeakable sin represented a perversion in which he could rediscover his old delights without feeling inhibited or guilty; quite the opposite: because it took him back to the chaos in which his neurosis impelled him to self-destruct. There, in the realm of ambiguity, he ran the risk of shattering the image of himself that allowed him to fit in with his father's moral rules and assert his authority over society, certain of his own worth and enjoying the social privileges so dear to his pride.

This would be the explanation Catalina gave Lina when finally she decided to tell her the truth. It was autumn, and the weather was still unpredictable. Many years had passed, and all that remained of their youth was a stupefied, unsentimental recollection. They met on the terrace of the cafe where they usually caught up whenever Catalina was in Paris, and they were perhaps exactly the way Divina Arriaga had imagined they would be at that age: Lina wearing her trademark blue jeans, with a few grey hairs she refused to dye because she thought they were well deserved and even earned; Catalina in the splendour of her immutable beauty, which committed the ignominy of asserting itself without any effort at all. Both of them were now calm and beyond hyperbole as they recalled the past, which emerged completely devoid of emotion and faded away into the distant hum of traffic and the fleeting scuffles of a few swaggering pigeons chasing breadcrumbs tossed from the next table. Less arrogant, perhaps, too—even if, on principle,

Catalina had hired a Rolls Royce and the chauffeur was waiting for her outside the square in his uniform—and capable, at
least, of recognizing the worth of their friendship amid all the
glitz and glamour where so many layers of vanity had been
stripped away like the layers of an onion. There was no real
curiosity in Lina's mind at that time, not even the desire to link
together certain events in order to remember them coherently
as she grew older in a world that sometimes seemed so full of
nonsense and confusion to her. But being familiar with
Catalina's code of conduct, she knew she would speak to her
about Álvaro Espinoza's death one day—not to justify her
actions, since Catalina had learned to answer to her conscience
alone, but to join together the dots for Lina if she ever wanted
to put the suicide in its true context, believing that by doing so
she was satisfying her need to find a logical explanation for
everything; in this way, she could write off the debt she
incurred fifteen years earlier, when she used Lina in a plot
whose inner workings had driven a man to self-destruct. That
was a need Lina no longer felt, since she had come to terms
with living in uncertainty a good while before Catalina; in
other words, she'd reconciled herself with the fact that she
lived in a universe full of questions for which there were no
definitive answers, and where no general law could be applied
to human behaviour. But that afternoon, Catalina wanted to
give her the means to construct a framework that would allow
her to make sense of Álvaro Espinoza's suicide, knowing that
for Lina, any act could be explained by pinpointing its causes,
whereas in Catalina's view, the trigger wasn't to be found in an
accumulation of facts, but in a kind of secret alchemy that
occurred in light of the facts, just a combination of miniscule
reactions and unpredictable associations that forever escaped
the conscious mind. Lina let her talk without admitting that
she shared this same opinion; she listened to Catalina explain
how this intuition had made her piece together the elements

that caused the drama, but then deny the inexorable nature of the outcome of her scheming. Because it was all there: the man and his pride; Álvaro Espinoza, facing the dilemma that was to shatter his arrogance. He'd sought power as a reward, and he caught it like a virus, not knowing that, in his desperate accumulation of glory and accolades, he was losing what he wanted most of all.

Power achieved prematurely, Catalina would explain, when his desires were still intact and doubt could still creep in if it occurred to him to consider the value of what he'd achieved and the price paid in order to get it. He'd played the game honourably as soon as he'd grasped the rules: in a hostile world devoid of compassion, where his mother rejected him with her absence and his nursemaid abandoned him by dying, the only person who'd been inclined to love him was his father, but only on the condition that he pursue a goal which meant relinquishing everything that gave him pleasure: the memory of his infancy in the company of a blond boy, both of them naked, cradled in the arms of a Black woman; the solitude he was driven to by the fear of having his nose put out of joint again; the embarrassment he experienced around the students at San Pedro Claver. He'd said goodbye to all these things through a formidable amnesia, which shook his memory like an implosion for years, muffling the images of his past amid a dull rumbling of discordant sounds. In such a state of despair, imagining his suicide would be the only way he could find the will to survive: death—a return to the space where he hadn't been born into coldness and indifference—would provide the inspiration for the only poems he wrote and a few philosophical considerations feverishly scribbled in the margins of a Marcus Aurelius book that Catalina found. He was seventeen years old at the time, and he truly believed that he was hearing voices: his ears were bombarded by the echoes of conversations between the people around him, plunging him into a state of confusion; but as well as the dialogues happening there and then, he could also hear the echoes of voices that had crossed paths in the past, and, sometimes, even the unsettling vibrations of his thoughts. Maddened by perplexity and consumed by fatigue, he found himself torn between his religious beliefs and the alluring argument that the stoic philosophers proposed, invoking the right to end one's own life in the name of human dignity, when a doctor friend of his father's examined him and he discovered that his ailments could be likened to a form of mental imbalance. Perhaps that was when he decided to fight against who he really was, by subjecting himself to the relentless discipline drilled into him by the Jesuits. Little by little, as the mists of anxiety seemed to be clearing, he began to steer his destiny, stacking up successes in his studies until he completed his professional training as a psychiatrist, which, although it did not make him particularly equipped to ease his patients' suffering, at least enabled him to run the only private mental-health clinic in Barranquilla. The desperation had pushed him to achieve a privileged situation, but his victory, far from reconciling him with life, only awakened a foolish craving for power within him.

He gained this power when he was too young—Catalina would repeat that afternoon—and couldn't yet come to terms with the frustration it produced, the infinite vacuousness: from the hypocritical flattery, to the women who surrendered themselves unwillingly, he felt more like a target of manipulation than a dominant subject, as if, from a certain point, dominance morphed into impotence. His father had been dismayed by the reversibility of power; he had discovered its illusion. There was nothing behind those images that flickered in the distance promising the laurels of victory, only new mirages whose purpose was to guide him along a path that had already been mapped out, making him sacrifice his desires so that society could continue to exist as it always had done: he hated disorder, but even more than that, he hated knowing that he'd been used; he only gained intense satisfaction from acting as a sovereign for a brief spell, setting targets and ticking them off through men who served him unwittingly; saying one thing to certain people and the opposite to others, or preventing any communication between them; pretending to be in possession of secrets shared by only a chosen few. This was how he'd managed to assert himself not only in his professional life but also in the political world, plotting and scheming until he became the governor of the province in the name of the Partido Conservador. That honour and so many others had been a salve for his old wounds, but it was also the root of the dangerous musings about his role as a tool in the hands of a society bent on preserving the status quo, an objective whose legitimacy he did not contest, even if, insidiously, an unfathomable rage crept into his heart.

It was in this period of uncertainty that María Fernanda burst into his life. And Henk, the handsome foreigner with his fine-featured face, as if delicately sketched by an ink brush and darkened by the passing of the years, making the paleness from his father's side fade slightly in an ironic tribute to his mother's blackness. Henk was hard to pin down, instinctively worldly, and his love of elegance had confined him to dealings with aristocrats and magnates whose wives he seduced for his work but also out of social duty. He'd grown accustomed to an easy life, full of the finer things and lacking principles other than those inherent to the role of dandy he'd always taken for granted, but now he was suddenly thrust into Barranquilla, in the heart of the tropics, where everything seemed extreme and where seducing a woman ceased to be a hobby and became a drama. Of course he never imagined such a thing would happen; nor did he imagine the risk he was taking by journeying to discover a childhood of which he hadn't retained the slightest memory. That was his first mistake: leaving behind casinos, castles and hunting expeditions in Scotland, as well as friends who only saw him as the cultured heir of a Dutch millionaire and his wife, a woman so melancholy she looked like something out of a Modigliani painting, to discover that the fact that he had been born from another woman's womb—a circumstance he thought of as an accident—condemned him to suffer the scorn of the middle classes of this inconsequential city that was splayed out on the banks of a river like a hideous caiman. No, not even in his dreams would he have envisaged that situation as he listened to Lina talking about Divina Arriaga's paintings, surrounded by the pine trees at his house in Boston. And if he had been able to envisage it, he probably would have laughed to himself like someone imagining being harangued by a group of screaming monkeys, all the while forgetting the ties that bound them to those same monkeys. Even if he'd understood it all, in other words, if he'd accepted how much the gaze of others could damage his self-esteem, he would have been comforted by the idea of a possible escape, not suspecting the pleasure that his aesthetic nature would take away from that confrontation, enslaving him—relatively, because he was always armed with weapons he could use to humiliate Álvaro Espinoza's pride: for example, by talking to him about Divina Arriaga's paintings, at the risk, of course, of seeing them disappear between his collector's hands. He never did, but this secret advantage allowed him to resist while Álvaro Espinoza succumbed.

Because a curious antipathy would be awakened in that man as soon as he disembarked in Barranquilla, which would not benefit his ego but would see his wealth multiply. He, Henk, (Lina told herself then) would have struggled to find a more venomous individual, whose motivations could only be explained by consulting a book about reptiles or pests that crawled in the shadows and ferociously attacked when least expected. Although to begin with he had felt slightly guilty about deceiving his foster brother—hiding his profession from him and his real reasons for being in the city—the uneasy feeling could not have lasted long, as long as it took for Álvaro Espinoza to recover from the trauma of Henk's arrival and to plan an offensive against him that was entirely uncalled for, because there was nothing he could hold against him, except being more cultured than him, and much wealthier, and having the face and manners of a well-to-do playboy who was accustomed to seducing men and women with ease. Perhaps Álvaro Espinoza's fury came from the murky guiderails of his subconscious, the place where sorrows his memory had chosen not to keep tossed and turned. In any case, the mere presence of Henk would be enough to violently shake the framework of his arrogance by showing him a ridiculous image of himself: a king of lunatics and provincial dignitary, as he yelled at Catalina the night when he lost control of his nerves and began to slide into absurdity. Henk, however, had kept his thoughts to himself during those long conversations in which Álvaro Espinoza boasted about his assets: he had agreed to accompany him to the brothels, staring indifferently at the women on display there; he also went with him to his mental-health clinic, where he was slightly irritated to see him parading around among the helpless creatures with the vanity of an Olympian god; and finally, at the country club, which had an air of childish pretence compared to the palaces in Venice and the Viennese castles to which he was usually invited. But he said nothing: just like María Fernanda, albeit for different reasons, Henk carefully kept his opinions to himself. He was there to act as the go-between for the owner of a fantastic collection of paintings who, as well as being a millionaire, was beautiful and seemingly out of reach. As bad luck would have it, she was married to his buffoon of a foster brother, and he would be forced to put up with the situation while the arrangements were put in place for the canvasses to be sold. The prudence he had learned as a *marchand de tableaux*, spurred on by the magnitude of the business prospect, and, most importantly, the impeccable social graces he had soaked up in the English colleges he had attended since being a child, made him impervious to the probing questions from the psychiatrist and his perfidies.

Perfidies were committed: Álvaro Espinoza, reluctantly dazzled by the refinement of the ghost who had come back to life on that cursed day, resolved to take advantage of his apparent naivety by wheedling a certain amount of money out of him, despite being immensely rich, so that he could expand his clinic, introducing him to the city's bourgeoisie by way of reward: it was a favour that Henk would have happily done without, but one that stirred up the worst demons of resentment inside Álvaro Espinoza. Hence his contradictory behaviour: switching from distrust to politeness, taking him to the brothels to introduce his best friends to him or leaving him in the lurch at the Hotel del Prado without explanation. The worst example of this happened the night when Álvaro Espinoza started to imagine that Henk was mocking his life's work: he'd hosted a cocktail party in Henk's honour, and then out of nowhere, under the influence of many drinks, he malevolently declared to everyone present that the man all the women were gawping at was the illegitimate son of a Black maid. The revelation had such a brutal effect that the guests, either disgruntled or downright offended, promptly said their goodbyes, leaving Henk confused and alone in a corner of the living room, bitterly discovering just how right Catalina was to hate her husband and be willing to give it all up to follow him instead. This was his second mistake.

Catalina hated Álvaro Espinoza without a doubt, but staying true to a motto that she would always respect, that love and work did not go hand in hand, she had no intention of joining her life with the life of that foreigner. Furthermore, even before she met Henk, she had mapped out his psychological profile with relative precision: of course, a collector who travelled around the world looking for rare, precious objects was going to undervalue anything that was too attainable and handed to him with no resistance; a playboy who was in the habit of visiting beautiful women could only be attracted to someone who escaped his womanizing ways by reigniting his jaded libido. Catalina's strategy would consist, then, in pretending to be seduced—although she wasn't and knew that she never would be, partly because she would have to do business with him later, and also because his excessive refinement extinguished any potential spark of desire on her part. But in the meantime, she needed Henk so that she could pass him off as her lover and humiliate Álvaro Espinoza. She, a woman who was usually reserved and so sagacious that nobody knew anything for sure about her love affairs, was going to invent this great passion, and, in the ultimate act of shrewdness, she was going to live it—not with Henk, of course, but with a rather strange man who had lusted after her in silence for years. The pretence of that love would alter her behaviour, making her unrecognizable; from nocturnal outings to emphatic declarations, where gaining complete possession of herself was all about overcoming prejudices, very little remained of the Catalina imbued with coldness, whom Álvaro Espinoza had always treated as a contemptible opponent. Now, for the first time, he was afraid of losing her, having suddenly discovered the vital role she'd played in his social advancement by joining him on political trips and appearing on his arm at receptions, helping him to make friends in high places. With the money she'd wrangled out of him after so many harsh words, she'd created a framework conducive to worldly life and the material wellbeing that was so pleasing to come home to when, after a day of work or a night of revelry, he wearily returned to the apartment. When Catalina was away, the staff ran rampant, the girls seemed anxious, and though people thought he was in the right, they gradually stopped going to see him. And Catalina seemed invincible to him: she did not respond to his insults and simply smiled at his threats. She wanted to leave him, that was all; she wanted to leave him for a mixed-race man, taking with her Aurora, the daughter he loved most of all. The world had suddenly lost its meaning for Álvaro Espinoza, because he didn't know who his opponent was; he didn't know that he had been pitted against Divina Arriaga's fortune, and it was breaking down his defences one by one. That treasure, which he would never find out about, would only strengthen Catalina's resolve and make Henk infinitely persistent.

Greed, however, was not the motivation for María Fernanda, who seemed to be determined to spend every last dime of her bounty to imprison him in desperation. At most, the money spurred her on when she was feeling discouraged, but the full force of her madness—Lina would hear Catalina say that afternoon while she watched the pigeons strutting about—had become focused on destroying that man, in a curious shift of mindset that no one, not even she herself, would have been able to predict; for some arbitrary reason, grinding Álvaro Espinoza to dust had become her final revenge upon society. Hence Catalina would speak to her about doubt fifteen years later; indeed, how could anyone imagine that a woman so impervious to any emotion wouldn't be content with making Álvaro Espinoza succumb to her whims as per the agreement she'd entered into with Petulia, taking her money and simply heading back to Cali; how could anyone predict that after giving Petulia the photographs that would allow Catalina to immediately demand their physical separation and the division of their property, she would actually decide to remain in the city.

Because that was what she did: without offering any explanation, she stayed there and set up home in a truly luxurious apartment, then began to hold parties resembling orgies and invite anyone she'd met during her time in the city. Those parties were a magnet for late-night revellers and prostitutes. In a haze of whiskey, sleazy lighting and vallenato music, a supposed relative of hers named Lionel reigned supreme: not so much effeminate as ambiguous, he could have passed for her twin brother and enjoyed telling obscene jokes in a slight Italian accent; nothing betrayed his homosexuality, and even some of María Fernanda's female friends could attest to his lovemaking talents, but the men, who kept enjoying themselves regardless and drinking to excess, completely uninhibited, said they felt uncomfortable around him. Álvaro Espinoza was aware of the danger that Lionel posed for him, and he hated him. In fact, he hated all of it: the apartment where that man swanned around playing the host without taking so much as a peso out of his pocket, and he hated the woman whose trickery he could not manage to shake off. For many months, María Fernanda had been a pit of torment for him: she was his mistress, and yet he did not feel like he possessed her; when it occurred to him to make a link between his feeling of emptiness and the restrictions she imposed upon him (this, he yelled to himself angrily) he would discover later, with renewed anguish, that he could not go without the delights that had been introduced into his love life. Then he rebelled against the sense of insecurity that such a vicious woman gave him—since he didn't dare to leave her alone for a moment, fearing she might sleep with another man in his absence—and still he refused to give her the financial support that, in principle, gave him the right to possess her exclusively or at least to demand the departure of Lionel, whose proclivities made him imagine the most aberrant relations between the two of them. The resignation of his will and his notoriously tightfisted ways were exactly what María Fernanda was counting on: all she had to do was be available and ask nothing of him, so that he would not get frustrated and stop wanting her. Meanwhile, Álvaro Espinoza felt his self-respect crumbling as he realized how, one by one, his resolutions went unfulfilled: every morning when he left that apartment, he vowed he'd never set foot in it again, and as soon as he got to his clinic, he found himself flooded with a longing to see her, to run and find her, catching her in the arms of the man who had no doubt paid for the excesses of the night before; but when he arrived back to the apartment, no one was there apart from the young man he didn't trust one bit, who slept in a bedroom full of gold fabrics and sequined cushions, his drowsy naked body always on show between two huge porcelain tigers. Lionel hated it when Álvaro Espinoza woke him up midway through the morning with his senseless fits of jealousy. María Fernanda, accustomed to using pills to lull her to sleep, began to tire of him bursting in like that, and one day she decided to pin a notice onto the door of the apartment announcing that she would only be receiving guests from six in the evening. This would be the detonator for the drama that unfolded.

Álvaro Espinoza spent that Saturday angrily brooding in his office, refusing to take phone calls or see any of his patients. When his secretary came in to offer him a cup of coffee, he told her to go to hell. No one could imagine what he was thinking during those hours, chain-smoking cigarettes and drinking the whiskey he stashed in his personal filing cabinet. Apparently, he phoned home, but the maid told him that Catalina had left with the girls to spend the weekend in Puerto Colombia. His friends recalled seeing him arrive at María Fernanda's apartment at around eleven, blind drunk and trying to give her a slap by way of a greeting. She dodged the blow, and he, losing his balance, fell to the floor. From there, he started hurling obscene insults at her, accusing her, among other things, of having perverted relations with Lionel, the kind based on the oral contact that satisfied their mutual corruption—until a very dignified Lionel loudly declared that he respected women far too much to touch them with even the tip of his tongue, inspiring a burst of laughter from the other people there. Feeling awkward, some men chose to play dumb while Álvaro Espinoza, assisted by María Fernanda, headed for her room; someone glimpsed him lying on her bed, apparently asleep. The revelries would continue as ever, with plenty of drink and vallenato music until dawn; some couples left in search of privacy, while others slept together in dark corners. María Fernanda had established the rule that anything could be given away but nothing could be sold at her parties, which is why Petulia, remaining true to her principle of never sleeping with a man for free, had given herself the job of pouring drinks and preparing the appetizers that evening, perhaps happy to resume the role of housewife that she'd played when she lived in El Prado. So she was the only one who noticed María Fernanda and Lionel going into the room where Álvaro Espinoza was dozing, and she was the only one who saw him emerge from the room later with the look of a condemned man: livid, his eyes darting around in fright, he lunged for the remnants of a bottle of whiskey, glugged its contents down, swiftly vomited onto the rug, shuddering as if gripped by a violent fever, and then headed for the door. Later, Petulia would swear she could tell exactly what had happened as soon as she saw María Fernanda come out of the room with her tie neatly knotted at her shirt collar, those dark eyes so devoid of emotion that they appeared to be stuck in the eye sockets of a statue. She felt it in her bones when she heard her calmly say: "Now he's sampled that pleasure, he knows there's nothing else like it."

And since sampling that pleasure meant he'd be doomed to seek it for the rest of his life, Álvaro Espinoza killed himself that Sunday, with the gun that Catalina had bought to protect herself from thieves and then carelessly left on the table the night before she left for Puerto Colombia.

PART THREE

I will send an angel before you and drive out the Canaanites, Amorites, Hittites, Perizzites, Hivites and Jebusites . . . Break down their altars, smash their sacred stones and cut down their Asherah poles."

These words could sum up man's inability to accept difference in others and the aversion that this difference caused, giving rise to so many conflicts, Aunt Irene would likely have said, if Lina had alluded to her tolerance, which travelling and reflection had transformed into a staunch scepticism towards any ideology that attempted to monopolize the truth. But from an early age, Lina had established a dialogue with her based not so much on affirmations as on suggestions and awful uncertainty, since the night she saw her for the first time, as Aunt Irene had been in Europe and Lina was in Barranquilla burning up with fever caused by a diphtheria so violent it seemed she would die before she was three. Lying on the bed belonging to her grandmother, who barely managed to conceal her dread as she paced between the bedroom and the living room awaiting Dr. Agudelo's arrival, she was overcome by the dizziness of a fever that might have been almost enjoyable were it not for the fact that she was also finding it incredibly hard to breathe in that room where, suddenly, Lina saw the figure of a woman appear, identical to her grandmother, only very tall and thin and dressed in a beautiful dark dress, as if made of black taffeta, who slowly approached her and, when she reached her side, placed a hand on her forehead, instantly inducing a deep feeling of peace. Lina would meet her again years later, no longer in a feverish haze, but in the house Aunt Irene moved into when she arrived in Barranquilla after having spent almost fifteen years away giving piano recitals all over the world, and she, Lina, had only to look into her eyes to know that she wasn't to bring up what happened during that critical night of her illness, so as not to spoil the game they were playing, the rules of which she had to discover for herself, only to accept that she would never understand them.

The former owner of the house was a rather eccentric Italian who had disembarked from some rowing boats in the very distant past accompanied by five so-called builders and a cargo of stones and statues the likes of which had never been seen before, and who, after walking around the area many times following the movement of a magnetized needle, people said, decided to buy a few acres of worthless land and on it to build the strangest mansion imaginable, for it was neither square nor rectangular, but round, and its foundations were laid out in a spiral formation. The only ones who knew this were the few people who took the trouble to go and watch it being built, because even before construction began, the Italian had his land fenced off with a thick stone wall, fifteen-foot high, guarded by a prowling pack of ill-tempered Dobermans. Among the builders, or 'freemasons' as the village priest called them with horror, there was one who had been educated in Spanish, and he was in charge of searching the region for the workers and carpenters who worked on the construction site for seven years until they finished that implausible house, with its round rose windows like a cathedral, and gargoyles that could strike fear into the most bellicose of spirits. The occupants kept themselves to themselves; they did not go down into the town or have any dealings with other people; as vegetarians, they ate the fruit and vegetables they grew in their garden, occasionally hunting rabbits and deer to feed their dogs, on which their peace of mind largely depended; in any case, the forest soon swallowed up the trail along which the wagons had travelled years before—carrying their belongings and construction materials, crates full of seeds, books, telescopes and even unusual musical instruments—until the trail became impassable. They lived so far from the main square and from what would later become the city and its residential neighbourhoods, that although people still spoke of them with apprehension at the end of the century, likening them either to excommunicated monks or members of some satanic sect, they had been all but forgotten by the time Aunt Irene graduated as a concert pianist and around "the Italian's Tower," as they used to call it in El Prado, modest little houses started springing up, the kind where no well-born person would have been happy to live. One enigma remained: the first occupants must have been long dead, and yet, on behalf of their heirs or whoever it was, a lawyer had been entrusted with keeping up the tax payments and discussing the installation of pipes and electric cables with the local authorities. The same lawyer, or his son, also showed up every time the tower was searched for reasons of national security at the beginning of both world wars, since there was always some fanatic claiming that it was being used as a refuge for German spies. But except for a guardian of pure coastal stock and the descendants of those unsettling Dobermans, the secret-service agents found no one and nothing, not even the furniture, upholstery, paintings and musical instruments that had appeared as if by magic when Aunt Irene took possession of the house as universal legatee, to the utter confusion of her sisters. None of them cared to know who their father really was—since parentage was established via the mother—but trying to imagine the author of their days being somehow connected to the unusual occupants of the Italian's Tower was a difficult step to take; difficult and particularly vexatious because it cast doubt on the perspicacity with which they undoubtedly believed themselves to be endowed. And yet they all remembered those horseback rides on full-moon nights, Irene leading the way as if she knew the path by heart and were being drawn by some dark force to the circular, walled building, where a servant would open the door when he heard them arrive, rounding up the dogs and lighting the torches that illuminated the garden through which they walked in single file, always behind Irene, as she was the only one who could locate and sidestep the traps laid for trespassers, the only one who could guess which tree or stone to look under to find the gift that the tower's owners offered them silently, without revealing themselves: jewellery boxes, books or music scores, which Aunt Irene practised devotedly on the piano, producing a deep music, unconnected to any kind of psalm or devotion, but directed with infinite intensity towards the heavens. At that time, Aunt Irene would have been about eleven years old, and they, her sisters, naively believed that her fame as a precocious pianist had soared over the rooftops of the Plaza de Nicolás to reach the hearts of men who were so indifferent to the world, and moved them. They might have also imagined other things, since at weekends Aunt Irene began to frequent an abandoned hacienda, which was overgrown with weeds and of little interest except for the fact that it was located not far from the tower, a detail that had also passed them by unnoticed, just as they did not notice, with the same overawed inhibition, the differences in terms of talent, sensitivity and character that distinguished them from their inapprehensible sister, whose passion for music kept her away from their games, and whose education their mother had decided to fast-track, in order to send her as soon as possible to Europe, preserving her intelligence from the intellectual poverty of their environs; an intelligence, or a certain understanding of life, which stood in stark contrast to theirs, the other five sisters, who were forced to take refuge in blind rationalism to protect themselves. This unequal treatment, and the fact it was not acknowledged—Lina would come to think at some point—had created bonds of complicity between them that made them feel guilty, bonds they tried in vain to shake off when Aunt Irene came to live in the city, taking possession of the Italian's Tower in a final desperate challenge to the family. Of course, they were never going to let such an affront become common knowledge, so for discretion's sake they resolved to visit her every couple of months, with a phone call and much deliberation beforehand about what time they should arrive and the kind of conversation that might entertain her; but any conversation seemed to suit her just fine, and over the years the sisters got used to talking amongst themselves, not noticing the condescending humour with which Aunt Irene suggested topics for discussion and then sat back and watched the argument unfold. Only her grandmother, Lina had noticed, seemed reserved: whenever they drove to the tower together in her wealthiest aunt's Cadillac, her grandmother would withdraw into a pensive silence that continued long after they returned home. She never explained the reason for her reticence, not even later, when she would go to visit Aunt Irene on her own and spend the whole afternoon listening to her performing Mozart or playing an old organ in search of haunting melodies that were amplified by the rooms, as if the tower had been designed as a vast sound box. They talked very little, but Lina always felt as if she'd discovered something through her silences or the way in which Aunt Irene always answered her questions with more questions, encouraging her to go beyond her perception of things to gain a new perspective or to acknowledge the limits of her own ignorance.

Curiously, it was Aunt Irene, and not her grandmother, that Lina would talk to about her problems with Beatriz. Not because Beatriz was Lina's friend, but because in a way she would never be her friend, despite her grandmother's best intentions: her grandmother had introduced her to the girl with striking blue eyes as the daughter of Nena Avendaño, who had been a childhood friend of Lina's mother's, and naturally, if Beatriz went to La Enseñanza for her high-school years, Lina should be responsible for introducing her to her group of classmates and explaining the ways of the school to her. The Avendaños had moved to El Prado only recently and lived close by, leading a seemingly harmonious married life that defied everything their critics had predicted about them on the day that Nena married Jorge, her first cousin. That wedding had set off an avalanche of rumours in the city: the two of them had grown up together under the tutelage of Nena's father who had adopted Jorge when his older brother died and had loved him like a son. They were given a strict upbringing, following Christian values to the letter; they were handsome and refined, and so similar to one another that, had it not been for the definite age difference between them, they might have been mistaken for twins. And suddenly it had turned to love, a provocative, urgent love that revealed the family's conflicts, their private life: Jorge didn't want to go back to Bogotá to finish his studies, Nena refused to eat a mouthful of food as long as her father insisted on keeping them apart; doctors, priests and friends all got involved. Wracked with anger, Nena's father finally consented to the marriage, but when he got home after the wedding, he had a heart attack and died that night, cursing the bride and groom in his final throes. In fact, marriage between cousins was commonplace for a social class that was determined to avoid miscegenation by all possible means, and always with the complicity of the church. There was something very different at stake here: his authority as a father, a father twice over, ridiculed twice over, stripped of the excessive rights to his daughter and the power over his nephew who had insidiously betrayed him. Hence the anger that put an end to his life, expressed in a curse that, everyone said, was supposed to haunt the guilty couple and prevent them from finding happiness. But they were all wrong: that passion developed into a quiet, intense pleasure, indifferent to anything that was happening around them. The children, all boys, kept on coming, and were looked after by nannies who kept them away from their parents in the many rooms of the Avendaños' mansion. Then Beatriz came along, a baby whose difficult birth and the irreparable damage she caused to her mother's womb—coming out with such determination that she tore organs and muscles—belied her fragility: she spent two years unwell, in her crib, forcing everyone to take care of her, while the relationship between her parents deteriorated. Whether it was because carnal pleasures were impossible with a woman whose vagina had lost the tightness required for male satisfaction, or whether Nena herself unconsciously feared another pregnancy, the fact was that Jorge Avendaño found himself in love with another first cousin of his, plunging Nena into a living hell. That happened long before they moved to El Prado, making a definitive break with the past and leaving behind the old family villa which was steeped in the memory of their incestuous love affair. No one knew about the calamity then, although Nena had already started doing her pilgrimages to the Virgin of the Convento de la Popa in Cartagena, and there were plenty of people who claimed to see her go out onto the main road, where she walked for days under a leaden sun alongside priests and all the city's religious fanatics, until she reached the foot of the hill and, on her hands and knees, scrambled up the rocky, scrubby path that led to the sanctuary. Such outlandish behaviour could have been down to a belated decision to reconcile herself with the spirit of her dead father by doing everything in her power to offset the curse; there was also talk of it being repentance for years of conjugal lust, in order to give the older children an example of a more modest kind of love, for those children could hardly have any sense of decency if, whenever they passed the bedroom where their parents spent all night and a good part of the day, they heard moans, sighs and other objectionable noises. Of course, they had no sense of decency—at least not according to the good, honest souls in the city—which enabled them to establish a fairly balanced attitude towards life; in other words, they riled anyone who tried to control them, they adapted to social norms to suit their own interests, and, since they learned about sexuality from an early age, in the care of their nannies, they easily seduced the women that fate landed in their path. Beatriz was different; unlike her brothers, she embodied all the ideals of a heroine from an exemplary tale: as soon as she entered La Enseñanza she immediately won over the nuns, who had never seen a more organized student, one so disciplined and devoted, capable of scoring top marks in every subject and an excellent grade for her conduct every week. Such perfection irritated Lina, who, after observing her for some time, unsure whether to brand her behaviour sanctimonious or downright idiotic, had discovered to her astonishment that Beatriz sincerely believed in the virtues of obedience: submitting to the orders of her elders seemed to be the only way she could free herself from the anxiety that an upbringing centred exclusively on the existence of sin and its natural punishment had created in her. This, Lina later thought she understood by answering the questions that her own questions elicited from Aunt Irene and which she refrained from asking her grandmother for fear of upsetting her, because everything that concerned Nena Avendaño seemed to cause her infinite sorrow: Nena had helped her to shroud her daughter, had been with her during the horrible days that preceded her death, and that was something that Lina's grandmother was not willing to forget. And it was a debt that, she, Lina, had to take on, helping Beatriz whatever the circumstance, without trying to understand her personality or evaluate her behaviour. This was particularly difficult for Lina, given her instinctive aversion to Beatriz's proselytizing, for it was not enough for Beatriz to always obey the nuns' arbitrary decisions and, like them, find every action sinful: talking to the cleaners, not going out to play during recess, messing around during mass, cutting needlework class, in short, all the little rebellions that made the repressive atmosphere of the school more bearable. No. Beatriz also tried to convince Lina and her friends of the spiritual benefits inherent to subservience, telling them that, on a smaller scale, it replicated man's submission to the divine will; moreover, their punishment should be accepted gladly, particularly if it was unfair, because then they could offer their suffering as a sacrifice to the Lord, gaining indulgences at the hour of their death. Her Sunday-sermon language and her habit of telling on anyone who had messed around whenever she was put in charge of the class when a nun left the room eventually made her so unpopular that Lina, much to her regret, was obliged to defend her. On more than one occasion she got her out of trouble or intervened on her behalf to calm things down, but one day Beatriz could avoid disaster no more: the school's pipes were being extended, and the workmen had left a wooden plank as a walkway over a relatively deep ditch; on top of this, and out of sight of the nuns, someone had placed another plank, forming a dangerous seesaw which a group of pupils were playing on. So when Beatriz appeared, they invited her to clamber up onto one end of the plank while they did so at the opposite end and jumped off it as soon as Beatriz had got on: all at once, the makeshift seesaw propelled her violently to the bottom of the ditch where she received a blow to the head that left her unconscious, and, when she came out of hospital and returned to school, her character was marked by a new trait: distrust. From then on, only Isabel and Lina went over to the Avendaños' house. It was a rather sad house, where Nena could be heard reciting prayers all day long, with Beatriz's voice answering like an echo as she learned the lessons by heart. Everything in it looked too clean; the tiles, furniture, curtains and beautiful old heirlooms could not have looked more impersonal if they'd been in the window of an antique shop. There were no radios, no pets, no plants or flowers; a kind of desolation emanated from that undisturbed orderliness, so unmoving that it evoked the decorous oblivion of a cemetery. Still hovering over the house, although she had died months before, was the memory of one of Nena's aunts, who had been responsible for Beatriz's education, if education meant terrorizing a child night and day with chilling stories of tormented souls who appeared before the living to tell them of their misfortunes and keep them from sinning. That unhinged woman, who had been thrown out of two convents after disastrous novitiates, had also dragged down Nena, who, not content with entrusting her aunt with Beatriz's upbringing, had also adopted the same trashy brand of mysticism by embarking on those pilgrimages to the Virgen de la Popa on which she would waste her beauty and youth, or what was left of them. She was not yet fifty when Lina met her, and she already had the skin of an old woman, her eyes clouded over with pain; all the trudging up and down the road to Cartagena made her stoop, the skin on the back of her neck darkened by the sun, and her knees, battered on the rocky path up the hill, were covered in scars and sores. From the very beginning, Lina felt an affection for her, one tinged with anger and pity. Having heard about the Avendaños' problem thanks to Berenice's trained ear for gossip, she found it unbearable that someone could suffer so much from someone else's indifference; it was disturbing to see how it manifested, how obscenely disproportionate it was. Yet Nena's helplessness and her complete lack of aggression made it easy for Lina to love her, and as the years went by, she would learn to decipher the confusing monologue that tumbled from her ruined mind. She didn't even have the words to help her understand the searing feeling of guilt she had as soon as she'd been left alone, without the protection of a pleasure to lose herself in every night, without the love that gave her worth by banishing her remorse at having felt nothing when her father died, when she heard him cursing her in his final throes. She just resigned herself to suffer blindly, in the darkness of a nameless ignorance, while she vegetated in a state that even her own children likened to madness, but which Lina chose to think of as a safe place where she, Nena, could at least cling to the hope that she might be able to change her destiny through magical rituals that could win the favour of the gods.

For Beatriz, on the other hand, her mother's fate was a terrible, intolerable injustice. Perhaps, subconsciously afraid to pass judgement on the father she adored, she did not try to look for the underlying causes for what happened; in any case, she'd had enough of seeing Nena returning from her pilgrimages, sunburned, with bloodied knees and the hem of her dress in tatters; hearing her praying the rosary, desperately pacing up and down the corridors at night; catching sight of the tracks of her silent tears; observing her lack of appetite at the dinner table; discovering the little white lies she told to try to appease her. Because Nena did not tell anyone about her sorrows, least of all the twelve-year-old girl who could not understand her and who was the only reason Jorge Avendaño agreed to spend occasional weekends at the house after securing some contract or other in the United States to justify his repeated absences. In reality he did very little work, living off Nena's father's inheritance and hiding his illicit love affairs from everyone, including the older children. Without meaning to, he had become a rogue, embroiled in a situation he did not know how to control, since he was neither prepared to earn a living by the sweat of his brow, nor could he do without the comforts to which he'd grown accustomed over fifty years of idleness. With his children studying in Bogotá and his wife transformed into an inoffensive weeping woman, he could afford the luxury of frequent visits to Miami, where the new object of his affections lived. And there, he could keep a yacht and live the high life without answering to anyone about the management of Nena's fortune, least of all Nena, who never asked for explanations. She was too soft for her own good, Lina would venture to suggest to Aunt Irene, who as usual was a closed book, and whose stony silence would prompt her, this time, to abandon easy platitudes and glimpse that rigid, vulnerable world of people who maintained a certain nobility of soul, expressed in subtle ways, such as taking refuge in derangement rather than admitting that the man they loved had acted dishonourably. Because if she had accepted that Jorge Avendaño was capable not only of lying to her but also of knowingly stealing from her, Nena would have been forced to admit the laughable nature of her passion for him and the indignity of having embraced that love, turning her back on a notion of honour based less on filial obedience than on a principle respected by the old aristocracy, which dictated that no one should ever do anything that could draw the attention of the riffraff to the family. They still lived in complete opacity; their descendants, lost in a society in upheaval, would have the bad taste to paint pictures or write novels.

So, Beatriz did not know why her mother suffered so much. Berenice surmised it with rather disarming common sense; having learned from Nena's maids that Jorge Avendaño never slept in his room, not even during the weekends allocated to Beatriz, she had easily guessed that there was a lover; who she was and where she lived, Berenice did not claim to know, but her long experience with the people of El Prado made her sure that it must be a close relative, because, in her opinion, Jorge Avendaño was only capable of getting tangled up in passions as fatal as death. Freud would have agreed with her, but Lina barely listened to her; at that time her primary concern was to see Beatriz as little as possible outside school hours without her grandmother noticing, and, if she couldn't avoid it, stoically enduring the atmosphere of that house steeped in pain, where that woman martyred herself while her daughter inflicted atrocious punishments on her dolls. Such was Beatriz's only distraction, and out of politeness, she, Lina, had to sit through grim rituals in which the most beautiful porcelain dolls Aunt Eloísa had imported forty years earlier and sold to Nena's father for considerable sums were symbolically tied up, beaten and sometimes crucified to cleanse their bodies of the sins Beatriz said they were guilty of, or to atone for offences so serious she could not talk about them.

"Because she doesn't know how to talk about them," Lina would hear Aunt Irene suggest one day, not looking up from the immense *Book of the Dead*, whose hieroglyphs she'd been showing her, teaching her how to decipher them; she said it not in an affirmative tone but a questioning one, as if she believed that Lina was capable of looking past appearances to discover the exact meaning behind the obscure symbol, the same way she had learned to find the meaning behind the complex figures in the book that lay open on the table. And suddenly, Lina had the impression that she was seeing things from a different angle, that she had been projected into a dimension so revelatory that she would forever recall herself sitting there in astonishment next to Aunt Irene, rapidly associating all the details that had vanished into her subconscious, recovered in a flash by her memory: Beatriz's games no longer struck her as a mechanical imitation of the example her mother had set, but an expression of a deeper, more worrying instability, as if another person altogether took hold of her when she was torturing her dolls. In a way this was true, because there was a gulf of difference between the outstanding student, bright-eyed and waiting for the first opportunity to stick her hand up and answer the teacher, and the girl playing with grim concentration in her room. From then on, Lina would see her own discomfort morph into curiosity: Beatriz inhabited two universes, distinct but not parallel in that they intertwined like two radio waves successively occupying the same frequency. Sometimes her intelligence worked its way into the macabre logic of her childish games, trivializing them; at other times, the morbid nature of her character turned her into a doll herself, and she would remain on her knees all through mass or sit extremely upright in her chair in class, not moving a muscle. As a result, Beatriz would soon become a subject of observation for Lina, even though she instinctively recoiled whenever Beatriz was around.

Because Lina could not avoid her, that much was clear: on the one hand she had her grandmother, insisting on the debt she owed to Nena Avendaño, and on the other she had Beatriz, inviting her to come over every day. Lina only enjoyed herself when she was accompanied by Isabel, who didn't hate dolls but, like her, preferred to go out into the garden and climb the branches of the hundred-year-old saman tree that had miraculously resisted the ravages of urbanization; hiding away in its foliage, they would invent fantastic stories while Beatriz begged them to come down, threatening and warning them about how inappropriate their behaviour was, especially if there happened to be any boys prowling around on bicycles and, in later years, in cars. The friendship with Lina's cousins, who abandoned their teenage misogyny as soon as they entered the final years of high school so they could try their hand at seduction, would, thank God, alter the situation: first, Beatriz agreed to go for rides in their cars or explore old, abandoned houses at night, and then, when she fell in love with one of them, her sexuality began to appear, burgeoning quickly and furtively.

It happened one December, during the holidays. They had made a habit of leaving Las Novenas and driving along the main road to Puerto Colombia until they reached the *ciénaga*, a shimmering mass of blue reflections; they got out of the cars and talked, amid the rustling of insects and the sudden flutter of a night bird they had disturbed; some couples sneaked off into the woods, not roaming too far in case they got lost, and staying there until the car headlights signalled that they should come back. Beatriz and Jairo Insignares hardly dared to hold hands: they had been sweethearts for about six months, when Jairo joined the other boys who followed the La Enseñanza bus in their cars, calling out flirtatious remarks to the girls, much to the indignation of the spinster tasked with keeping an eye on them. The flirting never did anything for Beatriz; at least outwardly she remained impassive, but her reaction would be different the day Lina passed on a letter from Jairo that contained a declaration of love so conventional that any of the other girls would have laughed. Beatriz did not laugh—quite the opposite: she kept the letter in the back of her religious studies book so it was as close to her as possible, and perhaps she began to dream, as much as any naïve young girl, and as far as her overly scrupulous heart would allow her. From then on she sat in the window seat on the bus: very pale, tense with emotion, she waited to see those cars appear so she could catch a glimpse of Jairo and stare at him intensely; one day she sent a message to him saying that yes, she would be his girlfriend, without really knowing what that meant, or only having a vague idea about it, because she sometimes went to the cinema on Sundays with Lina and had seen couples sitting together, giving each other long kisses as soon as the lights went out. Beatriz did not understand that those caresses, those first forays into desire, constituted the ultimate sin at her age. No one had told her this, and, like Catalina, she had not understood any of the allusions the priests were making when they roared from the pulpit, railing against the temptations of the flesh. Of course, it was forbidden to look in the direction of the boys perched on the school wall, and it was forbidden to see them behind their parents' backs, because to do that would mean to commit the despicable act of lying. But the only judge of Beatriz's private life was her own mother, and Nena Avendaño, perhaps trying to keep her away from the dolls, not only expressed no misgivings when she found out that she was in love, but also encouraged her to formalize the courtship a little, suggesting that she invite her suitor round to the house. Jairo, at first quite surprised and equally as daunted, got used to visiting her at weekends and ended up playing with the girls like just another friend, although from time to time, remembering his role, he brought Beatriz flowers or held her hand in the cinema. And things might have carried on this way were it not for Jairo's friends intervening, encouraging him to be more daring and, inadvertently, to satisfy some of Beatriz's desires, who was experiencing their love with the hazy ambiguity of an adolescent unable to leave her childhood behind for good. She had still not parted with her dolls: her favourite, the one with jet-black curls, spent most of the time tied to the bars of a window in front of the trees in the yard; Beatriz only locked her in a closet with the rest of the dolls if Jairo came round to visit, not so much as a sign of conciliation, but out of fear that her games would be discovered and she would become a laughing stock; the six months of courtship had made her aware of the opinions of others, albeit without fundamentally altering her conflicts with life and despite the furious turmoil that was raging inside her body. Furious and mute: nothing about Beatriz gave away her emotions, except the colour of her eyes, which went from blue to a dark, almost grey tone whenever she sneaked a sideways glance at Jairo from the bus window. Then December came, and with it, freedom in the nightly breeze blowing in off the swamp, and that strange sensation of existing in a motionless time, a time when the craziest of desires could be fulfilled. Following the example of the other couples, Jairo and Beatriz ventured into the darkness one night and gradually learned how to love each other; together they would discover the thrill of caresses and the giddy vertigo of kisses. Covered in sour sweat, eyes glazed over with excitement, they wandered back like sleepwalkers when the car headlamps beckoned; they smelled of grass and damp earth, looked distant and secretive. Those might have been the best days of Beatriz's life, Lina would eventually come to tell herself, when she was able to think about her calmly—that is, without being overcome with horror whenever she remembered her. Because until that point, Beatriz had never come so close to finding some kind of equilibrium, gradually leaving behind her disturbing games to venture into the well-defined order of adults, where pregnancies and domestic problems would have explained away her dichotomy, and carnivals and games of canasta would have tempered her foolishness. But destiny had resolved to reinforce the darker side of her personality instead, distancing her definitively from love and, in the process, involving Lina in the event that would affect her so badly.

More than a thousand times, Lina would regret taking Beatriz for a ride in her car that afternoon. She usually took a female friend with her, since that had been the condition her father gave on the day of her twelfth birthday when he finally decided to let her have the old Dodge, and Catalina and Isabel shared her joy of touring the heights of El Prado, where the streets were well laid out around still-empty plots of land where the noises of the city were muted, not daring to disturb their adolescent dreams. The dying engine seemed to be revived by the breeze and the lack of traffic; in the dusk, one could just make out the faint quiver of the city lights and the occasional cars cruising around with their headlights turned off, searching for spots to conduct clandestine love affairs. It was precisely one of those cars, a cream-colored Packard parked up in a dead-end street, which caused Beatriz to cry out and reach for the door handle, forcing Lina to slam on the brakes; the couple locked in an embrace in the Packard pulled away from one another in surprise, and as the woman ducked down, the man turned to look at them, but by then Beatriz was already running towards him. When she stopped at the window, she shouted something that Lina could not make out: Jorge Avendaño had just been caught in flagrante delicto, and by his own daughter, the girl he loved so much and from whom he could not expect the slightest shred of understanding. No doubt motivated by fear, and by the distressed pleas of the woman by his side, he started the engine without predicting how Beatriz would react: she leapt in front of the Packard, receiving the full impact of the sudden start and landing on the ground a few feet away. Lina had already jumped out of the car and made it over to where Beatriz lay, stunned by the blow and the pain of a broken leg, at the same time as Jorge Avendaño, who seemed completely unable to deal with the situation. Leaning over her, they both saw the woman sprint past them in a desperate bid to protect her identity. Beatriz saw her too, and managed to beg Lina not to say a word to Nena. A moment later she passed out, cursing her father, and as she did, her incredibly pale face wore a stern mask, bearing the same intractable expression as her ancestors in the old portraits that hung on the walls of her house.

Nena, of course, found out everything. Lina could tell by the way she held up one hand to silence her as she hurried into the hospital in El Prado with Alfredo, her oldest son; a firm gesture, yet full of tenderness, as if she wanted to spare her the humiliation of lying; she must have thought that she'd endured quite enough already that afternoon, when she found herself alone in the car, with Beatriz lying in the back seat, as she anxiously looked for someone who could help her. Because after depositing Beatriz's inert body in the Dodge and telling Lina to follow his car, Jorge Avendaño proceeded to drive around the streets until he spotted the woman, who was running about in a state of absolute madness, and then, when he finally managed to get her back into the Packard, he floored the accelerator and vanished around a bend. Lina could not believe her eyes. For a few seconds she sat there in a daze as a wave of rage took her breath away, then suddenly she remembered Dr. Agudelo, and decided to go to his office to find him. He had already left, and she had to scour half the city before she found him; since Dr. Agudelo thought Beatriz should be taken to hospital, they went to Las Tres Marías and, while he dealt with the formalities, Lina called the Avendaño brothers at the country club. She could not hide the truth from them: there wasn't a scratch on the Dodge, and she couldn't tell them it was an accident; she asked them, begged them even, to keep what had happened from Nena. But it was no use: the five Avendaño brothers were not going to miss an opportunity to finally expose their father's shady financial dealings, forcing Nena to admit, once and for all, that their marriage was a sham, and to regain legitimate control of her fortune as a result. This was accomplished without much difficulty: by threatening to reveal the name of his lover and his despicable behaviour towards Beatriz, the brothers managed to force Jorge Avendaño to hand over to them the assets that had allowed him to lead a charmed life for years, a lifestyle completely out of proportion to how much he worked. They could have demanded much more from him, and he would have given it to them; with Beatriz hospitalized because of him, and having lost her love forever, he plummeted into a state of depression that prevented him from putting up the slightest resistance to his sons' deal. In a way, they behaved honourably, even leaving him a decent enough personal income to enjoy an honourable retirement as an andropausal playboy, one who would live out his days on the golf courses of the country club, smartly dressed, and casting looks of doleful admiration at women. In exchange for these benefits, he would of course have to return to the marital home: to keep up appearances and to put an end to his wife's despair, which was the reason for the ridiculous pilgrimages everyone in the city was talking about.

And so everything was in order, the Avendaño brothers believed, perhaps with the candour of well-adjusted people who thought that resolving a conflict meant the slate was wiped clean. They did not understand that the long years of unhappiness had indelibly marked Nena, and, above all, they did not consider how that whole episode had affected Beatriz's state of mind. The teenage girl who left the hospital battered and bruised, with her leg in plaster, seemed to have lost the power of speech, so much so that Nena begged Lina to stay with her for a few days to try to coax her out of the mute state she had been in since the accident. Beatriz did not talk, she ate very little, and she lay awake all night. There was a dreadful intensity emanating from her stony silence, not a calculated or even deliberate silence, but one that was inevitable, almost inherent to the feverish mental activity she was experiencing, as if all her body's energy were being consumed in some monstrous process. Lina sometimes had the alarming impression that she could sense her thoughts, especially at night, when she would wake up startled and, in the dressing-table mirror, by the light of a permanently lit bulb, she would see Beatriz's wide-open eyes staring into space. Perhaps she was examining her points of reference one after the other, with a perplexity full of resentment; logically, it made sense that her core principles had suffered a considerable blow: lo and behold, her father, the symbol of order in her life, the figure at the centre of a rigid system of coercion and obedience, was behaving like a coward, violating the rules that had to be respected if he was to have any power over her; and her mother (the image she was supposed to identify with) was a hopeless victim, beyond even heaven's help. But Beatriz lacked Catalina's mental ability to question the values society had instilled in her and to start thinking for herself instead. Nor did she have Lina's sense of humour, which in the long run, could minimize the anxiety that was inextricably linked to a loss of certainty. Although the nucleus had broken up, its components were still there in her battered conscience, desperately trying to form a new structure. Until she found it: perhaps that dawn when, emerging from her depression, she went out to the yard carrying all her dolls, silently, without waking anyone, not even Lina, who had been sleeping beside her, and, leaning on her crutches, began gathering leaves and branches until she managed to light a bonfire that started to blaze with an ominous glow. Lina sensed it as she jumped out of bed, already guessing in that moment what her eyes would see a second later. And as she stood at the window, watching Beatriz flinging the dolls into the fire, she felt the strange, implausible certainty that she had witnessed the same scene once before: a young blonde girl, her expression angelic but devoid of any emotion, standing in front of a bonfire where dolls writhed and crackled in mourning amid the foul stench of burnt hair.

II

The Italian's Tower appeared like a question, an ironic reflection of the challenges faced by men. At its centre was a circular room whose walls consisted of mirrored panels alternating with open spaces that let in the light from the round windows in the rooms positioned around it; from top to bottom, from one side to the other, all the rooms led, either directly or via stairs and corridors, to the room where Aunt Irene used to spend her evenings. Apart from the piano, there was nothing else in that room, and yet it emanated a feeling of fullness, perhaps because the tiles formed a vivid mosaic of geometric figures painted in gold, blue and ochre on the floor, and the same colours and motifs were repeated on the ceiling, a thick stained-glass window that filtered the sun's rays, turning them into a still, golden light, reflected by the mirrors. Lina became acquainted with that room when she started going to visit Aunt Irene on her own, and from the first time she saw it, she felt that not only had she obtained a privilege, but she was in the presence of an enigma she could not decipher, as if the room had been designed with a precise but hidden intention that was off-limits to her intelligence. Only at the end of her life did she believe she had finally grasped the meaning behind the hall of mirrors, the reason for its shape, its curious layout: and with a hazy memory of it in her mind, she slipped, smiling, into the very specific dream of death. As a child, however, she was afraid to stay in the room if her aunt left her there, and she was even more afraid of venturing out and risking getting lost in the labyrinth of corridors. Because beyond its straightforward appearance, the circular room was surrounded by a maze of artifices designed to deceive the unsuspecting visitor, sending them into different rooms which all looked identical and were covered with wall-hangings that looked more or less the same apart from the stone borders that ran along the walls just below the paintings and tapestries, revealing a universe of figures chiselled by the hand of someone in the grip of hallucinations: trees with trunks sticking into the earth while their roots opened up to the sky, boulders defying gravity, suspended in the air over a flaming ocean, tiny men living inside the belly of a mermaid, winged fish, two-headed birds; all kinds of aberrant creatures among the symbols from probably forgotten alphabets and sketches of silhouettes suggesting an idea that would be developed much further on, in another room, following whimsical designs until it suddenly reached its definitive form, one that was not always accessible to understanding, but showing, through the expression of its totality or the symbolic formulation of its essence, the way back to the circular room, where Aunt Irene sat at the piano and played her favourite sonatas.

Lina would discover the clue offered by the stone frieze in a flash of intuition, one afternoon when she lost her bearings while crossing a corridor, and was going up and down stairs, round and round the rooms, unable to find her way, because they all seemed identical and Aunt Irene's piano resounded with equal intensity in all of them; she was unsure whether to shout for help or to try to contain herself, she suddenly noticed an image that looked familiar, not because she had actually looked at it before, but perhaps because she had seen it in passing and her memory had retained an impression of it: it was the outline of an insect gliding like a zeppelin over a shadowy city, but its menacing eye—which Lina recalled at that moment with astonishing accuracy—was not yet formed, and out of its socket came springs resembling antennae: one of them extended into the next image, blending into the tangle of foliage of the tropical trees there before finally merging with the branches of a mahogany tree under which a woman was cradling a translucent egg in her arms; a few steps further on the figure reappeared, staring out at a door Lina had never noticed before; the door opened onto a corridor which she proceeded to enter, observing how, along that particular frieze, the egg began morphing into concentric circles from which something resembling an androgenous being emerged and, before dividing into two distinct sexes, this being appeared to be inventing the insect itself, creating it with its imagination and so, gradually, by means of arabesques and pentagrams and other symbols, the insect started to take form, becoming enriched with details that made it more disturbing, metallic, armoured like an instrument of destruction. When Lina saw the insect fully formed, fixing its cold, hard eye on the sleeping city, she realized that she had reached one of the rooms that led into the hall of mirrors. From that moment on, she imagined she was having a silent dialogue with Aunt Irene.

Imagined, because she never knew for certain whether that assumption aligned with reality or reflected a secret delusion brought on by her aunt's total silence and the persistent shadow of those foreigners who had translated their dreams into stone before they died. It all began when Lina set out to understand her own thought process, if that was the right term to describe the jumbled activity going on in her mind, which as a rule was limited to a passive accumulation of observations from which she drew hasty and uninteresting conclusions, impeded by the simplicity of her outlook: when she finally acknowledged this seemingly insurmountable barrier, she could define the object of her focus, which, curiously, evaded her in a chaotic cloud of questions that revolved around one subject; when one day she managed to home in on it, she had the impression that Aunt Irene chimed in with a musical note. Yes, a musical note. That was all it took. This outlandish idea occurred to her when, after spending entire afternoons monologuing at her and only receiving polite but very brief remarks in return, she noticed how, at intervals, Aunt Irene would play a particular sonata. There were seven notes in the scale and seven open spaces between the mirrors, and so the step from this, to assigning each note of the key of the sonata to one of the seven entryways to the circular room, was one Lina happily took, favouring the arbitrariness of that association over her ineffective speculations. At any rate, she would come to realize much later, the friezes lining the walls were open to any interpretation, or rather, they could be read in a thousand different ways so long as one of the countless threads hiding in those intricate depictions was picked up, and even so, the main line of the frieze lent itself to an incredible number of readings, like those books that stay with a reader throughout their whole life, opening up new horizons for them as they grow older and more experienced. She spent years hopelessly trying to assign a note from the scale to each entryway, and still more years studying the maze of symbols, trying to single out the images specific to subjects that interested her. Sometimes, through patience and great humility, she managed to break the silence of the friezes; sometimes, they refused to speak to her, or did so incredibly slowly. Except in the case of Beatriz.

Beatriz, or her situation, was clearly depicted in the images carved in stone by the former inhabitants of the Italian's Tower; she was represented by an automaton, or a puppet, and sometimes a wind-up doll or a jack-in-the-box, whose distinguishing feature was his rigidity, the mechanical, disciplined nature of his movements; in his first appearance he was falling from the wheel of fortune on the tenth Tarot card, and in the second he was shielding himself from the light of the Hermit's lantern; from then on he could be seen making the strings that would turn him into a puppet that twitched with rage or pain, constantly staring at a sun so intense that it melted everything its rays touched; as he moved along, alternately dressed in the garb of inquisitor or victim, the automaton seemed to lose the tragic appearance of a tin soldier lost in a world of invisible obstacles as he acquired the form of a warrior, one increasingly attached to the thick armour that protected his body; suddenly he would collapse, and further along the friezes he could be seen on the ground or at the bottom of a cave, struggling hopelessly against the weight of his scrap iron; when the strings he was attached to pulled him back to his feet, he would stagger for a few moments before regaining his mechanical pace under the sun that deformed the objects around him. The automaton did not perceive reality, and neither did Beatriz; his armour kept him locked inside himself, preventing him from communicating with others, and Beatriz's armour did the same: he pursued a single objective, embodied by the sun that blinded him with its light; likewise Beatriz harboured an exclusive and excluding mysticism: the cult of the family.

Any sensible person would have believed that, after the accident in the Alto Prado neighbourhood, Beatriz was bound to question an institution that society had created in order to consolidate a system that put her, as a woman, at a disadvantage. In the end her mother could not have been more wretched, and the presence of a defeated but spiteful husband was not going to give her back the years she had lost to weeping and pilgrimages. Moreover, Jorge Avendaño had become morose and participated in family life as little as humanly possible, spending his days on the golf courses at the country club and his nights shut away in his room, drinking malevolently, methodically, until he fell asleep on the bed. With no apparent reason that would allow her to express her sorrow, Nena had retreated into a sweet madness of masses, prayers and processions. But Beatriz reigned supreme in this world of suffering.

Everyone, including her brothers, was afraid of the episodes she would sink into if anything about the ideas and behaviour of those around her conflicted with the imaginary order she herself had created; they were rather odd episodes, which began with a sudden fainting fit and continued with a total loss of appetite until her parents were forced to take her to the hospital. Confronted with this angelic-eyed girl who seemed intent on dying as if inhabited by some evil spirit, the doctors tried injections, transfusions and all the means at their disposal to combat the anorexia; when they finally succeeded in restoring her appetite, she complained of a searing pain in her groin that made her walk with a limp; the doctors could not do much about that either, other than venture into complicated psychoanalytical hypotheses, the substance of which they fundamentally opposed. With or without theories, they would have been amazed to learn that Beatriz somehow actually controlled her episodes: true, her capacity for suffering appeared to know no bounds and she could go for days and days without eating, impervious to the pleas, threats or promises they made to her. But the episodes were carefully controlled, managed even. For the time being, the problems only arose during the holidays or on the eve of a long weekend, since she was not willing to lose her status as top of the class; likewise, the pain in her groin disappeared as soon as the end-of-year ceremony drew closer, and she and Catalina would fight over who would have the honour of playing Jeanne de Lestonnac; also, curiously, the fainting fits always happened when her father was around.

Jorge Avendaño had fallen into a baffling trap. At first, he thought he was responsible for those afflictions, as there seemed to be a clear link between the accident caused by his cowardice and Beatriz's mental imbalance. Then the years went by, and at some point he must have noticed there was something amiss with his reasoning; that is to say, as he wandered the golf courses of the country club trying in vain to hit the little white ball—his caddy watching him, no longer with derision, but a look of pure boredom—and between the glasses of whiskey sipped in the darkness of his room, certain doubts would creep into his mind and unsettle him, until he decided to ask Dr. Agudelo for help. Having been brought up a Christian, Jorge Avendaño was inclined to accept that punishment was a consequence of sin, and he had racked up his fair share of faults ever since the day when, defying the authority of the man he regarded as his father, he had greedily committed a crime very close to incest. When, after many mistakes, it was his turn to be stripped of his ill-gotten power by his own children, his anger could be assuaged by the relief of seeing this affront as a form of expiation, the final thorn being Beatriz's conduct; provided, of course, that these episodes were down to a secret desire to torment him for a specific reason, such as his longstanding indifference to Nena's unhappiness, or the way he'd reacted when he was caught in the arms of a mistress. But here was the crux of the problem, the confusion that led him to overcome the natural reserve of every Avendaño and talk to a doctor about his private life: Beatriz did not have the slightest memory of that incident, which undermined any interpretation of it as being revenge and made the state of nervous tension her unpredictable trances kept him in unbearable. He spoke with astonishment, seeming to have discovered the power of language only a second before he opened his mouth, and giving the impression that he instantly regretted using it. Dr. Agudelo would tell Lina this not during what was to be their first conversation about Beatriz, but months later, when they had spent so much time in his consulting room analyzing the situation together and Lina finally realized her lifelong dream, born in the fever of diphtheria, of having a love affair with that man, with his gentle yet steady hands, and astute eyes behind the strict cordiality of his smile. Jorge Avendaño would never know how much he had gone up in her estimation for suggesting that Dr. Agudelo talk to her to try to understand his daughter's disorder. And certainly she, Lina, was able, if not to explain, then at least to provide some elements that might help to point the doctor in the right direction, since he was unable to see his patient and his only analytical material had been provided by someone too deeply involved in the conflict.

Without going into too much depth, Lina was able to make him see that Beatriz's alleged amnesia came from a desire to change the past to make it fit in with some illusory family history in which all her ancestors appeared as paragons of virtue, gallant knights in the service of the King and, later, of Independence, and matronly women devoted to their home or to the protection of the needy. Jorge Avendaño and Nena had loved each other since childhood, and nothing had ever stood in the way of their romance. What about his mistress? No, Beatriz had not forgotten her, but it was better to keep quiet about that momentary lapse of judgement; sometimes, when she was with Lina, she talked about that woman in a very cruel way, as if she were evil incarnate, horror itself. Because Beatriz's Manichaeism had intensified, assuming delirious proportions: as far as she was concerned, on the one side there were indecent women, odious prostitutes, soulless mothers, a whole satanic female universe conjuring up the ruinous darkness; and on the other, there were people whose behaviour conformed to the law she had entrenched herself behind, which consisted of a series of principles intended to safeguard the family's honour. She cared little about the religious, social or political origins of those principles, the interests they concealed or the injustices committed in their name; and so, when her brothers and uncles argued among themselves—while Jorge Avendaño quietly got drunk in his room—she advocated with equal intransigence for the Inquisition, Nazism or communism or whatever the topic happened to be, much to the astonishment of those listening to her, unaware of the hidden aspect of her statements and the organized intellectual structure that substantiated her reasoning: after much reading and a few compromises, Beatriz had secretly subscribed to the theory of evolution, albeit interpreting it in her own way, likening it to a process aimed at creating order out of chaos and concluding that all the repressive systems that had ever existed responded in different ways to the same progression in the fight against anarchy. No one dared to contradict her, of course, afraid they might suddenly trigger one of her episodes: as soon as she started speaking, the others kept silent, a little confused by her advances in the realm of ideas. Except for Lina: it was she who lent her book after book, without much enthusiasm because she knew that Beatriz would read them, not so much to follow the author's reflections as to stack up new arguments; when faced with the written word, she suffered a kind of innate colour-blindness in which she avoided anything that might break through the solid wall of her convictions. Álvaro Espinoza did something similar, but unlike him, Beatriz did not accept double standards, in men or women, and would not tolerate the slightest slip-up, either by herself or by others.

Things would have been easier if there had been some scientific or philosophical theory to back up Beatriz's way of thinking. Lina was willing to accept it as a starting point for a theory yet to be proved, provided it incorporated the notions of origin and purpose, that is to say, the concept of God; sometimes she seemed to find a parallel between her idea of matter organizing itself or having the intention of organizing itself, and certain images carved in the friezes of the Italian's Tower. But Beatriz categorically rejected the idea of there being any divine intervention in that merciless creation, whose sole aim was to achieve the original, immutable and happy order of the first particle a second before the explosion that had caused the expansion of the universe: there was, then, a quest for order which tended to suppress diversity in search of the primitive unity where good—conceived as the absence of evil—was found, and even denied in its purest state due to a lack of reference points. And nothing else; or perhaps, yes, something else, infinite cycles of dilation and contraction, whose meaning posed an enigma that could not be deciphered by intelligence. In any case, Beatriz did not intend to go into any more depth: this explanation supported her views on the need for a social order that could assimilate man—a supremely wayward and individualistic being—into the plan of matter itself, the same way that, years ago, when she believed in a God who doled out punishments and rewards, she saw every act of submission as a repetition of the reverence that was due to divine authority. At the time, however, her ideas were merely an exaggerated reflection of the religious principles of society, and any catechized illiterate person could have done the same, while her new creed—which quickly became dogma she only discussed with Lina—made her feel like she was one of the chosen few. Where were those men who could uncover the truth and suffer the consequences of such a revelation? Hidden away. Had they shown themselves, society would have crushed them. Society wanted simple, reassuring explanations, an all-powerful God watching over his children from the immensity of the heavens, a reason for life and death; since both these things were the minuscule reproduction of the process to which the entire universe was condemned by a law inherent to its essence, daring to call them absurd meant not only running the risk of inciting a wave of anger in people, but also, and in the best-case scenario, of making them think things that could give rise to total chaos, delaying the march towards the liberating entropy that those who shared Beatriz's lucidity sought through their efforts. Hence, the return to non-existence required absolute discipline, and the people who knew this were humanity's elite.

For years Beatriz believed that this knowledge ought to be reflected in some way, allowing the initiated to recognize each other as members of a Masonic sect; when she saw no visible change in her body, no mark or stigma capable of revealing it, she thought that her rigorous conduct would attest to her condition, and she began waiting for the sign that would allow the other chosen ones to find her; after endless dreams about letters that never arrived and gestures that no one made, she commissioned a jeweller to make her an unusual gold pendant with an engraving she'd designed herself, with the infinity symbol encompassing various religious emblems and mathematical formulas. Eventually she came to the conclusion that no one was inclined to consider the things of the Spirit in Barranquilla, that city of *mestizos* and fugitives, and she resolved to carry the weight of the truth by herself. She was fifteen.

There were advantages and disadvantages to her conviction that she had discovered the Absolute; the advantages immediately became apparent and were explained by her self-confidence: a surprising capacity for learning, finishing her daily tasks in half an hour of study so that she could devote herself to reading instead; a feverish intellectual dynamism that sometimes gave rise to subtle yet corrosive, acid-like analyses; and a kind of stoic attitude to solitude. All this, along with her obstinate rejection of any idea that happened to contradict her own. Fortunately, such ideas were few and far between. The world she had lived in until then was characterized, as she was, by Manichaeism, and in the fifties there were two ideologies battling for monopoly of the truth. On the one hand was religion, in whatever form, with its one true God, who was driven by homicidal tendencies towards anyone who tried to deny his existence, a reflection of the arbitrary father demanding the most servile submission from his children, curbing their sexuality in order to nip any passing fancy for independence in the bud; and, on the other hand, a materialistic mentality that had been best expressed by communism, also headed by another bearded patriarch, whose ideas—which were not always consistent with reality and were distorted to the point of producing a new doctrine—when put into practice created a climate of fear and repression that, in the whole history of mankind, had only been brought about by the inquisitorial courts of the Middle Ages. These two ideologies suited Beatriz: both had to rely on the family in order to establish some form of power in the name of their principles, and both tended to eliminate the disorder represented by so-called human freedom. It was as simple as that. And what about their founders, the messiahs, prophets and revolutionaries who, invoking the god of their ancestors or a materialistic creed, fought for a more just society? They were humble instruments in the service of a law they knew nothing about. All one had to do was observe how hopes crumbled in the face of reality, how illusions died when utopia gave way to the government of things.

Hearing her talk, Lina felt utterly powerless: she could never come up with the right kind of arguments to respond to rhetoric like that, and she lacked the mental discipline with which Beatriz memorized dates, facts and figures in order to turn her ideas into victorious phalanxes. She was filled with the same dismay when she listened to the long-winded speeches given by her religious uncles and, years later, the communists she would meet at university. At that point she did not know, and she would only discover much later, the terrible tax demanded by any dogma: a cannibalistic diet that began by devouring its followers' hearts and ended up stamping out all intellectual activity among them. Beatriz had taken up the cause of the Absolute too young, embracing it too rigorously, without having learned to smile inwardly to herself about it. The conviction of her superiority had definitely given her a feeling of omnipotence from which she drew the energy that allowed her to apply herself at school, to achieve her goals. But, once in possession of the truth, the source of so much gratification, she had to preserve it in its entirety, at any cost, avoiding the risk of exposing it to criticism from others. And others might not only be the people closest to her, including Lina, but also books that contained different opinions or subversive questions. So, gradually, she stopped reading, her ideas lost the sparkle of an intelligence fuelled by passion, and her discourse became more and more impoverished until finally it turned into a litany of negative precepts. Negative, but also fierce, compelling her to strike, viper-like, at anyone who dared to violate them. Although her mental fervour had cooled, the hatred from which it had bubbled up remained intact.

Hence the episodes Beatriz suffered every time someone behaved in a way that upset her, especially her brothers. Between her and the youngest there was a gap of almost eight years, exactly the amount of time that her aunt, exhausted by mysticism, spent ruining life for everyone in the convent during her last disastrous novitiate before arriving at Nena's house and taking charge of Beatriz's education. Spared the influence of that crazy spinster, and having been initiated early on in the game of love, the Avendaño brothers showed an instinctive penchant for freedom, managing to reconcile the social restrictions with their personal pleasures with such skill that it provoked the most terrible rage in Beatriz. By this point they had all returned from Bogotá, and they were having the time of their life at formal parties or nights spent carousing in brothels; sometimes they had girlfriends, selected from the few relatively liberated young women of the middle classes, in short, those who had studied in the United States or were strongwilled. And with them, they held get-togethers at their house, creating a warm atmosphere of muted lighting, boleros and blues, silences and whispers. Beatriz would shut herself away in her room, burning with indignation: she could not forbid her brothers from having their female friends over, nor could she find reasons to do so; after all, the order she so craved required marriage, which, in turn, required courtship. But evil lurked there, in the longings of those bodies caressing each other under the pretence of dancing in a dimly lit room, as dark as the swamp where, four years ago, she herself had discovered the first stirrings of desire. Cornered by the contradiction of her own logic, sensing the appetites she had so cruelly repressed in herself being expressed in others, Beatriz used anorexia as the instrument of her revenge. If she had been an inquisitor or a political commissar, she would have created a climate of terror worthy of the history books. But she was not, nor would she ever be: she had been born a woman, she had accepted the male law at all costs; without her knowing, power had been confiscated from her the moment she came into the world, and what little she had left of it, her rage against life had destroyed. Being one of the chosen few served no use in reality; there was no point in dreaming of being a member of an elite caste of chosen ones, who were invisible out of necessity and, consequently, unable to comfort her with their presence or lift her spirits when the black wings of pessimism unfolded. How dreadful existence seemed to her then, how futile all her efforts to lead the way with her exemplary conduct. Suddenly she felt as if the whole world were motivated by the purpose of sowing chaos, and in those moments a gesture or a simple phrase was enough to send her spiralling into one of her episodes, to the horror of those who had unwittingly offended her.

Lina defended the Avendaño brothers in vain, insisting that all men of their age and status behaved the same way: Beatriz thought that they secretly intended to torment her by ridiculing her principles, not realizing that no one knew what those principles were because her wariness prevented her from making them clear. At most, her brothers saw her as a sanctimonious prude who belonged in a convent, a little girl spoiled by her repressive upbringing, and they thought it was better to leave her alone and avoid any complications; deep down they blamed their father for having exposed her to the nonsense of that aunt of theirs, whose arrival had immediately caused them to flee to Bogotá; but when it came to Beatriz's episodes, like Nena's mysticism, they instinctively expressed their rejection through humour, not the sarcastic kind, but a distant, rather affectionate humour, with the nonchalance typical of people from the coast who are inclined to make fun of life in order to get the most out of it. Little could they imagine the things Beatriz imagined about them, how she spied on them, listened in on their phone conversations, rifled through their papers and even their underwear drawers; at night she would creep along the corridors, eavesdropping outside their doors, and if they happened to mention her in conversation, she would start turning whatever they had said around and around in her head, distorting it in such a way that the harmless throwaway comment became an insult; even if it didn't provoke an episode, this process of rumination left a trail of resentment in her mind, making her so aggressive that she infuriated her brothers. Something similar happened to her with everyone, but other people's reactions were not inhibited by fraternal feelings of any kind; the only reason she was not bullied at La Enseñanza was thanks to the protection of her natural allies, the nuns, and also because after the incident with the see-saw, she had learned the virtue of prudence.

Outside of school, however, the hostility she provoked could be unsettling. Beatriz saw it as magical, a kind of involuntary and unavoidable resentment caused by the superiority of her spirit. And there really was something irrational in the way people behaved towards her, as if her personality radiated a negative charisma, which abolished individual oppositions to

form a group, a horde driven by a tide of aversion, demolishing the fragile conventions that kept society afloat; perhaps
because they felt she was unyielding to any form of compromise, so implacable, so incapable of joining a group that her
very presence brought that hostility to the surface. Lina had
witnessed one of those vile attacks against her, like the one
Catalina had suffered at the country club during the newspaper beauty pageant. Catalina, however, had opened herself up
to the vengeance of the middle classes by embodying the
much-hated ghost of Divina Arriaga, naively but actively, by
proudly exhibiting her beauty; while all Beatriz had done was
refuse to take part in a game, like Lina and so many other girls
invited on the trip to Puerto Colombia that day. True, it had
not been an ordinary day; it was too hot, and the threat of rain
had been hanging in the air since dawn. Then things became
more tense, when the mothers in charge of supervising them
stumbled across Elvira Abondano making love to her
boyfriend among the logs washed up on the beach. They were
so horrified that, between urgently trying to hide a scandal that
was likely to come back at them like a boomerang, and taking
steps to send the culprit home as soon as possible, they left the
other youngsters with time to organize the strictly forbidden
game of spin-the-bottle. It was a game they played any time
they had the chance: the boys and girls would sit in a circle on
the floor and then spin an empty bottle in the middle; when
the bottle stopped moving, the direction of the cork pointed to
the person who had to get up and kiss a player of the opposite
sex, easing the way for romances and reconciliations, and helping some of them gradually overcome their shyness. One day
Lina would realize that her friends had unwittingly established
a group dynamic designed to rid them of any sexual inhibitions
by removing guilt, since everything depended on the unpredictable movement of a bottle, and the rules stated that
although a player could choose not to do anything when it was

their turn, they still had to allow themself to be kissed if someone else wanted to exert their rights. This particular condition
had always bothered Lina, who did not put much stock in
chance. For Beatriz, who was witnessing the spectacle for the
first time, the game was the height of hypocrisy. Lina was the
only one who knew how she felt, but the others guessed it
nonetheless; it was impossible to know how or why, because
nothing in Beatriz gave her feelings away; no gesture or look
betrayed her disapproval; she sat very calmly in her chair, and
then calmly got on the bus that would take them back to the
city. It was seven o'clock, and it was already dark. Suddenly the
light bulb that illuminated the interior of the bus blew, and a
mob of enraged boys and girls launched themselves at Beatriz,
wildly lashing out at her. When Lina realized what was happening, she started forcing her way through, doling out kicks
and punches without a second thought as she headed towards
where she had seen Beatriz sit down; there was a surprising
silence while it all unfolded; as she moved forward, practically
walking over her friends' bodies, they backed away as if they
were afraid of being identified; which was why, in the end, she
could only make out one of the attackers, a girl who left a lock
of blond hair in Lina's grasp. Beatriz was silent all the way back
to Barranquilla, gathering her energy for the predictable fainting fit that never materialized, simply because her father was
not at home. As she helped Nena rub ointment into Beatriz's
bruises, Lina ventured the explanation that she had been a
propitiatory victim, chosen arbitrarily and martyred in order to
unburden the community of its sins, because that day a couple
had been caught making love, and all of them had felt guilty to
some extent. Beatriz simply smiled with an indulgent expression. The Avendaño brothers didn't even look at her; their
pride wounded, they decided to deal with the insult in their
own way, and so, one by one, all the boys who had been on
the outing were challenged and slapped about, the innocent

paying for the sins of the guilty, thus reinforcing Beatriz's feeling that her family were the only ones she could count on.

Restored by this act of solidarity, the Avendaño brothers
were momentarily released from the obsessive gaze of Beatriz,
who, in the absence of any prey within her reach, turned her
attention to the maids and their behaviour. She had paid them
no mind before, judging them to be essentially beyond salvation, because they were born in sin, and in sin they procreated
with the shamelessness of females in the animal kingdom. And
she had likened them to animals during the first seven years of
her life, while she was under the influence of the frustrated
novice who believed that a different essence set them apart
from people of colour. The Avendaños had been white and
fair-haired ever since they came into the world; they had
arrived on the Iberian Peninsula leading their troops in
defence of the noblest of causes; together with the Queen of
Castile they fought against the copper-skinned Moors after
having quashed them during the Crusades two centuries earlier, hoisting the fierce boar of their coats of arms; their ancestors arranged marriages with the finest families in Europe and
some of them were able to print helmets on their heraldic figures; they were distinguished by their sense of honour and
their courage, and they never betrayed a single oath. What,
then, linked them to those bastards, tainted by the weak blood
of the Carib Indian and the diabolical blood of the Black
slave? Nothing, in short: the aunt did not see any connection,
even though common sense assured her that there were affini-
ties and her own religion obliged her to think of them as brothers. In Beatriz's eyes, they were so far removed from her that,
if someone had taken the trouble to explain the concept of
species to her, then without any malicious intention she would
place them in the same category as the missing link. However,
she would tell Lina, wide-eyed, how the maids fascinated her
when she was little: she dreamed of being one of them and

having lots of fabrics and trinkets; she wanted to wear her hair long, slather it in oil and comb it for hours in front of a cracked mirror; she wanted to smoke cigarette ends and douse herself in strong-smelling perfumes. The maids led a gypsy-like existence; they showed up in El Prado, coming from that godforsaken hinterland where her aunt saw thieves and prostitutes roaming free; dressed in garishly coloured clothes, they went from door to door asking for a job that would allow them to bid farewell to poverty, to the constant gnawing of hunger in their bellies, to a life of squalor in a filthy shack where men, dogs and chickens slept on the floor, and sometimes even a pig that was kept for lean times, greedily watched every night. In El Prado they were immediately given a bed, food, uniforms and a salary that they could save or spend on knickknacks. So why, then, did they leave? After a few months, for no reason at all, they would pack everything they had bought or received as gifts into a cardboard suitcase, and proudly return to their shanty towns. The aunt called it "laziness." "Lust," Beatriz declared, not even momentarily considering Lina's opinion, who could see in the maids' behaviour a craving for freedom so irrepressible that any material wellbeing was sacrificed for the pleasure of telling their bosses to go to hell, thus recovering the dignity that had been inexorably lost in servitude. She wouldn't hear it: the maids had appeared on Beatriz's horizon bringing with them the image of debauchery. Thousands of teenage girls were sold to unscrupulous men every year or lost their virginity to their mothers' lovers; by the time they were fifteen they were already responsible for a child, and by the age of thirty they had a brood of children in tow conceived with numerous fathers, thus increasing the poverty and disorder of society. Nothing could be done to combat their debauchery; even the church itself had failed. And when, driven by hunger, they finally landed an honest job, they spent their wages on powders, blushes and perfumes to attract men, setting off another cursed cycle of lust that would end with them falling pregnant again and immediately losing their job. No, freedom demanded a total inhibition of animalistic impulses so as to acquire the self-control with which an individual could clearly, lucidly, make a choice. The maids did not make choices: chasing momentary passions, they flitted from one lover to another, breeding completely irresponsibly. But, above all, they sinned, or in profane terms, they spread the virus of indecency wherever they went, even infecting the people of El Prado with it.

That was when Beatriz severed her last (and very tenuous) ties with religion and started to take an interest in Maoism, the only doctrine that addressed the problem of reproduction in practice by assigning one man and a limited number of children to each woman. Years later, convinced that the Latin American continent was going to become a seething human breeding ground like China, she came to sympathize with the city's first Maoists with terrorist leanings, even letting them hide explosives and weapons in her house in Puerto Colombia. But she was never entirely Marxist, insofar as she saw the masses as a simple instrument of the leader, an individual tenacious enough to impose his moral convictions on others. This assumption was what gave her the idea to launch a small-scale campaign of purification, spreading the word of God to the maids who worked for her closest relatives, her aunts on the Avendaño side, who gave her carte blanche at first, attributing such candour to her youth, and then, on seeing the disastrous results of the experience, politely asked her to restrict it to the maids in her own house. Poor Nena found herself suddenly without any staff: no girl wanted to work for a woman whose daughter took the liberty of intruding into her private life, spying on her when she went out into the garden at night to make sure that she was doing as she was told, not receiving nocturnal visitors or indulging in courtship in the shelter of the trees. Those two hours of freedom, earned after working non-stop, were not so much about seeking pleasure as they were about reclaiming their bodies from the clutches of menial labour. Gathered in groups, in the cool of the evening, the neighbourhood maids felt they were escaping the control of their mistresses, who subconsciously longed for the golden days of slavery, unleashing their pent-up aggressions on them (the aggression they were unable to express in front of fathers and husbands), until eight o'clock at night when they laid down their weapons and the all-important truce began, before the battle recommenced the next day. Separating the two factions was a neutral zone that stretched from the terraces, where the ladies sat in rocking chairs commenting on the latest gossip or some triviality, while across the garden, on the pavement, the maids revealed the family's intimate secrets and giggled about incidents they had witnessed during the day. The mistresses, sitting beside flags and banners bearing abstract nouns for the causes that had helped them to stave off the boredom as yet another day ran into another night without hope, had aged not only in their bodies, but also in that part of the mind where dreams and illusions surfaced; the maids, excited and smiling, regained a whisper of youth as they waited for the young soldiers to come and visit them before returning to the barracks at midnight. Between them was the garden, an area that their mistresses had forbidden them to enter (the signs, although faded, were still there) but in vain because nothing in the world would prevent them from violating it in the company of their lovers, pulling up plants and squashing the grass until they achieved the brief and wild spasm that restored something resembling justice. Everything that had been stolen from them in the house during the day they reclaimed at night in the garden, voraciously and playfully, because in the depths of their unconscious they recognized the price the other women had paid to gain the privilege of sitting in the rocking chairs on the terrace (next to the motionless flags and banners). This complicit understanding, which had been going on for years, ever since one person had found the means to put another person into their service and humiliate them, Beatriz tried to abolish in the name of principles that simply masked her frustration. The worst thing was that the anxiety of checking whether or not the maids were following her instructions only plunged her deeper and deeper into the luxuriant atmosphere of the gardens: from a window on the third floor of her house, armed with binoculars, she watched the nocturnal love affairs as far as the darkness would allow, her body contorted with anguish as she listened to the laughter and moans; when those expeditions were over, she would come downstairs aggravated and full of resentment towards the culprit, and then one of her episodes was never far off; that, or a new outpouring of advice and rebukes which would prompt the house girl to ask for her month's wages and leave.

That scene had already played out ten times when Armanda, Doña Eulalia del Valle's maid, grew tired of her whining and went to work for the Avendaños instead. In possession of all the aquamarines that Andrés Larosca had given to Dora and the brooches that Dr. Palos had given to Doña Eulalia in the distant past, Armanda had started asking herself certain questions about money and the most efficient way to get it; she was not going to ignore a maniacal girl's recommendations if they came with certain rewards: as soon as she understood Beatriz's apprehensions, she resolved to negotiate her chastity with her, night after night, convinced that it was better to do without the garden pleasures if, in return, she got her hands on the gold chains and bracelets from her jewellery box. Beatriz was overjoyed: in exchange for a few objects that were worthless to her, she could at last snatch a maid from the claws of vice and hold her up as an example to the others. In the space of six months, Armanda had become her plaything: she exhibited her, presented her and took her to the cinema;

after teaching her to read and write, she asked an incredulous Nena to give Armanda the afternoons off so that she could dedicate herself to her studies. Finally, she decided to use her to reach the other maids in El Prado by holding seminars where they would discuss the advantages of a moderate way of life. That was beyond what Armanda could do; sensing the danger, she diverted Beatriz's attention to what was happening over at the house of their new neighbours, the Del Puma family.

With that surname attached to him, Evaristo del Puma would have had to lock himself away in a monastery of Trappist monks to avoid the setbacks that were inevitably in store for him. He did something resembling this, hiding as much as he could at school, where he was the laughingstock of his classmates, who challenged him to demonstrate his courage and ended up beating him to a pulp, hitting him even harder for his cowardice; then, to escape from them, he took refuge in a modest business school and, with his rather dubious accountancy diploma, started his career. Shy and small like a little mouse, he would have remained in that insipid middle class so suited to his character if destiny (or a self-destructive tendency) had not led him to marry one of the Sierras: fiery women, precocious and tenacious in equal measure, thrust into adulthood at the age of nine, and still fertile in their sixties. People said that the marriage would never have happened if Lucila Castro's father had been in his right mind when Evaristo del Puma met her, because every man who had married a Sierra woman and had children with her knew all too well how much mental and physical stamina it took to please them. Unfortunately, Lucila's father was an old man by then, exhausted from endless years of marital passion and the desperate struggle to control the longings of his older daughters, whom, however, he had managed to marry off to men who, much like him in his youth, had the corpulence of bulls. And the same appetite. So the wedding went ahead. Evaristo and his bookkeeper's tie were eaten up within a year, during which time Lucila gave birth to her first child and proved once and for all that her husband was made of a different substance to her. So began her cycle of lovers. Many of them. So many that Evaristo del Puma chose to move away from the city under the pretence of collecting the debts contracted by the peasants of Magdalena with the firm he worked for; he would return home at the end of every month, preceded by a telegram detailing the precise time of his arrival and how many days he would be staying in Barranquilla; once, he came home to find Lucila pregnant and said nothing about it, then nine months later he attended the baptism of Leonor and moved to a village on the banks of the river for good.

It was later that an inheritance allowed Lucila Castro to buy the house next to Beatriz's and to put up her Black lover in it. Lorenzo was an enormous, quiet man who walked with the solemnity of an African king; he used to spend all day half-naked, his private parts covered with yellow shorts, only getting dressed at dusk when he went from car to car negotiating for the favours of his mistress. In fact, by that time Lucila Castro had already discovered that pleasure could become a source of income while continuing to be the wonderful reward the good Lord himself offered to those who accepted the facts of life in their simplicity: she loved to make love, and men knew it; her husband did not send her a penny, and the men were well aware of that. That was why, as soon as evening fell, they drove over to her house, turning off their headlights so as not to bother each other, and parked up outside, the line of cars stretching down the road as they waited patiently for the Black man to come out and announce that night's price, which could never be predicted; some of them waited their turn for months, either at the whim of Lucila or Lorenzo, who by way of explanation simply said in a calm tone of voice that many were called and few were chosen. He never lost his cool, Berenice recounted, delighted; he did not even listen while the others begged him to put in a good word for them: he looked beyond the cars and perhaps recalled his first encounter with Lucila Castro one night of Carnival, in the Barrio Abajo neighbourhood where no white woman had ever set foot; she with her reddish hair, her luscious, milk-coloured breasts, dancing frantically to the Mapalé as if Changó himself inhabited her body; and when the man with her began to draw back intimidated, realizing in his drunken state that it had been a mistake to take her there, he, Lorenzo, made his way towards her, chasing away the men who were starting to surround her; with a gesture from him, the *papayera* changed rhythm, the drums slowed down, the flute sounded out like a lament, and the burning longing of the woman clung to his skin and would never leave him. Since then, they had been united by a fiendish bond, but Lucila's amorous habits had remained unchanged. As Berenice explained, Lorenzo knew that no man in the world could satisfy the cravings of a woman who had discovered the depths of her sexuality and had the courage to accept it; besides, there was never a night when, upon her return, Lucila would not ask him to wait for her in bed while she took a shower, washing away the abrasive smell of her white lover until once again she became the lustful prey of Changó, whose sacred cry only he could recognize. And respect. Yes, Lorenzo loved women when the fatal forces of life were stirring through their bodies; he loved them with the most absolute fascination, following the unpredictable curve of their desires, the vertiginous fantasy of their passions; and he loved them respectfully, with the veneration that an old sailor feels for the sea. The other men could stay on land if they did not dare to take the risk, but not him. He had spent his whole childhood swimming in the green waters of the Caribbean island where he was born, surrendering to the cross-currents where sharks swam, to the huge waves that crashed foaming onto the beach, without the slightest fear, he told Berenice, because he already knew the day and hour when death would come for him: it had been predicted by his great-grandmother, who, with a snap of her fingers, summoned the voodoo gods and, in a sententious tone, announced in the same breath that he would have a passion for a white woman in whom the fire of his virility would burn without ever dying down. Lucila Castro was already in his thoughts the first time one of his female cousins slid across onto his sleeping mat one night and he felt his penis harden with an uncontrollable determination; he had waited for her through countless love affairs, patiently, until he saw her dancing in the Black neighbourhood on that night of Carnival. He couldn't care less, he said, about what people thought of their relationship, or about the filthy feelings she aroused in the men whose cars lined up in front of the house at dusk. The rest of the time Lucila belonged to him: she was his for the whole day, as often as he felt like taking her in his arms and igniting her desire with a knowing caress; that body letting go under his own commanding body plunged Lorenzo into total ecstasy, making him feel like he had been appointed by the magnanimous finger of Ochún. Besides, Lorenzo intended to take her away from Barranquilla: day and night she would be devoted to his carnal desires, day and night the pores of her skin would feel the heat of his urgent gaze. Lucila was beginning to come to terms with the idea of going to live with him in San Andrés, investing their savings in buying a business that would allow them to work together. And that was how their relationship was going when Beatriz started obsessively scrutinizing them.

It was a shock. The discovery that almost on her doorstep, although not on the same stretch of pavement, since Lucila Castro's house overlooked a different street—the procession of cars to which that shameless woman was giving herself, accompanied by her Black lover, caused Beatriz to suffer a wave of successive fainting fits. At first she did not understand what was going on: that is, the first time she walked to the end of the street and caught sight of the line of cars parked up with their lights off, while Lorenzo went from one to another muttering something to the drivers. Armanda had wisely refrained from giving her concrete explanations, so she only managed to establish the fact that around six o'clock in the evening lots of men pulled up there, spoke to Lorenzo, and then all of them left, except for one, who stayed where he was, waiting for Lucila to come out. Beatriz knew little about her, but if as a married woman she allowed herself to behave in such a way, there were no good conclusions to be drawn about her. All worked up, the next day Beatriz gathered her family to tell them about her suspicions and to ask them to intervene and put a stop to the scandal. The Avendaño brothers were beginning to exchange uneasy glances, when, surprisingly, Nena firmly put her foot down: no member of her family was going to interfere in their neighbour's private life, because Lucila had bought that house and what she did in it was no concern of theirs. Her brothers expressed their approval, relieved, and then Beatriz had her first episode. But it had no effect: Nena would remain unusually intransigent about it, saying that the situation of Lucila Castro's children should not be made worse. Such was her conviction, Beatriz then decided to spy on the children until she found proof of their unhappiness. But her efforts proved fruitless: Rafael, the oldest, had been forcibly taken by Evaristo del Puma and put into a religious school, from which he escaped as often as he could to go to see his mother and have fun helping Lorenzo make boats that miraculously popped open inside glass bottles. As for Leonor, who attended a secular school, she seemed fairly contented with her lot; she was a lanky little girl with very dark eyes and a gift for attracting animals; she liked to hang out in the yard of their house, which had been transformed into a tiny zoo, and watch the comings and goings of monkeys, birds, pigeons and peacocks, always nestled in Lorenzo's arms. Beatriz had discovered this after she had made a hole in the wall between the two yards. To catch a glimpse of her, Beatriz would lie down on the ground and spend hours watching the couple, the Black man and the girl, caring for the animals together, watering the plants or simply dozing in an embrace under a tamarind tree. One afternoon, one of Lucila Castro's dogs lunged towards the hole, revealing its existence with its yapping. Not a woman to be messed with, Lucila showed up at the Avendaños' house determined to find out which of their maids had the gall to do such a thing; she was greeted by Nena, who, when she saw with her own eyes that the hole in question had been made from her side, was totally ashamed and bewildered and apologized profusely to Lucila, promising she would move heaven and earth to find the culprit. Armanda could not stand up to the Avendaño brothers' interrogation; Beatriz was forced to admit the truth. At that moment, the rift that would tragically separate her from her family was formed.

She did not realize it; not then, or for a long time after. On her return from the hospital after her umpteenth episode of anorexia, she felt surrounded by a frosty, but not explicit, mistrust, the outlines of which she only managed to make out too late. She had no idea that, in her absence, the Avendaños had laid their cards on the table, finally expressing their feelings about their sister and her unacceptable behaviour, bent on catechizing the maids and spying on the neighbours. Beatriz had made their life unbearable, and her episodes showed that she was mentally disturbed. After years of silence, the words had been said. Crying, Nena listened to her husband and sons speak but did not dare to contradict them; even she, a woman whose immense suffering had made her sensitive to the problems of others, could not understand Beatriz's determination to prove what everyone saw but chose not to mention out of

Christian charity: namely, that Lucila Castro had been prosti-
tuting herself since her husband had abandoned her, leaving
her all alone with a daughter who was doomed to follow in her
footsteps if the gossipmongers had anything to do with it.
There were people in the city, in the long-standing families that
had managed to hold on to wealth and privilege, who reserved
judgement when a child's future was at stake. Nena was one of
those people. She was appalled at the thought of Beatriz lying
on the ground with a maid for hours, spying on Lucila Castro's
yard: no Avendaño (not even her husband Jorge) had ever
engaged in behaviour that was so dishonourable, so contrary to
the noble spirit of the family. However, it was difficult for her
to accept the solution that Dr. Agudelo suggested to her husband: to send Beatriz to a boarding school run by nuns, far
away from the conflicts that caused her episodes, and to
arrange the trip in such a way that it would not be seen as a
form of rejection or punishment. Nena did not want to be separated from her daughter just like that, but without her cooperation, the aim of the plan would not be achieved. So while
they waited for her to agree, the Avendaño brothers started to
gather information about religious schools that would be a
good fit for Beatriz's puritanism. In the meantime, Nena had
decided to give her a lesson in tolerance by taking her round
to Lucila Castro's house with a basket of fruit and sweets for
Leonor, to make her apologize again and let them know that
Armanda would be leaving. Lucila was most surprised by that
visit, and as a thank you, she gave Beatriz a South American
spider monkey that someone had given her that same afternoon.

The little monkey must have been used to relocating,
because he promptly made himself at home, turning the
Avendaños' yard into his territory. It was fun to watch him
jump from tree to tree and perform all kinds of pirouettes for
his favourite treat, a ripe plum; the Avendaño brothers built

him a rain shelter, and Lina brought him papayas from time to time. But Beatriz hated him: she had never lived with an animal before and she was filled with disgust at his brazenness. Plus, he frightened her. This strange being, so different and yet so similar to her, appeared to share her emotions, to imitate her gestures and, even more terrible, to scrutinize her: his eyes did not give her the furious or servile look of a dog, nor the brief and majestic indifference of a cat. No, his eyes just watched her, trying to capture her feelings towards him, that poor little monkey, doomed to seek out the sympathy of his new owners; perhaps he was only waiting for her to accept his presence so that he could safely free himself from the pleasure of swinging from tree to tree and listening in astonishment to the noises coming from the house, above all, the sounds coming from that object on which a round, black thing was spinning, and which, when he'd tried to inspect it, had earned him the worst spanking of his life. Getting punished for throwing something on the ground that had attracted his curiosity was par for the course when it came to humans; they were unpredictable, sometimes dangerous beings, although in all his experience as a spider monkey, he had never found any of them as vexing as the girl who now watched him without the slightest hint of kindness, and whacked him with a stick if he tried to eat the fruit off the plum tree. In fact, Beatriz had decided to educate the monkey by controlling his appetite and teaching him to relieve himself in a potty; her furious voice could occasionally be heard from the yard, followed by exasperated shrieks and the scuffling sound of an animal desperately fleeing through the tree branches. Then an incident occurred, though the version Beatriz told was somewhat jumbled: while trying to catch him, she had unintentionally wounded him and, since then, she had been the victim of his obscene animosity; there had been a wound, it was true, under his thick, reddish tail, and the Avendaños' new maid had used every trick in the book to get the little monkey's potty off his head: according to Beatriz, he had put it on himself to mock her authority. But it was difficult to imagine the spider monkey coming out of his nighttime shelter, climbing up to Beatriz's bedroom window and staying there, very still, staring at her until he woke her up; more incredible still to imagine he had the intention of terrorizing her by masturbating in front of her. The Avendaño brothers debated the veracity of these statements for a whole afternoon without managing to reach an agreement; finally, they agreed to organize a night watch without Beatriz knowing, in other words, they would observe the monkey during the night to see if he actually dared to commit such a brazen act. They appeared to take the matter quite seriously: either that animal was vicious, or Beatriz had become even more mentally disturbed. But, seeing as they heard her scream in terror one night when there was no monkey at her window, they opted for the second hypothesis, and decided to bring forward her trip to Canada, where they had found a suitable school. Meanwhile, Nena locked herself in the bathroom in tears, and Lina, who had been around animals ever since she was little, speculated about the intelligence of that monkey. But the deciding factor for the trip, to the absolute horror of the Avendaños, was the second incident involving the hole in the wall: one Sunday, after lunch, Beatriz ran into the living room where the rest of her family were having coffee and, before vomiting, crying and finally losing consciousness, she swore she had seen, through a new hole she had made in the wall of the yard, Lorenzo kissing Leonor's private parts. Utter chaos broke out: while Jorge Avendaño phoned the clinic and Nena broke into sobs, one of the brothers rushed out into the yard and scoured the wall until he found the hole. When he looked through it, all he saw was Lorenzo innocently pushing Leonor on a swing. There was no doubt in their minds: Beatriz was insane. That very afternoon her trip to Canada was decided, and Lina returned home with the spider monkey, to whom her grandmother gave the pompous and undeserved name of Merlin.

Six months went by before the monkey revealed his impertinence once again, contradicting the old adage that monkeys know exactly what they're doing. Having debuted in society, Lina was going out to cocktail parties and soirées almost every night instead of staying in and reading in a rocking chair on the veranda with Merlin on her lap. It was clear that Merlin disliked this busy worldly life from which he was excluded, and he showed his disapproval in a thousand different ways, from shrieking like a condemned man in the trees when she started getting ready to go out, to chucking fruit stones and other debris onto her dressing table. Then Carnival time came around, and Lina, as part of the Carnival Queen's entourage, was always rolling through the door in the early hours after dancing the night away, so badly in need of sleep that, as soon as she had removed her make-up, she fell into bed exhausted. Merlin took umbrage to this and decided to get his revenge in the rudest way possible: one dawn, Beatriz appeared to Lina in a dream, just as she had looked on the day she left for Quebec, very dignified, but staring at her in quiet desperation. In her dream, the airport had become one of the labyrinths in the Italian's Tower, and Beatriz seemed to be sucked into a swirling hurricane that, instead of rising upwards, descended to the depths of the earth. Lina woke with a start. And in that moment, she saw Merlin at her window, his eyes now malevolent and fixed on her, one hand on the grille and the other on his penis, slowly masturbating. To teach him a lesson, Lina whistled to the breedless, nameless dog, and Merlin scampered away through the trees in a panic. The monkey never went back to his old ways, but from that day on, Lina ceased to share the Avendaño brothers' opinion of Beatriz.

III

s soon as Aunt Irene moved into the Italian's Tower, Lina noticed the curious relationship she had with animals: she didn't think of them as an ornament or a nuisance, nor did she seek out their company to ease her loneliness, and she did not try to use them in any way; she simply loved them. And they, from the tiny mouse that wandered over the shiny piano lid when there were no cats around, to the imposing pair of Dobermans whose ancestors had witnessed the construction of the tower, seemed to feel at ease by her side, as if they saw her as an extension of their own existence. In a way they were right: Lina's grandmother said that even as a small child, Aunt Irene had the ability to empathize with even the tiniest of living beings, to get inside their bodies and share their emotions, enhancing her perception of things and that extreme, almost painful sensitivity of hers, which could be expressed through music alone and which only music allowed her to bear; at a very young age, her grandmother said, she would suddenly stand stock still, observing a bird in flight until she gave the impression that she was becoming one with the bird and watching the rooftops from the sky, flying away from the city, following the course of the river; or slipping inside an ant and marching along underground; or becoming an insect struggling desperately to free itself from a spider's web. Her mother would coax her out of those fascinating, distressing experiences by gently playing the piano, keying the notes from the score that Irene had stopped looking at to lose herself in the hidden consciousness of animals instead. As the years went by, Aunt Irene had to resign herself and accept the merciless side of life, but still, Lina was sure, she always rebelled against any act of cruelty: the two servants entrusted with taking care of the tower were instructed to take in any dog that had been stoned or wounded by the people of the neighbourhood, and to fill the cats' bowls to the brim in order to dissuade them from hunting rats or eating the eggs of the numerous birds that nested in the trees of the garden. There was something paradisiacal about the Italian's Tower, with butterflies fluttering around in the morning air and bats flapping their wings through the rooms at dusk. Things had always been that way in the tower, before Aunt Irene inherited it, before she was even born, even before the birth of the man who was probably her father. A walk through its underground passages would reveal glass vivariums where rattlesnakes, tarantulas and other species of poisonous bugs—the kind that any person in their right mind would have killed without remorse—lived out their natural lives; the first residents of the tower had simply kept them safe, writing down their Latin names and the correct way to feed them, driven not so much by curiosity or a spirit of observation, it seemed to Lina, as by the aim of establishing a certain harmony with nature, assimilating it or joining with it, like Aunt Irene, who had finally learned to accept life in its entirety. But although Lina did not know this at the time, or perhaps she could not express it clearly, ever since she was a child she had sensed that there was a direct link between the quality of a person's soul and the way they treated animals, as if the desire to protect creatures or not to cause them harm were integral to any form of moral advancement. That was partly why she immediately took a shine to that aunt, and why, later, she felt such disgust towards the Freisens.

Not the first Freisens who showed up in Barranquilla in around 1921: two half-mad French brothers, one of whom was incapable of recovering from the corrosive listlessness of the climate, and was shut away in his room by his brother until he died, while he, the elder one, would move heaven and earth to open a textile factory much like the one their uncle had stolen from him in Armentières, taking advantage of his lack of experience with legal loopholes. That particular Freisen hated the Germans, and their uncle, and he was missing a hand, which he said he had lost in the Battle of Verdun. However, when he learned Spanish, he started to speak it with a vaguely German accent, and he was tall, very blond and so skinny that a teacher could have taught an anatomy lesson on his naked body. His madness, which he talked about not entirely without humour, was something he had discovered in the trenches of the battlefield, while watching the soldiers who, suddenly, under the influence of daily terror, began to rant and rave as he had done throughout his first twenty years of life. Learning that he was deranged, he explained, was the beginning of his salvation, because from then on he could face the enemy that lurked within him, he could recognize its rhetoric and systematically do the opposite of what it told him to do: to cut a long story short, instead of accepting the money his uncle offered him by way of compensation, the logical choice would have been to stay in France and use a decent lawyer to recover his assets, and, in a country where twenty per cent of the young men had perished, to find an heiress with a decent amount of wealth behind her. But Freisen—known as El Manco on account of his only having one hand—would only adopt the puritanical bourgeois ways when it came to running his factory and becoming a millionaire. Everything else in his life was in deliberate defiance of all the values of abstinence and moderation instilled in him in his childhood: he had made Barranquilla his home, he said, because no other place in the world was such a polar opposite to Armentières, and a similar reason had surely prompted him to marry Rosario Ortiz Sierra, who had inherited from her mother a temperament that, on a nightly basis, could tear down the modesty inherent to the mental instability of every Freisen who had existed and would ever exist, with a wickedness that suited his most contradictory fantasies; during the day she played the role of lady, almost ethereal in her refinement, and by night she transformed into a femme fatale possessed by lustful demons.

Lina began to suspect it the day when she chased after a ball and ended up in the bedroom that belonged to Maruja Freisen's parents. She was surprised to see all the disturbing objects hanging from the walls and scattered about the room, from the incomprehensible mirror on the ceiling to the holes and phallic protuberances of the four statues, which resembled goddesses from ancient cults and appeared to serve as pillars; the room also looked out onto a private garden, where the bushes and garishly coloured flowers recreated the same elaborate, lust-filled ambiance. Lina stood there completely still, in a state of fascination similar to the feeling that sometimes invaded her when she contemplated certain rooms in the Italian's Tower; similar, but far more intense, because those items had not been used years before by men and women who were long-since dead and buried; they had been used by the very real Gustavo Freisen, whom she pictured striding into the office at his factory, and a very elegant lady who had bent down to kiss her on the cheek before leaving to play canasta at the country club, enveloping her in the languid scent of magnolia. Maruja's untimely entrance snapped her out of her state of shock; the couple's firstborn daughter was troubled to see that Lina had discovered her parent's erotic games, a euphemism she used after she made Lina swear not to tell anyone about the contents of the bedroom, then explained how each instrument was used and what it was for, not being boastful or mischievous but talking about the objects as if they were ordinary, even indispensable for any woman who considered marrying a

European man who had been messed up by puritanism. Almost twenty years later, in Paris, Maruja Freisen would awaken great passions in the world's wealthiest, most handsome man, refusing to become his wife and putting him through hell because he did not know how to kiss a woman down there, and, as she would later confide to Lina at the Select de Montparnasse, because she herself lacked the patience her mother and grandmother had demonstrated to fight the ravages of a bad upbringing every night: feminism had not arisen in vain. At that time, Maruja had already been widowed by a civil aviation pilot and treated herself to a long trip away with the insurance pay-out before returning to manage the financial department of her father's business. She had started her journey through the East alone and found that she needed to disguise herself as a man in order to visit Pakistan and Turkey without any hitches. With all this, her self-confidence seemed undeniable. When she arrived in Paris, however, she begged Lina to accompany her to the north of France, to the city where her family had settled after the Franco-Prussian war of 1870, almost as if she thought she might catch some mysterious virus when she met the uncles and cousins who were awaiting her visit with the same greedy expectation of any Frenchman expecting the arrival of an American relative. It was a winter of frozen highways; when they reached Douai they had to pull over to put chains on the tyres, and then, through the windscreen wipers battered by unrelenting rain, the city appeared at last, spread out beneath the infinitely sad sky as far as the main square, where the old Freisen house stood, ominous, reflecting the integrity of that bourgeoisie so proud of its virtue and tenacity. Maruja's relatives looked tense in their Sunday best; the hundred-year-old dust, disturbed by the sudden shaking out of carpets and soft furnishings, drifted across the fireplace in the living room; the fire was the only source of heat, casting a semi-circle of light into the darkness, which the feeble glow from the ceiling light, somewhere up there in the shadows, did little to chase away. Through a door decorated with a panel of pastoral motifs, in shuffled the last remaining Freisen descendants in an incomprehensible hierarchical order, all of them sharing the same family traits: they were pale, bony, lipless, and there was something excessively guarded about the way they moved, as if they feared they were inhabited by an unruly automaton; but there was no sign of the old predatory instinct, which was one of their ancestors' traits and the driving force behind their endeavours, and they might be thought of as offspring of a dying generation; none of them had married, and they were growing old together, abstemiously picking at the remains of some bitterly disputed inheritance. That room with its wood-panelled floors and walls had the gloomy smell of wax, conjuring the image of legions of maids harassed by many a Freisen wife, for whom housekeeping had been, from marriage to death, a way of escaping a nameless anxiety; in that room, Lina felt like she was with her grandmother visiting the dilapidated old houses belonging to her relatives, where there was always one room that was forbidden, out of bounds, and hiding behind the locked door was someone who did not want to be seen or had decided to give up the ghost. But those people—the melancholy ones, as her aunts respectfully called them—were surrounded by an almost sacred aura, because, before escaping the lofty pretensions of this world, they had stood out with their intelligence and sensitivity. They were not considered insane, but lucid, perhaps too lucid; their seclusion had to be protected and, when their bodies turned to piles of dust and their minds began to unravel from the constant darkness and lack of food, their needs had to be attended to, mitigating the suffering associated with their death as far as possible. The Freisens' attitude towards their family's outcasts was quite different, Lina said to herself as soon as she had caught a whiff of the atmosphere in that house and saw that group of cold, strict men and women, like figures at a funeral, walking in through the door in the panelling. It had taken her all of a second to grasp Maruja's secret terror, even if secretly it amused her to think about how the Sierra genes absorbed the Freisen genes without much difficulty and how the true incarnation of that terror was not only not there, but had most probably been locked in the basement or sent away from the house under some pretext or other. But it would appear, just as they had finished saying their goodbyes, after dining on a tasteless meal served with all the pomp and ceremony of a banquet, on chinaware solicitously wheeled out for the occasion. It appeared like a ghost and a caricature, in the form of a skeletal old man who, trembling with rage beside the car, cursed his relatives for having sent him off into the forest that day to chop wood so that he wouldn't be able to see her, Maruja, and warn her against the dangers of putting her virtue at risk by travelling alone or acting so brazenly as to reveal her status as a *métèque* who had tainted the family name. Then his speech became incoherent, but he kept on ranting without letting the girls past, his blue eyes wild and his long bones shuddering in a convulsion akin to St. Vitus' dance. The awful thing about his madness was not so much the sudden outbursts, but the fact that it was deeply associated with the Freisens' morphology, suggesting that there was something hereditary, almost ineluctable about it, because this old man was the ultimate Freisen, a replica of the first member of his lineage, who had raped and pillaged more than anyone else in that savage horde from the cold regions, until finally he imposed his leadership on them, spreading his semen in an act devoid of any tenderness. Neither he nor any of his descendants were tamed by Christianity, but from this new religion they drew the precepts needed to increase their power and the dismal purity espoused by the Castilians of the Spanish Court, an ideal which, after several generations of inbreeding, had morphed into mental aberration. The old man was still there, frothing with rage, when Maruja, who at first had stopped in horror, gave him the most offensive slap Lina had ever seen in her life, and the old man, shocked, ran off into the forest he had come out of, and out of which no Freisen should ever have emerged.

So, the Barranquillans had adopted one Freisen, whose daughter would feel compelled to go to the house of her ancestors and slap the archetype of them all, waving goodbye to the fear for good. And then came another on one of the first ships that set sail from Spain after the Second World War, arriving from the country where that Freisen had taken refuge with his wife and children as soon as the ill wind began to blow over the armies of the Third Reich, which he had served without being asked ever since the invasion, producing not only the tarpaulins for that army's trucks, but also the uniforms for its soldiers in his textile factory; he did this not out of greed, even if the Germans secretly funded his private Swiss bank account, but because he, Gustavo Freisen, was a man who valued hierarchy and order, and the Nazi ideology corroborated his principles. As did the dignitaries of the regime: he had seen the officers of the general staff of an armoured division enter the grounds of his house one Sunday, dazzling in the severity of their *feldgrau* coats with red lapels, their precise gestures, their gentlemanly demeanour; he had seen them bow chivalrously as they kissed his wife's hand and greeted him with respect, recognizing in him the natural ally who knew the secret purpose of that war. No, he was neither the conquered nor the vulgar collaborator, he had insisted to his cousin, El Manco Freisen, who could not understand the way he felt: El Manco had fled from a Europe torn apart, a continent so weak and at God's mercy that its longstanding enemies had managed to lead it into the deadliest of conflicts, the class war. Only one country, or its elite, warned of the danger; only one people, the Germans, had decided to combat it by attacking evil at its very root, those Jews deemed responsible for chaos, those corrupters of souls, murderers of civilization. From Marx to Freud, via Trotsky and the other rogues who had worked for the October Revolution until they gave the Asians the power to destroy the West, the Jews had been the hidden enemy, the plague of humanity. He, Gustavo Freisen, knew this, hence his adherence to Nazism.

Hence, too, his despair when he realized that the battle had been fought too late and he had to take refuge in Spain under a false name while the old Europe was beginning to perish: drained of its lifeblood once again, exposed to the demagogy of those agitators who would one day emerge from the shadows to plunge them all into servitude; corroded by guilt, that masochism which prompted men to punish themselves by destroying their finest achievements, or to view them with the spiteful eye of their enemies, the weak and cowardly, the dregs of society. No, El Manco was far removed from those concerns. He, Gustavo Freisen, had sensed it on the ship that brought him to Colombia, when he went out on deck one morning and was dumbfounded to discover that the Captain, who only the day before had been wearing a dignified and ceremonious uniform of blue fabric with gold stripes, had turned into an obese, sweaty character resembling an Italian baker, dressed in white and wearing ridiculous shorts, since the ship had passed into the tropics. The air was heavy with heat and humidity, and a smell of rotting seaweed rose from the waters that reverberated the sun's rays. All the rigour and discipline the crew had demonstrated as they glided through the fog of the North Atlantic was now fading into a kind of drowsy apathy. Gustavo Freisen felt enveloped by the humidity that clouded his glasses like an ominous mist; his shirt was pasted to his shoulder blades with sweat; his hands were wet, and he had trouble breathing that torrid, almost obscene smell, which evoked things he did not even dare think about. Accustomed to the austere winter greyscale in which a whole civilization had been forged and refined, his eyes hurt in that intense light, devoid of nuance or suggestion. Every day the ship went deeper into that sea of jellyfish and man-o-wars, every day the heat became more relentless, reducing Gustavo Freisen's ability to think. The other passengers had been passively adapting to the corrosive climate; the women were sensual, the children defiant. And night was already appearing in the sky crammed full of stars, a bright, foreboding moon, a heathen moon, ripe for debauchery; and already, near the ports, the chalupas were already bobbing towards them, laden with rowdy Black people selling sickly sweet, pungent fruits. The islands were lethargic with mosquitoes and neglect, and no one seemed to be in a hurry, not the *mulatos* drowsing on bundles of coconuts and bananas, nor the women moving from one place to another, their hips swaying provocatively. Seeing all those signs of decay, Gustavo Freisen told himself that if one of his cousins had willingly agreed to live in this place, there would be no point trying to tell him about the drama he had experienced on the European continent and the terrible demise of its values, because that continent and its values had surely ceased to matter to him.

Sure enough, El Manco did not understand much. He believed that if any society had to resort to genocide to survive, it did not deserve to exist in the first place. He could never really stomach the idea of the concentration camps, Maruja would tell Lina—especially given that the Jewish cloth sellers from Calle del Comercio were his best customers—nor did he forgive his cousin for having used his family business to serve the Boche, whose shells had torn off his hand. But being a man of good coastal stock, he played down the matter in the end, albeit after advising his relative to hide his past as a collaborator if he didn't want to get on the wrong side of the liberals, who were supporters of the allies and the majority in the city. Gustavo Freisen, like Doña Giovanna Mantini and so many other foreigners who reluctantly settled in Barranquilla, decided to recreate the atmosphere he had been brought up in, and to impose an army-like discipline on his children. He also led by example from the very moment the ship crossed the Equator, Maruja explained; instead of behaving like the captain, he appeared on deck wearing an impeccable white suit he'd had made to measure by a Spanish tailor, with a stiffly starched shirt and a black silk tie round his neck, an outfit that he would wear for the rest of his days, since he never allowed himself to dress in the garish guayabera shirts that El Manco sported on Sundays, nor in the pastel tones that became fashionable years later. Maruja said that she was surprised when she saw them disembarking from the ship: Gustavo Freisen, with his spotless suit and his face lobster-red from the sun, and his wife, sweltering in her freshly ironed linen suit, and then, behind them, the ten children respectfully following like little altar boys. The four eldest were almost albino blond and looked so alike that they could only be told apart by their size; they were born one after the other, leaving Odile Freisen's womb in such a state of fatigue that for five years she miscarried constantly until Javier was born, the only one of the brothers with black hair and a certain brawniness; then, the same year that Lina and Maruja were born, Ana came into the world, followed by four more boys who would put a definitive stop to Odile Freisen's reproductive capacities and her sex life with her husband, since he, following the Christian teachings on marriage to the letter, had never allowed himself to touch her outside of her fertile periods. On this subject, Maruja recounted with amusement how one time, under the influence of one of those cocktails her father made with fruit juice and lashings of rum, Gustavo Freisen had explained his view on marital relations to El Manco, boasting that he had never committed a sin against the flesh, in the sense that every time he'd touched his wife it had led to a pregnancy, which made it more or less twenty times that Odile Freisen had been persuaded to do the deed: ten times for the children, and the same again for the miscarriages.

But this was not of the slightest concern to Odile Freisen, who was a Breton by birth and affected by a congenital dislocation of the hip. The only daughter of a major shipbuilder, she had been very pretty in her youth but extremely self-conscious because of the condition that condemned her to limp, deforming her graceful body. Ever since she was a little girl she had felt the call of religion, she once confided in Ana, and she was probably harbouring romanticized dreams of a monastic life while her mother prepared a trousseau for her. At some point Lina would see the star piece: a night gown just like all her ancestors had worn, with sleeves down to the wrists and drawn tight at the ankles so that the future husband would not be able to pull it up, forcing him to use the only opening at his disposal instead, a sort of heart-shaped window at the pubis, embroidered with the words: "God wills it." And so as the mother sewed away busily, her daughter cried in secret, not because her hip condition prevented her from being courted at dances, but because she felt bad knowing that someday she would have to tell them she had decided to join the convent. Freisen's future wife must have been extremely naïve and her mother quite intelligent: congenital dislocation of the hip or not, with six hundred hectares of land in Normandy left to her by her maternal grandmother and three apartment buildings in Paris, the heiress was bound to receive a marriage proposal sooner or later.

When it did happen, her religious calling was instantly replaced by a desperate desire to have children, and lots of them, to show the whole world that despite her physical affliction, she was a woman just like any other, or more prolific, even: the successive miscarriages were her greatest sadness. Perhaps that was why Javier was so pampered and shielded from his father's violent rages. And maybe there was another reason: submissive as she was, Odile Freisen had already had plenty of years to judge or at least observe her husband, and either consciously or unconsciously, she must have been tired of his despotism; no doubt this initial realization was followed by a bitterness not devoid of hatred, not to mention the fact that Odile Freisen had turned into a woman during that time; then came the war, and while the members of her family, mainly her cousins from Normandy, either joined de Gaulle's camp or the Resistance, Gustavo Freisen disgraced himself by helping the Germans. That was when she began to despise him, Maruja said, because it gave her a concrete, rational reason to back up her hatred. Divorce was out of the question, given her religious leanings and the inextricable financial ties that bound her to that man, and so she was forced to follow him shamefully into exile, with her heart-nightgown packed away forever in the bottom of a suitcase, since the birth of her last child, two days before the fall of Stalingrad, had left her sterile for life.

With her fertility proven beyond dispute and her conjugal duties concluded by the grace of God, Odile Freisen waged a silent but relentless war against her husband, which would continue until her death. The first hostilities had become apparent when Javier was born and she decided to raise him alone, spoiling him and getting up in the night if he cried, without any help from the nannies who had taken care of the older children. This infuriated her husband, who insisted on giving the children Spartan treatment from birth; something as commonplace as showing tenderness to a baby or soothing it when it cried at night was already a defiance of the patriarchal authority and a demonstration of independence for Odile Freisen. So as a child, Javier was pulled in two opposing directions, between his mother's lap, where he found an ocean of complacency, and the exacerbated discipline of his father, whose image would help him to form his identity; the other brothers were unaware of this dilemma, simply because they were loved or accepted without passion; they had come into the world to appease a woman's complexes and justify a man's work and his sense of hierarchy. In a sense, they were merely objects. Javier, on the other hand, was always a symbol, and not only in the wordless war his parents were waging, but also as a man who felt the influence of two antagonistic worlds: the European, whose taboos had scarred him during the first ten years of his life, and the Caribbean, where those taboos tended to shatter in a burst of sunshine and sensuality. Of all the Freisen brothers, Javier would be the most conflicted: the older ones always remained nostalgic for France, and three of them would return to live there for good as soon as they were sure that their compatriots had drawn that cowardly veil over what went on during the war. The younger ones became party animals, one just wasted his time living like a playboy, and the youngest did not even bother to set foot in his father's factory, choosing to get rich by smuggling marijuana instead.

Marijuana would play an important role in Javier's life, much later, helping him to rid himself of his inhibitions. When he arrived in Barranquilla, at the age of ten, he was a spoiled and stubborn child who knew how to get everything he wanted from his mother; all he had to do was say "no" and dig his heels in, even if Gustavo Freisen beat him to a pulp while his wife was not there, because when she returned, Javier would show her the bruises from the blows he'd received, not saying a word, and his mother would fall into a silent rage and immediately block the Swiss bank account held in her maiden name, since that condition was one of the multiple and complicated legal arrangements imposed on her husband before the wedding. The experience of the First World War had taught Odile Kerouan's family that whether they agreed with it or not, it was better to keep part of their Naples assets in hard cash outside France, or even better in a neutral country like Switzerland,

and although half the dowry had been spent on expanding Gustavo Freisen's textile factory, the rest remained in that secret account, where the Germans would later deposit the money they paid for his services and which Odile never wanted to allow him to access.

Everything had gone smoothly for years, while Odile Kerouan remained her husband's docile and grateful servant. When the seeds of bitterness began to grow within her and she stood up to that greedy man, who was as cold-blooded as a shark, she discovered that she could resist his onslaught by refusing to sign cheques or documents; like Álvaro Espinoza, Gustavo Freisen had underestimated the evolution of a woman married by calculation and not without contempt. He never spoke about this to anyone apart from El Manco, that sulphureous-smelling relative who would somehow end up becoming his confidant. El Manco was the only person who could accept the real him without criticizing or judging his behaviour too harshly. And little by little, Gustavo Freisen got used to visiting him at his factory on Friday afternoons, to keep his finger on the pulse of the city, he said— because El Manco was aware of everything that happened in Barranquilla—but, deep down, to have someone with whom he could reminisce about places shrouded in mist and cold skies, where he had spent the best moments of his youth. Back then he was a bachelor, his mother was mingling with the high society of Lille, and he seemed destined for great things. He looked stylish, dressed in his tight-fitting jacket with its little wing collar as he courted a romantic mademoiselle from Broquemont whose family had the bad taste to go bankrupt. He remembered his jaunts in the countryside in the company of his brothers, the polite doffing of hats whenever the horse-drawn carriages passed each other between the poplars with green mossy trunks.

Above all, he remembered his house looking onto the austere

square whose cobblestones had been polished by the passing
of many men and many rains. He could hear the servants shuf-
fling around following the orders of an invisible butler inside
that house, the tinkling of a silver spoon and the majestic
tolling of the cathedral bell; when he looked out of the library
window and saw the slate roofs covered with the patina of
time, it gave him a pleasant feeling of perpetuity: ancestors of
his had gazed at the same stones, and, behind him, by the fire
in the hearth, they had read the same books that lined the
shelves; there would have been the same smell of freshly
rubbed wax, of burning logs amidst the peaceful colours of
winter. How Gustavo Freisen missed that light filled with
shades and half-tones, the closets full of lavender-scented
clothes, the portraits of his ancestors, who seemed to gaze
down at him approvingly from the walls: he too worked hard
and steadfastly to maintain the prestige of his house; returning
from the textile factory, he could savour the enjoyment of sitting in the living room that his distinguished, adorably worldly
mother had decorated with sienna-yellow curtains and opaque
globe lamps; he rested beside her, sipping an aperitif, satisfied
with his day, picturing the butler giving the final instructions to
the maids working in the kitchen or searching the damp cellar
for exquisite wines to pair with dinner. Oh, those French
wines, that pear liqueur, the taste, the smell of things created
over a long time, wisely aged: he would never have those again.
And as he uttered these words, Gustavo Freisen would pause
and hang his head while his cousin, El Manco, tried to divert
his attention to other topics, fearing that the conversation
would go on too long. Because then Gustavo Freisen might
start inveighing against his fate, and his longing for the past
would turn into a sombre exasperation that could set him off
talking non-stop for two hours: invariably, his mind made an
association between the pear liqueur and the memory of those
watercolours he brought with him from France, which, under

the harmful effects of a tropical fungus, had decomposed into a horrible mess of colours a month after he arrived in Barranquilla. How was anyone supposed to live in a country like that, where the paintings were leprous, the wines turned sour, and the sun seemed to glaze the landscape to the point that it resembled a mirage. And could one really call it a land-scape, that vermin-infested sea with sands so scorching that they blistered the feet, that fetid river of viscous water whose vapours seeped through the windows in his office at the factory, even though they were closed day and night to keep in the coolness from the air conditioning. The tropics reminded Gustavo Freisen of the most pessimistic passages from the Bible: vanity and corruption were everywhere, and the works of men were doomed to perish—one only had to look at that city full of cracked constructions, where termites inevitably devoured a building in under ten years. Nothing lasted there. Nothing perpetuated in that world without memory, without a past.

As soon as he arrived in Barranquilla, Gustavo Freisen bought a house that had been built by another Frenchman who had probably been driven mad by melancholy: it was a stately mansion, similar to the one his mother used to rent when they went to the Riviera during the summer, with a white façade, marble floors and many mirrors; it had three floors and magnificent bronze dogs adorning the banisters. He believed that in that house, he could allow himself the illusion of living in a civilized place. But it was in vain: when he looked out onto the balcony, he did not see gardens planted with palm trees and mimosas or sailing boats delicately crossing the blue waters of the Mediterranean but the sun bouncing off the faded roofs and cracked walls that housed the bourgeoisie of Barranquilla, a people who shouted loudly and emphatically, its intellectuals immersed in Byzantine discussions and its long-established families believing themselves to be relatives of

Alfonso XIII. Bourbons, no less, he repeated, as if humiliated by some insult, when one only needed to look at their faces to wonder what unspeakable couplings had engendered them. And suddenly he would look at his cousin, a little ashamed of letting himself get swept away by indignation, forgetting that El Manco had married one of those alleged descendants of the Spanish royal family. But El Manco smiled sympathetically at him: in that bitterness he simply recognized the symptoms of an illness that he himself had escaped, in a different time. He could picture his cousin as he was when he went to visit him in Lille before the First World War, as the heir to a considerable fortune, someone on whom all the gods seemed to be smiling. From him, El Manco had learned the art of obtaining obedience through persuasion, going out of his way to give his employees special treatment so as to avoid union strikes and complications; but in his cousin's case, this paternalism did not reveal any materialistic calculation but instead a desire not to betray his religious beliefs. Because at the time, Gustavo Freisen was profoundly Christian: he went to Sunday mass with his mother, and his moral integrity had earned him the respect of the elite of the North. That orderly and happy world, where a boss could afford himself the luxury of being loved by his workers, had been blown to pieces during the First World War: Gustavo Freisen had been one of the first to enlist, and three years later, El Manco had found him in a trench, covered with scars and medals: that beautiful and well-educated young man whose father had entrusted him with most of the management of the family business; the perfect gentleman who could impress the ladies and make a mademoiselle from Broquemont fall in love with him, the aesthete who could quiver at the sound of the bells or be moved by the smell of old books, had turned into a despotic leader, who made the men from his company tremble in his presence. He was beyond reproach, heading his troops as they attacked and exposing himself to danger with the recklessness of Achilles: he was righteous, so much so that it cost him his soul, El Manco explained to Maruja: he could not stand fear or cowardice, and since both were part of human nature, he had begun to despise human nature. El Manco lowered his voice when he spoke about the feats that had led hundreds of men under his command to their death and earned him eight palms on the ribbon of the War Cross: upon contact with pain, at the sight of blood, Gustavo Freisen had probably been possessed by the old demons of his lineage. What El Manco was saying was that no one could have imagined that wild-eyed captain falling in love with a woman or delighting in the smell of a book. Later, from his hospital bed, El Manco heard about him from other wounded men who came in moaning and wrapped in bandages, cursing Freisen's name. And that was all. El Manco had left the old France, never to return, while his cousin faced the economic depression, trying to start up the family business, going against the winds and tides of a factory that had been paralyzed for four years and cut off from its suppliers and customers; not to mention the suspicious prudence of the bankers—who were mostly Jews—and the chaotic political situation at the time. Gustavo Freisen stood firm, as tenacious as he had been when he fought the Germans, determined to give his mother and household back the level of wealth they had previously enjoyed, until debts and other financial problems forced him to ask for the hand of that Breton heiress, Odile Kerouan, whose dowry could not hide her obscure origins, for although her father had graduated as an engineer from the school of Arts et Métiers, her grandfather had been a simple ship repairman, one shrewd enough to end up becoming the owner of the company where he worked, and marrying the daughter of his main competitor.

Gustavo Freisen's mother's finely tuned intuition told her that though that money was necessary, it was too new. And so,

Odile Kerouan's married life began in even more thankless conditions. She had never expected much from men, and her strict moral principles instinctively kept her away from the games and seductions of love. She wept when her parents announced the date of the marriage, and she wept as she stepped into the church where the ceremony was being held. But from the revulsion she felt as an immature young woman, El Manco said, to what she had to endure later, there was a gaping chasm: Gustavo Freisen did not love women, and, like his mother, he despised outsiders; as soon as Odile Kerouan moved into the house in Lille with her extraordinary night gown, she no doubt found herself on the receiving end of animosity from both of them, and would have had to bow down to them repeatedly and suffer until the death of her mother-in-law, a character whom El Manco recalled without affection, comparing her to a provincial Madame Verdurin, an arrogant, peevish woman who would have gladly held a literary salon if her social prejudices hadn't stopped her doing so. She treated everyone badly, El Manco said, except her eldest son, with whom she had an emotional relationship that bordered on incest; this explained Gustavo Freisen's sexual scruples and the fact that he had married so late and out of sheer self-interest— which, incidentally, he never tried to hide from his wife, thus causing her to permanently resent him. Odile Kerouan, moreover, came from deepest Brittany; despite her religious upbringing, she had lived steeped in a magical world, where sailors heard the bells ringing from a city sunk beneath the sea, and the mist brought with it tiny and unpredictable beings that centuries of Christianity had failed to eliminate; she had been told about these *korrigans* frequently throughout her childhood and perhaps thought she had seen them dancing among the trees of the forest one moonlit night. What was she like, this nineteen-year-old girl, when she arrived in Lille to face a savage husband and a contemptuous mother-in-law? Filled with terror, El Manco told Maruja, capable of resisting, perhaps, but unable to fight back, since her parents had dispossessed her of everything, even of herself, when they handed her over to a man out of vanity, and that man received her as an object out of greed. Later, she was deprived of her sexuality through ignorance, and of her older children through infertility. Until Javier was born.

She must have been horrified to see how her husband was moulding her children, not daring to protest for fear of angering him or provoking her mother-in-law's humiliating remarks. No woman, El Manco argued—unless she had Freisen in her blood or was accustomed to barbarism—could allow the children that had come from her womb to be knowingly transformed into cruel and selfish creatures who took pleasure in the suffering of the weak. And she'd had to keep quiet while Gustavo Freisen systematically stamped out any hint of compassion or tenderness from his children, making way for the worst tendencies of human nature. What Lina and Maruja saw once, feeling like they were in a vile nightmare, Odile Kerouan had endured for twenty years and was still enduring when she arrived in Barranquilla, because the same thing happened again before their eyes, to the maddened screams of Ana. Perhaps the fact that there were two witnesses, and that Ana's only friends in the city had run off, horrified, to tell their respective families about Gustavo Freisen's sickening behaviour, was what enabled Odile Kerouan to demand her husband put an end to those abominations. Moreover, El Manco had taken matters into his own hands and immediately rushed over to his cousin's house to discover, astonished, the remaining evidence of the spectacle that had shocked Maruja so much. El Manco knew Gustavo Freisen too well and was not going to waste his time talking to him about humanitarian feelings or anything of the sort. He simply explained to him that, despite its racist blinkers, Barranquilla's high society was composed of two groups of people: the true aristocracy, descendants of Spanish noblemen who had settled in the region during the colonial period, for whom a needless act of cruelty was proof of unacceptable cowardice, and the others, who had worked their way up the social ladder through careerism and perseverance but were still considered by the former as low-class individuals, with whom interaction should be avoided as far as possible and reduced to mundane formalities. So Gustavo Freisen had a choice. He could either join the strongest side and be afforded powerful, unspoken protection, which meant receiving the latest news in good time, finding about governmental projects in advance and being invited to parties which were never reported in the newspapers, or he could join the nouveau riche who, despite being members of the country club or campaigning during the electoral periods in search of nominations that gave them the illusion of exercising power, were excluded from that secret aristocratic society, where the true power was hidden and he and his cousin, being foreigners, would never truly belong, but under whose wing they could prosper perfectly well.

Apparently, El Manco's words had an effect. It was never known for sure whether Gustavo Freisen had his doubts about the homogeneity of Barranquilla's bourgeoisie when he discovered the subtle divisions described by his cousin, but although mundanities were of no concern to him, he did not want to see his children go tumbling down the social ladder. Odile Kerouan had threatened to close the bank account again, and perhaps Gustavo himself was beginning to tire of so much tension: he was over fifty-five years old, and, in a certain way, he might consider himself defeated; as El Manco once pointed out to him, it was incongruous that he should allow himself to behave that way at his age, repeating the mistakes that had led to his downfall; whatever his ideological motivations for following Nazism had been, he should at least do his best to avoid another disaster and think of his children's future, who had already been deprived of their country and of the inheritance accumulated over various generations of Freisens: although the older ones might return to France one day, the younger ones would undoubtedly stay, they would become Barranquillans, and there would be no use in Gustavo Freisen rebelling against that fate. El Manco knew this, and he did not care, for that had been his intention when he settled in that sun-scorched city. However, he had seen the way many foreigners (Germans, Spaniards or Italians) formed ghettos to prevent their children from interacting with the people of Barranquilla, creating clubs and schools, forcing them to practise the language of the country they had left behind, and only succeeding in propelling them into the middle class that brought them all to the same level of staggering mediocrity. El Manco had been able to give his children the chance to move in the highest circles of that bourgeoisie thanks to his marriage, but if Gustavo Freisen insisted on bringing his children up like ruffians, he could be sure that he would never see them gain entry to that world. Money or the constant evocation of lost paradises were useless: sometimes, forming the cohesive identity required to assert oneself in life meant burying the past.

From then on, things became less strict in Gustavo Freisen's family. Thanks to the intervention of El Manco, who took the time to explain things to Lina's grandmother, she and Maruja started calling on Ana again. But for as long as they lived in the city, those older brothers produced an overwhelming sense of fear in Lina. Every time she was in a room with those dead-eyed, asthenic young men, she recalled the horrific spectacle they had staged. She could still see them there with Gustavo Freisen, their eyes gleaming malevolently as they surrounded the poor cat who was writhing wildly with pain, trying to protect her litter; they had not even tried to kill her first, to spare her the suffering of seeing her offspring tortured to death one after the other, because her desperation—Lina had understood this immediately—was precisely what gave them pleasure. And while the Freisen brothers bashed each kitten about, making sure to prolong its agony, Gustavo Freisen kept an eye on the mother, kicking her out of the way whenever she lunged. That stray female, who had been unlucky enough to choose that attic to have her litter, had probably done so on other occasions, afforded the protection of the house's former owner, so she did not understand what was happening: her kittens, terrified, their tiny eyes barely open, squirmed as they tried to escape those perfectly aimed blows that snapped their bones one by one: their meows were so high-pitched that they became a moan, blind despair, and she, the mother cat, beaten and bloodied, with one eye hanging out and her nose shattered, kept trying and trying as if all the energy in the world had been channelled into her battered body. Lina never knew how long she and Maruja spent watching the massacre before they reacted, grabbing some sticks that happened to be lying around in the attic, and pouncing on the Freisen brothers. The girls were both small, but their horror seemed to have given them brute strength: a blow to the back of the head knocked one of the Freisen brothers out cold, distracting the boys' father and allowing the cat to claw one of the other brothers in the face. Then Gustavo Freisen seemed to go mad: with an inhuman howl he killed the mother cat on the spot and violently hurled the kittens that were still alive against the wall. Maruja looked at him, livid with hatred. "Nazi!" she yelled, "Nazi pig!"

And grabbing Lina by the hand, she ran to the door.

It was six o'clock in the evening. They ran crying through the streets of El Prado, with the cat's piercing yowl still ringing in their ears. Lina felt as though she had just emerged from the depths of hell. The morning snack she had eaten half an hour earlier had turned to stone in her stomach, and she was struggling to get air into her lungs. She finally stopped by a tree, exhausted, to catch her breath. Between her tears she watched Maruja, who had stopped crying and regained the angry look her face had when she insulted Gustavo Freisen. "What's a Nazi?" Lina asked her. "You just saw one," Maruja replied. Though Lina did not realize it, the thing that people call ethics or morals, the thing that leads a person to unambiguously, uncompromisingly reject violence with their body, their instincts and their brain, had ingrained itself in her forever. The Freisens' arrival in the city had changed her life's trajectory. And, years later, it would do the same for Beatriz.

IV

When Lina got used to going to the Italian's Tower alone and to finding her way through in its maze of corridors and hallways, she began to remember the form and content of her dreams: the images that had haunted her during the night, only to vanish like the dew in the first light of morning, would anxiously creep back into her memory as soon as the great iron gate in the garden opened and she smelled the intense perfume of the jasmine climbing up the dilapidated gazebos and entwined in the branches of mahogany trees. That scent of jasmine made her feel like she was on the threshold of an unpredictable world where anything could happen, from remembering her dreams of the night before to seeing her aunt wandering beneath the green cascading ferns, while from the tower drifted the notes of the sonata, perhaps played by Aunt Irene herself. With its whimsical paths and that scent of jasmine, the garden lent itself to make-believe, inspiring the strangest of hallucinations. There were so many trees that their foliage formed a canopy, and not a single ray of sun could filter through the humid half-light, where plants bloomed in crepuscular colours; statues of women that looked like they were wearing masks had been covered in a tangled mess of vegetation for many years; dried-up fountains would suddenly begin to drip, and iguanas with iridescent crests and albino salamanders that detested the sunlight skittered through the cracks in man-made rockeries, which time had shaped into endless underground tunnels. But pervading all of this was the sense of unreality created by the illusion of seeing Aunt Irene's shadow in several places at once, and the memory of her dreams, whose significance Lina's aunt would help her to discover by gradually encouraging her to talk about them. Listening to herself, faced with the silence of that inscrutable and yet unquestionably attentive aunt, Lina got the feeling that she was opening doors that in other situations she would have thought it wise to leave closed, that she was revealing dark, violent emotions which had been concealed in the protective folds of her memory until then. To her, dreams seemed like a hook and line cast into seemingly calm waters with turbulent depths, where feelings writhed like lizards that had lived in the dark for so long they had lost all their colour. Lina turned those feelings into words with a combination of fascination and horror: they were a mirror, reflecting her true image and leaving her defenceless against her own contradictions. Inadvertently, she had descended into an inner vertigo and would never emerge, not even when she was able to talk about it years later, and although she had already learned to channel it when she was in the Italian's Tower. For Aunt Irene would also teach her how to use dreams to change the way she reacted to the everyday conflicts of life: if she could control her breathing and relax her body, if she shut her eyes and performed a slow ritual of concentration and forgetting, moving from one part of her consciousness into the next, the dreams would start to come back, like waves lapping the shore; then her memory would retrieve them, delving into the secrets contained in those dreams until the answer revealed itself. In this way, flight turned to fight, or failure to victory, and in this way, her most hidden desires were fulfilled. From that moment on, and defying all logic, her dreams ceased to be a passive expression of her anxiety, either because the anxiety disappeared or because her way of understanding it changed, as if acting on the effects might change the causes.

But there was no place for formal logic in the Italian's Tower, and there was even less room for it in the grounds that surrounded the tower, mirroring its structure; neither had any meaning, unless one abandoned the very notion of rationality to become wrapped up in flights of the imagination. And the garden was the place to do exactly that: in its shadiest corners stood gigantic mahogany trees with spindly, fragile-looking mushrooms growing at the roots: when she lay down among them, Lina immediately fell into such a deep slumber that within moments she could feel herself leaving her sleeping body and roaming around unfamiliar places; sometimes her spirit—or the part of her that was detached from her physical form—encountered beings from other walks of life, unrestricted by clothing, who swept her away on a dizzying journey to certain locations in space, not so as to offer her great revelations, but to share disconcertingly banal concepts with her. Lina did not understand why these entities insisted on impressing the idea of her insignificance in her mind, her own insignificance and that of all the inhabitants of the tiny planet where her body lay and where life, like a miracle, had developed: there she was—they seemed to be saying to her—a tiny pin prick among the infinite constellation of stars, and from there she could disappear, and her absence would make no difference to the dazzling pulsation of matter. Perhaps, like Aunt Irene, those voices were trying to convey the echo of a message that had been forgotten for thousands of years but would not be destroyed, not as long as there was someone listening to those echoes in the secret corner of a garden, knowing that she should pass the message on when she felt the first steps of silence approaching; as unclear as it was, her perception set in motion a mechanism that nothing and no one could stop, like a clock destined to tick until the hour of death, or a third eye that suddenly opened and remained eternally vigilant: because from then on there was no respite or rest, but rather a continuous interrogation, an eternal pilgrimage to the depths of the unconscious. Constantly forced to doubt herself, to doubt the justifications with which she tried to conceal her desires, Lina would see her narcissism withdraw, disoriented. Her pride, too: no reaction could be predicted, neither in herself nor in others, when human reality showed that it could not be reduced to the schemata of reason. Over the years, Lina would realize that simply glimpsing those illusions had altered her understanding of life by hinting at the existence of uncertainty. Aunt Irene and the garden, the dreams and their shadows would end up shattering the frame of thought that her grandmother had given her as a model. Much later on.

When the cracks presaging the inevitable rupture appeared in Barranquilla, however, it was completely unexpected. And those cracks appeared in connection with Javier Freisen, or rather, his marriage to Beatriz. Though Lina had her reservations, her grandmother had welcomed the news; barely heeding her granddaughter's objections, she declared that Beatriz had met her match in Javier Freisen, and Nena could swap her prayers of supplication for a *Te Deum* from that point forward. Content to imagine Beatriz happily on the road to marriage, she did not want to think about the motives that led a twenty-four-year-old man, in the prime of his life and as passionate as a fighting bull, to take an interest in a creature so dry that she evoked the frozen tundra of some distant planet. Because Lina knew full well that Beatriz's personality had not changed during her time with the Canadian nuns: she remained rigid and puritanical, and if there was anything she had learned, it was how to fabricate the image of an impassive person whose composure could not be disturbed by anyone. The Avendaño brothers thought that she had finally come to her senses, overcoming the troubles of an adolescence that had lasted too long. Dr. Agudelo told Lina that Beatriz's state of psychopathy was so extreme that she could even control the ways in which it manifested. And inwardly, Lina told herself that Beatriz would be better off selling her soul to the devil than marrying that man, who was pulled apart by two antinomian forces waging an all-out war inside his mind. Although she realized how vacuous this statement was, it was the only way she could explain the ambiguous nature of Javier Freisen's personality. He was impulsive like Benito Suarez—less crazy perhaps, but driven by the same desire to impose his will at any cost. And his was a capricious will, cemented over the years thanks to Odile Kerouan, who used her son's desires not only to humiliate Gustavo Freisen but also, most importantly, as a way to explore her own repressed desires. Javier had wealth and freedom, things Odile had dreamed of as a girl hindered by a bad hip, and then later, as a young woman confined to a convent. It didn't matter how many bicycles he broke or tennis rackets he lost; Javier could come and go from the house whenever he wanted, and he never had to answer to anyone. He was free to do as he pleased, but she, Odile Kerouan, was always there to be his confidante: with him, she savoured the pleasure of jumping onto the back of his motorbike as it roared to life, or gazing between the clouds at the silver wings of the small aeroplane he bought when he faked his date of birth to obtain his pilot's license. There were other things that Javier surely didn't talk to her about but which she could well imagine when she saw him heading out for the night with his friends, his pockets full of money destined to be frittered away in a haze of music and alcohol. Those banknotes, paid out by the fistful, had allowed Javier to hang out with older men while he was still young, learning the art of getting drunk in brothels and the right way to behave around the girls he met there. Petulia, who was a harsh judge of character, had taken a liking to him, claiming that he was a fiery sort who really loved women. Maruja and her sisters knew about Javier's fieriness all too well, because whenever they visited Ana they had to make sure they didn't end up in a room on their own, or else he'd suddenly come in, close the door and throw himself on them, his blue eyes gleaming in a way that made his intentions absolutely clear; only by shouting and hitting him had they taught him to be more respectful over time.

It was also true that he seemed to be in his element around women: he had joined Lina's group of friends since arriving in the city, agreeing not to abuse his strength in the slightly more masculine pursuits, and then, when his father bought the best house in Puerto Colombia, he would come and pick them up from Divina Arriaga's house early in the morning, and they would go horse-riding or swimming in the sea. All of this might have made him a fairly acceptable character, were it not for the other Freisen inside of him, who made an appearance from time to time, exposing a violent side no one had suspected was there. Lina saw this for the first time in the town square, when she witnessed him beating a bus driver to a pulp. The driver had stopped his bus to hurl obscenities at them, and in the blink of an eye, Javier jumped out of the car, wrenched the driver out of his seat and threw him onto the ground; were it not for the girls and some terrified passengers intervening, the driver would have ended up in the cemetery. Although Javier was seventeen years old at the time, he was already as tall as his father—but unlike his father, his frame supported a tremendous mass of muscle. Perhaps that was how Odile Kerouan had wanted him to be: a true descendant of those Breton sailors whose courage was not deterred when they heard the tolling of bells sunken beneath the waves. In any case, she had always defended his rebellious spirit: the first time he got into bother with the Jesuits, she sent him to Biffi College, and as the discipline imposed by the Congregation of Christian Brothers did not seem to suit him either, she decided to have him educated in a secular school where the pupils felt no guilt about insulting the teachers. Still, Javier had to deal with his father's antipathy; even though Gustavo Freisen did not really want him to fail, he expected that he would—that way he could regain some confidence in himself and the efficacy of his own pedagogical methods: of his first three sons who had settled in France, only one had managed to carve out a suitable living for himself; they never heard much about the second son, and the third had become a communist after covertly serving in an extreme right-wing party, and, in the ultimate affront to the family, spent his Sundays selling copies of *L'Humanité Dimanche* in the Place Maubert. Jean-Luc, the only one of that brood who had stayed in Barranquilla, showed signs of imbalance, flipflopping between episodes of total inertia, when he would lie in bed all day complaining of exhaustion, to spells of feverish activity levelled against the supposed laziness of the factory workers. Gustavo Freisen wasted a good part of his time undoing Jean-Luc's mistakes and trying to calm the infuriated leaders of the union, which, thanks to his shrewdness, had not yet been infiltrated by the communists. In addition to the problems caused by that son, whose upbringing Odile Kerouan had not been even remotely involved in, Gustavo Freisen also had to withstand the muted but tenacious vengeance of the Jews.

The city's Israeli community was extremely well organized. At its head were the rabbi and three millionaires who were set apart by the finesse of their diplomacy with local politicians and their strict obedience to biblical precepts; they were known as men of their word, even if very few people managed to speak to them, and they had managed to get hundreds of their fellow believers into the country between the two world wars. From the very beginning, new arrivals to the city learned that if they wanted to prosper they would have to quit their quarrelling and useless arguments, and demonstrate an unbreakable solidarity instead; if they had no money, they would also have to undergo a kind of initiation, which meant having to put up with the hardships of being a simple cloth seller in the Jewish stores on Calle del Comercio—regardless of their knowledge or qualifications—in order to demonstrate their ability to survive: in other words, their ability to create wealth in very squalid conditions. People viewed them with a combination of admiration and mistrust, because as exemplary as it was to see some poor man turn into a tycoon when only ten years ago he had been sitting on a stool, extolling the merits of his goods over a loudspeaker, everyone knew how exclusive and exclusionary that community was. It was different from the others, not so much because it had its own places of worship, clubs and private schools—the others had those, too—but because of its adamant opposition to its members marrying people of any other faith. That rule, the source of so many conflicts, had protected the unity of a people that had gone without a homeland for millennia, Lina's father told her, and it also allowed the Jews to keep their memory alive, their recollection of the wrongdoings they'd endured or the kindnesses they'd been shown. As a case in point, he told her about what happened to Divina Arriaga: none of Barranquilla's doctors could understand her strange affliction, and a few years after she arrived back in the city, she had received an unexpected visit from a renowned Jewish neurologist with whom the slightly Asian-looking maid would maintain a medical correspondence until she died. Divina Arriaga had not requested his services, and she had never even met him before. And all the neurologist knew about her was that she had helped a number of Jews escape the Nazis' clutches during the German occupation of France. As far as Lina's father knew, no member of the Israeli community had met the doctor or had been aware of his brief visit to Barranquilla. And the neurologist did not tell Lina's father who it was that had told him about Divina Arriaga's activities in the war, and then later, about her strange illness. But that doctor crossed the Atlantic to help her, and, from then on, he monitored the progress of her illness via letters the maid had sent him, and mailed over boxes full of medicines and powders in different coloured capsules, all designed to prolong her life as long as possible.

And so, it did not surprise Lina's father one bit that the Jews should swear to ruin Gustavo Freisen. As Lina's father was a friend of El Manco and his personal lawyer in some of his business affairs, he was entrusted with the delicate mission of asking the rabbi to grant the scoundrel forgiveness. He and the rabbi debated for a whole afternoon, both drawing on arguments from the Bible, a book which Lina's father fortunately knew by heart, just as he knew about the subtleties of the Semite soul, inherited perhaps from that grandfather of his, whose murder had almost brought about Cartagena's destruction. After that there was a gap of a few years, during which Gustavo Freisen's business seemed to go down the drain and the only way he managed to keep his factory afloat was by selling fabrics to the gringos at a loss. Sometimes, on his way back from the synagogue, the rabbi would stop in the street to talk to her father, and again the elaborate interpretations would return, leading them to converse in the manner of exegetes as the evening mosquitoes swarmed around them. But one Yom Kippur, the rabbi finally informed him of the decision that the heads of the colony had taken: they, the Jews, were willing to forget Gustavo Freisen's crimes on account of his family, but only on the condition that he provide tangible proof of his repentance, namely, by making a donation to the State of Israel. When he heard the news, Gustavo Freisen nearly died with rage. According to El Manco, he had become breathless, and suddenly all the bones in his body had started shaking; panting heavily, he was taken to a hospital where the doctor on duty had the good sense to give him oxygen instead of injecting him with some remedy that would have ended up destroying his already damaged nervous system. The Jews naturally found out about Gustavo Freisen's reaction, and although they agreed to do business with him after receiving the gift that Odile Kerouan judiciously donated to the State of Israel, they did so only so as not to betray the promise they made on Yom Kippur. But Gustavo Freisen would be reminded that his prosperity depended on the goodwill of the community every six months, when the new Jewish garment factories placed their orders with the cloth producers, and while his cousin El Manco was inundated with orders, he was forced to wait, biting his nails and secretly cursing the sons of Zion. He couldn't have suffered a worse fate: he had left his country, that France of old, whose sweet memory already seemed to have faded in his mind; he was feeling old before his time, ravaged by an erosive climate that was only fit for animals; he knew he was hopelessly cut off from the cultural milieus he once enjoyed, where people listened to symphonies with an air of solemnity and the publication of a book sparked a brilliant explosion of discussions. And he had gone through all this, only to find himself at the mercy of the very men he had fought against to the point of allying himself with the enemies of his homeland and becoming a renegade. After ten years in Barranquilla, Gustavo Freisen did not know what to believe, and the world seemed completely absurd to him. According to his faithful confidant El Manco, the worst thing was that he was so mired in mediocrity that he couldn't even see it: his younger children had never opened a book unless they had to study it, and they had no desire to learn about the past; they showed no interest in painting or music, except for those horrible Afro-Cuban rhythms and gringo rock, which was just as bad. Gustavo Freisen kept saying he was tired; he had tried so hard in vain to instil his offspring with some respect for European values, and he expended so much energy working in his factory and keeping Jean-Luc's stupidity in check that his wife had easily taken over the family's affairs, so now Odile Kerouan reigned at home like the rest of the women in Barranquilla, whose world she had joined in no time at all.

Because Odile Kerouan had learned that from a certain social level upwards, as long as the wives played down or paid lip service to their husbands' demands, the patriarchy in that city became a farce. Men could keep the illusion of holding all the power: their whims were indulged, and their opinions were never challenged. But between mothers and children, there was an infinite web of complicity from which fathers were excluded. Once they were married, the women offloaded their domestic chores onto their maids and entered the blissful idleness of afternoons spent at the country club playing cards until nightfall, satisfying their hunger cravings by ordering sandwiches, cups of tea and occasional alcoholic drinks under the guise of Cokes. This orderly monotony seemed to suit them perfectly; over and over they repeated the actions of the previous afternoon, of thousands of identical afternoons, until their minds went numb and their bodies became greedy for ham and melted cheese between two slices of bread, gradually getting chubbier and gradually increasing the measure of gin that the waiters at the country club mixed into the Cokes with exquisite discretion. Within that ordered existence, Odile Kerouan had discovered a freedom unimaginable to her European sisters, who were always under pressure from their husbands or families and deprived of those satisfactions, for no reward at all. But in Barranquilla, on the contrary, women had a considerable number of prerogatives: queens in their homes, goddesses in their children's eyes, they began to claw at their husbands' powers as soon as they were married, and when age or fatigue diminished the men's ability to fight back, they ended up possessing them completely. And no one challenged a situation which, to Odile Kerouan's mind, formalized the subtlest of compromises: a tacit agreement between the two sexes to live and die in peace. The sacrifice this pact implied did not seem to bother Odile Kerouan, who believed that sexuality was one of the aspects of human savagery that needed to be suppressed if the danger of falling into animality was to be avoided. She was well aware of the dreadful consequences of violence, and she had succeeded in eradicating it from Gustavo Freisen's behaviour. However, she was indulgent when it came to her sons' promiscuity, saying that experience had taught her how counterproductive excessive repression could be. Though there may have been ambiguity in her intentions, no one really cared: whether her friends were born there or not, they were married, like her, to wealthy foreigners who had settled in the city, and they formed a close-knit group over which wafted a light breeze of liberalism; besides playing bridge, they read the news in the local paper and some not necessarily recommendable books and, if they were feisty, had bouts of depression or indulged in secret affairs without any echoes. Whatever nationality they were, they all breathed in Barranquilla's air with relief and paid little attention to past prejudices that suddenly popped up in their conversations, like toads springing out of dark waters. Aware of how Odile Kerouan's marital relations had been, they shrugged when they heard her absurd comments about sex, not understanding that her remarks in fact conveyed the deep feeling of a woman for whom, for years, everything that fell outside the domain of productivity was a waste, a premise that she sometimes hazily recalled as she observed her own idleness and Javier's excesses.

Her spoiled son had grown more and more demanding, and the amount of money he spent on brothels and new flights of fancy became increasingly exorbitant. Odile Kerouan continued to open her purse for him, always grateful that through him she could penetrate the dazzling world of men. Javier was handsome and free: he had traded his motorbike for a sports car that raced along the main road to Puerto Colombia throwing up spirals of dust, and he was infatuated with a sailing boat named *Odile*, aboard which he defied the storms of the Caribbean with such courage that the fishermen of the high seas didn't know whether to call him brave or foolish. Lina, who was his co-pilot when he was in training for the sports car races, thought that Javier deserved both labels. Odile Kerouan, on the other hand, simply saw that penchant for danger as a trait he had inherited from many Breton sailors who, for generations, had learned to surrender themselves to the ocean, as if falling into a lover's arms. Sometimes she would go sailing with him, and the childhood memories would come flooding back to her: she felt young—she told El Manco's wife Rosario—and happy, with the breeze ruffling her hair and the air bringing the exhilarating scents of seaweed and iodine; out at sea, the waters of the Caribbean stretched before them in an infinite variety of greens, until they reached tiny secluded islands evocative of paradise; there, she and Javier would anchor for the night and sleep side by side under a mosquito net, listening to the rhythmic lapping of the waves. In those moments the past came rushing back, and Odile Kerouan realized how unhealthy her upbringing had been, caught between the nuns' puritanism and her parents' vanity; her life seemed sad, and she got the feeling that her sacrifices had been in vain; she was haunted by the desire to know why she had never thought about love when she was young and pretty—despite her displaced hip—and her presence at relatives' houses drew admiring glances; then she might have discovered the pleasures of youth instead of wanting to lock herself away in a convent until she lost all desire and let her parents marry her off to that man, who was as limp as an octopus washed up on the beach. Her musings led her to the humiliations she had suffered at the mansion in Lille, where the mother-in-law she despised had taken advantage of her naivety to ridicule her in front of her husband, who in turn only saw her as a walking womb for the Freisen family. This was the kind of thing Odile

Kerouan told El Manco's wife. Thank God she had Javier, she would say: Javier was her only consolation in the face of so much bitterness.

And Javier loved his mother; he liked to make sure she was happy, to help her erase those memories. Ever since he was a little boy, he knew she was his unconditional ally against the violent ways of Gustavo Freisen and his older brothers, who took pleasure in tormenting him, partly out of envy, but also because his inability to defend himself encouraged them to be cruel. Whenever they got him alone, he would tell Lina one day on the beach at Puerto Colombia, they would dunk his head into a tub of cold water until he nearly suffocated, again and again, trying to get him to do some degrading act or other in order to destroy his self-confidence. Lina listened, horrified. Javier looked at her with a smile. "They never succeeded," he said. And to Lina, his voice sounded as dangerous and defiant as a bull's horns in the ring.

But when he talked about his mother, his words always held a secret tenderness: it was thinking of her that made him decide to buy the sailing boat, and when he saw how happy she was on the little uninhabited islands, he convinced her to buy one of them. In those days, Odile Kerouan and her son lived completely as one: he confided his feelings and his experiences to her, and she granted his every wish. From picking her up so often from the country club in the evenings, Javier had ended up meeting her friends and became the beau of those women, who were somewhat past their prime and loved indulging in a little flirtation—innocently, of course—with one of the most attractive men in town. He would drive them home in the MG or ask them to dance at parties, stirring up ghosts of youth that they thought were dead and buried; suddenly they discovered the pleasure of smelling a young body, of being able to surrender to a muscular arm, and they began to forget the flabbiness of their thighs and the hours spent in front of the mirror trying to hide the damage the years had reaped on them, until Javier's strict indifference reopened the old wound; then, after the necessary mourning period, they took on a maternal attitude towards him, protecting him with broody jealousy: they would vie for his company, inviting him to their most exclusive cocktail parties, which were only attended by older, extremely wealthy and well-bred people. Those relationships allowed Javier to expand his customer base at the travel agency Odile Kerouan had bought for him so that he would have a decent means of earning a living without having to set foot in his father's factory. Javier had just scraped his high-school diploma at the time, and the agency was on the verge of bankruptcy, but three years later business was booming because the astute Odile had found someone else to sit at the cluttered desk belonging to a manager who only stopped by from time to time: a trustworthy man who was married and had five children to support: in other words, someone who actually had to earn a living.

Odile Kerouan had left nothing to chance in her unconscious mission to possess her son; always willing to give him whatever he wanted from far and near, even anticipating his whims, she had warped his character to such an extent that Javier could not stand anyone or anything getting in his way. But Odile Kerouan's big mistake was believing that he was eternally bound to her, as though a young man in perfect health would agree to remain in that state of uterine symbiosis for long, denying himself other loves and contenting himself with his sad routine of frequenting brothels. Javier had no particular interest in the women there, even though they were experts. He claimed he knew them all too well: he knew they were frigid and forced to satisfy the fantasies of their clients for money, never out of perversion; if they were lucky enough to rise to the rank of mistresses, they would try to create a dowry for themselves, consisting of a bed or a refrigerator, so that they could later disappear into the anonymity of a humble marriage. No, brothels were not a place where great loves blossomed, and as long as Javier continued to frequent them, Odile Kerouan was sure to monopolize his affections; sometimes, in her moments of depression, she imagined him married to a girl from a good family, and it felt like her heart had been stuck full of pins; then, to console herself, she resorted to the European notion of marriage as a simple financial transaction intended to increase wealth and perpetuate the family name. But imagining Javier falling in love was never part of her schemes; the mere idea of it was like a nightmare. They were happy together, weren't they? She was devoted to making him happy, wasn't she? She would ask El Manco's wife these questions, seeking reassurance; no one could love Javier the way she did, giving him everything without asking anything of him; no one else would be able to play down his flaws, by scraping away the stones in his path with her own nails. But Javier fell in love. And not with the double of Odile Kerouan—that is to say, someone who fell adoringly at his feet—but with the distinguished Victoria Fernán de Núñez, who had been pampered since childhood, with her mother, four aunts and a swarm of maids indulging her every whim—which were many and unpredictable, as the poor man from Caldas realized when he married her believing he had found El Dorado, only to find himself becoming the chief priest of an impetuous goddess to whom he would have to kowtow if he wanted to retain the privilege of managing her immense wealth. The Caldense was bold, but Victoria, born under the sign of Leo and enveloped in the aura of her wealth, was not impressed by anyone; she had learned from her mother and her aunts never to let a man control her, and even less her wealth. So, when they returned from their honeymoon (which she found less than thrilling) the Caldense started to submit accounts to her every month, and either because of this vigilance, which might earn him praise or reproach, or because of the trouble he had keeping up with Victoria's sexual appetite, his personality appeared to splinter over time, transforming him into a remarkable businessman on the outside, and in private, a child with a passion for collecting tin soldiers. Victoria brought back those little soldiers from her trips to Europe, where she purchased them or ordered them from retired craftsmen for colossal sums, while her lover at the time took her to heights of passion in which the thousand flowers of her insatiable temperament, always in search of new emotions, bloomed. She struck fear into the ladies of Barranquilla, because although she was not as refined and beautiful as Divina Arriaga, she had the same talent for fascinating men; perhaps not exactly fascination, but rather something similar to lust, because her complete lack of inhibitions and a hint of vulgarity picked up from God knows where, prompted men to peel off the last layer of their armour and reveal the fantasies that could not be satisfied in the brothels, or were out of the question with their wives. With her, however, the most horrifying forms of love could unfurl free of shame, and free of charge: Victoria refused gifts, convinced, she once told Lina, that any gift was a form of compensation linked to the decline of eroticism, and that receiving it meant admitting she had grown weary of a man's amorous behaviour, a precursory sign of monotony and, eventually, boredom. When, many years later, Lina happened to bump into her in Paris accompanied by her German playboy, who was undoubtedly her gigolo, she maintained the same reasoning but with a slight tweak; she was paying, true—by then age had reared its ugly head—but her lovers had to play into the fantasy, otherwise they would be given the boot; in other words, they would have to give up the sports cars and sumptuous apartments in luxury hotels. As Lina listened to her talk, amused by her cynicism and her devastating sense of humour, she couldn't help but think about the other Victoria Fernán, still graceful despite her years, slender from so much exercise—the woman Javier had fallen in love with, making Odile Kerouan miserable and ruining her relationship with her son.

Neither she nor her friends at the country club had suspected for a second the impact that the fiery personality of that ageing amazon would have on Javier, when Victoria would have been a perfect fit for any Freisen who was not entirely neurotic—in short, any one of them who was relatively unencumbered by those religions or ideologies which had always caused their sexuality to freeze over. Odile Kerouan succumbed to jealousy, and for the first time in her life she suffered a depressive episode; had she not objected to Javier's love affairs, she would have at least kept their close relationship; but like God's ways, El Manco said, the ups and downs of mental imbalance were unfathomable. Projecting herself onto her son, she had made a stand against time and death; by giving him everything he wanted, she had avenged herself for the things she had been deprived of, and by making him independent, she had obtained a piece of freedom. In fact, Javier had been conceived shortly after the death of the detested mother-in-law, when Odile Kerouan stopped feeling inferior in that house in Lille; she had not been unwell during the pregnancy, the birth did not take long at all, and rather than pain, it brought with it an unsettling sensation of pleasure she had never experienced before. Odile told El Manco's wife about her fear of Gustavo Freisen rejecting that black-haired baby, because despite her virtuous ways, she had fallen pregnant during a holiday when certain members of the Kerouan family were staying with them, including a cousin who was married to a male relative for whom she, Odile, felt a strong attraction. And besides being well-built, that relative had black hair. Odile Kerouan seemed to have shifted her desire for that man onto the sperm of the husband who impregnated her, somehow defying the laws of genetics, and somehow considering the new baby as hers alone, so different to his actual father and the other children she had formed in her womb out of duty or vanity and pushed out amid atrocious suffering and uncontrollable bleeding. Her love for Javier was never ambiguous, in fact, to be true to it, she agreed to modify her beliefs, becoming a tolerant and generous mother, instilling her own moral principles with the flexibility of a trapeze artist. Ultimately, there was nothing exclusive about this feeling, nor did it restrict Javier's sexuality, because through him Odile experienced pleasure by proxy and—this Lina thought she could sense years later—realized the fantasies she had suppressed for a period that most likely dated back to her childhood, when she lived with three of her first cousins: Jeanne, the future wife of the black-haired relative, and two other girls, whom Lina would find settled in Cannes, still united in the final glimmer of an ethereal and guarded love. It was Maruja who suggested Lina spend the summer with them when she found herself in dire straits, having lost her job as a translator, and the Breville girls took her in for several months until they found her a job through some friends, allowing her to continue roaming around Paris. Lina thought they were adorable from the beginning; they were like two candles in front of a veiled statue in an empty church, watching each other so that they burned down at the same speed, in line with some unspoken agreement to be snuffed out at the same time. Sometimes they would speak about the past, and Lina understood, despite their cautious language, that Odile Kerouan might have met with a similar fate to cousin Jeanne, a character the Breville girls talked about not without apprehension, using the word "intriguing" as a euphemism, because they were too well educated to insult her by calling her a *garce*. In any case, following a deliberate indiscretion by the same Jeanne, Odile Kerouan's parents made up their minds to send Odile to a school run by nuns, quashing her dreams of one day discovering the marvellous stone that would make her invisible, or the Lady of the Lake and her golden fortress inhabited by ten thousand women dressed in silk who knew nothing of men or the laws of men. Meanwhile Jeanne, orphaned and entrusted to the care of the Kerouans, gradually gained their affection until finally she replaced Odile in her mother's heart. That was Jeanne Breville's first betrayal in a long run of disgraceful acts that could have provided Balzac with the material for an entire novel and which, more modestly, offered Lina some insights to help her understand how pathologically jealous Odile Kerouan had been when she learned that Javier was in love with someone so similar in appearance to Jeanne, that cousin who had initiated Odile into certain illicit games and then ratted her out to her parents, condemning her to exile. All this, perhaps sunken in the darkest meanders of her memory, must have bubbled to the surface when she found herself ousted by Victoria Fernán de Núñez, precisely the only woman she could not love, for fear of bringing up that forgotten anguish. So, Odile went from understanding to despotism overnight; she became a sorrowful mother and began to irritate Javier with recriminations and begging, then when she realized how futile her jealous outbursts were, she ended up threatening to withhold her generosity, disregarding the fact that Javier still carried Gustavo Freisen's blood in his veins—despite her confused dreams of parthenogenesis—and it was not a good idea to poke the demon that slumbered inside him. Odile had also foolishly put the agency's shares in Javier's name, allowing him not only to cut the umbilical cord, but also to savour the delights of financial independence as he discovered a formidable talent for making money; from tourism, he moved on to the construction business and then to financial operations so fruitful that Gustavo Freisen began to open his eyes and take notice. That son of his had insulted him more than once: as a child he dared to treat his father with contempt by mocking his retaliations, and as soon as he reached his teens and found out how his father had behaved with the Nazis, his disdain turned into absolute hurtful repulsion, and he even had the audacity to call him a coward. That was the last time that Gustavo Freisen tried to hit him, because Javier flew at him, pinned him with one arm and whispered in his ear that his greatest wish was to have a reason to smash his head into the wall. From then on, they stopped talking to each other, or rather, Gustavo Freisen silently endured Javier's scathing comments at the dinner table, about the treachery of collaborators and the imbecility of those who allowed themselves to be ensnared by any ideology, repeating Maruja's indignant opinions word for word. But when Odile began to make life impossible for him and Javier proved to be a business whizz, Gustavo Freisen saw the crack forming, a way to gain not the affection but the cooperation of a son whom he deeply respected for his courage and who, in any case, was superior to that psychopath Jean-Luc, whose persecutory delusions had reached worrying proportions over the years.

Time, on the other hand, had honed Gustavo Freisen's capacity for calculation, as had the heartache he had suffered in that diabolical city; having learned the subtle art of patience, he could predict the way events would slowly but inevitably unfold; one day Victoria Fernán would tire of Javier, and that turbulent son would seek out power as compensation for his wounded pride, a power that only he, Gustavo Freisen, would be able to offer him, giving him an important position in his factory, which, thanks to his personal effort and despite the resentment of the Jews, was destined to become an empire with numerous branches. Jean-Luc lacked the stature to be imposing, and Javier would manage to guide him, while the only son Gustavo Freisen truly trusted, Antonio, was finishing off his studies at Harvard Business School. As soon as the situation became clear to him, Gustavo Freisen started singing the praises of Victoria Fernán and, when he was sure that his comments about her would reach Javier, he explained, confidentially of course, that he would prefer his son to be in the company of a highborn lady, instead of imagining him frequenting those hookers at the brothels swarming with venereal diseases. Disarmed by those intentions, Javier—whose intelligence sometimes appeared to be inversely proportional to his strength—decided to sound out his father's goodwill by asking if he could rent his house in Puerto Colombia for a few months. Then, much to his surprise, he was summoned by a notary to register the deeds in which Gustavo Freisen signed it over to him, paying the transfer taxes out of his own pocket and arranging things in such a way that it would not be detrimental to his brothers. Javier was happy: it meant he could say goodbye to Odile Kerouan and her judgements, and to the constant feeling of being watched, the obligation to always seem grateful. He still loved her, he would tell Lina, but he could no longer bear to live with her being so dependent on him, especially if pleasing her meant he had to give up the woman he wanted. And Victoria Fernán satisfied his desires beyond all expectations; she not only spurred on his masculinity but also taught him the secrets of female pleasure: with her, he said, he learned the science of rhythms, the art of daring, the alchemy of time; and the more he surrendered to love, the stronger he felt his character becoming, because strangely enough, the pleasure-taking Freisen was exactly as powerful as the castrated Freisen, as though only in extremes—whether of lust or of asceticism—could the Freisen men achieve the kind of intensity that had led them to command others, since the very first moment they managed to light a fire on the wild, frozen shores of the Baltic. Never before had Javier shown himself to be so efficient and dynamic, managing several businesses at the same time; like a yellow whirlwind, his MG sped from the banks of the Paseo Bolivar to the factories of the Industrial

Zone, from the airport, where he went to greet North American businessmen, to the Hotel del Prado with its bars bathed in air-conditioned gloom, where they discussed money in English. And as soon as night fell, the MG zoomed off to Puerto Colombia with Javier behind the wheel, eager to lose himself again between the avid, warm, juicy thighs of Victoria, who, feigning an illness, had declared that she had been forced to recover in the solitude of a seaside spa. That affair lasted as long as it was ever going to last: Victoria could not keep it up for long at the risk of causing a scandal that would be too much for Barranquilla's high society to digest, and since the man from Caldas could not stand to see her looking so exhausted, she agreed to go to Miami for a check-up in a private clinic, where she met an absolutely irresistible young doctor and embarked on a new love affair that kept her away from the city for well over six months. During that time, Javier progressed through various states of mind until he finally settled into the severe personality of the Freisens. His initial astonishment was followed by a violent feeling of anger that drove him, quite lucidly, to kick the furniture to pieces in the house in Puerto Colombia, and to write off the MG in a genuine accident from which he miraculously emerged unscathed. When he grew tired of getting drunk, getting into fights in brothels and cursing Victoria Fernán, Javier painfully began to reflect on the facts of life, using his best friends, Lina and Maruja, as sounding boards—and they tried in vain to talk him out of it.

But he was determined: even though his friends thought he was unprepared for the task, Javier wanted to understand the kinds of values that might have an influence on a woman of almost fifty, setting aside the subtle compromises that any woman of her age had to make in life if she wanted to protect her mental and physical integrity. Since he understood nothing, he chose to reject the enchantments of passion, devoting all his energy to achieving a secure financial position and entering, without realizing it, the field where his father was waiting for him. Gustavo Freisen did not impose any specific restrictions on him, certain that Javier's new responsibilities would end up calming his truculent spirit. And indeed, as the director of the commercial services of the Freisen industrial complex, there were many things he was not permitted to do, from dressing casually to causing scenes in brothels. His social life was limited to appearing at cocktail parties where he was expected to show his face, but the playboy those housewives and eligible young woman dreamed of had become a shrewd businessman who was always slightly cynical when he talked about the opposite sex. Working with his father cast a shadow over his personality, making it hard to recognize the Javier of the sailing boat in that straightlaced executive who hardly ever cracked a smile. He was plagued by paranoia: one day he would tell Maruja about how he'd had the feeling he was being persecuted during those years. But instead of being intimidated, fear made him grind his real or imagined enemies to dust. Gustavo Freisen decided it was best to leave him to it. Incapable of being prudent, Jean-Luc confronted him, and in doing so, committed a fatal error.

Javier hated Jean-Luc, seeing him as the embodiment of his other older brothers who had caused him so much suffering in his childhood, and the conspicuous carrier of the family's defective trait. While Javier grew up under the kind protection of his mother, Jean-Luc identified with Gustavo Freisen alone; the reason he stayed in Barranquilla was not so much to help his father with the business as to be close to that sullen and fierce force, which he had used as an example to forge his own will. El Manco said that despite having lived in the tropics for many years, Jean-Luc refused to eat fruit or salad or to drink water unless it had been boiled, and he always carried a small bottle of alcohol in his pocket for rubbing on his fingers whenever someone shook his hand; he had never visited a brothel nor indulged in a fling, because women horrified him: all the viruses and bacteria that threatened him lurked between their legs, and the serpents of evil slithered around in their souls. In addition to his fear of germs, he also had the most peculiar aversion towards workers, who he considered inferior beings due to miscegenation, and naturally inclined to baseness; as was to be expected, he imagined that the workers were fuelled by a merciless animosity towards him, and he suffered immensely, convinced that they were plotting against him. His delusions of persecution had reached such extremes that he suddenly refused to leave his office, and Gustavo Freisen had to drag him out of there, kicking and screaming. It was around this time that Javier started working in the factory, occupying a far superior position to Jean-Luc and immediately winning everyone over: the employees preferred having a boss who spoke without an accent, drank white rum and knew how to dance cumbia; at the weddings and baptisms he was invited to, Javier set aside any sense of hierarchy, only to regain it the following day without the slightest awkwardness. All his dealings with mechanics and fishermen had made him familiar with the locals, and, unlike Jean-Luc, he was not about to be intimidated if one of them muttered an insult as he walked by or gave him a grim look; knowing the coastal mentality, all he needed to do to settle the issue was call anyone who was feeling resentful into his office and talk to them face to face. He also showed that he was generous and willing to talk; his reputation as a righter of wrongs soon spread throughout the factory, and the workers began to take their demands straight to him without turning to the union. That, plus two or three wise innovations in the production circuits, had earned him the recognition of Gustavo Freisen, for whom profit was the ultimate sacred word. Jean-Luc, on the other hand, felt belittled; he tried in vain to warn his father that he was heading for ruin if he continued to accept Javier's methods. His hands clenched, his sweat-soaked grey hair plastered like molten lead to the back of his neck, Gustavo Freisen coldly contemplated that face, marred by twitches, whose chin, once well-defined, had softened over time. And Jean-Luc, humiliated, tiptoed away. Humiliated and confused: according to El Manco, the feeling of having lost his points of reference had pervaded him a long time ago, when they left Europe and his father seemed to bend to Odile Kerouan's will, and a new set of values was imposed on the family. And in that city, he could not have any friends: the young people of his age made fun of him because he didn't go to brothels and didn't like getting drunk, and the first time he attended a Carnival ball at the country club he swore never to set foot in there again: "perverted" was what he called it, the high-society women all made up and dancing to the beats of Black music, the men with their faces painted like clowns. He rejected that world of light and frivolity with every cell of his body, which was too white, too sensitive to the sun; the departure of his older brothers and an unfortunate misunderstanding with a hairdresser—who he thought was capable of understanding him because he had the same exquisite manners and spoke French—ended up plunging him into loneliness, and, like the hermit who, filled with dread when he senses temptation runs away to his cave, he desperately sought refuge in work. His office was clean, his secretary was elderly and efficient, and with his mere presence, Gustavo Freisen showed him which way to go, the high road that led to power: when he gave the order, dozens of people jumped into action, the machines sped up, and workers were hired or fired. From his desk he felt like the heir to a king, the vizier of a sultan, and when he wasn't being terrorized by the "nightmares," as his father called them, the world struck him as a formidable battlefield.

Alas, he did suffer those "nightmares": something in his throat, a claw-like grip that suddenly took his breath away, instantly making him feel his blood struggling anxiously through the arteries in his chest, as if his heart were expelling it in frantic eddies. The episode was accompanied by uncontrollable diarrhoea and was brought on by the persecution to which he was subjected, and which no one took seriously. For years Jean-Luc had been trying to identify the causal link between the first two phenomena, in other words, to find out if intestinal issues were causing the cardiac arrhythmia or vice versa, but nothing had come from his visits to doctors or from sending his faeces to laboratories in search of the nasty worm or disgusting amoebas that caused his colic, because the city's specialists insisted on telling him, contrary to all evidence, that his intestines were clean and his heart was in perfect condition. One of them, Dr. Agudelo, had been so incredulous as to start asking him questions about his intimate life and suggest that he should put an end to his chastity, and from that point on he trusted the doctors even less than he did the workers. In El Manco's opinion, Dr. Agudelo had shown too little tact: Jean-Luc had to remain chaste for the rest of his life unless he wanted to go mad, because no Freisen could get a glimpse of his own sexuality without falling into a pit of torment. And that was what happened: deprived of his only remaining human contact, of the relief of waiting for medicine to provide a solution to his problems, Jean-Luc's episodes intensified. He trembled as he remembered Dr. Agudelo and the malevolent questions he had asked, sowing so much confusion in his mind: his ailments were not the result of some nervous condition, he groaned, when the paranoia began to take hold and the elderly secretary rushed to tell Gustavo Freisen that his son had locked himself in the office again. However, putting these ideas together had a curious effect in the short term: Jean-Luc suddenly seemed to notice that if he went to the country club in the evening, he could meet his sister Ana's friends and chat with them, therefore giving everyone the impression that he was vaguely normal. That was how he met Beatriz and felt his heart beating without fear for the first time.

Beatriz did not even realize, still numb from the dreams envisioned at the school run by the Canadian nuns. She never knew why she had ended up there, and if she ever wondered about it, she must have thought that her parents had been blindly following the fashion of sending young girls from good families abroad to finish their high-school studies. There was no way she could speculate much on the matter either, as Lina understood it years later when she listened to her talking about her trip to Canada, because as soon as she got off the plane and felt those blades of icy air tearing at her lungs, the memory of Barranquilla seemed to vanish from her memory. That oblivion was what impressed her most: she became aware it was happening as she watched the snow-laden wind swirling against the windows of the car that drove her to the convent, and she slowly rubbed her bluish fingers, afraid of being made fun of by the other student next to her; it was a curious form of amnesia, because although she remembered everything, she could home in on her past without experiencing the slightest emotion; she immediately noticed how that past was transformed into an impotent yesterday that she pulled out of the shadows or returned at will, and she felt she was safe, escaping from a danger that had haunted her since childhood, one she found impossible to define. Then she felt something akin to bliss, *dicha*, although that word sounded over the top in Spanish and she preferred the term *bonheur* to express that particular state of mind, which was devoid of any form of anxiety. She told Lina that it was like having spent a whole life being unwell without knowing it, then suddenly discovering what it was like to be healthy.

It seemed there was no place for her old anxieties in that school: no one knew the Avendaños, and people frowned upon anyone who talked too much about themselves in conversation. Colombia was a pink region on the world map in the classroom, Barranquilla a dot next to the blue line of a river, and she, Beatriz, a Latin American girl who no one thought was capable of learning to speak two languages in less than six months, translating Horace from Latin into French and solving differential calculus exercises in English. But her studiousness earned her praise there, and her strict morals tended to be toned down in the company of those rich girls; for them, divorce was not a drama, nor was the fate of mankind an obsession: all they wanted was to be happy, to marry their brothers' friends, who would go on to become renowned doctors, directors of large companies and important politicians; they wanted to have two or three children and live in beautiful mansions in Boston or Montreal like their mothers, travelling to Europe every year to buy dresses, explore cities and visit museums. Beatriz had been disconcerted by the simplicity with which they embraced life. When she stayed with them during the holidays and observed the peaceful luxury of their houses, the transparency of their relationships, that sense of honesty about all of their actions, she occasionally wondered whether she had tormented herself for no reason; suddenly her plans to change the world seemed utopian—utopian and exaggerated: all that harmony was due to a long process of civilization undertaken by the peoples of the northern hemisphere, and not to the realization of an individual will. After much reflection, she began to liken the fact that she'd been born in Barranquilla to a cruel twist of fate and ended up fully integrating into Anglo-Saxon society instead. Her own friends, whom Lina would meet through her when she began to sell Divina Arriaga's paintings, still said this about her years later: Beatriz had adapted very well to the North American way of life. They remembered her as a well-mannered young woman who had no boyfriends to speak of, but who was always surrounded by admirers at parties; in particular, they remembered her brief relationship with the son of a Republican senator, which was cut short when she returned to Barranquilla. That boy, a cadet at the West Point military academy, had fallen in love with Beatriz after seeing a photograph of her that his sister had, and he instantly sent her the most passionate declaration of love; when they met after months of correspondence, Beatriz talked about converting to Protestantism. The young man wanted to get married, but she—and this no one understood—wanted to test him, and so she foolishly went away, leaving him so confused that after a while he started dating her best friend. That story, which Lina thought sounded somewhat far-fetched, would end up revealing its importance at a crucial moment of Beatriz's life: her failed attempt at separation. It explained many things, like the indifference she showed towards people when she came back to the city, and the slightly blasé smile behind which she seemed to be hiding a secret: Davy, the senator's son, was still writing to her, and she could picture herself somewhere far away from Barranquilla. Her aloofness, which Dr. Agudelo called psychopathy, was in fact the radiant contemplation of a dream in which, dressed as a bride, she walked with Davy through the arch of steel formed by the shining swords of the West Point cadets.

Among the smiles and camera flashes as she descended the steps of the church and tossed the bouquet of flowers to her friends, Jean-Luc and the other boys from the country club surely went unnoticed. Beatriz only went to the club to please her mother; the mundane existence in Barranquilla filled her with a weariness that she never tried to conceal; she did not know or want to learn to dance to the music of the coast, and at the first sign of vulgar behaviour, she went home. But her refined manners did not inspire derision, as they did with Isabel, because she had the Avendaño fortune behind her. The girl once scorned was now getting her own back: she was beautiful and rich, with a swarm of suitors buzzing around her. Her former classmates from La Enseñanza had already been married off to middle-class men, and the few women who moved in bourgeois circles by birthright tried to make friends with her. But it was no use: Beatriz was impenetrable. They had seen her coming home from abroad shrouded in a halo of mystery that made them intensely curious, with her blond hair gathered at the nape of her neck, her slim silhouette and the slightly absent look of the short-sighted; they had admired her majestic air at the debutantes' ball hosted by her parents, and then, expecting her to fall for one of the most eligible men at the time, almost no one had noticed how her discretion was turning into hermeticism. The Avendaños did, especially Nena. She, that woman who had suffered so much for her daughter, did not believe in the miracle of travel; having grown old with a heart full of sadness, she only saw the dark side of things; the death of one of her grandchildren and her husband's irremediable alcoholism had reinforced in her mind the conviction that the world was a vale of tears; in fact she cried every night remembering past calamities and imagining those yet to come, and it was only when Beatriz decided to return to Barranquilla that she took advice from a doctor to undergo treatment for insomnia; then she noticeably improved, and even agreed to update her wardrobe and dye her hair to an even white. But Nena's concerns were still lurking: even though Beatriz's serene state had been a pleasant surprise, she did not think for a moment that it would last long, and she was waiting for the signs of the storm right from the start.

The storm was a slightly darker shade in a sky that was always full of clouds; the darkening was almost imperceptible, like the disappearance of a very faint smile. Lina would later think that when Beatriz stopped receiving letters from the boyfriend she never told anyone about, she must have looked around and realized that her prospects were pretty bleak. The college diploma she had obtained in Canada, opening the doors to the best American universities, was of little use to her in a city where girls in her position did not pursue higher studies or work unless they were very poor or driven by an openly rebellious spirit. Since she did not fall into either category, her only choices were to remain a spinster or to get married, and in her eyes the men of Barranquilla must have cut a rather sorry figure compared to the charming West Point officer. In any case, she gradually stopped going to parties, finding one excuse after another not to leave her house, and in an attempt to quell Nena's anxieties, she discovered a sudden vocation for drawing and painting. She took correspondence courses from the United States and spent the whole day in her room in front of an easel, sketching faces and landscapes in charcoal, which began as a reproduction of the original model and then took on a tormented air as she worked on them; she had a talent for drawing, but she did not paint much, and deep down all she wanted was to be left alone with her pain. She did not talk about the senator's son to anyone, not even to Lina, who went to see her at Nena's request. The few boys who insisted on courting her ended up growing tired of her indifference, and in the end, Jean-Luc was the only suitor left.

The truth was that Jean-Luc wanted nothing from her, except to dispel the doubts about his mental health by showing his family he was the supposed bridegroom of a pretty heiress, whose lineage and distinction were taken as a given. Gustavo Freisen was overjoyed: El Manco's predictions were about to come true, and the concessions he had made to the city he hated, but on which his wellbeing depended, were finally going to bear the greatest fruit: one of his sons, the least attractive one, was going to consolidate their social standing by joining the Avendaño family. He suddenly decided to appoint Jean-Luc as production manager, doubling his salary—much to the indignation of Javier, who couldn't begin to imagine what Beatriz represented for his father. Odile Kerouan seemed willing to set her conjugal resentments aside and join her husband in the mission of reeling in this girl from a decent family, a girl who, moreover, had the advantages of being one hundred per cent white and speaking flawless French. So she encouraged Ana to invite her over to the house more often, gradually gaining her affection. Beatriz felt at ease in the Freisens' home: she found the atmosphere welcoming, she got to practise her favourite language, and she was showered with attention. Showing how subtle she could be, Odile persuaded her daughter to take an interest in painting too, turning one of the rooms in their house into a studio and hiring a fine-arts student to give them both lessons in perspective. In no time, Ana and Beatriz were the best of friends, and they went everywhere together in the car that Gustavo Freisen provided for them, with a uniformed chauffeur. In the evenings, Jean-Luc would accompany them to the cinema or invite Beatriz for dinner at the country club. Sometimes Lina would find them there, sitting at a grill table, looking very serious and barely saying a word to one another. Their relationship remained the same, a meeting of two lonely and somewhat unsociable people who preferred to keep their feelings to themselves; Beatriz was still carrying around the remaining shreds of her nostalgia, and Jean-Luc did not seem ready to take the next step: unsettled by the turn things had taken, he insisted on exaggerating the advantages of an unequivocal friendship, occasionally making remarks about his family's intentions, comments that were intended as jokes but which Beatriz found unbearable. The only one who noticed the ambiguity of the situation was Javier. As soon as he grasped what was at stake, he decided to win Beatriz over, killing several birds with one stone: he would get back in his father's good books, take revenge on his brother and get himself a suitable wife, one he could parade around in public and who would not deceive him like Victoria Fernán. But he did not know how to treat girls of his social standing, and he hated the hypocritical nature of courtship, with its stream of visits, serenades and declarations of love. So, he began to observe Beatriz the way one would examine a citadel before invading it, seeking advice from Maruja, who did not want to get involved in the matter because she thought his plan was foolish. At around the same time, Beatriz started to confide in Lina.

She had noticed, reluctantly and not without embarrassment, the interest she awakened in Javier; when those blue eyes of his brazenly swept over her body, she felt the blood flow to her cheeks and the awful sensation that she was losing her individuality and falling into the viscous anonymity of the species, there, where all human females eventually end up waiting for man's desire. In her belly she felt a pulsing beat she had never noticed before—this and other things, like how hard it was to express herself when he was around, as well as an undefinable drowsiness; she thought people could guess her emotions, and, sometimes, she sat there glued to the chair, imagining that her skirt was stained by the trickle of moisture that ran between her legs when, from across the table, Javier would not take his eyes off her. That experience had brutally changed the rhythms of her body: her period lasted longer than usual, erotic dreams awoke her suddenly in the middle of the night and stopped her getting back to sleep, and at the slightest change in temperature, she went from shivering with cold to hot flashes. Had she not been overcome with shame, she would have asked a doctor for help, given that she likened the manifestations of her amorous state to the symptoms of an illness, and though she confided in Lina, it was only so that she could be told a thousand times not to feel scared or degraded, regaining a little self-confidence in the process. But only a little, because every morning her vows never to return to the Freisens were shattered in a maelstrom of contradictory feelings: one day she said she wanted to give Javier the cold shoulder, then the next she wanted to nip his advances in the bud or show him that she was not intimidated by them.

Meanwhile Javier relished his desire like a privateer, without suspecting Beatriz's complicated feelings. Not particularly prone to reflection and rather ignorant of certain complexities of the mind, he simply followed his unconscious impulses, which had been revealing themselves with a rare perspicacity. The girl appeared to be in love with him, but if he treated her properly, he said to Maruja, he would be sure to see her rise up like an inviolable goddess; those scornful lips, those irascible eyes suggested a real puritanism that was impervious to masculine advances and even to any reproductive plans nature might have in store for her. However, at the slightest touch, Javier received an animalistic response from her: all he had to do was grope her in a corridor and she would wilt into his arms with the excited lustfulness of a cat on heat; he did not even need to resort to the tricks he had learned with Victoria Fernán, because Beatriz reacted less to the subtlety of the caress than to the violent way he did it to her, and she experienced her pleasure in a muted and solitary state of intoxication from which she emerged energized by a senseless hatred for him. It annoyed Javier that she was incapable of sharing her feelings, but he got off on violating the walls of her modesty over and over. It was all strangely entertaining, full of surprises, like riding the ghost train at a fairground. Every step led him inevitably to a more dangerous one, and he could never anticipate what Beatriz's reaction would be. He liked to create situations in which it was impossible for her to defend herself without causing a scandal. Once, for example, a group of friends had organized a bonfire down on the beach at Sabanilla; Beatriz had arrived in Jean-Luc's Buick, and Javier had gone off for a walk in the dark. It was an unsettled night, with lightning flashing over the sea in the distance. In the moonlight the waves broke over the shore in silver ripples, and the breeze seemed to carry the sounds of voices like echoes from an ancient shipwreck; feet sunk into the sand, sitting around the fire where corncobs and pieces of meat were roasting, they were listening to someone singing boleros accompanied by a guitar when a cold wind suddenly started blowing, and Beatriz decided to go and fetch her shawl from the car. Javier, whom everyone had forgotten about, must have predicted her reaction because he was hiding in the back seat of the Buick waiting for her; as soon as he heard her get in to the front seat, he reached round and pinned her to the seat with one arm, quickly slid his other hand between her legs and began fondling her, following the treacherous rhythm that Doña Eulalia del Valle had talked about. Beatriz did not even try to struggle: panic and anger clouded her mind, and she stared out through the windscreen at the glow of the fire, her only thought being that if someone caught them, she would die of shame right there and then. But no one came over, and as his hand continued delving into her most intimate parts, her body did not reject it; rather, after a few minutes that seemed like centuries, she would later say, in a complete daze she had felt her legs opening of their own accord and her hips moving in a swaying motion she could not control, until finally she felt her belly erupt in a wave of pleasure. The most insulting part came straight afterwards, when Javier got out of the car and lit a cigarette in silence.

In fact, Javier had gone out into the fresh air to try to suppress his own state of arousal. He was slightly startled; for him, pleasuring a woman was the same thing as possessing her; a second earlier, the proud virgin had been his, even more so than if he had penetrated her, and with that thought, his feeling of triumph gave way to a tenderness he dared not express: although he wasn't sure why, it seemed that things were about to change for them both and suddenly he wanted to take her in his arms and tell her how much he loved her; he threw his cigarette into the sand and turned to look at her, but through the darkness he saw her eyes blazing fiercely. Then, feeling bold again, he told her that the next time he would make her his, and if he discovered she was a virgin, he would ask the Avendaños for her hand in marriage. The response was swift: a gob of spit flew right at his face. Javier did not expect that. When he heard her opening the car door he thought she was going to slap him, and secretly, he would have admitted that a slap was well deserved. But spitting on him was something else. It was a declaration of war. As he watched her run off towards the bonfire, he swore never to touch her again and then left without saying goodbye to anyone.

Although his resolve did not last, the fact that he had even thought it was a sign that sooner or later he would distance himself from Beatriz. Javier was not excessively virile, not to that extreme: perhaps he considered it normal to have to overcome some resistance from women because he was convinced that, compared to men, women's desire took longer to ignite; but both sexes were equal when it came to pleasure, and it was up to each member of the couple to synchronize with what the other person wanted. This conception of romantic relationships, which was rare among Latin Americans of his generation, and which he would put into practice all the same years later, had no place for the depravity that tended to take hold of him when confronted with Beatriz's behaviour. In spite of himself, or not, he continued to be drawn in by the game she represented to him, and scenes similar to the day of the bonfire happened again: Javier never missed an opportunity to pleasure her against her will, and in the most compromising of circumstances. When he got tired of chasing her like a faun at parties and in gardens, of so many stolen moments of pleasure accompanied by fierce struggles, he decided to put her in her place by possessing her once and for all. The big fight he had with Jean-Luc would only hasten his resolve.

Jean-Luc, who seemingly chose to act as if he were deaf and blind, was browsing the social pages of *El Heraldo* one day when he came across a photograph of Javier and Beatriz leaving the country club together. He suddenly felt the old grip of anxiety once more: he was being deceived and made fun of—everyone including Gustavo Freisen had ganged up on him to further his brother's interests. After ripping the newspaper to shreds as his secretary looked on in alarm, he hurried to Javier's office to demand an explanation from him, and to make him promise to leave Beatriz alone. That was the only coherent sentence he could muster. He immediately lost all self-control: he started rushing around the office, his bones shaking erratically, and, enraged by the spectacle of his own impotence, he ended up hurling an ashtray at Javier. That was how the brawl started. The two brothers hurled punches at each other while employees and secretaries ran around like chickens looking for a place to hide; papers went flying, files were scattered, and documents were used as projectiles. His episode had given Jean-Luc tremendous strength, and after smashing a chair and overturning Javier's desk, he had got hold of a letter opener and was swiping at his brother like a knife thrower. But Javier seemed to be enjoying the situation; not only did he keep his cool, but he also whipped up Jean-Luc's anger by calling him crazy and sexually frustrated. Not even Gustavo Freisen's arrival served to defuse the situation; they carried on hitting each other, fuelled by the hatred accumulated over the years, for which Beatriz was just an excuse: they fought, hurt and insulted each other until Javier managed to get the better of Jean-Luc and then, with one last blow, left him lying motionless in a jumbled mess of papers.

Ana and Beatriz were sketching the rooftops of Barranquilla when they saw Javier enter the room, his jacket torn, his cheek bruised, and his knuckles covered with blood. They heard him say coldly that Jean-Luc had gone mad and that they should go and fetch Odile Kerouan from the country club and take her to the clinic where he'd been admitted. The versions of what happened next would be as numerous as the witnesses and protagonists. Ana claimed she had run out of the room and that then, realizing Beatriz wasn't next to her, she looked back and caught her in Javier's arms. Javier, on the other hand, said he had only blocked her path for a few moments but without trying to embrace her: he felt dirty and drenched in sweat, so he turned his back on her and went to his room to take a shower. After taking off his shirt, he put his head under the shower, realizing that the ashtray had struck him hard: he had a wound by his ear, and, as it clotted, the blood matted up his hair; he washed it, paying little attention to the stinging caused by the shampoo, and after drying it with a towel, he began to comb his hair in front of the mirror over the sink. He barely recognized his own face: beneath his reddened cheeks, his lips were pale and seemed to be pulled inwards, revealing the tips of his teeth. That was what Beatriz said: that his face had the look of the devil about it. According to her, Javier had dragged her to his room by force, and before he went into the bathroom, he had thrown her violently onto the bed; while she heard the sound of the shower running, she found herself possessed once again by that horrible sensation of existing in a body deprived of its own will; she struggled to her feet, and as she walked to the door, she was surprised by the evil face she saw reflected in the mirror. Before she could take another step, Javier jumped on her, hurling her back on the bed and yanking off her dress. Beatriz was paralyzed with fear: her father's face came into her mind over and over again; she realized that she was going to be raped, and she didn't want to lose her virginity. When she heard the buttons from her skirt rolling around on the floor, she screamed. Then Javier slapped her round the face.

Javier saw a gleam in her eyes that he knew all too well. He had managed to undress her from the waist down, but he could not prise her legs apart. The thought occurred to him that his victory was not to be had by raping her, but instead by forcing her to share the pleasure. That thought occurred to him, and suddenly he knew how to make it happen. Tearing the skirt into two pieces, he tied Beatriz's hands with one and tied the knot to the head of the bed with the other; then, when she was unable to move, he finished unbuttoning her blouse, exposing her breasts. He didn't even need to touch them, he would tell Maruja later that very night: feeling that she was tied up with her breasts on show gave Beatriz a dark excitement, betrayed by the trembling of her body. Slowly Javier undressed, proudly contemplating his erect penis: other men complained of being unable to maintain their erection for long, but he never had any problems of that sort. That sight made Beatriz tense up even more: her abstract concepts of virtue and maidenhood dissolved with the threat of physical suffering. Terrified, she heard Javier tell her that her vagina would open by itself, to become a cavern that his penis would slip into without the slightest resistance. Then she saw the belt and suddenly felt a sharp pain in her wrists: Javier had flipped her onto her front, placing a pillow between her belly and the bed, which was why she hardly noticed the first time it struck her: she would tell Lina, she was trying to reposition her hands by moving them as far as the tightness of the knot would allow; then yes, when she managed to forget about the pain in her wrists, her buttocks began to hurt, and she understood what Javier was murmuring to her: each whip of the belt was accompanied by an order to open herself wide, to open herself to him, in front of him. And little by little, choking with humiliation, she felt desire take hold of her belly in spite of the flogging, or perhaps because of it, while her legs obeyed the instructions issued by that arrogant voice with a lustfulness that made any attempt at thought impossible; she did not even notice when Javier untied her hands and made her turn over, still on the pillow, to look at her already eager vagina, throbbing between the golden hairs of her pubis like the tiny mouth of a hungry little animal. He penetrated her slowly, lifting her legs with his arms so he could slide into the warmth of her most intimate parts: the fiercely defended membrane gave way at the first assault, but Beatriz did not notice that either, because a dazzling joy, like an explosion, had launched her far beyond time and space, into the tumultuous vertigo where consciousness was lost and the convulsions of pleasure met the shadows of death.

V

For a long time, Aunt Irene had been a shadow for Lina, a space where her thoughts transformed into language and words reverberated back to her in the form of an endless, questioning echo, like streamers fluttering in the air ad infinitum; later, that presence turned into an absence, leaving behind the nostalgia of an abandoned path that once led to the ocean. Lina had felt her gradually slipping away into solitude, self-conscious and fascinated by the completeness of her own silence: she had finished the sonata she'd been composing for several months, and, with a distant look in her eyes, she serenely contemplated a world where memories had turned to ash and were flying through the air. Isolated and impenetrable, the Italian's Tower seemed to be getting ready to slip into a long slumber: the old furniture, the mirrors from Venice, and the sumptuous oil paintings and wall hangings started disappearing from the rooms, leaving for some unknown address in their old packaging; termites deposited their dark tunnels over the friezes whose language Lina had tried so hard to decipher, almost always in vain; suddenly aged, the animals hid themselves away in the darkest corners of the garden. Only the piano, reflected a thousand times by the mirrors in the circular room, stood there majestic and perennial, as if the heart of the tower were still beating and Aunt Irene's departure were just an illusion. Strangely, the servants seemed to be unaware that the tower was heading for ruin: the weeds were launching an attack on the main staircase, where the steps had been eroded

by the recent rains; no one had called a stonemason to repair
the cracks in the walls, and a damp draught swept through the
rooms, corroding woodwork and causing clusters of mould to
form on the curtains. Yet still the servants worked with patient
determination: they mopped the floors, and the place smelled
of creolin again; they oiled the hinges, and the doors stopped
creaking. It was almost as if they were waiting for some
inevitable event, hinting with all that incessant hustle and bus-
tle that the tower, despite its run-down appearance, was
preparing for one last ceremony before it secretly, silently collapsed into the inexorable voracity of oblivion. Lina's grandmother most likely predicted what would happen: she, a
woman who by then very rarely left the house and had not seen
her sister for two years, sent a letter which Aunt Irene did not
even open—after studying the envelope with a smile, she simply told Lina that of course her answer was yes, and that before
long she would let Lina's grandmother know when to come.
Other signs announced that shadowy forms were approaching,
edging ever closer; though a feverish smell rose from the dead
water in the garden, the large door at the main entrance had
been spruced up, and the trees lining the grove had been
pruned, their flowers in bloom; nine chairs and several freshly
polished silver candelabras had appeared in the hall of mirrors.

Always inscrutable, Aunt Irene gave nothing away, and Lina
refrained from asking for explanations; the stark whiteness of
her face and the intense glow in her eyes hinted that she was
not exactly preparing to leave for foreign lands; but this, like
so many other things, was not an appropriate topic to broach
with her. And so, Lina never mentioned the sonata that had
been the focus of Aunt Irene's attention in recent months;
although she knew bits of it by heart, she could not piece the
parts together coherently: certain lines of the melody sounded
like they were written for another instrument, and certain
modulations made no sense to her. All the same, she did not

dare to express her desire to hear the sonata played from start to finish; she had even given up on ever hearing it in its entirety. Hence her surprise when, early one evening, just as she came back from the tower, she was welcomed by her grandmother with the news that Aunt Irene would be performing the sonata for them that same night. Lina was overcome with a sense of foreboding: her grandmother was wearing a long black silk dress and the few pieces of jewellery rescued from countless shipwrecks, and whether it was because of her unusual attire or the small dark lace veil that covered her face, she had the same otherworldly air about her that Aunt Irene had had many years before, when she emerged from the fog of a fever. Her grandmother motioned her to her bedroom: laid out for her there on the bed were a ballgown and her kidskin gloves, and, next to them, a note from Aunt Irene inviting them to join her at half past ten that night in the Italian's Tower.

When she saw the uniformed servants in red livery and the torches lighting up the main garden path, Lina got the feeling that she had stepped into the past and that, for the first time, she was entering the site where, more than a hundred years ago, a group of men and women from very distant lands apparently wanted to establish a different relationship with life. Strangers to the vanities of the world, they were searching for an ideal that they never tried to impose and did not even attempt to put into words, simply alluding to it in certain ways, such as the shape of a tower and the strange scenes depicted on certain friezes—there, precisely, in those desolate landscapes, where everything was destroyed by the wildness of nature and the mercantilism of men—as if they accepted, with their wry lucidity, the ridiculous nature of any human endeavour. Perhaps it never occurred to them that the tower would last for so long or that other people driven by the same sensibility would live there, bequeathing it to their descendants until one of them, sensing the end was nigh, looked around and could find no one worthy of inheriting it; and that then, in tribute to the ones who had built it, this same person would compose a piece of music of staggering beauty and decide to perform it to an audience of nine strangers, just once, before tearing the score to shreds.

The sneaking suspicion that this sonata for piano and violin would be performed on one night only awakened strange resonances in the mind, like the recollection of something lost, of ancient rituals intended to allow the quiet contemplation of another person's consciousness, a fleeting understanding of the Absolute. Aunt Irene's invited guests, who looked as if they were attending a Venetian masquerade in their white leather masks, seemed to share the same disposition for introspection; they sat perfectly still in their chairs, in silence, their attitude conveying an unshakeable determination to conceal their identities; standing with his back to them and very close to the piano, the violinist quickly leafed through the score that rested on a mahogany music stand; his eagerness to run his eyes over it suggested that he was sight-reading. The hall of mirrors had never looked so uncanny or mysterious to Lina; suddenly she was confronted again by her childhood fears and the unsettling sensation that the room was haunted by invisible presences that were lying in wait, watching everything that happened inside it. That feeling intensified when Aunt Irene furtively walked into the room and took her seat at the piano. The first notes she played set the general tone of the sonata: a deep meditation, a low note, slowly progressing through a series of variations picked up by the violin, linking each new phrase with the last; nothing in that sonata allowed it to fit into any known genre, because it seemed to exist outside time and beyond time, probing the depths of infinity; its theme had sprung forth like a speck of light in a dark sky, reaching the proportions of a supernova in an explosion of rare intensity, and then, little by little, having explored the most varied contrasts of the melody, it collapsed in on itself and became inaudible, inaccessible, like a star that keeps its light to itself from the point of its implosion.

When Aunt Irene closed the lid of the piano, the room was filled with a stunned silence. That lingering music had evoked the terrifying expression of eternity, and it would have been outrageous to make the slightest sound under its spell. Exhausted, with his mask steeped in sweat, the violinist lowered his arms and bowed down before Aunt Irene in profound respect. Following his lead, the other guests stood up and paid obeisance. Lina noticed that her grandmother was on the verge of tears. Suddenly she felt crushed by an unbearable weight, as if the atmosphere of another world had invaded the hall of mirrors. For a few moments she closed her eyes and tried to control her breathing, and when she opened them, everything looked different: the violinist and the guests had disappeared; her grandmother, supporting herself on her walking stick with one hand, reached out pleadingly towards one of the adjoining rooms, where Aunt Irene was standing by an open window, tearing the score up into pieces that were carried away by the December breeze. But it was no use; the spectacle was over, and, in her own way, Aunt Irene was saying goodbye.

Lina did not know then that her grandmother, in return for hearing that sonata, had agreed to organize the most incredible simulation of a wake around an empty casket: it was her job to welcome the grievers, to mournfully accompany the hearse to the cemetery, and to watch the casket being lowered into the grave amid a shower of wreaths and bouquets of flowers. Later, spurred on by a delayed yet persistent curiosity, she would search in vain for the servants who were moving around blowing the candles out and collecting chairs and candelabras while, one step at a time, Aunt Irene made her way to the underground passages, with Lina and the weary pair of

Dobermans that refused to mate. They walked in silence, leaving behind them bedrooms and corridors plunged into darkness; they descended stairs and passed through the vaults where, many years earlier, Lina—stumbling upon those glass cabinets where creatures with deathly stings lived—had gained a glimpse of how all forms of life can be loved. Candle in hand, Aunt Irene kept advancing calmly and purposefully along staircases and increasingly damp tunnels that Lina had never even suspected existed. It smelled of earth and mould down there, and the air was beginning to rarefy. When they reached the end of a long passageway, she stopped and held the candle up to the frieze that ran along the wall. Lina moved closer to take a look at it. What she saw, she would never forget: an oval cavity, and inside it, with nothing there to hold it in place, a shiny metal object formed of two kinds of spirals that seemed to share the same centre, swirling in opposite directions until they came together again at their outermost point; in an allusion to duality, each spiral in turn gained a bluish phosphorescence at the points where it came into contact with the other, evoking a movement of perpetual pulsation or the illusion that the spirals were being impelled by their own indestructible force. Lina reached in to discover whether or not the object was attached to something, only to encounter the inhuman, inconceivable, fierce coldness surrounding it. Then Aunt Irene passed her the candle, with a smile. And while that thing pulsated before her fascinated eyes, Lina could hear Aunt Irene's footsteps retreating in the darkness, a door creaking as it turned on its hinges, and the terrible silence that was to fall upon the Italian's Tower from then on.

The next day was the funeral for Aunt Irene. Among the many people filing into the tower for the first time to offer their condolences, Lina spotted Javier and Beatriz. It seemed so long since the time when Beatriz was trying to find a meaning for life, and there was no point trying to talk about underground passages and friezes with this shadow of a woman, whose only interest consisted of passing for a model wife. Beatriz had changed: emerging from the storms of passion, she had taken refuge in the unyielding virtuousness of her youth, losing all vivacity of spirit in the process. That withdrawal had occurred in various stages, and in a way, Javier was to blame. Beatriz simply attributed the situation to their marriage. For her, the problem began twelve hours after she lost her virginity, when her head started hurting and an inconceivable nausea set in. Finding herself pregnant—she said to Lina around that time—and forced to get married against her will, she lost any capacity for desire, even the desire for life itself. Indeed, twelve hours after Javier raped her, he received a phone call from the Avendaño brothers wanting to set the date for the wedding, which they said had to happen as soon as possible and in the strictest privacy. People were surprised that two wealthy families were marrying off their heirs in such a low-key way, but since the Avendaños made sure that the baby's birth was announced exactly nine months after the wedding, the rumours did not last for long. Gustavo Freisen himself never knew about the mysteries of that marriage, which had disappointed him so much with its lack of pageantry: he would have preferred a big ceremony with gatherings and pre-wedding celebrations—in short, all the social events that would declare him triumphant after being secretly rejected by the city—rather than that discreet reception, which the Avendaños arranged to be held at ten in the morning, and that bride with red, puffy eyes, who could not disguise her devastation as she greeted the few guests in attendance. Gustavo Freisen didn't know what to think: she was the reason why Jean-Luc had gone crazy, and now, between tears, she was marrying the brother who had landed Jean-Luc in the madhouse for the rest of his life. The wedding itself seemed like destiny's way of making amends, but at the same time, it struck him as an insult to the memory of his son. All the same, the elegance of that house made quite the impression on him, and his bourgeois mentality humbly rejoiced when he discovered the row of portraits from which generations of Avendaños stared at him haughtily: as wealthy as the Freisens were, he said to El Manco, they did not have high-born ancestors who were capable of standing proud before a painter as though they were in the habit of addressing monarchs by their first names. Perhaps that was when he realized he'd forgotten the wedding gift and discreetly slipped a cheque for two hundred thousand pesos between the gifts laid out on an embroidered tablecloth; the fact that Beatriz did not even approach him to say thank you made him even more perplexed: that young woman either did not know the value of money and was a thoughtless individual, or she was conceited and had no regard for him whatsoever. El Manco eased his misgivings for a moment, commenting on the newlyweds' bashfulness and other nonsense of the sort. Gustavo Freisen would get used to Beatriz's moods over time, and though he would eventually thank her for giving him two blond, blue-eyed grandchildren, the ghost of Jean-Luc would always be hovering between them, filled with bitter resentment.

Talk would turn to Jean-Luc again later, when Javier decided to leave Beatriz. In the meantime, his father was the only one who visited him in Álvaro Espinoza's clinic once a week. That visit warranted special attention, because if Gustavo Freisen found his son unwashed, drugged up or complaining of bad living conditions, he would scream blue murder and threaten to send him to an institution in Medellín, and so, faced with the fear of losing his most valuable patient, Álvaro Espinoza made sure he brought his nurses in line. The rest of the family took no real interest in his fate, including Odile Kerouan, who felt a headache coming on as soon as she decided to go to see him, and Ana, who seemed to be under the impression that madness was contagious. As for Javier, he was secretly satisfied with his brother's confinement, and with having married the bride that his parents had lined up for Jean-Luc, not to mention taking on his brother's former roles in the company. Once he had avenged the cruelties he had been subjected to by that wretch in his childhood, his future opened up ahead of him, brimming with promise. Whether he liked it or not, Gustavo Freisen was entrusting his son with a growing number of responsibilities, and although Javier's brother Antonio was starting to prove himself to be the perfect manager, he still lacked the experience and presence to lead the workforce. Javier, on the other hand, knew how to run the show and make people obey his orders. He was good at talking to his staff and inspiring them to share his goals, reeling them in with his words. He knew how to motivate his workers, and as a result he had established an ingenious system of bonuses which were shared between the factory production units that succeeded in hitting a set quota each trimester; a hamper of toys on Christmas Eve and three boxes of white rum the night before Carnival awaited those who had clocked in and out on time every day, not to mention access to the company's cooperative store, where staff could buy items at a lower price than the market rate. Although Javier sought to increase his power, he never lost sight of the human side of things; his paternalism came less from strategic calculations and more from a kind of social awareness, which he had picked up from spending time with mechanics, prostitutes and fishermen; as far as he was concerned, the dispossessed did not deserve the life they led and had simply drawn the short straw. Javier did not pass judgements on society; rather, his bellicose temperament meant he was happy to accept the fact that there were always winners and losers, but if he could help someone, he would do so with the same fighting spirit he had used to destroy Jean-Luc and to conquer Beatriz. He had come to resemble a warrior, more prone to action than reflection, bored by routine, spurred on by a challenge and capable of brilliant flashes of intuition in combat. The business world was the perfect place for him to use his leadership and organizational skills, all the while papering over the frustrations caused by the marriage, which in those days he told no one about and perhaps he did not even perceive; it had to be a confusing feeling of dissatisfaction, expressed through sudden fits of rage against Beatriz, which he immediately regretted, annoyed at himself and slightly troubled to witness her descending into those terrible episodes of nervous depression, when she refused to eat and stayed in the same room for four whole days, neglecting her duties to the children while Nena sat beside her, crying, and Dr. Agudelo tried to bring her out of her languid state by giving her drugs with unexpected effects. Dr. Agudelo had told Javier that she was fragile, and they both took refuge behind that tenuous explanation to pretend that they had forgotten the past: they acted as though the passion between the couple had never existed, as though desire had never propelled them towards one another with wild anguish; they never alluded to the incident that had hastened their marriage, and that silence had the air of drowned man decaying in the depths of the water; entwined in the fibres of a bitterness that Javier resisted with the resilience he had honed at work, but which Beatriz sunk into every morning as soon as she saw the sun rise through her bedroom window, leaving behind another sleepless night to endure the tedium of another day just like the last in that house in Puerto Colombia where Javier had insisted they live; she had very few visitors in that house, and none of the good, reliable maids wanted to work there; it had no air conditioning, and even the water was rationed at times. In her daily struggle against the dust that covered the floors and the damp that ate away at the walls, she was always the loser; the desire to give that house an elegant appearance had quickly left her, but her frantic need to keep it tidy and very clean did not. Cleaning was an obsession for Beatriz: she washed the woodwork, hunted down insects, scrubbed trays and saucepans. She hated those Saturdays and Sundays when Javier's family came to visit them, ruining her entire week's work with all their comings and goings from the beach. She hated the sand that seeped in through the cracks in the windows and doors, and she hated the August rains, because they flooded the garden, splattering the terrace with mud, and the December breeze, which sprinkled the taste of salt on the crockery. The household chores had a strange ability to calm and infuriate her at the same time: she could spend whole days peacefully fighting against the dirt and instilling good manners into her children, patiently taking care of them, washing and ironing their school smocks (which were always immaculately white) and tidying their toys away time and again. And then suddenly, she would find all that housework unbearably vacuous: any maid could do the same job, and any nanny could look after the children. What had those dreams from her younger years done for her? They had led her to that exhausting, thankless routine. She had already discovered how unjust it was that there was no reward for housewives who toiled day and night without receiving any pay and whose devotion was taken for granted. It was completely hypocritical, she said to Lina: society wanted to ease its conscience by concealing the fact that half its members were treated like the slaves of former times. And though this knowledge could have been freeing if she kept it in mind, it quickly vanished under the weight of her woes, because she was miserable and she wasn't going to spend her life cooped up inside her own four walls, looking after the children. She was suffering, she wanted to die, and so she slowly slid into a state of depression; one day she stopped eating and stayed in bed, until finally her frailty reduced her to the state of pupation in which she seemed to find peace. Dr. Agudelo insisted on telling Javier that the solitude of Puerto Colombia was partly responsible for her depressive episodes, but there was no point explaining to him how a more fulfilling social life would ward them off. Javier would not budge: deep down, he believed that Beatriz was unstable, and if he did not dare to say it openly, it was because the drama with Jean-Luc was still too fresh in his family's memory. Moreover, he did not want to accept any responsibility for Beatriz's behaviour or entertain any discussion that could take him back to the memory of the first throes of their love. Yes, he had married her out of duty, he said to Maruja, but that marriage gave him certain rights. But his wife had refused to let him into their bed, saying that she was afraid of losing the baby; and then forty days after Nadia was born, when he tried to assert his marital rights again, he was confronted with a stiff, frigid body that made his penis sore when he penetrated it, causing another pregnancy and confining him to chastity once again. The problems didn't end there: Beatriz agreed to take the pill on her gynaecologist's instruction, but he could not have his way with her because of the risk of causing her horrendous pain, cystitis and vaginal infections, for which he had to take her to the doctor, feeling deeply ashamed. Normal women didn't behave like that, he dared to say to Maruja one time. And Maruja, brash as ever, reminded him of how those hands used to be able to drive that same body wild with pleasure. Incensed by her remark, Javier called her perverted, and for two years the two of them stopped speaking.

Those were two tough years for Javier: he had lost weight and was beginning to acquire the vulture-like look typical of the Freisens; sometimes he would complain of indigestion or exhaustion, and he could feel himself twitching uncontrollably. His sexual urges had dwindled, like a prostrate monk after a long period of abstinence and penitence. He no longer tried to enter Beatriz's room, and strangely, in his own way, he felt jealous. It was jealousy that made him shut her away in that house in Puerto Colombia from the start, trying to remove any temptation for her to surrender to the touch of some other man who could fathom the complex workings of her lust. This became clear in his moments of rage, when he insulted her confusedly as soon as he got anywhere near the forbidden parts of that ghost of a woman, before backing away, shocked at having treated the mother of his children so badly—he told Maruja on the day of the argument—but furious deep down that he had to resort to trickery to get something that by rights was already his, through marriage. In the end, Beatriz understood the truth: the death of her pleasure was what was at stake. She understood it by likening it to a mutilation, and she said the same thing to Lina, crying from noon until sundown as she summed up the story of her life with a sharp, agonizing lucidity, like a flower that bursts into a thousand colours when its petals begin to fall: she remembered her childhood under the iron rule of that aunt who had been kicked out of the convents, those horrible evenings when she trembled in fear as she listened to her talk about souls in Purgatory, and her glee as soon as she saw her father walk through the door and went running straight into his arms, finding peace and tenderness, the kindest of refuges; she also remembered what happened in the Alto Prado neighbourhood and her oath to never expose herself to the kind of anguish that Nena had suffered. In that brutal, painful kind of psychoanalysis, when for the first and last time she tried to get to the bottom of her conflicts, she recognized that she had run away from the cadet from West Point because he represented the unsullied, beloved father, symbolizing a kind of respectability that had no place for sex: for some reason, she could only desire men she found abhorrent, like Jorge Avendaño when he left her on the backseat of Lina's car to protect his lover, and Javier when he made her writhe with pleasure, unscrupulously cheating his brother in the process. She talked about all these things in an extremely tense state, her voice cracking with emotion, her body racked with spasms that preceded each new wave of tears, unwilling to accept any words of consolation, any explanation that could trivialize her masochism by accepting it as part and parcel of the experience for generations of women who had been abused by the patriarchy for centuries. Completely exhausted, she finally agreed to go to sleep in her bed and slept the whole night through. The next week she slept with Víctor, an alleged revolutionary who was not to be trusted, losing herself once more in the sensual pleasures that her husband denied her.

Víctor was the illegitimate son of an important rancher who worked for Bolívar, whose land stretched across the border that marked the point where men ceased insulting each other with words, and fought with knives instead. Acknowledged before law by his father, from whom he had inherited his treacherous nature, Víctor completed his high-school education in Cartagena, gaining qualifications that prompted the rancher to send him to the capital so that he could become a lawyer and take care of defending his properties against invasion by the campesinos, and at no charge. But Víctor did not even pass his first-year exams in law, because he enjoyed frequenting bars and hanging out with easy women more than attending his classes at university. In any case, his professors and classmates chose to avoid dealing with him very early on: he had a reputation as a thief in his lodgings, and later he was accused of the cold-blooded killing of an old loan shark who was demanding he repay his debt. Although he was not reported to the authorities, Víctor thought it wise to get away from Bogotá for a while; he had heard talk of guerrillas in the Eastern Plains, and he helped to organize expeditions to hunt down *indios* in the Amazonian rainforest, where he caught a strange disease that rendered him impotent—some said it was from having sex with a dead native girl, others said it was because he had been struck in his private parts by a vengeful arrow; the bottom line was that he returned to Bogotá with his pockets full of money and suffering from an illness that resisted all known antibiotics. He was twenty-three years old at the time, but he seemed much older because of the lines on his face; he was almost bald and his teeth were rotten because he was terrified of dentists. When the rancher found out about his adventures, he threatened to go looking for him in the capital himself, along with a bodyguard famed for his ability to handle a whip. Without further ado, Víctor enrolled in the Free University of Colombia, where he learned Marxism by the book, found out that he was a victim of society and discovered an honourable way to unleash his violent side in the student protests. In other circumstances he would have turned into a thug, but by the grace of Marxism he had become a revolutionary. His young classmates saw him as a hero, whereas the student leaders viewed him with mistrust. Of course, the Partido Comunista decided to sign him up, but Víctor would not bow to any form of discipline, and, when his comrades from the cell asked him to make a statement of self-criticism, he took advantage of the first opportunity to publicly call the *pacos*, the members of the Colombian communist party, a bunch of cowards, shouting over a microphone that the revolution was a matter for men, men with real balls—forgetting the damaged condition of his own. It didn't really matter; no one would have dared to remind him about it anyway. By then he had made a name for himself as a braggart and was always leading the protests with the most hot-headed students who were willing to take on the police armed with knives. They booked him, he accused the communists of betrayal, and he switched sides from the Universidad Libre to the Universidad Nacional. For a while he slipped under the radar, and then later he joined a group of virulent Trotskyists whose ideas he adopted in the blink of an eye. Since the armed struggle was in need of funds, he robbed the small branch of a bank and was forced to go into hiding; then his new comrades discovered a unique side of his character: the pleasure he took in seducing their women, taking advantage of their hospitality and the sexual misery they were condemned to by the puritanism of the revolution. Thinking of him as an invalid, they forgot he was cunning. The first incident happened when he was staying in an apartment owned by a philosophy professor whose wife had dropped out of her studies to devote herself to the cause and the household chores. Her name was Mirian, and she lived her life shrouded in a resigned mutism, no longer remembering the dreams she used to have as a student, when she was determined to get the degree that would secure her independence and make her feel that she was making her way in society on her own merit. That philosophy professor seemed so sure of himself, so impressive in his conviction that he possessed the complete truth, and he changed the course of her life. With him, she was going to fight for a better world by creating a classless society and universal "fraternity"; but she would have been well-advised to consider what that term boiled down to in practice, because once she was married with three children in tow, her existence was limited in the same way as all the women who were excluded from that association of brothers, whose objectives remained the same despite the changes that were introduced in terms of ideology and language. Uncompromising when it came to his principles, the professor stopped her hiring a maid, and as a moralist, he balked at certain erotic fantasies which he classed as bourgeois vices. And Mirian ran herself ragged, typing up her husband's revolutionary texts and taking care of washing and ironing shirts, darning tights and looking after the children. She was almost a shadow of her former self when the professor invited Víctor to stay in the modest apartment where they lived. She welcomed him passively, but not without reticence, perhaps thinking about the burden that the presence of another man represented. If Víctor noticed, he said nothing on the subject, and since that place appealed to him after staying in so many squalid boarding houses and so much rushing from pillar to post on the run from the police, he decided to be on his best behaviour, washing his own clothes, helping her with the household chores and, little by little, becoming her confidant. It couldn't have been easier: women put up with too much frustration to resist the temptation to talk if they found someone who was willing to listen. For this same reason, he, Víctor would prevent women from reaching important positions in his organization; for this same reason, he loved them in his own way. Every woman, he would tell one of Lina's friends in a rare moment of weakness, made him think of his mother, living in a shack, chopping firewood in the bush; he remembered being wrenched out of her arms before the rancher bent her over and mounted her like a horse. Víctor's mother loved him immensely; she was beautiful once, but years of working in the hot sun and a poor diet made her toothless and blackened her skin, taking her from him when he was eight years old; after that, the rancher's wife took care of raising him until he was sent to Cartagena, and he had fond memories of her too. Added to this hint of sympathy that women inspired in him, his own impotence brought with it the art of knowing how to make love to them; deprived of an erection but not of desire, he quickly learned certain secrets of female pleasure: when a woman was satisfied, he said, she would always be generous, forgetting about the man's physique and even being grateful for the lack of penetration, which forced him to resort to more sophisticated methods without shrinking from the complexity of erotic games. The day the professor caught him on top of his wife in his own bed, their mouths greedily buried in each other's genitals, he almost had a stroke. Víctor saw him out of the corner of his eye, gasping for breath by the door and powerless to react; and so he continued with his duties until he heard Mirian's stifled groan, then he got up and started to get dressed, indifferent to the scene that was erupting between husband and wife.

As his friends scrambled together to use their dialectics to cast light on that terrible incident, they concluded that comrade Víctor had been a victim of seduction at the hands of a false revolutionary, and with the complicity of a communist doctor, they placed Mirian in a mental asylum from which she would never leave. Víctor went to stay with a sociologist, and soon he was up to his old tricks again; the next time it was a student of economics, and gradually, with all the scandals and arguments that broke out, the group began to disband. Meanwhile, Víctor had earned the trust of a very wealthy old liberalist, a former supporter of Gaitán who had been in political exile during the conservative dictatorship. The man had exquisite manners and very pale eyes, and had been educated in England, inheriting a fortune in the form of haciendas scattered throughout the country. His youngest son took after him; just like his father, he felt guilty about having so much money, and his remorse had prompted him to join the Partido Comunista; he was always at the front at protests and trying to earn forgiveness for his origins, taking blows from the policemen—who hated him for being a communist and a millionaire—and ending up in jail, where his comrades left him to rot in order to toughen him up; he got out thanks to the intervention of some liberal senator who was friends with his father, and he would be back in there again as soon as the Partido decided to organize a new protest. Ten years of beatings and stints in prison had left him so unstable that he fell into Víctor's trap, and when finally he managed to get away from that fiend by handing over a million pesos as a ransom, the only way he could find peace was by joining the Hare Krishnas; he would grow old dressed in salmon pink, shaking tambourines in the streets, his head completely bald except for

416 - MARVEL MORENO

one lock of white hair. Yes, Víctor was a real nightmare for Don José Antonio del Corral and his son.

The Del Corrals owned a large secluded hacienda close to the Sierra Nevada de Santa Marta, which they had left in the care of a foreman with whom the *indios* got on reasonably well because he respected their customs and knew how to make the most of their slow way of working; a mixture of *mestizos* and descendants of warriors, those *indios* had lost their legendary fighting spirit after smoking so much of the marijuana they grew on the slopes of the Sierra Nevada, a strain that would later achieve notoriety in the United States under the name "Colombian Gold"; in the meantime, they led a peaceful life, working the land in their own way; in return for their work, they received a third of the hacienda's output and various inventions introduced by that white man with the crystalline stare, who occasionally made it out there with various animals and mules carrying fertilizers and unfamiliar seeds. In a sign of deference to the *indios*, the white man did not give his instructions directly to them but to the foreman, who in turn relayed the instructions, telling them about the new bull stud that would produce a breed of cows that made more milk, or why it was a good idea to plant those trees bearing extra-sweet fruits, which were highly prized in the market at Santa Marta. And so it was. For years, Don José Antonio del Corral had made La Carmela his refuge and the main testing ground for his innovations, and now the hacienda was fully stocked with good pastures and livestock with an excellent yield. Were it not for his heart problems, he would have spent his older years staring at those awesome skies, where billowing masses of blue clouds pushed towards the snow-capped peak of the mountain. But at his age, even travelling to La Carmela exhausted him, and apart from the *indios*, no living soul roamed around the area. That, the solitude of the hacienda, was the first thing that caught Víctor's attention when Don José Antonio started talking to him about his favourite property; no one knew its exact location, and it appeared on the map of Colombia as a godforsaken place covered in rainforest. Víctor decided that it was the perfect place to train for the guerrilla life, and somehow he persuaded José Antonio Junior to ask his father if he could use the La Carmela, and to go there with him and a group of revolutionaries who considered themselves Maoists.

They arrived there with books by Che Guevara and Mao, and the best of intentions: to get up at dawn, wash themselves in the cold river water and climb the mountain with rifles and backpacks; in short, to enhance their physical and mental endurance so that they would eventually form a functioning guerrilla unit and could head for the bush. But it was a madhouse, and six months later, they shot the foreman and had turned despotic, forgetting the sage advice of their revolutionary guides and treating the few *indios* who had been unable to flee as slaves. That friend of Lina's, who would speak to her about Víctor years later, blamed the failed mission on the objective conditions in which they tried to achieve it: the comrades were too poor and had been corrupted by all the luxury and comforts; Víctor had taken care of everything else. He was the one who came up with the idea of staying in the Del Corral mansion instead of camping out in the bush, where the real training would have begun; then he had a shipment of whiskey smuggled in, saying it would help with the cold nights. Between the alcohol and the lack of political indoctrination, which Víctor banned because he thought it was pointless, the group eventually lost its morale; they spent the whole day sleeping off their drinking binges or committing the most outlandish, random acts; they roasted a calf for every lunch, much to the dismay of the foreman and the shock of the workers, who had never seen such wastefulness; they wolfed down chickens and suckling pigs, bananas and cobs of corn with shameless gluttony. Since tyranny always begins to exculpate itself before it is imposed, Víctor convinced himself that those *indios* were devious at heart and could only be educated once the revolution was triumphant; meanwhile, they would have to serve them, the representatives of the proletariat, contributing to the cause with their assets and hard work; it was clear that Victor and his comrades would attack the workers' property sooner or later, because at the rate that they were plundering La Carmela's resources, before long there would be no edible animal left alive. They didn't allow the animals to reproduce, even killing the pregnant females. This is what riled the foreman, who took his gun one afternoon and walked into the room where Víctor was snoring in bed, then kicked him awake and ordered him and his gang of bandits to leave. Víctor immediately understood the seriousness of the situation. That maniac looked ready to kill him, whereas he hadn't so much as cleaned his rifle in three months, and so he promised to leave that very evening, assuring him that his men were ready to establish a new guerrilla base elsewhere; then a few hours later, the foreman was tried by a revolutionary tribunal chaired by Víctor, and the next day he was executed for being a traitor to the people's cause. Terrified, the *indios* hid their women and tried to flee, leaving their life's work behind them; there were gunshots and fatalities; those who didn't manage to take refuge in the rainforest had to surrender to the rifles. Little by little, La Carmela fell to ruin and José Antonio Junior slipped into a state of nervous exhaustion. Víctor had made it clear to his father that he would shoot his son if he dared to alert the military, and so it went on until he received a million pesos in exchange for his son's release. After making a fortune trafficking marijuana, he settled in Barranquilla and devoted himself to smuggling harder drugs.

Beatriz had been dead for almost twenty years by then, and Víctor laughed as he recalled his old Maoist friends and their grand plans: during the first months of his sojourn in La

Carmela, and before the true revolutionaries who had initially joined him on the mission deserted the cause, he had received weapons and instructions from a mysterious major who believed that terrorism was the best way to destabilize the bourgeoisie. So, he had decided to organize a wave of attacks on the anniversary of Gaitán's assassination: the explosives would be dropped off on the beaches of Puerto Colombia, and Víctor would have to find a safe place to hide them. That was when he discovered Javier's house, which was off the beaten track and so luxurious that the police would never think to go snooping around there. It was the home of a pretty, blue-eyed girl, who was undoubtedly miserable because she went out walking on the beach at sunset, downcast and always alone, looking like she had been crying all day. Víctor decided to try his luck; his hairpiece and elegant white linen suits gave him the air of a playboy, and so as not to startle her, he started sitting on a bench at dusk, staring melancholically out at the ocean, with a book by Sartre or Marcuse in his hands. One day he approached her, and from then on, they spent many an hour discussing existentialism, Maoism and sexual liberation. Although Beatriz was unaware that Víctor memorized the simplified explanations of various philosophical texts before each meeting, she did not fail to notice that man's lack of refinement, because with a certain movement or a remark, the would-be intellectual suddenly gave way to the rancher's illegitimate son. Víctor changed tactics as soon as he realized: he talked to her about his unhappy childhood and about the misfortunes he had suffered as a young boy; he declared his love for her, reading poems by José Asunción Silva in a low voice; then he moved on to Neruda, in whose name he was ready to sacrifice himself for the revolution. From time to time, and at odds with the romanticism of his language, he would suddenly grope her, plunging her into a quagmire of confusion: this stranger inspired desire and revulsion in her at the same time, and she was ashamed of both feelings. To escape the dilemma, she told herself she was in love with him. When they finally slept together, she discovered the delights of unbridled lust, uninhibited by the embarrassment of showing that side of herself to a man of her same social standing, who would condemn her citing his own principles. For fifteen days she experienced an orgy of pleasure amid false declarations of love and real tears of regret. Emboldened, Víctor allowed his masks of the sophisticated intellectual to fall away one by one until he disgusted Beatriz. Then they remembered their obligations: the armed struggle was waiting for him, and she had her children to look after, so by mutual agreement, and not without sorrow, they decided to part ways; but out of guilt for the secret aversion she felt towards a man of the people who was going away to fight in the revolutionary movement, she agreed to let him use the basement of her house to hide the explosives meant to destroy the capitalist society. Víctor had accomplished his mission with flying colours.

Beatriz came out of that affair filled with a complete revulsion towards sex. The pleasure of orgasm, she would tell Lina, was no compensation for the humiliations she had to endure in order to achieve it: it was too short, the build-up was full of anxiety, and it left her racked with guilt; the thing she detested about eroticism was precisely what Dora and then Catalina had discovered one day, fascinated: a transgression, a way of asserting oneself, of momentarily silencing the will, to discover the dazzling silence of the Absolute. But Beatriz experienced her sexuality like men, caught between a fear of the instinct that reminded them of the part of their nature they loathed, and an irrational hatred towards the simple truths of the body; she likened desire to a diabolical possession that deprived her of her free will, and pleasure to a terrifying disintegration of the mind. Afraid of lowering herself to such a degree again, she tried to resign herself to her fate and come

up with a whole strategy to escape the depression she suffered
in the face of married life; and so, turning to Vaseline and the
pelvic floor exercises her gynaecologist had recommended,
she finally eased Javier's jealousy; she then convinced him to
take her to Nena's house every day, where she could leave the
children while she went to the beauty parlour or to play
bridge at the country club; at seven in the evening she began
to cram herself full of tranquillizers, and Javier would come
home to a placid wife, as if detached from everything happening around her.

Incapable of imagining what led to that change, Javier felt
happy: he had a respectable job, two beautiful children and a
submissive wife. Now they could make love every night without her body's rejection getting in the way of his appetite;
sometimes, in the raptures of pleasure, he asked her if she was
enjoying it too, and Beatriz, stupefied by the tranquillizers,
invariably replied by saying that she loved him. In a way, she
was telling the truth: a strange feeling had started to mask her
bitterness; she called it love for lack of another name, and it
was expressed by the constant fear of losing the only man she
thought she could count on in life. Javier seemed like a
paragon of virtue after her dealings with Víctor: he was decent
and generous, and he never lied or took advantage of anyone's
weakness; he would never hold a poor old man to ransom by
threatening to shoot his son, like Víctor had told her he was
planning to do, in a display of power. Javier adored the children, and ever since Beatriz discovered the benefits of
Vaseline, they had made quite the happy couple; he had given
her a chihuahua, valuable necklaces and rings as gifts; he was
determined to buy her an apartment in Barranquilla, and on
Saturday afternoons they went out together to order furniture,
which started to accumulate in their spare room; they brought
back rugs and chinaware from a trip to Miami, and they
picked out a Limoges dinnerware set from a French catalogue;

they were the envy of the town, they were invited to all the best parties, and, for her birthday, Gustavo Freisen bought her a car. Spending time at the dressmakers' workshop or sitting around a bridge table was boring, true, but González, the country club's sharpest waiter, knew that when she asked for a Coca-Cola, that meant he should serve it with two fingers of gin. And between the gin and the tranquillizers, she couldn't think straight. Nor did she want to.

By the time she attended Aunt Irene's funeral, she was convinced that she truly loved her husband; she called him at the office several times a day and suffered beyond words if he was late coming home. Javier insisted that she drive to Puerto Colombia in her own car, but she chose to wait for him at Nena's house instead, exaggerating the dangers of driving with two children at that time of night. Her mother, the only person to notice how she rinsed her mouth out or chewed breath mints when she got back from the country club, said she was right. And from feeling so pampered and protected, from suppressing her rebelliousness and denying her sexuality to such an extent, Beatriz became a shadow of her former self, trembling at the sight of a mouse and summoning the doctor if one of her children so much as sneezed. The children's health was another of her major concerns, and for that, Gustavo Freisen was profoundly grateful. He adored those fair-haired grandchildren, whom he saw as the justification for all his efforts. He said this same thing to El Manco: apart from Antonio, his own children hadn't amounted to much; Ana had married an out-and-out *mestizo*, and his youngest two, Miguel and Jaime, were in with Barranquilla's intellectuals, a bunch of homosexuals and stoners. Sitting in the wheelchair he had been bound to since suffering a stroke, Gustavo Freisen could hear them coming home at night with their friends and holing up in an air-conditioned living room to drink and smoke pot until dawn. Irate, but afraid that another stroke might finish him off, from then on he tried to distract himself by working on a giant puzzle with a thousand tiny pieces: it was the repro-duction of a Degas painting, and he never managed to finish it. Odile Kerouan, on the other hand, was more conciliatory; Miguel's effeminate ways and Jaime's marijuana did away with the last remaining traces of the Freisen personality, that horri-ble surliness that lurked in all her children and would sud-denly emerge, distancing them from her, as had happened with Javier. Odile Kerouan never imagined that life would have such a disappointment in store as to see the apple of her eyes stupidly fall into the trap designed to help Jean-Luc find a wife. Javier—who, thanks to her Swiss bank account, would have been able to travel the world with her, visit wonderful countries, eat in the best restaurants and stay in the most famous hotels—had become the husband to a nobody whose only achievement consisted of having given the family two fair-haired, blue-eyed children. Only in this regard did Odile Kerouan share Gustavo Freisen's sentiments; his grandchil-dren filled her with tenderness and an unspoken pride: they were beautiful, friendly and, most importantly, white. Beatriz cared for them with devotion and showed no qualms about leaving them in their care, thus expressing a desire to rein-force the ties that bound her to her in-laws. Ultimately, there was nothing Odile Kerouan could hold against her other than the fact that she had married Javier.

The critical remarks started when Javier wanted to leave Beatriz, not showing the slightest bit of pity for her despair. Later on, Lina would find herself thinking that he had in fact abandoned her the very day of their wedding, or to be more exact, the first time he tried to possess her body, failing to real-ize the complexity of her desire. Javier was still young at that time and could not just keep getting away with violating the Freisen family values—that subordination to sexual morals and the hard work that venerated the achievement of ordering others around and being obeyed, of calling the shots and feeling important—sacrificing his freedom like Álvaro Espinoza in order to hold the power. Not one for introspection, it took him years to notice, but now, when there was no one to stand in his way, surrounded by respectful employees and efficient secretaries, he caught himself longing for the sound of the unfurled sails of his boat flapping in the breeze. He had made his peace with Maruja, and he invited her to lunch almost every day because their respective factories were close by; he no longer talked to her about his marital problems, but of the dazzling greens of the Caribbean or that sun, which covered his body in salty sweat and shimmered on the water like the reflection of a god. Now his greatest desire was to sail at his leisure and see the coastal mangroves shrinking out of sight, leaving behind the stretch of water where a few boats were still silhouetted and gannets or seagulls wheeled overhead. Out there, facing the horizon, he lived in the present, not thinking about the past or the future; out there he had only himself to rely on, and his ability to circumvent the ocean currents or to detect the slightest change in the wind, his strength to hoist or lower the sails at just the right moment made him feel like he was living intensely, discovering the full power of his body and the sharpness of his reflexes. He remembered the creaking of the ropes in the rain, the constellations shining in the sky and guiding him at night, the different kinds of seaweed that created the illusion of sleeping cities at the bottom of the ocean with their phosphorescence, the reefs aglow with corals, and those moments when he felt his penis stiffen in the warmth of the sun, when, lying out on deck, he looked up at the sky as it blurred into a golden glow. He wanted to be free and to escape the routine of work, to discover his virility reflected in nature once again. But Beatriz was standing in his way; she represented everything that he had suddenly begun to despise: monotony, conventionality, the cold, stiff love of the bourgeoisie. That placid vagina, smeared in Vaseline, was so far from the thrills his own penis longed for. And she, the possessive wife, seemed so miserable compared to the passions he could now feel in his heart. Intoxicated by the visions he had once had on a hallucinogenic trip, when his younger brothers prepared a cocktail of drugs that gave him a glimpse of paradise, Javier did not heed Maruja's protests, but nor did he reject them; instead, he simply asserted his right to life, attributing the past to an error of youth. Beatriz was frigid, and her jealousy was delusional. She wouldn't leave him alone for a minute, and she insisted on waiting for him every evening at the Avendaños' house to make him go back to Puerto Colombia with her. By doing so, she was depriving him of male company, and as he explained to Maruja in a serious tone, men needed to meet up, tell each other jokes and go to whorehouses together. If he had been a more cultured man, he would have also mentioned the shacks that were out of bounds to women, or the recruitment of young men in more recent times. But his sun-worshipping and nostalgia for the savage horde were not signs of nascent homosexuality, as Maruja assumed; rather, they were early manifestations of a fuzzy desire which was waiting for something on which to project itself, relying on vague fantasies until it manifested on a dock at the fishing club, where he worked every weekend to make his boat seaworthy again. So, Beatriz would have to resign herself to being left alone on Saturdays and Sundays, not noticing what was sprouting in Javier's mind, or rather, thinking that it was just a passing mood. Her husband had been on edge for a while, and the silliest little things drove him up the wall; it seemed he had given up on his plan to buy her an apartment in the city, the children were getting on his nerves, the latest tub of Vaseline had not even been opened. She could cope with all of this by upping her dose of gin and tranquillizers. But those interminable Sundays in Puerto Colombia—in a house that was always empty because Javier's absence kept family and friends from visiting—gave her time to think, making her question her life and the various trials and tribulations that had landed her in this situation. The lack of reading and conversations had dulled her mind, and now her thoughts drifted from anecdotes to recriminations; as Javier became more cutting and aggressive, she tried in vain to concentrate on *The Second Sex* or the most recent work by the North American feminists, but those books, instead of comforting her, left a bitter taste in her mouth and made her feel that she was to blame for her own fate; moreover, she struggled to grasp certain assumptions that alluded to authors or theories she knew nothing about, and the solutions she found there struck her as ridiculous or implausible in the context of Barranquilla; sexual liberation, which was all the rage at the time, reminded her of the sorrows of her own experience, and Víctor had shown her the darker side of the revolution. She closed those books, telling Lina that she was tired of all the utopias and complications. Javier would come back, and she was going to wait for him.

Meanwhile, Javier would find out why people say the first step is always the hardest. With the *Odile*'s keel repaired after several months' work, the thought of returning to Puerto Colombia on Saturday evenings seemed ridiculous when he could keep repairing the on-board instruments with an electrician who agreed to continue working until midnight. After that, he would go drinking in that dark living room cooled by five air conditioners, where marijuana and cocaine circulated on silver platters and his brothers played host to the city's most eclectic characters. He spontaneously decided that the factory could do without him on Fridays, reducing the days he dedicated to work and Beatriz to four out of seven, because from Thursday night he settled in at his parents' house, sleeping in his old childhood bedroom, much to Odile Kerouan's covert glee. Crushed, Beatriz had backed down without a fight for fear of sparking those fits of rage in which he insulted her wildly, accusing her of wanting to emasculate him, being frigid and preventing him from living; she no longer knew what to do: the slightest remark from her prompted a barrage of shouting and insults, plus Javier's logic was so shallow and ill-intentioned that it did not allow for any form of reasoning, and, she would tell Lina, she felt a strange lethargy coming over her. Her depression had taken a different path: instead of manifesting itself through anorexia, instantly receiving attention and treatments intended to fight it, her melancholy cunningly lurked in the background while the events that would later justify its explosion kept mounting up. Over the years, Lina would compare her depression to a surprisingly sagacious virus, which, after familiarizing itself with all the antibiotics capable of counteracting it, had resolved to remain invisible, waiting for its host organism to completely deteriorate so that it could pounce when no defence was possible. Because from the moment when Javier started hanging out with his younger brothers, his coarseness kept increasing without meeting the slightest resistance from Beatriz. Now he turned up at the house in Puerto Colombia at all hours of the morning with his friends, looking to continue their mammoth drinking sessions; he bad-mouthed the Avendaños, publicly ridiculing their alleged lineage; he made Beatriz put up with commoners and sour-smelling men with booming voices who vomited in the garden—not to mention their wives, all servile middle-class women who were willing to downplay the worst humiliation from their husbands in order to hang on to them. She also had to welcome Jaime's female friends, these new young, headstrong women who came from the same milieu but were determined to rebel against the established values, who adored marijuana and practised a certain form of sexual liberation. Pioneers of female emancipation, they were defiant in their attitudes and excessive in their opinions, and had no time for people who accepted compromise. Almost all of them would finish their university studies, get married then divorced; they would take lovers, and as soon as their first grey hairs appeared, they would decide it best to grow old beside the last love in their lives. But back then, in the full bloom of youth, their intransigent ways meant they could not understand Beatriz, and they simply saw her as the carbon copy of the mother who was waiting for them at home, whose anger they would have to deal with by grumbling and telling lies. Javier encouraged their insolence in front of Beatriz, partly to humiliate her and partly because the girls' desire for freedom echoed his own sentiments; he felt young again around them, not oppressed by the restrictions of marriage. They smelled fresh, he told Maruja, and unlike Beatriz they were full of vitality. Now that the *Odile* had been repaired, he would take them sailing with him during the holidays, teaching them how to navigate the ocean and sail a boat; they would go to San Andrés and Santo Domingo, and to the small island his mother had bought years earlier; they would learn to dive and go exploring the remnants of famous shipwrecks, which he could locate after reading Exquemelin and the stories of old fishermen. "They're off to find Morgan's treasure," Maruja joked, taking Javier's exploits with a pinch of salt, because as far as she was concerned, it was all very childish and in no way a threat to Beatriz's security: she was all too familiar with those girls, who were close friends of her youngest sister, María Eugenia, and she knew that though they were free and easy, they were unlikely to get involved with a married man. However, in a roundabout way, her sister would end up being the one to complicate matters.

María Eugenia was perhaps the most intelligent of the Freisens, and definitely the most rebellious. Since the age of fifteen, she had decided to spend the holidays away from her family, travelling around the country with North American hippies on a quest to find magic mushrooms. On a trip to San

Andrés she found out she had a distant relative who was the same age as her and had already racked up enough sexual experiences to turn Casanova himself green with envy. Her name was Leonor, and she was the daughter of Lucila Castro. She had inherited her mother's fieriness, several properties in Miami and the best store on the island, specializing in luxury products. With the help of her widowed aunt and two sisters of the faithful Lorenzo, Leonor kept on top of her store, determined to enjoy the pleasures of life without ever resorting to prostitution. It was as though she had two different personalities: there was the disciplined business whizz, who stood firm in her disputes with the island's traffickers by day, and a sensual nocturnal self, who selected her lovers based on mysterious criteria. When María Eugenia met her, it forced her to radically rethink her views: studying guaranteed independence, those mushrooms dulled the senses in the long run, and sexual liberation by no means liberated women: instead it made them all completely available to men, who kept making love to suit themselves, unconcerned with female eroticism—and now, thanks to the latest theories, they could even get out of the work of seducing them or the humiliation of paying. María Eugenia was awestruck with admiration and suggested that she come to spend the coming Carnival season in her house. Not particularly interested in the men from the continent but sniffing out an opportunity to sell a sizeable shipment of smuggled goods, Leonor accepted her invitation and went to stay with the Freisens.

For Javier, meeting her and falling in love with her were one and the same thing: he found her beautiful, fascinating and strangely aloof. In fact, there was something about Leonor that attracted men and scared them at the same time—a bit like Divina Arriaga, Lina would hear one of her uncles remark, wondering, not without astonishment, how she could be so cultured and elegant when she had been raised by a wayward mother and a practically illiterate Black man, on that island where there was nothing to see but cocktails and tourists. But that wasn't how things really were, Lina would realize years later, when she ran into Leonor in Siena, dining across from the Piazza del Campo in the company of an Italian count. Leonor invited her to join them at their table, then back to her friend's house, not far from the square, and they talked for hours: they were united by their friendship with Maruja and they both shared a nostalgia for the Caribbean. Dropping her guard a little, Leonor recalled her past, from the time when Lucila Castro went to stay in San Andrés and sent her to study in Germany on the advice of one of her lovers, to her ill-fated stay at the Freisens' house. She told Lina that she had lived in various European countries, changing schools to suit Lorenzo's whims; every year, when she returned to the island for the holidays, he performed a strange ceremony, tossing snails onto the map of the old continent to decide where she should go, then when she completed her studies, she decided to stay in San Andrés, because that was where the remains of Lorenzo and her mother were symbolically laid to rest, both of them having perished in the same shipwreck. But after what happened with Javier, she opened her business in Miami and then later in Bali, where she was getting ready to travel as soon as she had wrapped up some business. Like Catalina, Leonor had not changed a bit: she was still very beautiful, with her short hair combed back and her eyes—a very dark, deep brown—bright with intelligence; she did not wear make-up, and although there was nothing deliberately flirtatious about her movements and expressions, she had an aura of seduction about her, a kind of voluptuousness that clung to her skin, something intimate and strong like a perfume. One could guess from looking at her that she was sensual yet lucid, and capable of terrible coldness if her interests were at stake. She raised an eyebrow so subtly that it was barely perceptible, and her friend left the table; then, switching from French to Spanish, she asked Lina for news about Javier. She listened to the story without batting an eyelid: Javier desperately searching for her in his sailing boat, exploring the Caribbean islands one by one and, five years later, being struck by the fatal disease he caught from the sun, covered in bandages like a leper, still calling out her name from aboard the *Odile* as he sailed past the fishermen on the high seas, who trembled with fear at the sight of that skeletal figure and his boat with its tattered sails, both of them—the man and the boat that everyone thought were dead and gone, and the vision of them there—portentous ghosts. "I never said I'd live with him," was the only remark Leonor made, swiftly changing the subject.

Lina did not question the truth of that statement for a second. Right to the end, there was almost something excessive about Javier's passion, and she herself knew that sometimes love for one woman served as an excuse to destroy another. Yes, she regretted not having guessed sooner, when Beatriz would still respond to logical arguments and was willing to discuss such matters, analyzing the different sides of the situation, its possibilities and consequences. But it never occurred to either of them that Javier's feelings might not be reciprocated by the one he was ready to give everything up for; they didn't even know the name of the woman who had him consumed by a desire so strong that he even spoke to Beatriz about her, asking her to get out of his life; had they known then that the fires of that passion existed only in his imagination and were not shared by his lover, the whole thing would have turned into a ridiculous drama: those juvenile cravings for freedom, those barbed comparisons and that triumphant air about him when he got back to the house in Puerto Colombia after disappearing for a week on his boat. But once the scandal was out there, Javier could not backtrack for fear of becoming a laughingstock. Hence his reluctance to disclose the identity of his great love, and hence Maruja's amusement when she found out. In fact everyone laughed, but not for the same reasons: the older men thought Leonor was a prostitute, confusing her with Lucila, while Javier's friends were surprised by her self-confidence and had her down as a nymphomaniac. Only a few people in the city, among them Maruja, found out the basis for Leonor's romantic dalliances: she refused to accept the kind of erotism that focused on an organ that stood proud and quickly emptied itself, leaving women with a sense of frustration and men with a sad taste in their mouths; instead, she sought out those rare men who had learned to make love a different way, joining in the woman's orgasm time and again, controlling their own desire and maintaining their erection for as long as possible—not in the name of religious principles or to wield some sort of sadistic power, but to infuse their whole being with eroticism, before finally plunging into a timeless sensuality and vibrating to the cadence of female rhythms. So basically, Maruja would say to Lina, laughing: an atheistic tantrism. And when she noticed that she was still staring at her aghast, she added: "Don't worry, she'll be sick to the back teeth of Javier by now."

But even then, it was already too late. Lina realized this when she turned up at the house in Puerto Colombia an hour later and found Beatriz slumped in a corner on the terrace, staring vacantly at the last reflection of the sun on the ocean. She was very pale; she looked at Lina as if she didn't recognize her, and then, straining to speak, she asked her to look after the children. Huddled by the door, holding each other, Nadia and Javier Junior looked like they'd been crying all day: they were still in their pyjamas, and hadn't eaten since breakfast. Lina bathed them, made them a meal and stayed with them in their room until they fell asleep. When she got back to the terrace, she found Beatriz sitting in the same position on the floor, her arms wrapped around her knees, and her vacant eyes staring into the darkness; her body was quivering slightly, her forehead was burning up but her hands were frozen. A shawl and a glass of gin finally prompted a reaction. "Did you know that I'm crazy?" she asked Lina all of a sudden. Then, as she sipped the gin and smoked one cigarette after the other, she told her what had happened: Javier had told her the name of his lover in a fit of rage, and she thought she had lost her mind; well, at any rate, she had lost all sense of time. She remembered yelling, "Why her, why her, of all people?" before everything started spinning and she collapsed onto the bed. When she came to, Javier had disappeared, and the children were still asleep. Without thinking about what time it was, she drove into the city to get some support from her family, to cry in her mother's arms. Only when she saw Nena in her nightrobe did she realize that day was dawning. Summoned by Jorge Avendaño, her brothers came over to the house; she heard them murmuring on the veranda but she did not dare to move, she told Lina, she couldn't utter a word. Strangely enough, in all the mental turmoil, she couldn't understand why Javier's revelation made her feel so miserable when, for the past three months, he hadn't missed an opportunity to hurt her by telling her about his lover. Her brothers reminded her, and in a rather brutal way, when she mentioned Leonor's name. From the moment they had walked into the room where she was sobbing in Nena's arms, they seemed to take pity on her: they listened to her tale, furious with Javier and his despicable behaviour. But when she revealed the identity of his mistress, Beatriz noticed a strange change come over her brothers: they started glancing at one another out of the corner of their eyes and asking her abstruse questions about her state of mind and whether she felt like she was being followed or watched. Beatriz sensed the truth and decided to sound them out, accusing them of insinuating she was mad so that they wouldn't have to confront Javier. And then one of her brothers erupted and reminded her how, years earlier, she had tormented them by spying on this same Leonor and making up absurd stories about a masturbating spider monkey and a Black man kissing a little girl between the legs. Beatriz told Lina that she had felt her heart for the first time: she felt it beat, stop for a moment, then start pulsating again; a horrible pain stopped her breathing, as if all of a sudden, some creature had lodged itself in her chest and was grasping at the back of her neck with its tentacles. She no longer wanted anyone's help, she just wanted to be left alone; a thousand thoughts were running around her mind, but the pain prevented her from being able to think; she watched with relief as her brothers left the room, then gulped down some aspirin and tranquillizers until finally she regained control of her body, and after calming poor Nena down, she made her way back to Puerto Colombia. She remembered giving the children breakfast, but then nothing after that.

For once in her life, Lina tried to make her face up to reality. Yes, her brothers had thought she was mentally disturbed ever since she told them about Merlin, the mischievous monkey that had also tried to make a mark on her; likewise, they had sent her to Canada on the advice of Dr. Agudelo. And now Javier was cheating on her with Leonor, who in turn had been introduced to sexuality by Lorenzo as a young girl. But she, Beatriz, could do something about it. She could bid farewell to the past and start another life elsewhere; she had money and her health, no one was forcing her to stay there, passively enduring Javier's insults. Eventually Lina offered to explain the situation to the Avendaños, and the next day the whole family gathered at Nena's house, including Beatriz, who, growing in self-confidence, managed to express herself coherently and told them she wanted to leave her husband and move to Miami with her children. Reassured by her words, the Avendaño brothers arranged to meet Javier after consulting a lawyer to assess the legal aspects of the situation and prepare the documents needed for the children to leave the country. To everyone's surprise, Javier did not put up the slightest resistance: he signed the papers that they presented to him, agreed to start the proceedings to make their separation official, and offered to pay Beatriz alimony on his own initiative.

To all appearances, everything was in order. And yet Beatriz remained in Puerto Colombia, prostate with apathy and brooding over the ruins of her love life. And still Javier could not contain his desire to see her and talk to her about Leonor. An unhealthy relationship had developed between the two of them, because he needed to flaunt his romantic exploits; it was as if he wanted to cement them in someone else's memory, specifically, in a memory from which they would never be erased. That was what the lucid part of Beatriz understood, the part that came to the surface in Lina's presence, when she had to express herself reasonably and find the real explanation for everything. This same Beatriz accepted the existence of the other woman but could not escape Javier's influence because he provided her with justification for the thing that she would have otherwise had to accept as a delusion in her mind; she lived full of fear; she was afraid to leave the house and afraid to stay, to remain in a place where people were doubtless laughing about her misfortunes, or to move to Miami and face a thousand new problems; it terrified her to spend the night lying awake trembling with anguish, or sleeping thanks to the pills and entering the horrible realm of nightmares. Suddenly, in the garden, she would be surprised to hear strange voices coming from the ocean; sometimes she thought she could see a man's face peering through the shutters. Worst of all, those hallucinations had an echo in reality: when the sounds began, her chihuahua howled and scratched at the door, and likewise, Lina had seen the man. One night, Lina had noticed someone's eyes shining through the window, and so she went out into the garden armed with a stick; but the man did not even move: he kept watching Beatriz, as if hypnotized, and he only left when she threatened to call the police; his facial features and the way he walked were typical of men from the Colombian interior; he was young and rather good-looking, and he had probably felt drawn by the presence of a beautiful woman living in a secluded house. Beatriz had a different take: she reasoned that this man had to be one of Víctor's friends, who had been told about her sexual perversions and was coming to rape her and to collect the explosives that no one had claimed until then. When that poor devil caused an uproar by stripping naked on the beaches of Puerto Colombia, his photograph appeared in the press along with a caption saying that he had been locked up in the mental asylum because he had gone insane: the article called him "harmless." Far from feeling reassured, this just gave Beatriz something else to worry about: the asylums were not secure, he would escape and come looking for her; on more than three occasions she saw him standing outside the shutters again, and on three separate occasions she got Lina to phone the asylum pretending that she was a journalist, to check that the man had not absconded. But there was nothing she could do about the voices: suddenly, in the middle of a conversation, Beatriz would seem to disconnect from reality, on high alert to something only she could perceive; then she would burst out crying, as if her heart were breaking. She never told Lina when this happened; but in one of her lucid moments, she'd explained to her how the voices coming from the ocean told her that life was pointless and only in death would she find peace. However, her children prevented her from dying; she could not entrust them to her mother, who was too old, nor to Odile Kerouan, who had taken Javier's side from day one, with inexplicable ferocity. The only time that Beatriz had ever tried to ask her for help, Odile had unleashed all the bitterness that had been building up in her heart, more or less accusing her of having seduced her son without thinking about Jean-Luc's feelings. All this malice prompted her to make the most absurd contradiction: she criticized Beatriz for being an unworthy wife because Javier wanted to leave her, and at the same time, she accused her of being unable to adapt to the liberalism of the era and clinging to Javier in the name of outdated principles; although she did not say it to her directly, she dropped hints that she only had any time for her because she had given the family two children, and in this way she was repeating—perhaps unknowingly—the behaviour of her own mother-in-law from Lille, whose sarcastic remarks had caused her so much suffering in her youth. That conversation had driven Beatriz to despair: all the kindness that the Freisens had shown her was pure hypocrisy because they simply saw her as a breeder. She would never let them have her children, not them, nor Javier's lover. She no longer dared to trust anyone: her husband was unfaithful, her in-laws looked down on her, and her brothers thought she was mad. And her own mind, riddled with anxiety, was increasingly losing touch with reality. Lina offered to call Dr. Agudelo for her again, since he was someone she could speak to without fear of being betrayed.

Dr. Agudelo's visit lasted three hours and had an immediate impact. Beatriz decided never to be Javier's confidante again, and that it was time to commence the proceedings to leave for Miami. The fear of having her visa rejected because of her relationship with Víctor faded as soon as she walked into the American Embassy and was met by a clerk who was also a friend of the family. For the first time in a month, Beatriz dared to venture out of the house and go to the beauty parlour, where Angélica, the hairdresser, gave her a warm welcome and assured her that the whole city was on her side and applauded her decision to leave. She called Isabel, Maruja and Lina and told them to join her, and they got the party started by cracking open a bottle of champagne. Someone brought grilled sandwiches from the country club and Lina phoned Rosario Miranda, a relative of hers based in Miami, who straight away offered to meet Beatriz from the airport and put her up in her house while she looked for a job. It was three o'clock in the afternoon when they parted ways, slightly tipsy and pretty happy, promising that they would go to Puerto Colombia that night. Beatriz had to buy the tickets and get some dollars on the black market, then stop off at Nena's house to cheer her up and collect the children. She would wait for them there, she told them as she got into her car. When she walked past Lina, she smiled. A strange feeling came over Lina; she had always seen that face inclined to severity or sadness, twisted with rage or in pain, but she had never seen it smiling; for a few seconds she found herself calmly recalling the friezes from the Italian's Tower. "Nonsense," she muttered to herself, starting up the engine of her new car, "I've just had too much champagne."

Henk was waiting for her at the Hotel del Prado to introduce her to an English art collector who was interested in a Van Gogh painting in Catalina's collection. The negotiations went on until seven o'clock in the evening. When Lina said goodbye and reached Nena's house, she walked into complete chaos: Isabel looked like she was having one of her worst days, Maruja was insulting Odile Kerouan, who seemed to have lost the power of speech, and Nena was crying as she hugged a photo album that had been torn apart; in a corridor, Javier was looking completely drained as he struggled against the well-aimed fists of one of the Avendaño brothers. It took Lina more than half an hour to get anyone to explain to her what had happened, and the story made her sense that disaster loomed. Gustavo Freisen had accepted the breakdown of his son's marriage without any great reservations, merely remarking that poor Jean-Luc was languishing in a mental asylum because of that wedding; but no one had dared to tell him about the agreement made between the Avendaños and Javier and what it entailed. He had resigned himself to the absence of his grand-children during the past month or so, believing that they were sick with whooping cough, and he had sent for an attorney to come and assess the situation. The situation could not have been worse: his son had a lover he flaunted in public, and his daughter-in-law had not left the marital home at any point. Furious, Gustavo Freisen instructed the attorney to recruit two ex-policemen as detectives, whose mission it would be to monitor the house in Puerto Colombia until they could prove—or if necessary, fabricate—Beatriz's infidelity. But apart from that madman and the doctor who had spent three hours with her the previous afternoon, not a single man had been to see her. The doctor's visit intrigued Gustavo Freisen: his grandchildren had whooping cough, yet no one tended to them, and here Beatriz was, calling a doctor known for his abil-ity to treat mental illnesses. The strategy was decided: he would tear his grandchildren away from that woman on the pretext of her being mentally disturbed. Right there and then, the attorney refused to implicate himself in the matter and promised to bill him for his services the next day. But Gustavo Freisen was not going to let himself be disarmed just like that: he called Javier to demand that he put a stop to his love affair and take his children back, and then, when he found out about the pact he had made with the Avendaños, he cursed him and vowed that he would cut him off and kick him out of his house, threatening to immediately make him pay him back the money that he had taken out of the factory as a loan. Javier left, slam-ming the door behind him: in the grip of rage, he got into his new MG and raced down Avenida Olaya Herrera, and when he reached Paseo Bolívar he saw Beatriz's car parked outside a travel agency. He screeched to a halt and got out of the MG: in front of Beatriz's terrified eyes, he smashed in the car window, opened the door and grabbed the papers, all of them, the pass-ports and visas, the dollars she'd just bought, the document that authorized her to take the children out of the country. And when Beatriz ran to stop him, he slapped her hard across the face, yelling that he was going to take the children from her and have her locked up in the same clinic as Jean-Luc.

"Why did you do that?" Federico Avendaño was asking him now as he kicked the stuffing out of him. And Javier, hunched over in the hall, his face messed up by the blows, answered him feebly, "I don't know." Like him, Odile Kerouan couldn't understand why she had turned her back on Beatriz when she saw her in her house, taking the photographs of her and her children out of the picture frames. Javier had phoned her from the fishing club, explaining that he had taken the documents and asking her to tell Gustavo Freisen that everything had been dealt with. Odile passed on the message to her husband and went down the stairs to go to the country club, where a table of bridge was waiting for her. She found Beatriz in the living room, tearing out photos with a calm resolve that emphasized the crazed look in her eyes. Odile didn't think she had seen her until she heard her stutter, "Aren't you going to do anything?" And straight away, as though answering herself, she said, "No, she won't do anything." By then Beatriz had lost control, Odile Kerouan told Maruja: she had left for the country club, and instead of meeting up with her friends, she stayed in her car for hours until she suddenly came up with the idea of going over to Nena's house. Odile only realized how serious the situation was when she noticed that the photo albums and picture frames at Nena's had been stripped of their photographs too.

As she listened to them talk, Lina was paralyzed with hatred; if she'd had a gun in her hand, she would have fired it at Javier and his mother without the slightest bit of remorse. All of them, including the Avendaño brothers, seemed to be incapable of thinking with their brains: they were wondering where Beatriz had run off to, whether or not to call the police, whether perhaps she was at Dr. Agudelo's clinic. "Imbeciles," Lina yelled at them, suddenly remembering about the explosives. "Why the hell do you think she destroyed the photographs?" Maruja instantly understood. "My car's faster than yours," she said to Lina, catching up with her in the garden. And they headed for Puerto Colombia while the Avendaño brothers dashed to their cars, followed by Javier and Odile Kerouan. No other journey would ever seem as long to Lina; at no point did Maruja take her foot off the accelerator, but to Lina it felt like they were never going to get there. As she struggled to breathe the balmy night air, she cursed her lack of foresight. Not once in that terrible month had she considered the danger that those explosives posed: Víctor had shown Beatriz how to store them to avoid an accident, and in doing so, he had also taught her how to cause one. "Faster," she begged Maruja, scrutinizing the shadows on the horizon and trying to guess what Beatriz was thinking, entrenched as she was in that mindset and determined not to let anyone get their hands on her children. As they drew closer to Puerto Colombia, she could sense Beatriz's desperation in her own mind: following Dr. Agudelo's advice, she had made a huge effort to drag herself out of her torpor, she had gone to the bank, the embassy and the beauty parlour, and when the difficulties seemed to be subsiding and the road of life was opening up in front of her, with the image of the cadet from West Point inching back into her memory, Javier had destroyed her meagre dreams, under pressure from that venomous father of his, Gustavo Freisen.

Finally they made it to Puerto Colombia and turned up the narrow path leading to the house. For an instant they glimpsed the dark, ghostly house rising up beside the ocean, on top of sand dunes chirping with crickets, fragile and fleetingly snatched from the blackness of the night by the glow of the headlamps. They glimpsed it before that terrible deflagration shook the car, striking them in the face, bursting their eardrums and damaging their retinas with the immense bubble of fire that tore through the house from the inside out, wrenching doors and windows from their frames and sending the splintered roof flying through the air in a terrifying, unreal way, like something out of a dream. And then the flames rose high into the sky in a wordless, desperate plea.

EPILOGUE

Years have passed and I have not returned to Barranquilla, that place where our grandmothers arrived in a cloud of hot dust, on mules laden with their furniture and yearnings for the oldest cities of the Caribbean coast: at that time, Barranquilla was nothing but a sweltering hamlet with no history of its own, apart from the sad tale of having exacerbated the symptoms of Bolívar's illness as he travelled to meet his death.

Sometimes, at night, I think I can hear the weary plodding of the mules that carried their belongings, and I think about the world our grandmothers left behind, where patios bloomed with vines and daguerreotypes faded on the walls of bedrooms. Those women came with memories, so many memories. We used to hear them talking about their world, not thinking that our own—so easy and frivolous, revolving around a club pool and Carnival dances—would also become part of the nostalgia of memory.

Sometimes, at night, when the fever grips me again, I think that, like our grandmothers, I dwell among memories. All these years in Paris have not been able to erase them; on the contrary, it seems the fevers and even the cold that cuts like a knife outside the Metro station on my way home from the hospital insist on taking me back to the city of El Prado, to the breeze that always came in December, to the evenings when, sitting round a table at the country club, with the sun beating down outside on the golf courses, my friends and I amused ourselves trying to predict our destinies with a deck of cards.

No card could have foretold the extraordinary twists and turns our destinies would take, not mine, nor the other girls', and especially not that of Benito Suárez. My own grand-mother—who seemed to have a prophetic ability to figure out the inexorable hidden paths in each person's life—would not live long enough to be surprised by Benito Suarez once again, or at least by the news of him that arrived year after year, first from the rainforest, then from the far reaches of the Orinoco and finally from the desert of La Guajira, where he would die. He wanted to see the ocean one last time, he told a local woman from the village where the anthropologist had gone to stay. The anthropologist, who in turn told me the tale, did not understand why I took such an interest in that poor devil, a hermit, a good man, she said, his hair now shot through with grey, who roamed the desert curing the *indios* without taking a cent from them, who penned poetry and sobbed in his ham-mock at night, calling out for Dora, the woman he had once loved.

I sometimes think—always at dusk, when the fever comes and the cooing of the pigeons on the rooftops dies down—that the labyrinths of life hold undecipherable enigmas, just like the stones of the Italian's Tower. Having helped my grandmother to die as per her instructions—dissolving the powder from all the capsules, which she was supposed to take only once a day, then carefully refilling them with talcum powder so that Dr. Agudelo wouldn't notice—I was surprised to learn how Aunt Eloísa had decided to celebrate the end of her own life: in the middle of a party, raising a glass of champagne to toast with her daughters as fireworks exploded all around her, and horns honked to usher in the new year.

But there was nothing unpredictable about what happened to Catalina. When I see her pictured in *Vogue* alongside that daughter with those dazzling golden eyes, who looks like she could be her sister, at Régine's or some other chic New York spot, resplendent and cold as an iceberg, surrounded by other socialites, men just as impervious to the frailties of the heart, I think how she's fulfilling the destiny that Divina Arriaga had predicted for her, in that gloomy bedroom where she hid away until she forgot the past.

Many things have changed, it seems, in the city I left forever after my grandmother's death. Many things. Our houses disappeared around the same time that the *marimbero*s arrived in Barranquilla: men from the desert of La Guajira who got rich trafficking marijuana and cocaine, who would build marble palaces and shoot each other dead in the streets in the name of old tribal vendettas, before being absorbed into the city just like the immigrants, peddlers and fugitives from Cayenne many years earlier.

In time, the sons of those *marimberos* would come to Paris: rich, young, handsome, talking an English honed at Harvard, they wore white tuxedos with a red rose in their lapels to the summer gala parties, with the self-assured manner of their fathers as they moved through the sand dunes with a machine gun tucked under their arm. They were accompanied by the new wave of girls from Barranquilla, who were already liberated and spoke to me with a certain fondness because they were vaguely aware I'd once written a book condemning the oppression their mothers had suffered. There was nothing submissive about these young women: they didn't wear make-up, they kept a couple of grams of cocaine stashed in their powder compacts, and they made love with an air of nonchalance, much to the dismay of their lovers who felt like cherries absent-mindedly picked from a plate. Perhaps only I understood that the frenzied way they feasted on men they chose and devoured without tenderness or compassion was simply a form of revenge unwittingly taken by that generation of women on behalf of so many others. The carnivorous young women passed through Paris; they passed through, then they left and returned to Barranquilla. Over the years they would discover the fear of loneliness, and then they would agree to live with just one man. Perhaps their daughters will learn that love is not found in promiscuity, nor eroticism in drugs, and, like Divina Arriaga, they will know how to tell these things apart, recognizing that both play a sacred, initiatory part in the long pilgrimage that allows them to glimpse the infinite, and then to be humbler, and eventually, to come to terms with life.

Time would help me understand many things: Aunt Irene's silence, certain words my grandmother used to say, Aunt Eloísa's smile. At one time I wanted to die, in Deià, a village in Mallorca. It was night, and the freezing winter wind dried my tears, mocking my sadness. I had decided to end it all and was wandering the empty streets of that ghost town, when suddenly I heard the music of a violin: behind the closed shutters of a large house, someone was incessantly repeating a musical phrase from Aunt Irene's sonata. I stopped for a moment, and as soon as the instrument fell silent, I sang the next line, which the violinist, after a moment of hesitation or perhaps shock, hurried to pick up again. I ran away, but there was no need to run as no one followed me, because, like me, the violinist knew that this sonata had been composed to be heard only once before vanishing into the shadows of oblivion. I saw my decision was an absurd dream: I was reminded that we all have an appointment in Samarkand.

Years have passed. I have not returned, nor do I think I will ever return to Barranquilla. No one here even knows its name. When they ask me what it's like, I simply say that it's by a river, very close to the sea.